ALSO BY KATHLEEN TYAU

A Little Too Much Is Enough

MAKAI

KATHLEEN TYAU

Makai

BEACON PRESS • BOSTON

Beacon Press
25 Beacon Street
Boston, Massachusetts 02108-2892
www.beacon.org

Beacon Press books
are published under the auspices of
the Unitarian Universalist Association of Congregations.

First Beacon Press edition published in 2000

Printed in the United States of America

05 04 03 02 01   8 7 6 5 4 3 2

This book is printed on acid-free paper that meets the uncoated paper
ANSI/NISO specifications for permanence as revised in 1992.

Text design by Abby Kagan

Library of Congress Cataloging-in-Publication Data

Tyau, Kathleen.
    Makai / Kathleen Tyau.
    p. cm.
    ISBN 0-8070-8345-3
    1. Hawaii—Fiction. I. Title.

PS3570.Y35 M35 2000
813'.54—dc21

00-044422

FOR PAUL

CONTENTS

Every place has its own wisdom. Come.
Time we talked about the sea,
the long waves
"trapped around islands"
—Michael Ondaatje

I was a child and she was a child
In this kingdom by the sea,
But we loved with a love that was more than love—
I and my Annabel Lee—
—Edgar Allan Poe

MAKAI

1

RIDING TO SEA IN COCK-A-ROACH

Annabel Lee is coming, and I'm not going to be cheap. I'll buy a new dress and we'll go out dancing. Annabel Lee and me, Alice Lum, still best friends after all these years, not just old married ladies. It's been seven years since the war ended, and I miss the music, miss the dancing. The men holding me, spinning me around, my high heels clicking to the beat.

But instead of music, I hear my husband, Sammy, snoring. He whistles through his nose, like a teakettle coming to a boil again and again.

Wake up, Sammy Woo. The rain has stopped. Annabel Lee is coming tomorrow. You promised to take me shopping in town. A real town, with more than one store. Not like this place where I am stuck. Hana, Maui. Out in the sticks, where the road stops, where you can't get the ocean out of your head.

Look at him smile. He must be dreaming something good. How can he sleep with all his snoring? He gets mad if I wake him up. When I ask what he's been dreaming, he says, I forget.

How can he forget? Me, I remember everything. Sometimes I wake him in the middle of the night and tell him what I'm dreaming, so he can help me remember in the morning. But when I go back to sleep, my dream is gone. Maybe that's why he's smiling. He is dreaming my dream.

The sun is bright, screaming through the windows.

All that rain, for so many months and days. This is my home. Underwater. It rains in my sleep, in my worst nightmare. My nightgown, the sheets, my husband, Sammy, my daughters Beatrice and Lurline—everything, everybody I touch feels damp. My whole life turning into mildew.

But this morning, sun on my face, on my arms. Tears from the sky no longer falling. My bare feet creaking across the kitchen to the back door. My face pressing against the wet screen. Dew evaporating off the grass and the ti leaves. The clothes steaming on the line. And, rising over the ohia and the guava and the banana trees, a giant rainbow. The biggest rainbow I have ever seen, landing right on top of my papaya tree. And now look. Count them. Three new papayas. Three of them, yellow and green. When Annabel Lee comes, they'll be just right for eating. She and Sammy can each have one, and my girls and me can share. Beatrice can eat half a papaya by herself, and I can mash some of mine for Lurline to suck.

My mother was right. What kind of man takes his family where there are more mosquitoes than people and no good places to shop? When we left Oahu to move to Maui, my mother said, You go outer island, might as well go mainland. We never going see you now.

I haven't told her about the first time we drove the long, winding road out here to Hana. How I threw up the whole way. How scared I was every time we crossed a stream, right through the water, no bridge. I cannot tell her the road isn't road. Just dirt and gravel that washes away in the heavy rain. I cannot tell her about the flash floods, what the locals call Big Water. Big Water because it rushes down from the mountain all at once, like a toilet flushing. Big Water, washing away everything that gets in the way. The trees, the rocks. Everything.

We live in a cottage in Sylvester Kaleheo's back yard. The house is small—only one bedroom—but we don't have to pay rent because we fixed it up ourselves, and we can use all the yard we want. Sammy works on Sylvester Kaleheo's fishing boat, and he likes that better than maintenance crew at Hickam Field. He likes the fish, the wind, the waves, the rain. The way the rain makes everything clean. For him it's like starting over again and again. Brand-new every day.

I write to Annabel Lee in my head.

Dear Annabel. I close my eyes and see her name. Not her married name, Annabel Whitlow—I cannot call her that—but the way she wrote her name in school. With the Annabel and the Lee running together to make Annabelle, with the last *e* forming a long curlicue under her name.

I write to her in my head, not on paper. Never on paper.

Dear Annabel Lee. Just think. My Sammy, our Sammy, is a fisherman. Sammy, the slop boy, the water boy. Now a fish boy.

He got so sick his first time out. He spent day number one in the water tied to the boat, but now he walks, talks, smells like fish, and guess what we eat for dinner every night.

Beatrice cries when she sees me cutting the fish stomach open. She doesn't like what comes out. Sometimes eggs. Orange, like seeds. I scrape them into a bowl and bury them in the garden next to the pigeon coop. The eggs make good fertilizer for my bok choy and green onions.

I grow vegetables and Sammy raises homing pigeons.

He ties messages around their legs before he lets them go.

Property of SAMUEL WOO
Hana Maui Feed ONLY
Pigeon Food NO Bread
SEND BACK HOME

He gives them fish names—Aku, Ahi, Ulua, Mahi-mahi—like that. He says those are good-luck names, so the pigeons won't drown. He sits out in the yard every night, waiting for them to come home. Sometimes after the girls go to sleep, I sit out there with him.

He doesn't like it if I talk. If I talk, he says, Go back inside. But he likes when I scratch his arm, if I touch real light. I cut my fingernails short for the girls, but I save one long nail for Sammy. One long and filed smooth and round, not too pointy on the tip. That's what he likes. My long nail scratching his arm softly in the dark.

Dear Annabel Lee. We raise rabbits too. Rabbits are easy. All they do is make babies, but they're hard to trade. We end up giving most of them away. My girls and me, we won't eat rabbit. Sammy says it's just like chicken, but he's wrong. Rabbits taste like where they live. One time I thought I was pregnant again, but it was just the smell of the rabbit hutch.

You can sleep with me in the bedroom. Sammy can sleep on the couch. Your boy, Wycliff, can share the futon with my daughter Beatrice in the little nook next to the kitchen. Our baby, Lurline, sleeps in a drawer.

We can stay up late and talk, just like we did in the dorm at the Priory.

Oh, Priory. I wonder what the Sisters would say if they saw me now. Alice Lum, now Mrs. Samuel Woo. Fisherman's Wife.

You haven't seen my dinette set. It's the only thing new, my parents' wedding gift to us. I still have your phonograph and the records you gave me. I have the clothes you sewed for me too. They don't fit me anymore, but I can't throw them out. Remember how we always wore the latest style. I bet you still have your figure, not like me.

Living out here, I've been getting real sloppy. Wearing fat clothes. Muumuus and dusters. Talking pidgin. I better start talking good again. Sister Martha Verity would be mad if she heard me now. I don't want the neighbors to call me stuck-up Priory girl, but I want Beatrice and Lurline to speak good English. I want them to get a good education, go to college on the mainland, and be anything they want, not just a wife.

You won't recognize Sammy. He's not a boy anymore. He's big and strong from working on the boat. He loves his girls. He doesn't say it, but I know. And he can't say I don't take good care of him.

Makai

. . .

I start so many letters to Annabel Lee, but I never mail them. I rip them in half, envelope, paper, the whole thing at one time.

Lurline is hungry this morning. She sucks my nipple so hard I almost cannot breathe. She makes so much noise, like she can't get enough.

I take her outside to visit the papaya tree. The rainbow makes her hair look red. She has her daddy's wavy hair. His high forehead, too, but she has my nose. His lips, the way they curl. My dimple on her left cheek.

The neighbors think I'm lolo, hanging my wash outside in the rain. The sheets, the towels, Sammy's BVDs, Lurline's diapers. But I don't care. Let them call me what they call me. Who is the sun drying clothes for now?

My breasts are sore, my stomach feels queasy. What is it that I am forgetting to do? It was here, in my head, when I walked over to the back door, but when I looked out, it was gone. All I can think of, all I can see, is the rainbow. The rainbow falling on my papaya tree.

Sammy sleeps like my babies, on his stomach. His skin is brown except for where his T-shirt and shorts cover him during the day. He looks like one of Beatrice's paper dolls, with light skin for clothes. His okole rises up from the sheet like two loaves of sweet bread. He hates when I tell him I love his okole. He thinks I should prefer what he's lying on in front. But not when he's sleeping. When he's sleeping, I like what's behind. I like to press my stomach against his okole. When I have my rags, the heat from his body takes away my cramps. I like to lick the muscles on his back. The salt from his skin settles my stomach.

Three weeks ago he started sleeping without his BVDs. He got mad because I poked my long fingernail through the holes in his shorts. He wouldn't wear the new ones I bought him from the Sears catalogue. He said I ordered the wrong kind, Jockey shorts, too tight around the crotch. He likes them loose. He likes for everything to hang.

I'm afraid Beatrice will climb in bed and find him all naked. But I don't want to lock the bedroom door. There might be a fire or the girls might have bad dreams.

Annabel Lee is coming to visit. She's bringing her son, Wycliff, but not her husband, Coy. I wonder if the boy has his father's green eyes, his father's light brown hair, his way of walking, like he is floating. So much I still remember.

Ever since her letter arrived, I have been growing the rest of my nails to match the one that's already long. Tonight I will paint them Everlasting Red.

Sammy's awake. He rolls onto his back. Another part of him is also waking. I see that look on his face. No fishing today. He wants me to come back to bed.

Cannot, I tell him. Annabel Lee is coming. You promised to take me shopping.

Shit, he says. Shit.

I go into the bathroom and put the toilet seat down. I leave the door open so he can hear me going. I sit for a long time before I flush.

I'm going to buy a new dress, not fabric to sew, but a brand-new, store-bought dress, the latest style, something to match my red slingback pumps. Last night I found mildew growing in my good red shoes. I scrubbed them with alcohol and dried them on the kitchen table under the fan. You can't buy shoes like these in Hana. You can't buy shoes like these on the whole island of Maui. You have to go to Honolulu if you want something fancy, and even then it's hard to find.

I'm going to buy a sirloin steak too, big enough for Annabel and me to share. A nice T-bone for Sammy. He and Beatrice like to chew the bone. I can fix hot dogs for the kids. I'll buy black olives in a can.

Some potato chips too, and make onion dip and clam dip. I'm tired of squid and tako for pupu. I want red wine with a cork. Italian. Chianti, pronounced with a *k*.

We'll have baked potatoes with sour cream and bacon and some chives from my garden. I'll cook Sammy a pot of rice. I'll make salad too. Not cole slaw or macaroni, not watercress. I want real head lettuce, the mainland kind, iceberg. Plus cucumbers and tomatoes and eggs. Deviled eggs.

It's the rain that makes me fat. I see the rain and all I want to do is eat. I want pound cake, lemon pudding, banana cream pie. Haole food. Salty food makes me bloated, fish makes me stink. I want butter and sugar. Eclairs, long johns, jelly doughnuts, a bakery cake. Chocolate dobosh with white frosting and pink roses.

I'm twenty-nine years old, but not for long. My birthday is two days from now. When you cross over to thirty, you need your best friend to help you celebrate. Annabel Lee is six months older, so she knows how I feel. Not exactly skipping, but tugging my rope, ready for something exciting to come along and pull me off my feet.

Sammy is still lying in bed when I come out of the bathroom. I try not to look at him. The sheet covers up to his belly button. His chest is bare and smooth. His arms are folded behind his head. He watches me take off my nightgown and put on my duster. I turn my back so he can't see my front.

He says, I going play softball today With the boys.

But you have to take me shopping. What if I get stuck? You know how the truck always stalls.

Only when you driving it.

And then I cannot make it start.

You flood the engine, that's why. Just tap the accelerator. I told you no press so hard.

All I need is one dress. Some food. Some meat. I can't feed Annabel only fish, fish, fish.

He throws back the sheet and walks over to the window. He stands before the glass, scratching himself for all the neighbors to see. He waits for me to complain, but I don't care. He struts like a rooster to the bathroom. Leaves the door wide open. Nothing at first, because he has to wait for himself to go down. Then finally, a loud, wide stream, like a woman going.

I hate the truck, I hate the name—Cock-a-Roach—what kind of name is that? But it was cheap, so we couldn't say no. It needed new brakes, new clutch, new everything. Sammy replaces one part, and another one breaks. He tells me that every time he fixes something, the rest of Cock-a-Roach gets jealous. I'm jealous too, seeing him throw good money at a piece of junk. The back window is gone. I have to cover it with a shower curtain. The door on the driver's side is broken, so we tie it shut with a rope. But the rope is thick, and I can't undo the knot when it's time to get out.

Sammy says, Just tie a bow. When you come back from town, I'll fix it.

Beatrice loves to ride in Cock-a-Roach. Lurline sleeps all the way to town and back, but not Beatrice, who will soon be five. She likes to stand between my legs. One time she almost fell right through a hole in the rusted-out floor. Lucky thing I was holding her at the time. When we got home, Sammy nailed a board across the hole. I was so mad I couldn't sleep. Beatrice woke up crying, and I stayed awake that whole night, carrying her, rocking her, my legs shaking the whole time.

Beatrice can go to the toilet by herself now. She can brush her teeth and put on her pajamas. She can't wait to see her Aunty Annabel. She wants to show off her new panties. Annabel sent them Christmas before last, but they didn't fit. She can finally wear them now.

Beatrice is a big girl, wearing panties.

Look at how she sits straight and tall in the front seat of Cock-a-Roach, holding my red sling-back pumps on her lap. Lurline sleeps in a basket between us. Just the three of us girls, going to town. Bouncing along on the road full of rocks.

.   .   .

The sun is bright and hot and rising fast. The sky blue except for a few big clouds where it's still raining up in the hills. The rain sinks into the ground, into underground streams. The streams run through the roots and the rocks. The water bubbles up into pools aboveground. The whole mountain is like a sponge soaking up water, the valley like a sink filling up.

So far, so good. Cock-a-Roach still chugging along. The steering wheel feels light, not heavy at all. Lurline cries from her basket.

Give Sister the bottle.

Beatrice sticks the nipple in Lurline's mouth. Lurline sucks the bottle. Beatrice sucks her thumb. As long as they don't bite themselves from all the bouncing around. As long as they don't cry. Beatrice sits in the crater formed by my okole, by all the okoles that have sat there before us. The crater is wide, too wide for her small hips. She slides from side to side.

Put Mama's shoes on the floor.

She drops them one by one. They clank on the wood that Sammy has nailed to the floor of the truck.

Hold on tight. Hang on to the springs.

What stream is this? Number two or number five? Losing track. Cock-a-Roach swaying like a boat. The rocks big and slippery under the wheels.

Next time *he's* taking us to town. Next time we'll go the long way around. The winding road, on the windward side, even if it makes me sick. The only good thing about going the back way is seeing Haleakala all naked. No trees, no jungle. Everything out in the open. Nothing hiding. Nothing to be scared of.

Sing to the baby. Sing to Sister. Ring around the rosy. A pocket full of posy.

Cock-a-Roach rocking back and forth like a cradle.

Beatrice sees the rainbow first. Falling across the road, across the running water, like a bridge in the sky.

See how big the rainbow is, just like in our back yard.

And we are driving right into it. I hope it means good luck.

Now I know what's wrong. When I first saw the rainbow back at the house and steam was rising off the clothes. It was Sammy's BVDs. I was so mad that he was still wearing the old ones that I hung them on the line far away from the house, where all the neighbors could see.

Too late, Sammy Woo. They've seen the holes in your underwear. They know how brown and old they are.

He must have seen his BVDs hanging on the line. He must have gone outside in the rain last night and picked them, because they weren't out there when I looked this morning.

But they were hanging for five days. Five, Sammy. As many as the fingers on my hand.

He's scared for her to come. He doesn't want Annabel to see him now. I should be the one who's scared. I should be the one.

My knuckles turn red and white and red again as I grip the steering wheel. I reach for Lurline. Need to cover her with the blanket. Need to keep her warm.

The wheels slide around on the rocks. The steering wheel feels funny. So heavy I cannot turn it anymore.

Beatrice stares at me. Fish eyes. She wants to know why I am laughing. I can't stop thinking about Sammy's BVDs. When the Big Water hits the side of Cock-a-Roach, Beatrice's eyes are open wide, but mine, mine have narrowed into half-moon slits.

COMING LIKE WAVES

Last night my daughter Beatrice came home from the mainland with her boyfriend. She brought him home, to our house on Oahu, to sleep with her. She's thirty-two, old enough to know what she wants, and I guess it's not her husband, Frankie.

This is not the Dark Ages, I tell myself. This is 1979 and people sleep with each other left and right these days. At least she got married before getting pregnant with Emily.

Poor Emily, poor baby. She's the one I worry about. Sammy said she cried so hard when Frankie took her to his parents' house. She didn't understand why she couldn't have her mommy. Beatrice cried too when she saw the empty crib. Frankie was in such a hurry, he didn't even take Emily's blanket. Just diapers and some clothes, that's all.

Beatrice called Frankie on the phone and screamed at him to bring Emily back. He told her he would come by in the morning for his things. She could see her daughter then. Beatrice tried to argue, but he hung up the phone. I heard the click clear across the room.

In a way, I don't blame him. He goes to the airport to pick up his wife, who has gone away for six weeks of training—all the way to Georgia, so she can learn how to shoot a gun—and when she comes home, she has a brand-new dress and a haole boyfriend. And worst of all, the boyfriend is tall and good-looking, and she says she has loved him all her life. Frankie was pretty decent, all in all. He didn't even yell. He likes to think things over before he decides what to do. Cool head, that's what he has.

Not like Sammy, who says, What the hell? Where's the bastard going to sleep?

Maybe I expect too much from Beatrice. She's a college graduate, after all. She has a political science degree from U.C. Berkeley, not like Lurline, who's a little bit slow. Now Beatrice is a U.S. customs inspector, a GS-7, and rising fast. They don't let just any old body search for drugs and carry a gun. She's a modern girl, almost a women's lib. She even keeps her maiden name. She says Beatrice Chew is too much. It's hard enough being a Woo.

But sometimes she isn't smart.

I should have said something at the time, but all I could think of was I have to change the sheets. If only Frankie let me put fresh ones on that morning, before Beatrice came home, then I wouldn't be so upset. But Frankie said, The sheets still clean, Mom. I only slept on them twice.

Mom. That's how he calls me. His mother, Aggie Chew, she doesn't like that, but it makes me feel so good. Still, here I am wishing I had new sheets. Even the ones on my bed are too old. Sammy doesn't care what color the sheets are, and neither does Beatrice, but you don't know about these mainland boys. Besides, this mainland boy is the son of my best friend, Annabel Lee.

Sammy got mad when I sent him to Wigwam to buy sheets. I told him two sheets, full size, percale, so I don't have to iron. Blue, not pink. And make sure one is flat and the other one fitted. Plus matching pillowcases. He grumbled because I was so fussy, but of course it wasn't just the sheets I was worried about. For one thing, I'd rather have a whole new bed. Queen size, so the boy won't think we're cheap. A bed that has no past.

How can Beatrice do this? And just when I thought she and Frankie were finally getting along again. No more arguments late at night. I thought the quiet meant peace and loving, but maybe they were just giving up. Letting their marriage leak slowly, so nobody could see or hear it happening, and then all of a sudden, flat.

Why does it have to be so complicated? Annabel's son looks like a good boy. He's so big now, I hardly recognize him.

Beatrice scolds me for calling him Wycliff. She says, He goes by Wick now, Mommy. Wick like the candle. Wick, Wick, Wick.

She expects me to call her by a nickname too—Beet, not Beatrice, what her friends call her—but I can't do that. I feel like I'm calling my daughter Squash or Potato, and what does that make me, the mother of an It? At least Beatrice is not as bad a name as Wycliff. His father, Coy, hated his name—Cornelius Wycliff Whitlow the Second, spelled with a Roman numeral II. How could he and Annabel let their son be number III?

I don't understand so much.

I hope I can remember to call him Wick. He has Annabel's thick hair and her dark skin, but I can see his father in the way he looks at my daughter Beatrice. His eyes so green. And the way he talks to her. His voice like a whisper.

Sammy will like him better when he gets a job.

Rain falling on the roof, coming into the house through the windows which I better get up and close. Wet on my face. My heart beats so fast when I wake up to the rain. I have to lie still for a moment to make it slow down.

I can hear the water running down the drainage canal across the street. Sammy says we're safe, living up here in Pearl City Heights. Our lot is twenty feet higher than the neighbors' down below, and we have a stone wall, but sometimes the water is so loud it's like we're back on Maui. I have to kneel on the bed and look out the window to make sure we're not.

Sammy's side of the bed is empty. I can hear him hammering outside in the garage and it's not even six o'clock. I wish he wouldn't pound nails so early in the morning.

He fell asleep on the lanai last night. Him and his bottle of Johnnie Walker Red. I better get up before the phone starts ringing. It will be Gracie Todama, our neighbor next door. She can hear everything over the fence, but she won't come right out and ask. That's how she is. As if she doesn't have enough troubles of her own. Gracie's daughter could be such a pretty girl if it wasn't for what she calls herself. Toad, instead of Amy. Toad and Beet. They're best of friends, and no wonder. Gracie feels like I do, that it could be worse. Instead of just ruining their names, they could be hippies. They could be lost.

Get up, Alice. Don't be a lazy bum. Check the windows in the girls' room to make sure the rain isn't coming in. It looks so strange, the empty crib. In the twin bed next to the crib, Lurline sleeps curled up, the sheets twisted all around her. She smiles like everything is still the same. She doesn't even notice that Emily is gone.

Two weeks ago I came into this room and found Emily standing up in her crib, hanging on tight to the bars. I said, Oh, look at you! Wish your mommy could see.

I picked her up and put her on the floor to see if she could stand by herself. She took two steps and fell down. I felt so bad. My granddaughter walking and her mother gone. I put Emily back in the crib and I didn't tell, not even when she walked for Frankie that night. All I could think of was what my Beatrice was missing, being away from home for so long.

Emily looks like Beatrice when she was small. Every time I go into the girls' room and see Emily in her crib, my heart stops for a moment, and I think, Oh no, my daughter Beatrice hasn't grown up too. And then I remember it is Lurline who is slow, Lurline who will always be the baby and live at home. Lurline who has gone far away in her head.

I changed the sheets last night when they were taking a shower. Good thing Sammy was outside so he couldn't hear them. First Wick went in and then Beatrice went in after. I could tell by the feet. I heard the toilet flushing, the shower running, no talking, like they were already an old married couple. She didn't even go in there with Frankie. She always locked the door. Sometimes I could hear Frankie knocking and calling to her, but she never let him in, not that I know.

I hope they will be quiet, so the neighbors don't hear. Gracie Todama doesn't gossip much, but she might just a little this time. It's bad enough with Sammy drinking out there and calling Beatrice a slut and a whore. Maybe if he hears them take a shower, he'll remember when we did the same thing, before the girls came along.

It's because of Wick, because he's Annabel's boy, because he's Coy Whitlow's son. That's why Sammy's mad.

Sammy says he doesn't love Annabel Lee anymore, but I remember how he looked when I gave him back his mother's jade bracelet. The bracelet he gave Annabel to hold for him when he went off to war. He didn't cry, not then, but he did later on.

Maybe I worry, but I'm not dumb. He thinks I don't know what went on that time on Maui, after the girls and I almost drowned in the flash flood. Him and Annabel Lee, in the kitchen drinking, smoking, talking, and me in the bedroom with the kids, listening, crying. And then the door closing, so I couldn't hear them, what they were doing. Just the rain.

The rain coming through the screen, wetting the living-room floor, but I'm not going to scold Sammy for leaving the sliding door open last night. Better rain where I can see it and hear it and feel it.

The water in the drainage canal doesn't sound too loud yet. Not like when we had the hurricane and the water sucked Clara Mitsuoka right off her back porch.

Clara Mitsuoka drowned, but not me.

Me, Alice, I'm lucky. I know where everybody is. My husband, my daughters, even my granddaughter is safe. But Annabel Lee—she thinks her son is home in Florida, watching the house. She doesn't know he's with us and that he's not going back. Poor Gracie too. Her daughter Amy Toad is hitchhiking someplace in India. The time before that was Australia. Gracie never knows where her girl is off to next. I feel sorry for Gracie. Her husband, Mits, drinks too much, and he goes out to bars, not like Sammy, who drinks mostly at home.

I hate it when people come and go. To my mind that's always trouble.

•   •   •

Sammy says I worry too much. He says I'm the one who makes myself sick. I tell him it's because I'm a Pig and that's what a Pig does. Somebody has to worry.

Worry is a funny thing. I worry crooked, never straight. Many of my worries are old, not just new, and they keep on coming like waves. Just when I think everything's okay, I'm floating and feeling so good, here comes another one. Big one, small one, I never know which. That kind of worry gets a person down. How can I carry everything inside? How can I keep afloat?

My love for rain is wrong. I used to hate the rain. The Big Water, what it did to us. How come I'm still alive? I have everything—my girls, my husband, my house—but still I'm so afraid.

My daughter Lurline is the only one who sleeps through it all. Twenty-eight years old and she's still sucking her thumb and hugging her favorite blanket. Her breasts are bigger than mine. She won't wear real pajamas. She likes only baby dolls. Black see-through nylon with a lace bikini. I have to sew red thread on her panties so she doesn't wear her sister's clothes. Beatrice doesn't like for Lurline to touch her things. She even put a lock on her bedroom door to keep Lurline from snooping around. Frankie had to make me a key so I could get in there to clean. I made him promise not to tell. Frankie is a good boy. He goes along.

Look how the sun comes through the blinds. It cuts Lurline up into little strips. Light and dark, light and dark. I'm afraid to touch her. She might fall apart.

In the bathroom I find one towel wet and crooked and falling off the rack. Another towel folded up nicely. In the tub, a wet facecloth clogging the drain. Beatrice's new dress lying on the floor beside the hamper. Her bra and panties. Gray cotton panties with a white elastic waist, like men's Jockey shorts, except not as much fabric. Why does she have to dress like a man? Inside the hamper, his white shirt and khaki slacks, rolled up with a pair of real Jockey shorts inside. Half of me wants to pick them up, to see if he smells like his father, Coy.

Coy Whitlow, truck driver from Georgia. Coy Whitlow, good dancer, good friend.

I feel so close to Annabel now. I hope she doesn't worry too much about all this. She didn't used to worry, but I bet she does now.

The orchid lei I bought for Beatrice at the airport lies on top of her hairbrush. The flowers are tangled with strands of hair. Her straight black hair and his brown and curly. I bet she even lets him use her toothbrush.

I stuff the dirty things into a pillowcase and carry the whole thing to the back door. The lei I hang over Beatrice's high school graduation picture on the end table in the living room. She looks so pretty in this photograph, not like later, in college, when she threw away her makeup and let her hair grow long. I made her send this picture to Annabel Lee, along with a graduation announcement. Annabel sent twenty dollars and a nice card back. She wrote to Beatrice: I can't get over how much you look just like your mother. That made me feel good. That Annabel Lee remembered me looking like that.

I keep Annabel's letters in a shoe box. The box that used to hold my favorite red sling-back pumps. My shoes are down with the crabs, but the box is still good. I just have to put Scotch tape over the corners now and then.

I read her letters when I can't sleep. I answer her in my head.

Dear Annabel Lee. I can still hear you talk. I can still hear you laugh. The way you pronounce every syllable so carefully, like English is brand-new. Some people think you're being stuck-up, but I know it's just how you talk. Like words are bells you ring.

Sammy won't let me read her letters out loud, even when they come to both of us, like at Christmas or on our anniversary. I send back cards with just our names. I have too much to say, so I can't say anything. I buy cards with thoughts close to mine. For my dearest friend. So many miles, so many years. An ocean cannot keep us apart.

She writes: Alice, when are you coming to visit me? The airplanes go faster now. Florida is not as far as you think. You don't know the meaning of far.

Sometimes she drives two, three hundred miles in one day, just to go visit somebody, and then she drives all the way back home. All by herself, now that Coy is gone. I don't want to go if she makes me do that. That's six hundred miles, twenty times around the island.

Annabel Lee reminds me of when I was brave. When the Japanese attacked Pearl Harbor. When we lived under martial law and worked for the Army. All those leis we made for our brothers and friends going off to fight in the war. Too many goodbyes.

I'm so glad I had girls. Goodbyes are not the same with daughters.

Annabel Lee is wrong. I do know what is far. Far is more than the miles you can go in one day. Far is my daughter Lurline, who cannot tell me what she thinks. Far is my older girl, Beatrice, who can but doesn't, at least not all the time. Far is my husband, Sammy, who talks to himself, who talks to everybody but not me, not like I want him to talk. Far is my friend Annabel Lee, who hardly comes home anymore. Far is everything I'm not, every place I don't go.

Me, Alice Lum, now Alice Woo. I am the only one who stays home.

YEAR OF THE HORSE

Annabel Lee is a Pig. I'm a Pig too, and so is Beatrice and my mother. That makes four of us who should be all the same, but look how different we are.

Sammy is a Dog. I thought he was a Pig when we first met, but then I found out he flunked fourth grade. A Dog is loyal, but stubborn too. That's him all right. It's the loyal part that worries me. Who or what is he really loyal to? In Sammy's case I think it's fishing. Fishing and his mother, because his mother is dead. His father too. If they hadn't died, his whole life would be different. Mine too. Sammy would have been a happy man, we wouldn't have run away to Maui, and my girls and I wouldn't have almost drowned.

I have Annabel to thank for getting me back home to Oahu. Annabel and my brother Michael, who came all the way from Michigan to help us pack and move. Michael is a Ram, wise and gentle, the kind of person you want to confess to. Not like a priest, but almost.

I'm loyal too, in my own way. I never give up hoping for the best. I'm an optimist, but not exactly, because I'm still scared when I leave the house. I don't go out much, only where I have to. Sharlene's Shear Shop in Pearl City. My parents' house in Kapahulu. Sammy shops for me at Foodland. Beatrice buys our clothes. I only go to the beach if the water is flat and I can sit right by the lifeguard. People think I'm scared of water, but it's not just water that makes me nervous. It's being surrounded, ambushed, like in the cowboy movies. I hate having too many things to choose from. I can never make up my mind. If I say yes to one thing, that means no to another. I feel sorry for the animals in the zoo. I could let them all out and not think twice.

When I take a shower, I need to face the spigot. I don't like water falling on me from behind. When Annabel came to see us on Maui, after the girls and I got caught in the flash flood, I couldn't even wash my hair. She had to pour water over my head with me still lying on the bed and the basin on the floor. She made Sammy go outside so he couldn't hear me cry. She got water all over the sheets, then afterward she rubbed my head and sang to me so I could sleep.

The only thing I don't mind is the dark. Sammy says I give him chicken skin, the way I can sit in the dark for hours. When I'm outside in the sun and I close my eyes, the inside of my eyelids turn yellow and red like a traffic light. But in the dark, there's only one color. Black and only black.

Year of the Horse, 1930. My father's birthday. My mother begged him to take the day off from setting bones, but he refused. His doctor's office was in the back parlor of our house in Kapahulu, so he planned to keep on working, even though my mother had invited all our relatives and friends to come over that day for a birthday party. Hard times called for a good party is what she believed. Better to act rich, so prosperity can find you. You'll be the one all dressed up, ready to live.

She said to my father, Today you rest, Dr. Lum. Today you celebrate.

She always called him Dr. Lum, even to his face.

My father pulled his black cap over his ears and padded down the hallway to the back parlor. My mother grumbled as she tended to the pots steaming and boiling on the stove.

All a time work work, she said. No good. No good.

A long butcher's apron protected her new dress, shiny and made of gold silk brocade. Too fancy for home, but she wore it anyway. I watched her barter for the dress in Chinatown. It was a good trade. One dress for her and a new red blouse for me in exchange for one week of housecleaning plus a visit to Dr. Lum plus a large box of Chinese pretzels that she let me help her fry in the outside wok.

Seven o'clock in the morning and party guests were already show-ing up at the back door, yelling through the screen. Into my mother's hands they shoved boxes of manapua and roast pork. They gave me bags of fruit to carry into the kitchen. Bananas and papaya and guava. My favorite kind of mango, Hayden. My brothers' favorite, Pirie.

All day long they trickled in—uncles and aunties, cousins and second cousins, my mother's mah-jongg friends, and dark, wrinkled men from my father's plantation days. The bachelor men, my mother called them. They knew my father when he first came over from China and worked as a cook. They said his soup was good, but noth-ing compared to the rubbing liniment he brewed from herbs and bourbon. They lined up after supper, waiting for my father to rub yok jow into their bruises and soothe their aching bodies. Tit Da Ee Shang, they called him. Doctor of sprains and fractures. Bone healer.

My mother protested each gift of food. Oh, you. Why you bring so much. But she smiled as she carried each box to the long table in the dining room. Then she yelled at me: Alice, hurry up. Get tea for Aunty and Uncle.

I hated pouring tea. I rushed, spilled tea on the floor, on my toes, on their toes. I did not like standing among the grown-ups, listening to their loud chatter, feeling their calloused fingers pinch my cheeks and brush my bangs out of my eyes. I liked the li see money—shiny pennies wrapped in red paper—but not the kisses or their wrinkled cheeks.

As soon as I could break free, I ran to the front door, where my father's patients were waiting. That was my real job. Ushering his patients into the back parlor.

I loved the back parlor, the darkest and best room in our house. This was where my father, the bone healer, performed his magic.

He sat on a big wooden chair with a straight back and a hard seat. The chair rested on a pedestal, like a throne. People stood in front of him, waiting until he reached out and touched the part of their body that was sore. He always knew where the hurt was, without them having to tell him.

His hands were large and belonged to a man twice his size. His fingers looked like chicken bones, thick at the knuckles, skinny everywhere else, but strong. When I was younger, he could lift me with just his two baby fingers. He held me with his arms straight out, not even shaking, and me dangling in the air until my mother scolded him to stop. Aiiyaa, she said, broke hand, broke hand, then no more work. He never answered her, just lowered me slowly to the ground.

But now I was seven years old, too big to carry, but finally old enough to help. I squatted in the corner of the room and watched my father work.

The boy had fallen off a mango tree. His father put a bottle of bourbon on the floor next to my father's throne. The boy whimpered when Dr. Lum reached out, but he didn't cry. Dr. Lum did not press very hard, just moved his fingers lightly over the surface of the boy's arm. Sometimes his fingers lingered in one place a little longer, then moved on. He worked with his eyes closed and then leaned back in his chair when he was done, his eyes still shut. The boy's father poked his son's arm lightly.

Still sore?

And the boy, excited now: No more. All gone.

What you say?

Do jay, do jay. Thank you, Dr. Lum.

What you do?

The boy bowed his head. The father bowed too and thanked my father over and over again.

I led them out to the hall, where they squinted as they walked back out into the light.

My father stood up. He waved his hand at me, so I knew he wanted his pipe. Not his tobacco pipe, but the other one he kept in a secret drawer. It wasn't going to be a long smoke, not like when he went downtown, but just a little one that blew away when he turned on the fan. I wasn't supposed to let anyone into the parlor then, so I went out into the hallway and sat in front of the closed door with my arms folded and a stern look on my face. I acted like nobody was allowed in there but me, but the truth is, I was locked out too.

While I waited, I pretended I was the one with the broken ankle or the arm in a sling, and Dr. Lum's big hands touched only my leg, my body, and left all the others to suffer and rot. Sometimes I pretended I was Dr. Lum, with his high forehead and hollow cheeks, what people called horse face.

Better to look like a Horse. Better to be born in the Year of the Horse, like my father, than in the Year of the Pig, like my mother and me. Pigs love to feed people. Pigs love lots of company and noise. From my mother I inherited my moon face. My short legs, my crescent eyes. But it is the Horse who succeeds, the Horse whom everybody admires.

My mother hated when I wouldn't talk. She said I was just like my father. Hard Head, Tight Lip.

The older children picked on me, trying to get me to scream. When I did, they laughed and ran away. They wanted me to run to my mother and complain, but I never did.

I healed the cats and dogs in the neighborhood, the ones that would come to me, and after a while, most of them did. I sat and waited for the babies and the younger children to come to me too. I closed my eyes and ran my fingers over their tiny arms and legs. If I was very quiet, I could even hear the little bones go click click click right into place.

CHINAMAN'S HAT

Maybe we have the wrong day, the wrong flight. Maybe Frankie wrote it down wrong. But it's April 1, 1979—how could I forget April Fools' Day? Besides, it was Beatrice's handwriting on the calendar. The backward scrawl because she's left-handed. The red ink so we don't forget.

Beet arrives 1:15 p.m. United.

She's saving miles for a free trip to the mainland, plus Sammy likes to go to the Red Carpet Room for drinks.

Lurline thinks going to the airport means visiting the fish. She loves the carp. Red, orange, and blue carp, like Christmas lights shining underwater. She drags me over to where Sammy is squatting by one of the pools in the garden down between the runways. He wiggles his fingers in the water, like worms. He hates all these fish swimming around loose, but he's not allowed to catch them. When he sees me coming, he stands up and sticks his fingers in his pockets. He jingles his keys and coins.

Lurline points at a red carp. She likes red fish the best.

Yes, I see it. Pretty.

I wish I could tell her the truth, that red fish give you nightmares. I wake up screaming every time. Sammy scolds me for waking up the girls, then he conks right out again. Before I can go back to sleep, I have to eat guava jelly and toast. Guava jelly, not strawberry jam, not at night. Strawberry is too lumpy going down.

Lurline leans against her father, lays her cheek on his shoulder. She's almost as tall as he is, taller than me and her sister, Beatrice. Whatever part of her stopped growing, it wasn't her legs. She wears one of Beatrice's old miniskirts, which barely covers her panties. She likes for me to shave her calves with Sammy's electric razor. She likes the noise. She likes for me to pretend I'm driving a car up and down her legs.

The plane engines hurt my ears. The way they squeal like a pig going to slaughter before they take off, and then again when they land. Sammy says that's just the way they make them now, but I still don't like it.

Beatrice's husband, Frankie, carries the baby plus her diaper bag. Emily grabs Frankie's wire-rimmed eyeglasses and pulls them off his nose. He pries her fingers off his glasses and whispers into her ear. He points at the door where people are coming out, one, two at a time. The tour guides next to us hold up signs. Aloha, Bill and Lois Drews. Aloha, Mr. and Mrs. Tolopka. Emily squirms in Frankie's arm. She wants to come down. I can see she' s getting ready to scream.

Something tells me Frankie needs his hands free. He's nervous about seeing Beatrice. Sorry for the silent treatment he gave her before she left for Georgia.

I wave at Sammy to come and get his granddaughter. Carry her, take the diaper bag, keep her from crying. Don't want Beatrice to see her baby like this.

Frankie pulls out a cigarette. Marlboros in the cardboard box. He strikes the match and waits for the black to leave the flame. His hand shaking, his cigarette too. Beatrice gave him a gold lighter with his initials, but he still likes matches better. He and Sammy stock up whenever they go out. They give me the matches to hold for them. I keep them in Sammy's brandy snifter and in Beatrice's pottery bowls. I read all the names. All the places they go that I never go. My travelogue.

Wait till Beatrice sees Frankie's haircut. She didn't like his sideburns and ducktail, but this is much worse. Frankie says the music in the barbershop was a little far out and the barber wore dark glasses and clipped to the beat. Frankie says, Don't worry, it'll grow back in a while, but I'm not so sure that's soon enough. His head looks smaller now, and the grease makes his hair stick together so you can see his scalp underneath. I wish he wore the baseball cap I gave him for Christmas, but Emily keeps pulling it off his head. But even with a hat, he'd still look like a Chinaman. Too Chinese, too pake. Beatrice won't like that.

Frankie blows big smoke rings in the air. First one, then two, then three. Like a powwow.

First thing I notice is, she's wearing a new dress. A sleeveless scoop neck with a full skirt, white with big, bright flowers all over. A Marimekko print, floral, and I thought she hated floral. Plus she's holding hands with a man. He's hapa-haole but not local. I know him from someplace, but I can't think of where. He's carrying a funny-looking suitcase. Long and black and round on one end.

Frankie says, Wait here.

I'm not moving. I'm staying right where my feet are stuck.

Sammy comes over by me. He's carrying Emily, who's sucking her bottle. What's up? he says. Who's that?

I tell him, Frankie says wait, so I'm waiting. Must be somebody he knows.

The man's hair is brown and wavy, pushed back behind his ears. He holds his hand out to Frankie for a shake, but Frankie is rude and doesn't take it. They stand there talking, so I can't hear, and I keep hoping Beatrice will call me to come over. I won't go unless she calls.

Sammy says, What the hell, what's going on? but he stays right by my side.

I'm glad we're at the airport, not at home. With all these people around, Sammy won't talk too loud, he won't make a scene. Neither will Frankie. Not like the actors on TV, and I'm glad.

I wonder what's inside that bag. Maybe a tennis racket or a shovel.

Frankie throws his cigarette on the floor. He doesn't even step on the butt, so it's still smoking when he walks back to us. He doesn't say anything, just grabs Emily from Sammy. He takes the diaper bag too.

Beatrice hurries over to us. The man stays behind, watching her overnight bag. She wants to hold Emily, but the baby won't go to her. Emily's face is blank, like she doesn't recognize her own mother.

Frankie says, Don't force her.

Beatrice says, Just let me carry her.

Emily starts screaming, and Frankie says, That's it, we're going. He turns around and walks toward the terminal with Emily, the diaper bag swinging from his shoulder. Now it's like TV.

Give her time, I say to Beatrice. She's just shy. She'll come to you when you get home.

Beatrice starts crying on me, and that's when the man comes over. Beatrice tries to introduce me and Sammy, but Sammy's face is shut—a who-do-you-think-you-are kind of shut—and he won't shake hands either. He says, I better go help Frankie with the bags.

I don't have leis for both of them. I only have an orchid lei that I bought for five dollars at the airport lei stand. The first time I ever bought a lei from the airport because I was too lazy to make one. I feel so cheap. Doesn't look good, giving a lei to my daughter but not to him. Won't catch me buying leis again. Look what happens when I do.

Beatrice crying and saying, Don't you remember Aunty Annabel's son? Give the lei to Wick, Mom. Give it to him.

Annabel's son.

He has to bend over twice. First, so I can put the lei around his neck. Then, so I can kiss him on the cheek.

Coy Whitlow's boy.

He says, Thank you, Aunty Alice, and I'm so shocked by his voice. It's like his father, Coy, talking to me after all these years. He looks like Annabel Lee, but he has Coy Whitlow's Southern drawl. He's so grown-up. A handsome young man.

But what's he doing here? Why is he hugging my daughter? Why is he kissing her on the mouth, like she belongs to him, not Frankie? I'm so confused.

·   ·   ·

At the baggage pickup, Beatrice says I can ride with them in the taxi.

Sammy's not talking. Just standing by the door waiting for me, and I'm glad to see that his hands are in his pockets. Frankie and Emily are already in the car. I know I should go with them, but Beatrice grabs my arm. She needs me to stay with her.

We sit in the back seat of the taxicab. Annabel's boy and me with Beatrice in the middle holding both of our hands. The seat feels greasy. Good thing I'm wearing Capris and don't have to sit on the cushion with my bare legs. The taxi driver puts the funny-looking suitcase in the trunk, along with Beatrice's luggage. Beatrice says Wick doesn't have any bags, only his banjo. That's what's in there, not a shovel. She says if I want he'll play it for me when we get home. I don't know what to say. I've never heard a banjo before.

The taxi driver watches them kiss in his rearview mirror, and I stare at the moving numbers on the meter and wonder who's going to pay. I have only three one-dollar bills, two quarters, and five matchbooks in my purse.

When we get to the house, Frankie has already come and gone with Emily. After Beatrice calms down, Wick brings out his banjo. He says to Lurline, What songs do you know?

Beatrice says, Play "Michael Row the Boat Ashore." She likes that one.

I'm glad Beatrice is being nice to her sister. The banjo sounds good, just a little bit loud. He plays with his thumb and two fingers moving at all different times.

Sammy is outside, drinking beer and slamming things around in the garage. I should fix him something to eat, so he doesn't get drunk, but it doesn't feel right, walking away while the banjo is still going.

Wick plays "Five Hundred Miles" and "Ticky Tacky Boxes," and then he plays a fast song that I don't recognize. His banjo gets real loud. For sure Sammy will grumble. He won't say anything now, but I'll hear it tonight, just me alone.

That was "Foggy Mountain Breakdown," says Wick. A real banjo song, not like the others.

Beatrice looks at me. I'm not saying one word. She's laughing and crying. Her eyes are swollen and black underneath, where her eyeliner has smeared. She says to Wick, Maybe you should play something slow. What about "Amazing Grace"?

He says, You okay, babe? You want me to stop?

She says, No, play. The music helps.

She sings along with him. "Amazing Grace, how sweet the sound." Beatrice has a low, deep voice that matches Wick's, which is a little high for a man. He has the kind of voice I like, a voice I've heard before. When I close my eyes, I can go way back. A day like this that I should pray to be over, but I'm humming along. Gracie Todama will love this song because it has her name. Maybe tomorrow I'll ask him to play it again for her.

Chinaman's Hat. The tide was out when we waded out to the island. It was me and my brothers—Russell, Michael, and Joe-Joe—plus two of my boy cousins. The water was so shallow, I could pretend that I knew how to swim, that I was bigger than five years old. The seaweed tickled my neck and wrapped around my toes. The seaweed was my shawl, and me, a beautiful mermaid.

The island looked just like a hat, a coolie hat, pointy on top and flat all around. That's how it got its name.

The Chinaman floated to China, said Michael.

Nah, he wen drown, said Joe-Joe. That's how come you only see the hat.

Russell said, Shut up, don't scare her, but it was too late.

My brothers and cousins swam over to the reef, where it was deep, and I stayed on the sandbar to look for shells. I watched the boys jump off the reef and swim all around where I couldn't go.

Alice, Alice, they shouted. Come by us.

I shook my head. Didn't want to get salt water in my eyes. Wanted to stay where I could touch bottom, where I could see right through the water to all the pretty coral. Plus I could walk around the island if I got tired of one spot.

The sun was hot and my fingers were wrinkled. I was getting thirsty, and I had to keep climbing farther and farther up the rock so the water didn't come up above my waist. My brothers and cousins were still playing out by the reef.

My mother waved at us from the beach. I waved back. Then everybody was waving. My mother, my aunties, but not my father. He was pointing and talking to one of the uncles.

My uncle scared me when he swam up from behind. I was high on the island now, watching the boys. He shouted at them.

Better come back, he said. Tide coming in.

My uncle gave me a piggyback ride to the beach. I clung to his neck and kicked my feet to help him go faster. He made my brothers and cousins swim in front of us, like a parade, except that Michael and Joe-Joe got farther and farther behind and my uncle was too busy to scold. When we reached the sand, I looked out toward the water. I saw Joe-Joe but not Michael. My mother was screaming, my father standing with his arms folded. My uncle dropped me to the sand and then ran back in. He swam past Joe-Joe. I began to scream like my mother for my brother Michael, Michael.

When we got home, my father gave Michael good lickings for almost drowning. Only Michael, nobody else. He hit him on the head, on the back, on his legs. Michael didn't cry, but my mother cried, and I cried too, feeling every blow as if it were my own.

5

ALL THE LITTLE BONES

Wick is the April Fool. He has nothing to wear, just what he wore on the plane. When he didn't get off in L.A., like Beatrice thought he was going to, his luggage got left behind. His bags are still waiting for him in the Los Angeles airport. At least, that's what he hopes. Me, I'm keeping my fingers crossed, although I wish we knew last night. Sammy could have bought Wick some shorts and underwear when he went to Wigwam for the sheets. These kids just don't think ahead. They want to live now, not tomorrow, even if it means wearing yesterday's clothes.

Beatrice says, That's okay, Wick can wear Daddy's clothes until we have a chance to go shopping.

But I don't think Sammy will like this idea. I wonder too what poor Wick is thinking. He sits on the couch wearing Sammy's Bermuda shorts, four inches too big, and Sammy's T-shirt, so tight I'm ashamed to look.

Beatrice digs in a box of Frankie's clothes and pulls out a pair of jeans. Before I can stop her, she grabs the scissors and cuts the legs off to make shorts. I can't believe she's doing this, cutting up her husband's pants. Is this my daughter? How did she get so mean?

She says, Here, try these. The jeans were loose on Frankie, but on Wick they are just right. Beatrice makes him turn around to show off his nice okole. She rolls the bottom of the T-shirt so his stomach shows, and then she leans over and gives him a big Blow Fat, right above his belly button. The noise makes him jump, makes me jump, and Wick grabs Beatrice and lifts up her blouse so he can give her a Blow Fat back. Lurline climbs on the couch next to them. She wants to Blow Fat too.

I can't watch. I have to go in the kitchen and sit down.

Beatrice spends all morning packing Frankie's clothes in boxes. She just throws them into the boxes, any which way. I have to take them out and fold them right.

I'll never hear the end of this from Frankie's mom. She's probably down at the clubhouse right now, crying on the senior citizens, telling them it's all my fault. That Aggie Chew. First, she nags until she gets me to tell her how old I am. Then she tells everybody in the Golden Age Club that I am old enough now to join, even though I'm younger than her, younger than all of them. She says I need to get out of the house, so my girls can have a chance to grow up. She says I need to start dancing again. She knows from her sister-in-law, Barbara Chew Harimoto, what a good dancer I am. I finally say okay just to shut her up. As long as I don't have to show up at the club, I don't mind paying my dues. She knows I don't like to go out. She's still mad because her son and my daughter came to live with me, not her.

Frankie, Frankie. He's being interrogated now, but if I know him, he's not saying much.

I should have seen what was coming. Beatrice going out with her friends for drinks after work. The way she bosses Frankie around. The way she leaves all the worries for him. And Frankie just letting her come and go, never complaining out loud. She's been asking for a fight, begging for a good reason to stay home, besides her duty as a mother and a wife.

It's not like Frankie doesn't care about her, but it's not the kind of caring that she wants. He has a way of showing love that she doesn't appreciate. When he washes and waxes her car, when he irons her uniforms at the same time he does his shirts, she doesn't even say thanks. She only complains because he doesn't buy her floral bouquets anymore, like he did when they were dating. And she hates when he checks the TV schedule before he takes her out to a movie.

She says all she wants is a little romance, and what does Frankie do in answer to all her grumbling? He shops. He researches what he wants to buy and then he goes out hunting for it. It could be anything—a painting, a pair of pliers, a record album. He brings it home like a trophy and it keeps him happy for days.

That's how he got all those shoes. Beatrice has filled two boxes already and still has more to go. He even has the shoes he bought on the mainland, when he was going to St. John's College of the great books in New Mexico. The shoes were too good for school, so he brought them back. But he still doesn't wear them, because his feet get swollen in the heat and he wears one size bigger now. He even has a pair of ski boots. Heavy plastic, like what the astronauts wear. He let me try them on once, outside on the lanai. Sammy grumbled: No fall down, unless you like go hospital. And no broke the concrete. So Frankie gave me his ski poles to hold, and even Sammy had to admit that I looked cute in ski boots and shorts.

Frankie wears stacked heels, just like Beatrice. Some of his shoes are four inches tall, which is good for him, but I have to shake my head. He owns a pair of black-and-white wing tips too. He doesn't realize those shoes always remind me of Wick's father, Coy, from when we danced together during the war. Frankie bought the wing tips when he managed the Chinese restaurant in Santa Fe. He could have become half partner if he didn't move back home to marry Beatrice. What we give up for love. Now he's selling shoes at Reyn's in the Ala Moana Shopping Center. He's the youngest, but number one in sales, and he can buy all the shoes he wants at 15 percent off.

Wick borrows Sammy's slippers to wear when he goes to the store. His feet stick out over the front and back, and I worry he might stub his toes. Wick's feet are big, size eleven. What Beatrice calls humongous. His toes are long and pointy, not Vienna sausages like Sammy's and mine. Beatrice laughs and shakes her head, so Wick puts his loafers on. They're old shoes, scuffed all over, and they need a good polish. He even wears them barefoot. No socks.

Shoes, shoes. My father's kingdom came from shoes, not from setting bones. He built another throne in Chinatown before the war, this one for shining the shoes of the men who were arriving in Hawaii by the shipload. Mostly sailors and soldiers, but also sheet-metal workers, welders, and other men who worked in the shipyard at Pearl Harbor. When I went to the market with my mother, I squatted on the sidewalk like the old men and watched them. Pak gui, my mother called them. White ghosts. They were scary all right—the way they roamed the dusty streets of Chinatown like dogs in a pack—but they didn't look like ghosts to me. For one thing, they were every color but white. Their faces pink and red and black, their hair yellow and orange and brown, their eyes blue and green. Their long legs were real, the hair that grew all over their arms and poked out the front of their shirts, the smell of sweat and shaving lotion, beer and cigarettes. The only thing like a ghost was the smoke that blew out of their noses and mouths and circled their heads like clouds.

At first, my mother nagged my father to get a job as a chef. Not a cook. Head chef. She wanted him to work at the best Chinese restaurant on the island, at Lau Yee Chai in Waikiki. She couldn't exchange the food and whiskey my father's patients gave him for everything we needed. She wanted to send my brothers to college and me to private school, if she could save enough money for tuition.

But what my brothers and I wanted most was an automobile. Our very own American car, a Ford, shiny and black, so we wouldn't have to ride the streetcar all the time. We could drive around the island and visit all our friends and relatives, especially the ones who lived in the country. My mother's mah-jongg friends would be surprised when we dropped her off at their houses, and so would the ladies at church. A new automobile would make my mother high society, and she liked this idea.

My father said he would never drive the car, even if we could afford to buy one, but he went down to Waikiki anyway to apply for a

job at Lau Yee Chai. My mother ironed his khaki pants and white shirt and made him wear shoes instead of slippers.

Russell can drive the car, she said. And then later on, Michael and Joe-Joe.

We cleaned house while my father was gone. I helped my mother scrub the kitchen, the bathroom, the floors. Then while my brothers and I washed the windows, inside and out, my mother started cooking. She wanted to feed my father all his favorites when he came home, if he didn't start work that very day, of course. She cooked salted duck eggs, bitter melon with black beans, and harm ha pork. The odor of shrimp sauce and garlic filled the house.

But when my father came home, he was barefoot. He scrubbed his feet while my mother asked too many questions. How come they didn't hire him, how come his pant cuffs were full of sand, what did he do all day, where were his shoes? My father refused to answer. He shook off his pants on the steps, then retreated to the back parlor. His cave.

We sat down to eat, but nobody was hungry, except for Joe-Joe, who loved harm ha pork and ate the whole bowl by himself.

Five days later, my father was shining shoes in Chinatown.

My brothers and I helped set up the shoeshine stand on the sidewalk in front of an herb shop on Maunakea Street. The owner of the shop, Mr. Chung, was my father's good friend. My father sent many customers to Mr. Chung, so he was happy to help out. When my father wasn't shining shoes, he could sell herbs. That way he wouldn't always have to stand outside. It didn't look good for a bone doctor to be working on the street. My mother was glad to hear this. Shining shoes wasn't exactly what she had in mind when she urged my father to get another job.

My father nailed a chair to a wooden platform. It reminded me of the throne he sat on while setting bones at home. He waxed the chair until it glowed, then let me try it out. I could see everything from up there. I could look right into people's eyes and spy into their shopping bags. I could see the sailors coming, their thick white caps nearly tipping over onto my lap.

I painted a sign:

SHOESHINE CHEAP

My father couldn't read or write English, but he told me what to say. My mother criticized the sign. She said, How much cost? Cheap not free. So I painted the coffee can too, in big black letters.

On the front: SHINE 5¢

And on the back: THIS MEANS U.

Everybody had a job except for me. Russell moved boxes in a warehouse, Michael delivered milk, Joe-Joe sold newspapers, my mother baked shortbread and Chinese pretzels, which she sold in big glass jars. I wanted to help my father polish shoes, but my mother said it was a boy's job, so Michael and Joe-Joe went down to Chinatown after school to help. Joe-Joe walked up and down the streets with a shoeshine box, but Michael helped my father at the shop.

I got to visit the shoeshine stand when my mother shopped at the market, but that was all. I envied my brother Michael so much. I wanted to squat next to the throne like him and wait for shoes to clean and polish. My father stood inside, spying through the window. He didn't go out until a customer appeared. Then he made Michael watch while he demonstrated how to clean off the dirt, how to put on the paste, how to buff until he could see his face in the leather.

When school let out for the summer, my mother finally gave in.

You can hold sign, she said. Watch can. Make sure they put money. No touch feet. No touch shoe. And stay away from the pak gui.

My brother Michael sat on the stool, waiting. I shook the sign and watched for shoes. Black shoes with black shoelaces, brown shoes with brown shoelaces, long shoes, wide shoes, some shiny, most of them dusty from the sand and the gravel and the dirt.

Michael didn't look up until the shoes stopped in front of him and my father came out of the shop.

I envied the men sitting on the throne. All they had to do was sit and close their eyes while my father and brother did all the work.

My brother's fingers were stained from the shoe polish and from the pencils and chalk he used to draw with when my father wasn't looking. He scratched on the sidewalk, on the dirt, on butcher paper. Shoes without feet, shoes marching, shoes close together like mountains in a range.

My father's fingers were dirty too. Black under his fingernails, black on his fingertips. Fingers that were my father's eyes, fingers he used to heal fractures and sprains.

Sometimes my mother brought us snacks. Coconut-filled buns and candied fruit for Michael and me. Hot tea, dried fish, and salty lemon peel for my father.

My mother was very happy with the money we brought home. While we washed our hands in a bucket outside the back door, my mother counted up the cash on the kitchen table. She let me help her stack the coins. Most of the money came from tips. Sometimes men gave us whole dollar bills. Gambling money, Michael told me. They snapped the paper money in half, the long way, before they stuffed it into the can.

My mother didn't know that sometimes my father massaged feet while Michael polished shoes. My father made the men come inside the store, where they sat behind a screen and soaked their feet in a basin of soapy water. He pulled their toes and shook them one by one. He rubbed the bottoms of their feet until they groaned. My father's stained hands and their big, lumpy feet. They closed their eyes and smiled, so happy. My father pressed all the little bones and the big ones too, clear up to their knees.

They paid him good money for that. They gave me money too. Nickels and dimes. Whole quarters, my own two bits. They called me Honey and Sweetie. My father told me to bow and say thank you, but I was afraid to bow. Scared they might pat my head. My mother had a good nose for anything bad. She would know if they touched me, and then I wouldn't get to keep the money.

I loved the herb shop. Loved the dark room, the strange odors in every jar, and the burning incense on the counter. If Michael came inside, my father twisted his ear and made him go back outside to wait for customers. But me, I got to sit behind the counter. I spun myself on the stool, high off the ground, around and around, until the room got dizzy and everything was double. Two of my father, four hands, twenty fingers, and more than I could count in the jars along the wall. Things I couldn't even name. Things you make tea with and swallow to make you feel good again. Herbs and leaves. Twigs and lizards and bones.

When we got home, my mother made me strip down in the shower, and then she washed me from head to foot, like I was still a baby. I complained, but I loved the way she lathered me with soap, all white and bubbly, the way she rubbed me with the rough towel, my skin turning red. Her strong hands scrubbing and cleaning every inch that was me.

6

WHAT A GIRL TELLS HER SISTER

Annabel Lee wanted to have only one baby. But she lost the girl inside her after she and Coy got married. Then she gave birth to Wick, and after that she couldn't have any more.

The way her son follows me around the house. He's grown-up, over six feet tall now, so it makes me feel funny. The way he talks to me, just like a lady friend, telling me how he feels, what he likes to eat, asking me what to wear, how he should talk. He won't sit down unless I'm sitting down, and he stands up when I walk in the room or get up from the table. At first it was like Queen for a Day, but now I just want him to stop. It makes me nervous, the way he pays so much attention to what I'm doing. Beatrice says it's his Southern upbringing, polite, sweet talk, and all. I guess I should remember this from when Annabel and I went out with Coy, but it's different now, being the mother. What you notice, what makes you worry. I wonder how much Wick knows. I wonder what he's told Beatrice. It would be like Annabel to tell her son everything, but how much of it is true? When Beatrice asks me about Wick's father, I tell her Coy was just a friend, a good friend during the war. She doesn't suspect anything, although she ought to know that being a mother doesn't make you immune from doing stupid things.

I want Wick to go out to the garage and make friends with Sammy, but he won't go near him, not without Beatrice around. Not that I mind that much. In the morning after Sammy and Beatrice go off to work, Wick stays home and keeps me and Lurline company. He even helps me clean house. He's good at vacuuming, even more careful than Frankie, and he sings while he mops, so I can't complain too much when he forgets to take off his shoes before coming in the house.

Sometimes I wonder if Annabel raised him to be the daughter she couldn't have. She's always been jealous of my girls. She used to say if I wasn't going to come visit her on the mainland, then I should send the girls over by themselves. She wanted me to put them on the plane and give the airlines her photograph so they could see who was responsible at the other end.

As if I could do that.

My mother calls to find out what's going on, but of course she already knows and is checking just to make sure. I thought maybe she heard about Wick from Frankie's mother, Aggie, but no, she tells me it was from her friends at church. She wants to know if Beatrice and Frankie are going to get divorced, and I can already see the smoke. Between my mother and Aggie Chew, I don't need to hire a plane to go up and write our family troubles across the sky. Why waste money? By tonight, everybody from Wahiawa to Aina Haina will already know the whole scoop.

Aggie Chew calls me too. She's upset because all of a sudden she's the main babysitting popo, not me. Now she can't go to the clubhouse any old time she wants. She says, I just called to see how you doing, Alice. Just because of these kids don't mean you and me have to be strangers.

What she really wants is for me to take Emily every morning, plus three, maybe four, afternoons a week, so she—Aggie—can go dancing down at the clubhouse by the Ala Wai Canal. She has two big dance exhibitions coming up, so she needs extra time for practice. She says she knows I understand why she wants to keep this just between the two of us. That means don't tell Beatrice, and especially don't tell Frankie.

Aggie Chew makes me feel bad just for letting things happen, so I'm shaking when Beatrice comes home. As soon as Wick stops kissing her, I blurt out everything.

Beatrice is tired. Her eyes are red from crying. I can tell she stopped by to see Emily on her way home from work, and now she wants to get out of her inspector uniform, take a shower, and forget. Emily is finally coming to her, which makes things even harder for Beatrice now. At first she was hurt when Emily ignored her, but now it's the opposite—Emily won't let go. She clings and cries when Beatrice has to leave. Frankie says, It's all your fault, look what you did, she's all confused.

Frankie's talking more now. Beatrice doesn't report everything to me, but I hear more than I need to from Frankie's mother.

Beatrice looks at me like I'm her last straw. She says, Oh, Ma. I told you I'm taking care of everything. Don't let those blabbermouths get to you.

She stomps down the hall to her bedroom, and Wick follows close behind.

Blabbermouths! That's what she calls her mother-in-law-soon-to-be-ex. That's what she calls her own popo—my mother—and the ladies at the First Chinese Community Church. Sometimes I think she's not my girl, the way she doesn't care what people say.

He kisses her too much, I think.

It's all happening so fast. Beatrice says the divorce will be final next week. The waiting period is only seven days. Beatrice filed the papers two days after she came home from Georgia. One week, that's all it takes to get divorced nowadays, and it took her and Frankie ten years to get married. I almost gave up hope of being a grandmother. But by next Wednesday, that's it. Over. Pau.

She's giving Frankie full custody of Emily. She says having the baby was his idea, so now it's up to him to raise her. I'm sick when I hear this. She's afraid the baby will get in the way. She doesn't want to lose the loving, and who am I to tell her the loving can go, baby or not. Maybe things will be different for her and Wick.

But I know she goes over to the Chews' house after work, hoping to see Emily before Frankie comes home. I see the empty boxes on the back seat of her car. The ones the new baby toys came in. And I notice the stuffed animals leaving Emily's crib one by one.

I just don't want her to have regrets.

I hear them in the bedroom before supper. Beatrice crying, her voice muffled, so I know she's talking into his chest. He's rocking her, then singing her favorite song, "Killing Me Softly," and pretty soon I don't hear crying anymore.

When they come out of the bedroom, she's all smiles again. She's wearing her blouse and panties and skipping down the hall to the bathroom, shouting, Save some pupu for me, I'm so hungry the horse better watch out.

First day of my freshman year in high school. My new school, St. Andrew's Priory, an Episcopalian school in downtown Honolulu. I begged my parents to drop me off before we got to the main gate, so the other students wouldn't see our car, wouldn't see the crocheted doilies on the dashboard. My mother tried to pretend the Ford was new, not a secondhand jalopy that we bought with shoeshine money, but that car, it jerked and popped, especially with my father driving. Plus I didn't want my mother to talk to the nuns. Didn't want the Sisters to see how excited she was. If I turned into an old maid, if I ended up in a convent, it would be my mother's fault for listening to her church-lady friends and making me go to this private school for girls. All girls, only girls.

On the ride into town my mother said, Wash you face, you ears. You hair once a week. Wear slipper in the shower. Wash you panty in the sink. Roll um up dry in the towel. Call me now when get you rags. I like know when get you rags.

.   .   .

The Sister with the soft voice, Sister Mary Clementine, asked a tall and pretty hapa-haole girl to take me upstairs to my room. The girl was my roommate, Annabel Lee. Her eyes were wide and tapered, her cheekbones high. Her hair was reddish brown, thick and wavy all over and sticking out, even though she wore it pulled back into a bun. On the way to our room, Annabel Lee showed me the dining room, the lavatory. The baby dorm too, where she stayed when she was younger. She said, When we're juniors, we'll get to babysit.

I felt old all of a sudden. My life as the youngest, as the baby in my family, the only girl, suddenly over now.

Up in the room, Annabel said, This is your cot and this is mine. She got the bed by the window because I was new. She said, You can borrow my alarm clock, just don't wind it up too much. And don't call me Sissy. Only my family calls me that.

On my pillow lay two carnations, one red, the other one white, with the long stems still on. She picked them from the governor's yard next door. She picked them just for me.

I said, Thank you. I didn't know the governor grows carnations. You sure this isn't stealing?

Don't be silly. The governor didn't grow them. His gardener did. Besides, they're red and white, our school colors, so he must want us to have them. Otherwise they're just going to die. At least these two are for a good cause. To celebrate your coming. Why, don't you like them?

Of course, I liked them. Nobody had ever given me flowers before. Leis, but not my very own carnations with the stems still on. She showed me how to trim one inch off the bottom of each stem. She put the carnations in a glass of water and placed them on my trunk so I could see them when I went to sleep and when I got up first thing in the morning.

Walking down the path to chapel with a white handkerchief on my head. I didn't have a veil like Annabel's yet. A veil that I could tie around my neck so it wouldn't blow off in the wind.

This is stupid I feel so stupid why do I have to wear this napkin I'm not a nun I'm not married to Jesus I don't even know how to pray.

Annabel told me when to stand, when to kneel in church. She opened my prayer book to the right page. She let me share her hymnal.

Annabel Lee's fountain pen scratching across the page. We were supposed to be asleep, not sitting by the window, writing in our diaries by the light of the moon. Annabel wrote with royal-blue ink, never black. She had a dark blue spot on the knuckle of her middle finger and a big callus from writing so much. I had a callus too, but mine was black from writing with a pencil, so I could erase.

Annabel Lee said I should write with ink. She said, A diary is supposed to be what you are thinking at the time. You're not supposed to change your mind. The way you feel is how you feel.

But what if I make a mistake?

Just tear out the page. Throw it away.

I can't do that.

Sure you can. You think too much. That's why it takes you so long to write. Don't read what you write. Keep on going no matter what.

The way her pen flew across the page, her handwriting big and taking up so much space. She ended her sentences with exclamation points, and she signed her name after every entry. She signed Annabelle, with the Annabel and the Lee running together and the last e forming a wavy line under her name.

Annabel Lee was half Chinese, one-fourth Hawaiian, one-fourth Scotch. When I told her I was only Chinese, nothing else, she said, Well, at least you know where everybody is.

I didn't know what she meant by that, and I was afraid to ask. I knew she had a mother, a beautiful hula-dancer mother, and a father who owned a restaurant in Chinatown. When her parents came to take her home for the weekend, she was always so happy to see them, especially her mother. I watched them from the window. Her mother hugged her, and they whispered and laughed, like sisters.

Her father didn't say much. He followed them until Annabel's mother turned around and smiled and waved for him to come. When he walked up to her, she kissed him, right there in the courtyard, in front of the coral cross.

Pearl Hanohano asked Louisa Chun, and Louisa Chun asked me. I rushed back to the dorm to pose the question to Annabel Lee.

If you could marry a young and poor man or an old and rich one, which one would you choose?

Rich one, of course, said Annabel Lee.

You would marry an old man?

No, I said rich.

That's not how you're supposed to choose. You have to pick young and poor *or* old and rich. You cannot have both young *and* rich.

I didn't say young. If I have to marry at all, he just better be rich.

Annabel Lee sent me a note in study hall.

Let's sneak out early for lunch. I want to get to the piano before Marjory Cunningham.

How?

Tell Sister you have your rags.

Not me, you tell.

NO, YOU.

My legs shook when I approached Sister with my lie. But when I went to the bathroom and checked my panties, sure enough, there was blood.

Annabel Lee could play anything on the piano. She could play from notes or by ear. All you had to do was hum the song and she knew what keys to hit.

Let's be the Andrews Sisters, she said.

I thought there were three sisters.

You can sing one part, I'll sing two.

Her voice like a bell. Ringing every syllable, loud and clear. She could even sing without the piano. All she had to do was play the first note, and then she could sing without looking at the words. Right into my eyes. Like the song was for me. Only me.

The choir director, Mr. Cody, caught her playing the organ before choir practice. She played "Georgia on My Mind," slow and loud and sexy-like. Mr. Cody was an Englishman with a wooden leg and a cane, so we heard him stumping down the aisle. But not Annabel. She had her nose in the keys. He waited until the song was over before he coughed. Annabel flew off the organ bench and ran all the way to her place in the choir.

She sang soprano in the front row. Mr. Cody assigned her the number one spot.

Annabel Lee wasn't boy crazy, not like the other girls who had boarded at the Priory since they were small. I wasn't boy crazy either. We both had older brothers who took us hiking and fishing and let us play ball. If we wanted boy friends, we could get them anytime.

At lunchtime we danced in Queen Emma Hall. We took turns dancing the boy's part. Annabel said if she had to choose between a boy who couldn't dance and a girl who could, she would always pick the girl. The other girls hated when Annabel made them dizzy by twirling them around so fast. They didn't like when she tipped them way back at the end of the song so their hair swept the floor. They were afraid she might let them go, and she never promised that she wouldn't.

Every now and then boys came over to dance with us. They marched off the bus looking so solemn. Eighth grade, ninth grade, boys from Kamehameha and St. Louis. They all wanted to dance with Annabel Lee, even though she was so tall. She knew how to make them look good, even the ones who stepped on her toes. She was pretty, and they liked that. But she would let them have only one dance apiece. One, and then they had to sit down and let the next one ask.

Sister Martha Verity found my panties soaking in the bathroom sink. She marched into the dining room while we were eating breakfast and said, To whom do these belong?

They were white lace panties. Huge. The girls laughed and looked around the room for the girls who were fat. I wanted to faint. I wanted to fall and crack my head wide open so they would have to carry me away.

My mother bought my panties big, so I could grow into them. She said all her lady friends wore this kind. I had to close the waist with a safety pin. I didn't wash them unless I was alone in the bathroom. I squeezed them dry and hung them under my towel. Sometimes I wore them wet all the way back to my room. But that morning, I forgot.

When Annabel looked up and saw my panties, she said, I'm sorry, Sister. Those are mine.

She walked up to Sister Martha Verity, took the panties, put them in her school bag, and sat back down. She sprinkled sugar on her toast, like nothing had happened. Nothing at all.

The girls called Annabel Sissy Miss Prissy because of the way she walked into the room. Like she was a model or a beauty queen contestant. They imitated her when she wasn't around. They laughed at me when I stomped out. They thought I was going to tell her what I saw, but I could never tell her. Never.

Annabel taught me to say Roman Catholic, not just Catholic, because Episcopalians are Catholics too — Anglican Catholics. She said Father Peter was a minister not a priest. And we had Holy Communion but not confession. A bishop, not a pope.

I had so much to learn. Annabel Lee helped me memorize what I needed to know and more. The Jubilate Deo and Gloria in Excelsis. The Apostles' Creed, the Lord's Prayer. The verses in Ecclesiastes about a time for this and a time for that. I wanted to be pious and pray on my knees all day and eat the Body and drink the Blood from the shiny silver goblet that Father Peter wiped with a thick white napkin before he pressed it to my lips. I wanted to sing the way he sang. All in one note, all in one breath.

•　　•　　•

The bells rang at noon. No matter where we were—in class, in the hallway, in the bathroom—we stood up and faced the bell and recited the Angelus.

BONG Hail Mary full of grace the Lord is with BONG Blessed art Thou among women Blessed is the fruit of Thy BONG Holy Mary Mother of God pray for us sinners BONG and at the hour of our death Amen BONG Mary full of grace the Lord is with Thee BONG art Thou among women blessed is the BONG of Thy womb Jesus Holy Mary Mother of BONG pray for us sinners now and at the hour of our BONG Amen Hail Mary full of grace the BONG is with Thee Blessed art Thou among women BONG is the fruit of Thy womb Jesus BONG.

I counted the bells. After the twelfth ring, it was time for lunch.

When I went home to visit my family on the weekends, I felt so guilty because we didn't pray. Even my mother, who went to church, didn't pray out loud at the dinner table. I had to say everything to myself. When I ate at Annabel's house, we prayed together out loud, her mother too, and Mr. Lee never acted as if we were doing anything strange. When Annabel first came to stay overnight at my house, I hoped she would pray with me, so my mother would get the idea.

But instead, Annabel said, The food looks so ono, Mrs. Lum. And then right after that: I like your dress, where did you buy it? Pretty soon the two of them were talking like old friends, and after dinner my mother showed Annabel all the clothes in her wardrobe. Annabel sat on the bed and watched my mother model a green dress that made her look like a frog. Even my father said so. Annabel grabbed a white belt and a gold brooch and showed my mother how to make the green less solid. They spent one whole hour mixing and matching my mother's outfits while I washed the dishes and swept the kitchen floor.

Before we went to sleep that night, we prayed. Just Annabel and me. She said it was okay to skip a few. It wasn't like we were Roman Catholics and had to confess.

•   •   •

One day I found two pairs of panties in a brown paper bag sitting on my pillow. They were plain white cotton, like what all the girls wore. And just my size. I looked at Annabel.

I don't have money, I said. I can't pay for these.

No need pay, she said. I told my mother they're for me. She lets me give away my panties if I want to.

What do the Sisters do when they go inside their house, do they pray all the time, what do they wear under their habits, are their heads really shaved?

Annabel Lee stole from the Sisters' clothesline one brassiere and a pair of cotton panties, both of them gray and limp and enormous. She tried the panties on in the toilet stall. Both of her legs fit into one hole. We stuffed our neckties into our mouths to keep from laughing. At lunchtime we sneaked through the fence into the governor's back yard and hid the underwear behind a mock-orange bush.

What a girl tells her sister: Act like nothing happened. If they call on you, don't look away. Look right between their eyes.

Annabel Lee pulled the cotton bedsheet over her head. She lay on her stomach, propped up on her elbows. Her hair was pulled back, so the sheet pressed against her forehead and around her cheeks like a nun's habit. That made me laugh, the thought of Annabel Lee as a nun. The flashlight lit up her eyes, her face.

Oh, my darling Cody, she said. My heart beats for you.

The thought of Annabel with the old choir director made me scream. I had to bury my face in my pillow so the Sisters didn't hear me laughing. We were not allowed to close or lock our door, so the Sisters could check on us any old time.

We took turns reading with the flashlight. Annabel said we could read anything, but not Jane Austen. She was sick of novels about women looking for husbands. We had to read enough of those in English class. She said, Here we are at a girls' school, trying to pretend we don't care about boys, and they make us read these stupid books.

Marriage was stupid, but not love. True love.

Her voice like a bell, ringing through the hot night. No breeze coming in the window. I rolled from one side of the bed to the other to keep myself cool. I was finally drifting off to sleep when she said, Now it's your turn.

But I couldn't read like she did. I stumbled over the words. I raced through the verse. She liked for me to read Edgar Allan Poe, of course. His poem about Annabel Lee. It was a morbid poem—the girl dead and all, gave me the creeps—but Annabel loved that poem, especially the part about love and the soul. She said our souls would be like that, never severed, even in death. Our souls would always stick together because we were sisters in spirit, and I liked that.

What a girl tells her sister: Speak like you mean every word. Like you believe in what you're saying. That's what it means to live a passionate life. That's how I want to live. Passionately. Every single minute.

My mother had to get sponsors to send me to the Priory. We couldn't even afford to buy a real trunk. My father built me one from wood scraps. He painted it orange, because orange covered up the different kinds of wood he used.

When Annabel Lee saw my trunk, she said, You're lucky yours is so bright, not dull and boring like mine.

But I loved her trunk. It was made out of real wood, all the same kind, so it looked good even without paint. Besides, it was an antique, an heirloom from her Scottish grandfather. She wasn't nice to that trunk. She hid food inside it. She slammed the lid so hard, the hinge broke off. She carved a heart on the top and in the middle, she scratched the initials RLS.

RLS stood for Robert Louis Stevenson. That's what she called her grandfather. RLS. Louis.

Annabel's hair was the color of horses, a reddish brown, mahogany. Every morning she combed her hair into one thick braid or swept it up into a bun. And every night she pulled the ribbon off and let her hair fall loose again. The opposite from what I did.

While she brushed her hair, I rolled mine into small, tight circles, then pinned them flat against my head. But in the morning, when I took the bobby pins off, my hair went straight right away. Annabel tried to put my hair up like hers, but my hair wasn't long or thick enough, so I had to go back to my same old look. Hair parted on the left, pins horizontal, one on each side. Every bit of me that wasn't round looked square. Square hair, square collar, even my camisole had a square neckline that cut across the V of my middy blouse.

How come you have so much hair? I asked her one night.

She said, Because my mother always gives me lomi lomi. I'll show you.

She washed my hair in the sink and massaged my scalp so hard I was afraid for what little hair I had. Then she twisted my hair into tight braids, still wet, tied the ends off with rags, and made me go to sleep like that.

The next morning she untied the rags and told me to bend over and shake.

Don't comb, she said. Don't brush or pin it back.

The waves lasted all the way through breakfast. All the way through chapel. When I walked into the bathroom, the face in the mirror startled me. It was me, flushed and sassy and wild. It was me because of her.

Annabel said, Bet you too chicken to climb the ylang-ylang tree.

The ylang-ylang tree grew in the middle of the courtyard. Everyone would see us.

I said, I can if I want.

Prove it, then, she said. Prove it.

She climbed and I followed. We hung upside down, but the other girls couldn't see anything because we wore shorts underneath our skirts. All they could see was Annabel's long hair coming down through the middle of her skirt, her laughing face, and me, holding my arms tight around my blouse, too scared to laugh. They watched us from below, from the windows, from the top of the steps. Chickens all waiting for us to fall down or get caught or expelled. But we didn't fall or get caught. We didn't get kicked out of school.

•   •   •

We smuggled bread and butter under our blouses and ran to the lanai upstairs. There we read poems and ate bread and drank the grape juice that Annabel brought from home. The poem we always read first was "The Rubaiyat of Omar Khayyam." The bread was our Loaf; the juice, our Jug of Wine; and we, each other's Thou, singing over the boughs of the ylang-ylang tree below.

My other favorite tree was the coconut tree that grew right through the roof of the Waikiki Theater, where we went sometimes for movies on Saturday afternoon. Annabel said the tree was fake, but it looked so real to me. Outside, the coconut leaves soaked up the sun, while inside we squinted in the dark to see who was there. Maybe we'd spot a boy we knew, or one we hoped to meet. Maybe even the love of our lives, like Annabel used to say, as we put on eye makeup in the ladies' room. We sat up in nigger heaven and pretended we were Ginger Rogers dancing in the arms of Fred Astaire or Merle Oberon yearning for her Heathcliff, Laurence Olivier.

We also went to the YWCA on Richards Street to swim. When Annabel found out I could only dog-paddle, she signed me up for beginner lessons. During open swim, she helped me practice my strokes. Sometimes we just talked and treaded water, and I got so I could tread water for twenty minutes at a time. I had strong legs, and I was a good floater. Annabel said it helped that I had an okole that bobbed like a cork.

What a girl tells her sister: We're supposed to be leaders and go to college. Not just get married and have babies. That's why we go to the Priory, not to public school. So we can learn to speak good English. So we can be smart like boys. Smarter even.

I wanted to be a nurse. An RN. Annabel Lee wanted to be a dancer and a dress designer too. She wanted to design costumes and ball gowns. She said we had to find a college where we both could

study. Maybe in San Francisco or, better yet, New York. As long as we were going away, we might as well go far.

New York. Fifth Avenue. Broadway.

The Sisters taught me religion, but Annabel taught me how to dream.

Annabel and me, walking to Chinatown after school. Down Hotel Street, Maunakea Street, past the bars and barbershops, the little stores with crates of dried food spilling out onto the sidewalk, the fat Hawaiian ladies stringing leis, and the men, of course, always them. Our long white cotton middy blouses hugging our hips. We rolled up our black wool skirts at the waist to show off the lace on our slips. We knotted our black neckties low, at the very tips. The sailors always looked twice at us, then smiled and winked, because of the way we were dressed—like them, but not. They swung their long black neckties at us. Annabel swung hers back, and then we laughed and took off running for her father's restaurant, Fat Lee Wo. Annabel's hair flying loose behind her, our ties and wide collars flapping, our legs, our hearts pounding.

We tried on five colors of lipstick at Kress's before we decided which ones we liked best. Glamour Girl red for Annabel Lee, Princess pink for me.

I drew them over and over in my diary. The profile of a girl. Her high forehead, pointy nose, voluptuous lips, curly eyelashes, long hair. The profile of a stallion. Flaring nostrils, big eyes, wild mane, the bit in his mouth.

7

DRESS WITHOUT A BODY

Wick doesn't want to call his mother, but I tell him he better or I'll never hear the end of it. Annabel still doesn't know he's followed my daughter all the way to Honolulu. She thinks he's home in Florida, watering her flowers and watching the house. She doesn't even know yet that Beatrice was in Glynco, Georgia, at customs inspector training camp. Wick says my letter is still sitting on the kitchen table, waiting for Annabel to open it up.

He dials long distance to Baltimore, where Annabel is visiting her friend Judd, who is a doctor. Not just any old doctor, but a plastic surgeon.

Long time to be in Baltimore, I tell him. Beatrice was in Georgia for six weeks. Doesn't your mother have to work?

Sure, he says. She sells real estate when she's home. She and Judd went on a Mediterranean cruise and then up to his cabin in Maine.

I'm thinking doctor, cruise, must be serious.

I'm also thinking Beatrice must have called Wick and told him where she was. They wanted this to happen, and yet they sit on the couch, holding hands, like they are together only because of luck.

Wick doesn't like to bother his mother when she's at her boyfriend's house. He says she gets mad if he calls at the wrong time. But now should be okay. Sunday morning, eleven o'clock, which means five o'clock East Coast time. If they're at home, they're drinking cocktails

before going out to eat. They eat in restaurants most of the time because Annabel doesn't like to cook.

Speaking of food, I hope Wick will hurry up and dial before Sammy comes inside for lunch. I don't want him to ask who's paying for this call.

Wick speaks loud and deep into the phone. He says, Hi, Judd, this is Wick Whitlow. Is my mother there? Yes, I'm fine. Everything's fine, sir.

When Annabel comes on the phone, his voice gets soft again.

He says, Hi, Mom, I'm calling from— Yes, the house is— You said you'd be— While you were—

He tries to tell her the whole story, but his sentences are only half. He talks quicker now.

Yes, it happened that fast! But it's right, I know it is. I'll get another job, okay? Aunty Alice says we can stay— I know. Just until we find an apartment.

Finally, he's quiet. I can hear her voice from where I'm standing, not what she says exactly, but it's not hard to guess.

Wick says, She's getting a divorce. I can't help— It's not all my fault. Don't get— Yes, Aunty's right here. Do you want to talk to her?

He hands me the phone. Me, why me? I shake my head. Don't want to talk to her when she's like that.

Beatrice says, Talk to her, Mommy. Please.

She calls me Mommy, so I can't say no.

Annabel says, Alice, you folks okay? What the hell is going on?

Nothing. Everything's fine.

That's not what I just heard. I can't believe they did this. I had no idea. Did you know what was going on?

Oh no. Not me.

And here I thought he was at home. All my plants. My flowers are going to die. I guess he told you I'm in Baltimore.

Yeah, he told me.

What else did he say?

Nothing. He said you were visiting your friend.

Judd. He told you about Judd?

Little bit. How was the cruise?

She sighs. I guess I have no room to complain. Listen. Let him give you some money for food, okay? If he doesn't give you enough, I'll send you some.

No need money. We have so much food. He eats like a bird.

She laughs. She says, Make him give you something anyway. I want him to get a job. How is Sammy taking all this?

Not bad.

I bet. Where is he? Why don't you talk?

He's outside. Working on the house.

Listen, Alice. Don't let Wick take advantage of you. He still doesn't know what he wants to be when he grows up. He hasn't seen RLS in so long.

Mmm.

Let him wash his own clothes. And tell Beatrice not to pick up after him. I didn't know those two were so close. What about her husband? What about the baby? Oh, I'm so sorry. Those crazy kids.

Mmm.

Let him cook, too. And he knows how to clean house. Don't spoil him. I've tried so hard to raise him right, and this is what I get. I can't even go away for a little while.

Sammy cooks too.

Well, in case Sammy doesn't feel like cooking. Or make him take you out to eat. I'll send some money. Let me talk to him. I'm sorry about everything, okay? You take care. I'll talk to you later, when I get home.

I don't want to hear the rest, so I go into the kitchen. Wick doesn't say much this time, and then Beatrice gets on the phone. Her voice is small. She gives short answers and then is quiet in between. After they hang up, Beatrice says to Wick, Jesus Christ, your mother is a fucking interrogator!

Wick laughs. She is, but you know what? I think she's glad I'm here.

He kisses Beatrice again and again. Right there on the couch.

Is this where Frankie went wrong?

They don't see me staring. They don't see me thinking it's time to go ask Sammy what he wants to eat for lunch.

Annabel's husband left her for a man. But that's a terrible story, so if anybody asks me, I tell them he ran off with a waitress. Coy's a truck driver, on the road all the time, so that's not too hard to understand. I never told Beatrice the truth, but I guess she knows now.

Wick asks me what's all this about Robert Louis Stevenson, is that who his grandfather really was? He says his mother only talks in a circle, and I don't know what to say. Sometimes I think she must still love Coy. The way she calls him RLS.

Poor Wick. He wants so much to be Hawaiian. He is part Hawaiian—one-eighth—but he wants more than blood. He wants the family too.

Tell me about the King, he says. Tell me about my great-great-grandfather. Kalaniopuu.

I wish he wouldn't say the King's name out loud. He can almost pronounce it too. Like he's been practicing his whole life. I can just imagine what Annabel has told him. That he has royal blood, that he's descended from a king. I'm not superstitious, but sometimes I worry that the real family of King Kalaniopuu will find out and get mad. But I can't tell him it's just a story. That it isn't true, because maybe it is.

Too bad his grandma is dead. Dora Kaiulani would be so happy that Wick has finally come home and wants to know about his family. She wouldn't worry that the boy doesn't have a job. She would say, Alice, you know why this happened. You and Sissy are so close, your babies cannot help but love each other too.

I can hear her talking. Dora Kaiulani. I can hear Wick and Beatrice too. They have more love than they know what to do with. It's a crazy love all right. I can feel it in my bones.

.   .   .

On Monday morning after Beatrice goes to work, Wick tells me he wants to go out. He has ants from staying home, waiting for the divorce, which is final tomorrow. I draw a picture for him on how to catch the bus so he can go to the Bishop Museum. I show him where to transfer, where to get off. I tell him when he gets off the bus to walk makai one block to get to the museum.

Makai, I repeat. Make sure you go makai.

He says, What's ma-key?

The way he says it—ma-key—comes out meaning "dead." So I say it again louder. Makai. That means toward the ocean. The opposite way from mauka. Mauka is toward the mountain, yeah?

He nods, but I can tell he's confused by the way he pushes out his lips. So I draw another picture, this one of the island with a mountain range running down the middle. I make waves all around to show the ocean. Then I draw arrows as I talk.

This way mauka. To the mountain. Makai. To the sea.

He goes over to the living-room window and looks out. From our house we can see all the way to Pearl Harbor. We can see the gray ships and the blue water.

He says, So that's makai.

Yup.

And mauka is that way. He turns around and points out the sliding door of the lanai, up toward the highlands.

That's right.

He swings his arm around the room and says, But the ocean surrounds the island, so makai is everywhere you go that's not mountain.

Nod.

And if that's the case, then there are a whole lot of ways you can go. I might add that it's all controlled by sight. But what if I can't see the ocean or the mountain? What if there's a building in the way? What if it's nighttime? Then what?

He stands there grinning, the little smart aleck, and I'm getting this funny feeling, like I've been here before. That day Annabel and I waited two hours for Wick's father, Coy. Coy was waiting for us on the mauka side of the Royal Hawaiian Hotel, while we sat on the beach wondering why he was so late. We finally gave up, thinking it must be another one of those times when he failed to show up without any explanation. But when we walked around to the other side of the hotel, there he was, pacing up and down the sidewalk.

Wick's eyes are bright and open wide. He still wants an answer. So I tell him what we told his father, Coy, what I know he won't like to hear.

You better ask somebody. You better ask for help.

Bishop Museum is a good place for him to start. He can look at the statues and see what Hawaiians used to wear a long time ago. He can see how people lived and what they ate, and maybe he will recognize himself. His dark eyebrows, his thick hair, the body of a warrior, a hula dancer, a surfer, even with so little Hawaiian blood. Beatrice says he's light on his feet because of tennis, but I don't think it's only from that. He tells me he wants to dance the hula and play Hawaiian music too. He can already pluck the melody to "Little Brown Girl" on his banjo. Dora Kaiulani would be so proud.

Annabel Lee was born with dancing in her blood. That was the story I heard from early on, from Annabel, then from her mother.

Dora Kaiulani said her grandmother danced hula for the King of the Big Island, Kalaniopuu. That was before Captain Cook came along and tried to kill the King. That was before Kamehameha conquered the islands. King Kalaniopuu would have been old, but not too old for what it took. Some people said it was only talk, that the King wouldn't sleep with a common woman, but Dora Kaiulani's tutu wasn't common. She was more royal than all of them. She was the best hula dancer too.

Dora Kaiulani called Annabel by her nickname, Sissy. When I went over to Annabel's house, I had to practice getting used to that name. Annabel said, My mother calls me that because I take after her. Her mother called her Sissy too. Could be worse, but I won't let them call me Sister.

Dora Kaiulani said Sissy's dancing blood started before she was born. At birth she was not zero. She was zero plus her mother plus her tutu plus her tutu's mother. When you added all that up, Sissy's dancing blood was as old as all of them put together. It was not like the other kind of blood that could bleed away. Sissy's dancing blood would stay with her forever.

Dora Kaiulani said, You can dance all you want. Hula, ballet, ballroom. Any kind.

She put her hand over her left breast. Just remember where it comes from.

Me, I had no nickname, no dancers in the family, not that I knew of anyway. I didn't even know my own popo, who was still in China, so I loved it when Dora Kaiulani called me Sweetie.

Sweetie, what the soldiers called me, like it was my name from long ago.

A wedding dress hung on Annabel's bedroom wall. It was her tutu's wedding dress, white silk fading to yellow and brown, with tucks across the front of the bodice and a double-tiered skirt.

Why is that dress nailed to the wall? I asked. Why don't you hang it in the closet?

It doesn't fit anybody, said Annabel. My mother couldn't fit it when she married my father, so she put it on the wall. For good luck.

Good luck in my house meant red paper, oranges, roast pork, money. Not a dress hanging on the wall. A dress nobody could wear anymore. How could a dress bring luck?

Annabel said, RLS bought the dress in London.

I said, Which RLS? The real Robert Louis Stevenson or your grandfather?

Annabel said, Look at this picture and tell me what you think.

She pointed at the picture on her dresser. It showed a haole man with a long black mustache and a little bit of hair on his chin. Then

she brought out a gold locket and opened it up. The picture was very small, but it looked like the same man.

I said, Is this your grandfather?

She said, You can't tell the difference, can you? You don't know who is who, so you have to believe me.

She snapped the locket shut and put it back in her jewelry box.

After supper I lay on the mat and watched Annabel and her older sister, Emma, dance the hula. Dora Kaiulani beat the ipo and chanted in Hawaiian. Warm air rustled through the trees and blew across the lanai. The girls swayed in their pretend skirts, Dora Kaiulani's scarves tied around their hips. I didn't understand the song except for the end. Haina ia mai ana kapuana. And now I'm at the end of my story. But I could tell what was happening by watching their hands. They told a story of the mountains, the moon shining beyond the reef, the rain falling from up high, the ocean waves crashing down below.

As we lay awake in bed that night, Annabel said, I like when we dance on the beach. Just my mama and me. Not Emma, because I'm the best. We dance at night, in the dark. The salt water is good for blessing. But my father doesn't like it. He's afraid we might drown and he won't be able to find us in the dark.

Annabel Lee scratched my arm as she talked. The way she drew her fingernails across my skin. So light and soft, and yet I could feel it clear through to my toes.

I dreamed about the dress without a body. It flew off the wall and out of the house and down across the valley. I tried to run after it, but I couldn't move my legs. I woke up perspiring. Annabel lay next to me, snoring gently. The dress on the wall looked like a woman without a head. I got out of bed and went into the kitchen to look for something to eat. Some cake or pudding. My mother said bad dreams meant that my stomach wasn't content, so I needed something sweet to make it happy again.

As I tiptoed through the house, trying to find the kitchen in the dark, I heard a voice singing. It was Dora Kaiulani. I followed her high voice into the living room and through the screen door to the lanai. From there, I could see into Annabel's parents' bedroom.

Dora Kaiulani was in there dancing, wearing nothing except her panties. Her face glowed, her large hips rose and fell like waves. Her thick brown hair sprayed over her shoulders and down around her breasts. Her breasts were very large, bigger than my mother's, and her nipples were huge and dark, darker than any nipples I had ever seen. Her panties were white, made of silk. I knew because I had helped Annabel fold clothes. I had pressed Dora Kaiulani's silk underwear against my cheek.

I couldn't see Mr. Lee, but I smelled his cigarette.

I was shaking when I climbed back into bed. Shaking because I had been spying and because I didn't get anything to eat. I lay in the dark for a long time, wishing I had even a banana, my eyes closed so I couldn't see the dress on the wall, trying to stay awake, afraid of what I might dream. I kept thinking about what I had seen. Dora Kaiulani, naked, and so beautiful, much more beautiful than I ever hoped to be.

I saw my mother naked only once. She was sitting on the toilet holding her stomach and crying, but she wouldn't tell me why. There was blood on the floor and on her panties.

My mother slept in a long nightgown, like me. She saved her curls with a black hairnet. She didn't dance. She didn't even sing, except at church.

The next morning I woke to the sound of mynah birds. So many of them, squawking in the jungle behind the Lees' house. They lived up in the hills, near a trail that crossed over to the windward side of the island. From where I lay I could see the tops of the trees. Dora Kaiulani was singing in the kitchen and frying eggs and Portuguese sausage for breakfast. Annabel came into the bedroom as I was getting

dressed. I spread my nightgown on the bed and smoothed it flat against the sheet. It looked very strange, empty like that.

I told Annabel about my dream. How the dress flew off the wall and went all the way down the valley. Makai. How I tried to run after it but couldn't.

Too bad, she said. I fly in my dreams all the time. Everything is green and brown. Except for when I'm flying over the ocean. Then everything turns blue.

I said, You're not scared of falling down?

No. If I did, I'd just wake up.

She made me wear her mother's bloomers, so the mosquitoes wouldn't bite me when we went to pick guava. The bloomers were too big for me, but I loved the feel of the soft cotton fabric between my legs.

Dora Kaiulani wore her long hair up in a crown, always covered with fresh gardenias or orchids. When she kissed me good morning, she left the shape of her lips on my cheek.

I traced those lips in the bathroom mirror. Those perfect lips. I rubbed the red into the hollow of my cheek like rouge. Like blood.

SLOP BOY

Sammy tells me he can't sleep under the same roof as a gigolo. That's what he calls Annabel's son. Gigolo, not Wick, and never anything to his face. He talks to Wick and Beatrice through me. Where they going? he says to me. Him and Her Majesty—that's what he calls them, and when he's drunk, he says a lot worse.

I tell Beatrice, Never mind your father. You know how he gets.

Beatrice pays for half the mortgage plus gives me money for food and utilities every month, so Sammy can't complain that much. If it wasn't for her, he wouldn't have enough money to buy his boat and all the fishing gear. Not to mention the extra motor and all the other parts that he has to replace every year.

I have to give Beatrice credit. She's not like me. She doesn't feel guilty, and I know it's not because of the money. She doesn't believe that true love is wrong. She says all the other times were unreal, and she must have been out of her mind. The English professor she lived with at Berkeley. The hippie guy she brought home for spring vacation who took a bath only one time. When she finally moved back home, scored high on the Civil Service exam, and started dating Frankie again, Sammy and I were so relieved.

Being a U.S. customs inspector is not easy. You have to guess who might be hiding something, and then you have to find it. I don't like to think about my daughter touching all those crooks. So filthy. She only has to search the women, but that's not exactly clean. She says she can't give me all the details, because all their procedures are top secret. Just as well, because I don't want to know. At least the pay is good. Frankie doesn't make that much selling shoes.

Frankie is Beatrice's old boyfriend from her Priory days. He's a nice Chinese boy, graduated from Iolani in the top 10 percent. Frankie is a poet too. He's writing a book, his second one. He says when he finally gets published, I can have an autographed copy all for myself, because I am his biggest fan. Beatrice better watch out, because all the talking that Frankie's not doing is going down on paper someday. Besides, when he does say something, he's tougher than you think. When he found out Beatrice and Wick went to look at condos, he said he wouldn't let her see Emily anymore. He says Sammy or I have to be here or he won't let his daughter come to the house, not if Wick is around. That's what makes Beatrice mad. What Frankie is insinuating.

Trouble is, Frankie can do it. Full custody means a lot more than no dance practice for his mother, Aggie Chew.

It's a big surprise to me when Beatrice says it was Frankie's idea to have a baby in the first place. The whole time I thought it was because Beatrice's clock was ticking. Now she wants to know why I didn't tell her how much a baby would tie her down.

The way she looks at me, as if I've been dragging my anchor for thirty years.

Sammy's building an apartment over the garage. He started to put up the beams while Beatrice was away in Georgia. It was supposed to be a surprise for her when she came back. Before the tables got all turned. What Sammy wanted was for us to move into the apartment, so Beatrice and Frankie could have the house to themselves. Them plus Emily and Lurline, of course. I told Sammy, Better wait and ask Beatrice when she comes home. After all, she's paying half the mortgage. But he went ahead with the plans anyway. One bedroom, one bath, plus a kitchenette in the living room. Too small, but he wants to live simple, throw everything away that we don't use or let Beatrice keep it downstairs for us. He had to go down to City Hall five times just to get all the building permits.

He's proud because he got an ohana permit, which lets you build the extra house for family, but I don't know what family he's talking about. Frankie and Emily are gone, and now Beatrice is looking around for someplace else to live. Every piece of wood he saws, every nail he pounds, makes me count how many of us are left, how many rooms will be empty when he's done.

I want him to offer Beatrice and Wick the house. I want him to talk, make the boy feel welcome. That's all.

Sammy comes to bed acting all lovey-dovey and expects me to feel the same way back. I don't mind the liquor. I don't even mind the day-old whiskers on his face. I just wish for once he'd ask me in a nice way, not just fall on top.

Afterward he goes to take a shower and he doesn't come back. I wait and wait, and I'm feeling bad because I couldn't make my mind go away the whole time.

He's up there, in his apartment. That's how I think of it. It's Sammy's apartment, not mine, not ours. I wouldn't care so much if he was sleeping in his boat. A fifteen-foot boat is not comfortable, but he loves that boat. It's like a cradle to him. But the apartment is a different story. The roof isn't even up. He's sleeping out in the open, under the stars. All by himself.

From early on I told the girls they have to let what their father says go in one ear and out the other. I wish I could take my own advice. I feel sorry because he's an orphan, but sometimes I just want to scream, especially when he cries over his mother's jewelry. I have what my own mom gives me, but that's mine, for my girls.

Sammy says he only wants what's coming to him, what he would have gotten if his mother hadn't died when he was a baby. He blames his father for abandoning him instead of sticking around to fight for him. Now Sammy says he's going to outlive all the aunties and uncles on his mother's side of the family. Every time one of them dies, he waits by the phone for the call after the funeral. He thinks he's got something coming. He thinks he'll inherit his mother's jewelry after they all kick the bucket and he's the only one left.

The bed is so big and empty.
He doesn't even have a TV up there.
Am I that fat?

The shower is going again. Seems like the shower is going all the time now, with just one more person in the house. Especially in the middle of the night, when they come home late, when I'm trying so hard to sleep.

Sammy doesn't believe me when I say I loved him from the first time I saw him carrying slop from Annabel's father's restaurant.

Slop boy, I say to him when he's kissing me. Slop boy, when he's being sweet.

Stop saying that, he says to me.

So I say it in my head: Slop boy, slop boy.

He doesn't want to remember that time of his life, but I do. That was before everything. Before he was the slop boy. Before he fell in love with Annabel Lee. Before Pearl Harbor was bombed and they all went away and left me behind. If I could go back, that's where I want to go. Back to before the war, when I was stuffing wonton at Fat Lee Wo and Sammy was carrying slop. He says he was only doing it because he had to help his uncle. It wasn't his real job.

He doesn't understand. So I say it every time, when there is a time. Slop boy, slop boy. So he knows.

Honolulu Chinatown, before the war. Not Beatrice's Vietnam War, but mine, the Second World War. Chinatown was still noisy and busy then, but in a different way. More people on the street than in automobiles. Bicycles and dust. Music from the honky-tonk bars. Narrow alleys crowded with carts and children playing in the dirt. Chickens pecking at scraps, soon to be slaughtered and sold. Laundry hanging from clotheslines strung across the balconies. Old ladies hobbling around, men squatting on the sidewalks, smoking, watching everything go by.

I worked in Annabel's father's restaurant, starting in the summer of my freshman year at the Priory. When I met Sammy the following summer, I was already a cook's helper, working in the kitchen making dim sum, not just sweeping floors.

My mother liked the food I brought home from Fat Lee Wo. Steaming noodles and dumplings, chicken, roast pork, sometimes duck, all of it free and already cooked so my mother could spend more time playing mah-jongg or helping out at the church.

Sometimes I took food to my father's shop. Just a little, so he wouldn't be too obligated to Mr. Lee. It was bad enough being in debt for all that I took home. My father's business included shoe repairs now. He had expanded into the shop next door and had added two more thrones, plus a screened booth where customers sat while he massaged their feet. It was very hard for him, restricting himself to their feet when he knew everywhere else they were suffering too. He still hid this part of his business from my mother. She thought all the money was coming from shoes.

Michael still did most of the shoe-shining, while Russell helped my father with repairs. Joe-Joe continued to hawk in the streets, bringing back customers with worn-out soles or run-down heels.

While Michael polished shoes, my father stood behind him and inspected. If Michael left any dull spots, my father made him shine the whole shoe again and again. It was painful to watch. Michael looked so much like my father. The way their faces shut down. The way their brooding sucked all sound away, so there was only a dark hollow where there should have been a voice.

I was glad to have a job of my own at Annabel's father's restaurant, the second-biggest restaurant in Chinatown. Everybody ate at Fat Lee Wo who couldn't get into the restaurant that was number one.

Annabel said not to even say the name of the other place, not to even think it, or her father wouldn't let me work there anymore.

I loved the kitchen at Fat Lee Wo. The noise. The steam. The long white butcher's apron that tickled my shins. The small mountains of garlic and water chestnuts, pork and shrimp. The slippery dough rolled into long noodles and smooth round balls. The cleavers chopping so fast my fingers hurt to watch. The dumplings molded into half-moons, money bags, and crowns. This was art, and a person could really live on this kind of art.

My favorite job was stuffing wonton. The cooks said I was good because I knew not to put too much filling in the wonton pei. Not like Annabel, who was too generous and always in a rush, so her bloated wonton blew up in the broth. Annabel in her pretty dresses and her hair pinned with orchids, paying more attention to her face than what was going on with her hands. They sent her out front to help at the cash register, but me, Alice, I had my own apron and shared a hook with the youngest cook. And lucky for me, because if it wasn't for the wonton, I wouldn't have run into the slop boy.

My slop boy. Sammy Woo. I met him first, before Annabel Lee.

I saw him from the back. His legs were a little bowed, but not so bad that I minded. Not when I saw his thighs, thick with muscle, and his bare back, when his shirt crept up as he bent over to dump the slop. I waited as he poured the slop from the can in the kitchen into his metal bucket. I stood behind him, carrying a heavy bowl of filling for mah tai soo, which I did not want to drop. I couldn't go forward until he moved, and I was afraid to back up. Too many cooks behind me. So I lifted the bowl higher, to keep it out of the way. Just then one of the cooks yelled at me—she was carrying a big pan of steaming noodles. I jumped at the sound, the slop boy turned, and my bowl of mah tai soo filling fell right into his bucket of slop. Slop and mah tai soo filling spilled all over us, all over the floor.

Sorry, sorry! I said, as the cooks scolded in a dialect I did not understand. One of them slapped him on the side of his head.

No, I said to her. It was an accident. He didn't do anything.

I didn't even know his name.

He knelt down on the floor and began scooping up slop with his bare hands. I ran to get the mop. The cook took it from me. She used the mop to push us out of the way so she could clean up the mess herself.

Give me the bucket, she said to him. Go wait outside. She tilted her head toward the back door. You, she said to me. Go wash.

He stood up, his T-shirt barely covering his belly button. His eyes narrowing into slits, his lips squeezed tight. If he was mad at me, I didn't blame him. I wanted to faint from the smell, from looking at him.

Sorry, I said. It's all my fault.

Never mind, he said. He looked less mad, and I felt a little better. Then he headed for the door.

I wished Annabel were there. She would know what to say. She would know what to do. Me, I just watched him go, then washed my arms in the sink. My arms and my face and my throat and the back of my neck, even though there was no slop back there. How stink I was all over. Slippery, sloppy, wonderful stink. Only my brothers were allowed to get filthy, sweaty, shoeshine dirty. Just me in my crisp white blouse, ironed and washed, and my skirt with the pleats pressed flat. But now my apron, soaked clear through, the front of my blouse, my legs, covered with grease and gravy and everything rotten and smelling so bad it hurt to breathe. I couldn't stop grinning, and then I was laughing. Alice, Alice, slap your face.

I ran out the kitchen door to look for him, but he was gone and the slop bucket too.

Slop boy, I said to myself all the way home. Even Annabel didn't know who he was. She said, He takes out the slop, for goodness' sake.

I daydreamed all the way home, missed my bus stop, and had to ride all the way up Kaimuki to the end of the line and then back down again.

Slop boy, when my mother asked me where I had been and how come I stunk and why was I so late. I didn't even remember to bring

home the box of noodles that the cooks had fixed up for me until I walked in the kitchen and saw everybody waiting.

Slop boy, as I undressed and pushed my clothes down into the basin of soapy water.

Slop boy, I got you in trouble. Letting the water run and run until my mother started pounding on the bathroom door.

The cooks teased me when I came into the restaurant the next day. One of them said, Your friend never come for the slop today, just the old man. She cackled and went back to peeling garlic.

Slop boy, I'm Alice. I said it every night, as I pulled my nightgown up around my waist so I could feel the cool sheets on my hot skin.

I still didn't know his name.

I didn't see him again until the football game between Iolani and McKinley. Iolani was our brother school, and Annabel was a cheerleader, so we went to all the games. Usually I sat in the cheering section and yelled until I was hoarse. For this game, however, I sneaked over to the McKinley side after the first quarter, so I could visit with my public school friends. One of the girls gave me her black-and-gold pom-pom to wave. Go Tigers. I rolled up the waistband of my skirt and borrowed some lipstick. That's when I saw him, down on the field, carrying water instead of slop.

Who, him? Sammy Woo? Lucky he stay water boy 'cause he nevah went make the team. Yeah, he can run like hell, but him and Masa? The quarterback? Them guys no see eye-to-eye. He no like go where Masa like throw, yeah? So the coach wen pull him off the team. Tough luck, yeah? Now he can see and hear everything, but no more nothing for do. Yeah, he still carry slop. Why you like know?

If I hadn't gone to the Priory, I would have gone to public school, to McKinley, like Sammy Woo. I might even have been in class with him. I would have seen him every day. Just the thought of that made me sick.

Ask him to the picnic, said Annabel Lee. She meant the picnic for the Iolani football team that she and the other cheerleaders were organizing. I was helping with the food.

Cannot, I told her. You ask for me.

Yeah, she said. Sure, Howie will like that.

Howie Harimoto was the Iolani quarterback, captain of the football team. Everybody knew he had his eye on Annabel. Howie could have had any of the girls, but Annabel was the one he wanted, because she knew how to play hard to get.

Annabel thought for a while, then she said, Well, who's doing all the work after all? And bringing most of the food? I can invite anybody I want.

You think the other guys will get mad?

Then for sure we better ask, so they don't get swell head.

But what if Howie thinks you invited Sammy for yourself?

What do you care? You want me to invite him or not?

I nodded, but the way she was smiling made me wonder.

He didn't show up at the picnic until after we started eating. We saw him running up San Souci Beach, but we were picnicking across the street. Annabel waved and yelled, but Sammy ran right past us. He dove into the surf, still wearing his T-shirt and shorts, and paddled way out, until all we could see was his head and arms and feet splashing. Somehow it made me feel better knowing that he could swim. He caught waves for almost half an hour before he finally came out of the water. He took off his shirt and sat down on the sand with his back facing us. The way his back was heaving, I could tell he was breathing hard, which made me breathe hard too.

Annabel nudged me with her elbow. Here, she said. Go give this to him. She handed me a bottle of strawberry soda and a plate piled with sushi and noodles and teriyaki chicken.

You come with me.

No, go by yourself. Talk to him. Don't be so shy.

She gave me a little push.

Go ahead, she said. Go. And don't say anything about the slop.

All the way over I told myself, She's right, he doesn't want to hear about the slop, so don't say anything, just say, Hi, I'm Alice, but when I got there, guess what popped out.

Remember me? I said. I'm the one the slop fell on.

He looked confused.

At Fat Lee Wo, I added.

Oh. You. That was you? He smiled and shook his head. Sorry, yeah?

It was my fault. I'm Alice. Alice Lum.

Alice whose hips are too big in these pants but Annabel said I should wear them tight and my hair too flat from perspiring in the sun and all of me smoky from the barbecue and my stomach fat from eating and drinking too much while waiting for you to come. I told myself you weren't going to come so if you didn't it wouldn't matter, but you came you came you came.

He was trying not to look at the plate of food I held in my hand. The chicken leg was about to fall off.

Oh, sorry, I said. Here. Annabel Lee said to give this to you. That's her over there. She's a cheerleader.

I know, he said.

You know her?

No. I know who she is. Tell her thanks for me

He took the plate and the bottle. He stuck the bottle in the sand. I turned to go back to the picnic site.

Aay, Alice?

Yeah?

Thanks. He lifted his chopsticks full of rice and smiled.

I thought of him looking at me as I walked back to our picnic site. Don't run, I told myself. Don't let him see your fat thighs jiggle. He said, Alice Aay Alice. He remembered my name. I was so nervous, I stubbed my toe as I crossed the road. My legs were shaking as I collapsed on the picnic blanket with a big smile on my face.

Well? said Annabel. What did he say?

He said thanks for the food. I couldn't stop grinning.

What else?

I shrugged.

Did you ask him to come by us? Did you? Oh, you!

She had to go over and ask him herself. She walked over there like she had all the time in the world. She dropped to the sand slowly, with her legs folding neatly right under her. Why did I let her go by herself? Why was I so chicken? Because I wore these stupid pants. Because I knew I couldn't talk like her. Because I was stupid dumb dodo stupid.

She waved her arms in the air while she talked. I knew she was exaggerating and making eyes at him. She pointed at his plate, like she wanted him to keep on eating. Eat up, she was saying, I can get you some more.

I wanted him to eat too. To eat and not look at her. At her hair, her breasts, her legs. She was too tall and her mouth was too big, but that never stopped the boys. Her wide hips looked just right in her shorts, her bright yellow shorts cut to look like a skirt. She copied the design from a magazine. I had to help her with the hem. She hated sewing by hand.

One of the other cheerleaders, Barbara Chew, made me jump when she came up behind me and said, Who's that guy with Annabel? She pointed at them on the beach.

I said, Just a friend. Somebody I know.

Barbara said, Oh yeah? Somebody *you* know?

Sammy put the plate down and covered it with a scoop of sand. Annabel brushed off the back of her legs. He watched her, and then he stood up too and they began to walk down the beach, away from us.

Barbara Chew said, I wonder where they're going. You sure that's your friend?

I didn't know which one of them she meant.

.   .   .

Annabel Lee didn't go with Sammy until after her mother, Dora Kaiulani, died, not until after the funeral, and I couldn't hate her then. But before that I did.

You're jealous, she said. Admit it.

No, I'm not.

Oh yes, you are. You're mad because he talked to me.

Who said I was mad?

I guess you better invite him yourself next time.

Maybe I don't want to.

Okay, then don't.

I won't.

Up to you.

She didn't even ask to copy my math. She asked Priscilla Young, who she knew was just as smart as me. At lunchtime she danced with Priscilla too. She tried to teach her to rumba, but Priscilla stepped all over her toes.

Annabel had the nerve to invite Sammy to Barbara Chew's birthday party. Him and two other McKinley boys. They sat outside on the stone wall and didn't come in until Mr. Chew went outside to see what was up. Sammy told Mr. Chew that Annabel Lee had invited them as a surprise for Barbara, and Mr. Lee believed him. Barbara went along. She said hi to Sammy as if she knew him. The boys brought a birthday gift too, a small white box with red ribbon that Barbara shook and held close to her ear before she opened it up. She waved the little coin purse that was inside so all of us could see. She opened it up and three dimes fell out. Dimes because it's bad luck to give a wallet without money inside.

Oh, you guys, she said. You guys.

Aay, Alice, he said when he saw me. I was serving punch. I acted as if I was expecting him the whole time.

Aay, Sammy. Annabel is over there. I pointed.

I wanted him to see her flirting with Howie Harimoto, flirting with all the football players, so he could see the way she was. Sammy looked, but he didn't say anything, just stared until I felt sorry.

I said, You want something to eat? Try the noodles. They're real ono. They came from Fat Lee Wo. That's where I help out sometimes. I guess you know. You still working for your uncle?

I didn't recognize my own voice. I couldn't believe it was me talking. I sounded like her, like Sissy Miss Prissy, who I hadn't talked to for almost a week. A whole week.

Which uncle? he said. Slop or chickens?

Slop, I said, and bit my lip. Oh well, he said it, not me. Broke the ice. I wanted to scream, wanted to ask him about the chickens. Wanted to know everything about him.

Instead, I said, You have to try the spareribs. Barbara Chew's mother makes the best sweet-and-sour. Come, I'll show you where the food is.

We ate outside, sitting on the stone wall. Me and Sammy and our fingers all sticky and him pretending he wanted to wipe his fingers on my dress and me slapping his hands away and us talking about everything. School. Football. The chicken farm where he worked on the weekends. How many eggs a chicken could lay in a day. How you could tell an egg that was going to hatch from one that wasn't. He told me his grandfather wanted him to quit school and stay out there on the farm, out in the country, but Sammy wanted to graduate. He wanted to stay in town, even if he had to carry slop. I felt great, him confiding in me like that.

Annabel didn't know about the chicken farm. She asked me a million questions when we got back to the dorm.

I didn't want to tell her anything.

What's the big secret? she said.

But my lips were sealed.

Listen, she said. Look at me. I let you wear my clothes and use my makeup. I teach you all my songs and how to dance. I sew for you. Everything I have is yours. I tell you everything I know. Come on, Alice. Who's your friend?

•   •   •

I don't know why I was her friend. The way she promised but lied, the way she gave but took away. She was so pretty and rich, but only a part of me was jealous of that. The rest of me wanted to be just like her. To have all the luck. To be spoiled like hell. Most of all, I wanted to be bold like her. To dream. To believe that I could have whatever I wanted. The other girls didn't like her, but I knew it was because they wanted to be just like her too. She made everything that was hard look so easy. It didn't stop her if something was scary or difficult. She just wanted it even more.

Eat some of my root-beer float, she said to me at the soda fountain in Benson-Smith. I was mad at her because she made me go there when I told her Sammy was probably over at Kress's, where the soda was cheaper.

Come on, she said. I can't drink the whole thing myself.

No, I don't want any. I waved her spoon away. My stomach was queasy and I had a headache. I had failed the pop quiz in algebra, my second-best class, and I hadn't seen Sammy since Barbara Chew's party. I went over the whole party in my head, everything he said, everything I said, trying to figure out what I had done wrong.

Suddenly she yelled, Sammy, Sammy. Come over here.

I looked up. How come I didn't see him? Why did you call him?

Quiet, she said. He's coming. Act nonchalant.

He walked over to us, smiling.

Aay, Annabel Lee, he said.

He said her whole name, Annabel Lee. Like that. Then he looked at me. Aay, Alice.

I smiled halfway.

Open your mouth and close your eyes, she said to Sammy. Go ahead, close and then open.

He obeyed. How did she do that?

She began to feed him her root-beer float. He smiled, his eyes still closed. She said, Don't look now, not until I say you can.

I watched for only half a glass and then I left. Ran all the way back to the dorm.

.   .   .

She stayed on her side of the line and I stayed on mine. I drew the line with chalk down the middle of the floor. The way the line went, she had to move her bed away from the window, and I made sure she did. I gave her back her alarm clock too. And then the next morning I woke up way before her, so she had nobody to help her get to breakfast on time.

A boxer bitch abandoned a litter of five pups under our house. When I got home that weekend, I found the puppies playing under the kitchen table and rummaging through the living room. I picked up one of the dogs, pressed him against me, let him lick my face. My mother waved her broom.

She yelled, No touch! Get worm! Outside! Go!

My parents gave all the dogs away to the neighbors, except for the one nobody wanted. We named him Peanut because he was the smallest in the litter. My mother said we had to keep him outside, but Peanut cried, so Joe-Joe sneaked him in. Peanut wandered through the house after Joe-Joe fell asleep. He jumped in bed with Russell and Michael, and then he crawled under my quilt. In the morning, he woke me up by licking my face. I took him outside and Joe-Joe brought him back in again at night. This went on for a week, until my mother smelled dog on the sheets.

The next time I came home to visit, Peanut was gone. My father took him to the country, to my uncle's farm in Waipahu. It wasn't as far out as Wahiawa, where Sammy worked on his uncle's chicken farm, but there was still plenty of space for Peanut to run around free.

We went to visit Peanut a couple of times. He was so big we hardly recognized him, not small like the other dogs who stayed in town. He barked when he saw us, but he didn't run over.

But he knows me, I said. He knows me.

He's a watchdog now, said my uncle. Best one I ever had.

PUPULE QUILT

Lurline follows her sister's boyfriend all over the house. She hangs on to Wick's arm, his leg. Sometimes she even tries to sit on his lap. This makes him jumpy, and he looks worried, as if I'm going to scold him, even though I know it's not his fault. He's afraid to touch her, afraid to make her cry. He tries to get away. He says, Please don't do that, but she doesn't listen. I tell him not to smile like he's enjoying the attention, but when she tickles him, he can't stop laughing.

She's not that way with all men, just the ones she likes. The way she creeps up on him. The way she stands right behind him and rubs herself against his back.

You have to give her something to play with, I tell him. You have to say sit, stay, lie down. You have to treat her like she's your cat or dog. She wants to be your pet.

He says, I can't do that, but soon enough he can.

I make him drive up to Waimano Home, up in the heights above our house in Pearl City, to where the retarded children live. We park the car and watch the children play on the swings. Some of them are much bigger than Lurline. Lurline slaps the car window. She wants to get out and go over to play with them. I give her my watch to hold. She likes to follow the second hand around and around with her finger.

Wick says, Beet told me about this place. She said she used to come up here sometimes. With Lurline.

He looks at me. He knows something he better not tell.

But I already know what Beatrice was thinking. It's what I want sometimes too. To leave Lurline here and never come back. Everything would be so different then.

We sit there for a long time, just watching.

Wick buys a ukulele with his lost-baggage money. He says he can play any song as long as somebody can sing it for him, but I hate to sing when anybody's listening. He plays the ukulele with the banjo picks, so it sounds even louder. He knows "Little Brown Gal" and "Tiny Bubbles." Beatrice teaches him "Princess Pupule Has Plenty Papaya," which he likes a lot, so he plays it over and over. He buys Lurline a plastic ukulele, so she can play too. Her ukulele goes out of tune real fast, but she's happy strumming along. He even lets her play his banjo, until Beatrice gets jealous and cuts off the strings.

That Beatrice. She sure has a temper. When she comes home from work and sees Wick sitting around playing music and Lurline hanging all over him, she starts yelling the minute she walks in the house. At Lurline, at Wick, at me. She says something mean like, Am I the only one who works around here? Or, Do I always have to tell you what to do? Just like she's our mother. Then she goes into her room and slams the door, and if Wick doesn't go in after her, he's out with the dogs for the rest of the night. I hate to say it, but she's bitchy most of the time, and not just from PMS.

I don't know why she gets mad at Wick. He's trying so hard to do the right thing. He helps me out around the house, and he looks in the newspaper every day for a job. It's not his fault if Lurline likes him. I like him too. Isn't that what Beatrice wants? Maybe Lurline gets him a little excited, but I can see in his eyes how sorry he feels for her. How she makes him want Beatrice even more.

Wick is getting so tan. He could almost pass for local now. Every morning, after Sammy and Beatrice go to work, we rush around like mad doing the laundry, cleaning the house, and then we pack lunch and go swimming. I have to go too because Sammy will kill me if Wick cracks up the Fairmont.

At first we went to Ala Moana, but the water there is too flat for Wick. He wants to go surfing at Waikiki, but I'm scared of all that traffic. Somebody might dent the car, plus I can't park parallel, and all those shops and people on the sidewalk make it hard for me to concentrate on the road. By the time we get where we're going, my head is splitting and we have to turn around and come back home.

Finally, I let Wick drive, but he has to promise to go slow. If the cops come, he has to say I got sick, that's why he's driving. But I try not to think about cops or Sammy, just where we're headed so we don't get lost, and I don't tell Sammy about every place we go. Ala Moana is what I say, if he asks, and I cross my fingers when I do.

It's so hard to decide where to go. Wick looks at the map and says, What about Pearl Harbor?

Can't swim there.

How about E-wa?

He says E-wa, without pronouncing the *w* like a *v*.

Too much seaweed.

Maybe Ha-lei-wa? He says that wrong too.

Too far, that's way out past Wahiawa.

He looks disappointed, so I finally show him how to go to Hanauma Bay. I let him drive the scenic way, around Diamond Head, and he likes that. When he sees the big blue bay, he's so excited he wants to carry everything down to the beach in one trip. His backpack, the mats, the cooler, the snorkeling gear. Lurline and me, we carry only ourselves and the towels.

Wick's swimsuit is the bikini kind. I try not to look. It's blue with a gray dolphin on the front. Lurline laughs and points at it, and I have to slap her hands when she gets too close.

I don't like for Lurline to go in swimming by herself, but Wick keeps a good eye on her. She's not scared of the water that girl, not like Beatrice and me. Sammy made them take swimming lessons, but still Beatrice doesn't like to swim. She doesn't remember the flash flood, but I know it's from that. What she hates is being under, feeling trapped.

Annabel's boy, he's like a fish. Diving and then coming up when I least expect. I hold my breath the whole time he's down there. He likes to stay under for a very long time. I can't stand to watch, so I go for a walk. Not too far. Not out on the rocks.

Beatrice cannot believe her ears when Wick tells her where we go. I can hardly believe it myself. She says, Mommy, that's good, I'm glad you're going out, but still she doesn't come with us. Maybe on the weekend, she says, but on the weekend they sleep too late.

Every new beach we go to is like a missing piece of my life. All my years of staying home, and now an adventure every day. I'm exhausted by the time I fall in bed, but the next morning I'm up and at it, ready for more.

Wick says if I trust him to drive all the way to Hanauma Bay, why not go just a little bit farther. Like Sandy Beach.

Sandy Beach no good, I tell him. Too dangerous. Only kids go there.

But when he comes in from helping me hang the clothes on the line, I say, Okay, we can go Sandy Beach, but you better wear something else.

I can't explain, so I point at the cover of his surfer magazine.

Better if you wear shorts like this. The long kind, yeah? And slippers too. Only haoles wear sandals. And maybe you should leave your backpack at home.

When I finish my lecture, I'm shaking and he's laughing, but he listens to me. He can't wear slippers, though. The thong makes him sore between the toes.

Never mind, I tell him. Better you go barefoot anyway.

Let's make a pupule quilt, Dora Kaiulani said to me and Annabel Lee. The haoles call it a crazy quilt, but ours will be part Hawaiian, so we have to name it right.

We started the quilt in our junior year, but Dora Kaiulani died before we got it done. We were always getting sidetracked by all the clothes we wanted to sew. Dora Kaiulani said that was okay, because we could use all the scraps from the dresses for the quilt. The pupule quilt wasn't the main thing while you were making it, just in the end.

I remember in the beginning how we rummaged through the sandalwood trunk and the dresser drawers to see what we could find. Annabel and I pulled out yard after yard of cotton, linen, silk — even wool. Mothballs fell from the folds and rattled onto the wooden floor.

This fabric too good, said Dora Kaiulani. All we need is scrap. Let's see what else we can find. I know. Mama's clothes.

She pulled a faded muumuu out of a box.

This is what Mama wore after we came back from San Francisco. Day in day out, she wore muumuu instead of dress. And then before you know it, muumuu was all she could fit. Here's one more and one more, and look, my father's bow tie. He always wore bow tie, bow tie, and white linen for a suit, even if he was only staying home. Too bad I don't have his suits. Mama cut them up after Louis was gone five years. She was so crazy, she made dish towels from his pants. And this is her shawl, so long it reached the ground. She was cold all the time until she got fat.

Dora Kaiulani held up a girl's dress. It had dainty tucks across the front and a wide sash tied in a bow in back.

Look how small I was when we went to California. I'm saving this for my first granddaughter, cross my fingers and hope to God. This fabric no good for quilt anyway. Too slippery, and it might bring bad luck. Sixteen grandchildren, that's what I want. Four from each of my children. That's not asking too much.

Annabel Lee begged me to go to Sandy Beach with her. She said it was a good idea because this guy from Kam School was going to be there and she wanted to see him again. I didn't want to go. Sandy Beach was a long way out, and the surf was very rough, with a strong undertow. I didn't want to get slammed around. Plus I had to lie to my mother again, like I did every time Annabel got one of her bright ideas.

Finally Annabel said, I think Sammy might be going too.

Oh, I said. How do you know?

Somebody told me.

Who?

I begged, but she wouldn't say. I had to go and find out for myself.

It was just me and Annabel Lee and all those boys. The boy from Kam plus his cousins from Kahuku, who Annabel didn't tell me were going to be there too. Their pidgin was so heavy I could hardly understand them, but it didn't matter, because they ignored me. I sat on the sand by myself and watched Annabel bodysurf with the boys. I worried whenever she didn't come up for a while, but I didn't have to worry that much. She was tough, that girl. Even though she kept getting knocked down by the waves, she kept swimming back out for more.

The top of my head was hot from the sun shining on my black hair. The rest of me was starting to burn. When she finally came out, I said, He's not coming. Let's go.

No, she said, we have to wait. He promised me he was coming.

This was a different story than before. I didn't know what to believe.

Sammy finally showed up, driving his uncle's truck, crates and buckets rattling around in back. He had to lie to his uncle to borrow that truck. The other boys stood around looking at Sammy and trying to figure out what was going on. I was afraid they would start a fight, but Annabel made me get in the truck fast. She sat in the middle. I sat by the door, wishing I'd had time to put my blouse on over my swimsuit. Sammy pressed the accelerator to the floor, and we took off, Annabel laughing and me sucking in my stomach and hanging on to the door.

•   •   •

Dora Kaiulani pulled two slips out of the bag. Two silk slips with black lace around the edges. Silk, not cotton.

She said, Here's one for you and one for Sissy. Emma already has her own. Try them on.

I said, But it's not my birthday for three weeks.

You want me to keep it till then? Okay, then, don't be silly. Just put it on.

My slip was too long, but Dora Kaiulani said, Never mind, Winnie can fix the hem. She can take off the lace and hem it up and put the lace back on again. You might as well try this on too.

She pulled out two gold chains with a pearl on each one. Both chains were the same length, both pearls the same size.

I had to hide the necklace from my mother. I could wear it only at night in the dorm. I tucked the necklace inside my nightgown and fell asleep with my fingers pressing the pearl against my throat. When I woke up in the morning, I reached for the pearl to make sure it was still there. Sometimes I woke up in a panic because I couldn't feel it, but the pearl had simply run around to the back of my neck.

Sammy wanted to buy shave ice for us after school.

I said, No need. I can buy my own.

But Annabel Lee said, Sure, I could go for one.

I said, Okay, I'll share.

But Annabel didn't want to share. She wanted a whole cone, all her own, so I ordered a small. I didn't want to waste his money.

He paid for the shave ice all in pennies. He poured them on the counter, and counted them, one by one. The shave-ice man made him step to the side. I felt so bad, like we were robbing his bank. Annabel acted like people bought shave ice with pennies all the time. Sammy ordered strawberry and so did I. Annabel asked for a rainbow shave ice—strawberry, vanilla, and coconut. She ate the whole thing so fast, and then she started on his.

Aay, go way. He laughed, but he let her take all she wanted. It made me sick to watch.

When his shave ice was all gone, she said, Buy me one more.

No, I said.

You don't have to have any, she said. Sammy and I can share. She looked at him.

He smiled and ordered one more, another big one. Paid for it with a whole dollar bill and got loose change back.

You stinker, said Annabel, punching him.

He laughed and let her hit.

I want rainbow again, she said. I don't like only one flavor.

She invited him to her house for supper. He walked all the way up the hill to her house and was sweating when he got there. Dora Kaiulani made shepherd's pie. Mashed potatoes and corn with meat on the bottom. Sammy was so hungry he ate half the pie. Annabel only nibbled at her food. She told her mother she wasn't hungry, but I knew it was because her dress was so tight she could hardly breathe. She put on that dress while I was helping her mother in the kitchen. And all I had to wear was my stupid shorts so I could sit on the floor and help her sew, because she never warned me that he was coming over too.

How come you don't talk to him? asked Annabel. I work so hard to get you two together, and then you won't even talk.

The words got stuck inside me. What I was going to say to him. What I was going to say to her. I wrote everything inside my head. I planned it all out, and then when the time came, I couldn't say a thing.

A picnic at the beach with our McKinley high school friends.

Sammy said to Annabel, What you got for eat?

Me? she said. What makes you think I brought this food for you? Why don't you ask Alice? She made musubi for you. Alice, show him what you made.

He tasted one of my rice balls. Then he said to Annabel, Aay, you know what? Alice musubi taste more ono than yours.

Annabel threw her rice ball at him. It hit his face and dropped on his plate and knocked his food on the ground. He sat there stunned for a moment, and then he said, You asked for it. Before I could say anything, she got up from the blanket and began to run. He ran after her, her screaming and him throwing pieces of my rice ball at her. She was fast, but he caught up with her right away. They got rice all over them, and Annabel shouted at me to come and help her. Then she dove into the water, clothes and all, with him following, neither one of them looking to see if I was coming.

Just cut the fabric any old way. No worry about straight. All you have to do is fit the piece into the square someplace. See how easy. I like this kind where you don't have to make it so perfect. Real Hawaiian quilt is hard work. Even the kind your mama sews is too much trouble. She has to cut all those little circles. That would make me pupule for sure.

We hiked all the way out to the edge of Hanauma Bay to see the Toilet Bowl flush in the lava rock. I didn't need to see it to know how it got that name, but everybody was going so I went too. We walked behind our McKinley friends. Annabel made me walk in the middle, between her and Sammy Woo. They talked over my head.

Sammy said, You heard what happened to Milton Mau's uncle?

Annabel Lee said, No, what?

Somebody wen kill him with one hammer.

A hammer? You joking.

No, for real. He was lying in bed and somebody came inside his house and hit him on the head. They looking for the guy now. Milton and his father and his uncles, all them Maus. Spooky, yeah?

Annabel said, How do you know it was a man? Maybe it was a woman.

But he wasn't even married.

Who said wife? Could have been his girlfriend, said Annabel. His lover. His mistress.

Lover, she said. Lover, mistress, right over my head. Right out there with the water splashing up high on the rock. The sky was so blue and the sun too bright. I wanted to close my eyes and disappear, fall off the edge. If I drowned, she would be sorry then, especially if Sammy jumped in after me.

Hurry up, said Annabel. You're always getting far behind.

Dora Kaiulani held the faded dress against her body so we could see what it used to look like when she wore it a long time ago.

See how hungry I was back then. No wonder Sing's father felt sorry for me when I walked into Fat Lee Wo. The restaurant wasn't built yet, just the kitchen where they made manapua. Sing's father was the owner then. I told him I like sell manapua down by the wharf. I figured I could eat while I worked. He just laughed at me. He said only men could sell manapua. Only men could carry the heavy buckets. I said, Those old futs. Who like buy from them when they can buy from me? I said it just like that. He laughed, but he could see how smart I was. I stood up straight and made my chest go out, so he could see that too. That's how I got the job working in the wagon down by the wharf. He even gave me a ride down to the pier every day. To show all the men who was boss. Sometimes I think he like keep me for himself.

She dropped the dress and laughed. She said, That's why Sing won't let Sissy work in the plate-lunch wagon! He's scared she'll run off with a fisherman.

Annabel got the football boys to give us a ride to the dance at the Palama school gym. She said for sure Sammy would be there.

I don't want to go, I said.

Don't you want to see him?

You're the one he likes.

That's not true. When you're not around, he always asks about you. He's shy, that's all. Both of you are so shy you make me sick. I'll

help you sew a dress. My mother has some fabric we can use. I'll
make it even prettier than mine.

But on the day of the dance, Dora Kaiulani began hemorrhaging.
The doctors didn't know what was wrong. Annabel wanted to go
home to help her mother, but Dora Kaiulani said, No, Emma can
help me. You stay in school.

We never made it to the dance. I read to Annabel that night in the
dorm. Whatever she wanted. Short things — mostly poems — because
she couldn't concentrate on anything long. She didn't want me to
start a novel in case she had to go home unexpectedly. I read Browning and Dickinson, but not Tennyson, not Poe, and then I sang to
her and rubbed her back until she fell asleep.

Dora Kaiulani wouldn't stay in the hospital. She insisted on coming home. She wanted to plan Annabel Lee's seventeenth-birthday
party.

Annabel said, My mother says we can have ballroom dancing.
She's already hired a real live band, and we're going to have bids.
Bids! And everybody has to come dressed up or my mother won't let
them stay. She's even hiring instructors to give lessons beforehand.
Can't you just see it? She's going to make everybody dance!

She hugged me and began twirling me around the room. We
danced on her bed and then we danced on mine. When the other
girls came in to find out what was going on, we were sitting on the
floor holding each other, both of us laughing and crying, and then
just crying.

Our brothers helped us string paper lanterns and streamers over
the lanai and across the back yard. We decorated the house and the
garage with plumeria and orchids, ti leaves and ferns. Mr. Lee
catered everything — fancy Chinese dishes from his restaurant, plus a
whole table of roast beef and real haole food. White bread sand-
wiches without the crusts. Canapes which were like pupu, except
you weren't supposed to chow them down. Caviar that looked like

papaya seeds. Petit-four cakes, chocolate bonbons, a big bowl of mixed nuts already cracked. Even bottles of champagne in buckets of ice for the adults. Dora Kaiulani's plan was dance first and then we could eat. And then dance some more.

She sat in a wheelchair, her hair swept up, the crown circled with tiny white orchids, her face powdered and rouged. She wore a long purple evening gown that her dressmaker Winnie had sewed for her. The fabric was a rich embossed satin that I'd seen in one of her dresser drawers. Mr. Lee wore a black tuxedo with tails. He looked pretty snappy, all dressed up, although he kept wiping the sweat off his forehead. Both of Annabel's brothers wore tuxedos; my three brothers came in borrowed suits. Sammy's outfit looked borrowed too. It was too square in the shoulders and wide at the waist, so he looked like a box, a gift box I wished I could open. Annabel wore a white ball gown with a big organza ruffle around a very low neckline. The boys joked that her ruffle looked dangerous. If one of them got too close when they were dancing, he might bounce off. Her eyes were outlined with black eyeliner, darker than I'd ever seen, and she had painted her lips a pink so pale that it was almost white. As scary as she looked, she was more beautiful than ever. Like an angel or a fairy.

The Priory girls stood in one corner, watching the Iolani boys, who had their eyes on my girl friends from McKinley. The McKinley boys stayed off by themselves, except for Sammy, who was helping my brothers carry some extra chairs off the truck. The boy from Kam School, who bodysurfed with Annabel at Sandy Beach, sat listening to Dora Kaiulani tell one of her stories. I could see she was in pain, because her lips moved very slowly and she didn't talk with her hands.

Finally Dora Kaiulani rang a bell and said, Ladies' choice. Come on, girls, don't be shy.

Annabel walked toward Howie Harimoto, but Barbara Chew was already asking him to dance. Annabel swished past Howie, past Sammy, past all of them, until she reached the boy from Kam. As she pulled him toward her, he hugged her close, then spun her out and

around. They made a good-looking couple, her like Cinderella and him tall and handsome in his blue uniform.

Me, I took my time, because all the girls knew where I was headed. He was smiling when I got there, his jacket unbuttoned, sleeves rolled up, all the squareness melting away in the heat. My true and only target: Samuel Woo.

Everybody danced with everybody. No wallflowers, no spectators. Dora Kaiulani made sure of that.

I danced with Sammy for three sets in a row. After I asked him for girls' choice, he asked me back for two more. One of the other girls came by finally and said, No be so hoggy, Alice. Some of us like dance with him too.

I laughed and said, You can have him. Sammy protested, but I made him dance with her. Before I had a chance to sit down, Milton Mau grabbed my hand and said, Come on, Alice, my turn now.

It was the best dance, the best birthday party.

Sammy was helping Mr. Lee carry out a new bowl of punch when I went off to look for Annabel and her mother. I saw Howie Harimoto dancing cheek-to-cheek with Barbara Chew and the Kam School boy crouched behind a table pouring champagne into his glass, but I couldn't find Annabel or her mother anywhere. Just Dora Kaiulani's wheelchair, empty except for one small white orchid that must have fallen out of her hair. I picked it up and ran inside the house.

I found them in Annabel's room. Dora Kaiulani lay on the bed, still in her dress, although Emma was loosening up the neck. Annabel looked up at me. Her eyes were red. She said, Go back and keep the party going, Alice. Mama needs to rest.

The drawers were stuffed with fabric. Shiny satins, silks fine and smooth. Starchy linens, wool in mothballs.

Annabel spread fabric out all over the floor of the sewing room. She laid her pattern pieces on top. The house was quiet. I could hear Mr. Lee snoring from the little room off the kitchen, where he slept after Dora Kaiulani passed away. Nobody slept in the big bedroom anymore, not since the funeral. The door from the bedroom to the lanai stayed shut.

I watched Annabel pin the pattern to the fabric. All she wanted to do was sew on our weekends at home, even though she couldn't wear the clothes to school. My mother felt sorry for Annabel—losing her mother so early in life—so I was allowed to stay overnight more often to keep her company.

Annabel said, I'm going to use this wool for a jacket and skirt. Then I'll make a shirtwaist dress out of the cotton print. No, not that one. The one underneath, with the red flowers. Do you want me to make you a skirt? Just pick out the fabric you want and tell me what style.

Don't you want to try it out with muslin first?

Why bother? There's plenty of material.

How come your mother had so much fabric?

She was saving it for our trip to the mainland.

What trip? You never told me about a trip.

I'm telling you now. We were supposed to go after I graduated. She wanted to take me where RLS took her.

How come you call your grandfather RLS but your mother calls him Louis?

Louis is what Tutu called him. That's what they used to call Robert Louis Stevenson.

I thought, Oh no, not that again, but I kept my mouth shut.

She went on. See, my tutu also danced hula for the royal family. That's how she met Robert Louis Stevenson, when he came to visit Princess Kaiulani. Princess Kaiulani was just a girl, but Tutu said you should have seen the way he looked at her. Tutu wanted somebody to love her like that, and then she met my grandpa, who was Scottish too. But then my grandpa went away and didn't come back, and Tutu started calling him Louis, so we did too.

What about the real Robert Louis Stevenson?

What about him?

Don't people get confused about who your grandpa was? Like me.

Annabel sighed. She sat back on her heels and said, I don't know. I'm not even sure they were married, and sometimes I wonder about the name. It's like she was trying to tell us something. I only know what my mother told me, and you know how she was. Louis, RLS. What difference does it make anyway? You know who I'm talking about.

I gathered up the scraps that fell away from her scissors. I said, I guess we should save these for the quilt.

No need, said Annabel. Doesn't matter anymore.

No, I'll put them in the pupule quilt box. You might want them later on.

Every time Annabel cut out fabric, I picked up all the scraps and put them in the box. Just the good pieces, the ones that were big enough for adding to the quilt. The rest I threw away.

PUKA NIGHTS

Turns out Sammy is not an orphan after all. For thirty-three years I have been listening to him cry over his mother, who died when he was a baby, and now I find out he was adopted. Sammy's aunty, Ethel Pang, tells me he isn't even Chinese. He's the second son of a Japanese couple from Palama.

Aunty Ethel comes to visit me on Thursday morning, while Sammy is at work. She expects me to eat while she tells me all this. I'm in shock, and all she can say is, Eat the malasadas while they're still hot. She brings out an envelope with the adoption papers to prove she's telling me the truth.

She says, Sit down, Alice. Stop fussing around. I have enough tea.

She expects me to tell her how Sammy is going to take the news. Is he going to get mad or what? She thinks maybe I should be the one to tell him, since I am the wife. So he can process the information in private. Process. She's no dummy, this Aunty Ethel. Her husband is an accountant, and she's his office manager, but now they're both retired. They're going on this long trip to the Orient, so she wants to get all her business squared away.

While she tells me about her itinerary—Singapore, Bangkok, Hong Kong—I can feel the malasada dough turning into rock inside me. I take a big sip of tea, but my teeth chatter on the edge of my cup. Lurline plays with the bracelet on Aunty Ethel's wrist, and I have to interrupt and say, Stop that. Stop.

Aunty Ethel says, You like my bracelet? It's scarab. Here, you can have it.

She takes off the bracelet and gives it to Lurline, just like that.

I say, What do you say to Aunty, but Lurline doesn't hear me. She's too busy dancing around the kitchen table.

Aunty Ethel says, Never mind, it makes her happy. Just listen to me, Alice.

There's a long hair growing out of the mole over her lip. I watch it move like a whip as she talks. She says all her brothers and sisters know the truth about Sammy, but they kept it quiet all these years. She's the only one with a guilty conscience, but she couldn't say anything until Big Uncle died. None of her brothers want Sammy to know, but she's not scared of them, only Big Uncle, and now he's dead. Her sisters don't have the guts to tell Sammy. She's the only one, but now she has to leave for the Orient next week, and there's so much to do before they go.

Think about it, she says. I just want you to know before I leave. In case something happens and I don't come back.

She puts the envelope back in her bag and I help her walk down the driveway to her car. The way she kisses my cheek and hugs me so tight before she leaves. Her gray hair and the cough she hides behind her hand. The tears in her eyes. She's like the old folks. Going back to China to die. I should ask if she's feeling all right, but all I can think is, if what she says is true, that makes my girls only half Chinese. And my granddaughter, Emily, only three-quarters. That means I am the only one who's Chinese all the way.

My mother will faint. Aggie Chew will talk.

And Sammy. Sammy hates everything Japanese. Our TVs are RCA. Our appliances, Kenmore and Amana. Our cars, Ford, Scout, and Dodge. If my mother didn't buy me a Toshiba rice cooker, I would still be burning rice.

I just don't know. I cannot even think.

When Sammy's aunty drives off in her silver-blue BMW, I know I better have a good story for my neighbor Gracie Todama. I'll tell her about the scarab bracelet, but I can't tell her the truth.

•   •   •

Sammy wants to know where Lurline got the bracelet, so I have to tell him his Aunty Ethel came to visit. I wait for him to ask me what she had to say, but all he wants to know is if the scarab is real or fake and how much is it worth.

Beatrice says, I know about scarab. It's a bug. Just like in the Gold Bug story by Edgar Allan Poe.

Gold? Sammy's all ears.

Yeah, the gold bug is part of a secret code. They drop it down a skull, through the eyes, and then they find the buried treasure.

Treasure?

It's just a story, Dad. There's actually a lot of symbolism involved. There's a tree, like the Tree of Life, and the eye of the skull means something too. I forget exactly what.

Never mind about the tree or the eyeball, says Sammy. Just tell about the treasure. Tell about the gold.

His eyes light up and he forgets to ask me about Aunty Ethel. It makes him feel good, hearing about the treasure. That's all he cares about, what he gets in the end, never mind the middle. He's thinking Lurline's scarab bracelet will bring him luck.

I don't dare tell him I've read the story too. I had forgotten about it until Beatrice reminded me, and now I feel better, knowing there's a story. That's why he wants to inherit his mother's jewelry. Not just for the jade and the gold, but for the story too.

Sammy keeps his mother's jade bracelet and my good jewelry locked up in a safe out in the garage. He doesn't trust the bank. He says they can look inside your safe-deposit box any old time, and if they steal something, by the time you find out, it's long gone. I don't like him keeping my jewelry out there, but it's better than the way he used to hide his mother's bracelet when he was a boy, under a rock up in the valley. He uses a combination lock, not a key, so we don't have to worry about hiding the key. The combination is four numbers—his birthday plus mine.

That way we won't forget, he says. Easy to remember.

The way he says it, I know he's thinking, Always the same number. Not like me. I'm thinking about us, locked together. Locked, without a key.

I have to sneak and give my jewelry to Beatrice. I tell her to hide what I give her and act as if my mother gave it to her directly, because he's so jealous of what I have. He says I should see his mother's jewelry. All of it. The gold, rubies, jade. Better than anything I own. He has a good memory for what he saw only as a baby.

Just like I thought, Sammy likes Wick better now that the boy has a job working in the lounge bar at the Moana Hotel. It's only part-time, but the tips are good. The coeds will love this hapa-haole bartender with a Southern accent. He wears a little badge with his name. He doesn't even have to make up something catchy. Wick is plenty good enough.

He goes to work before Sammy gets home, so they don't have much chance to talk. But when Wick comes in at two in the morning, sometimes Sammy is still out on the lanai, and I hear them talking until 3 or 4 a.m. Beatrice waits in the house and gets mad, of course. Wick brings Sammy silver boxes of Chivas Regal, and Sammy is happy that Wick likes liquor, not like Frankie, who drinks only ginger ale, ginger ale. Sammy feels good because Wick brings him only the best. I'm just hoping the boy doesn't steal.

Wick looks so handsome in his work uniform. Red aloha shirt and white slacks that look good with his tan. I don't know how he keeps from getting wrinkled when he squeezes his long legs into the used Volkswagen bug he bought from the Star-Bulletin ad. He calls his car Beet Two. He's proud because he doesn't need a big car to hold his surfboard on top. He wants everybody to know he doesn't surf long board anymore.

He and Beatrice fight sometimes. She yells and he pretends not to hear. She yells some more, and he starts playing the banjo. Then she runs into the bedroom and slams the door, and he finishes the song before he goes in after her. Sometimes she comes out and lies on the couch, and I cross my fingers that he'll take her back in. Almost always he does, but not every time.

She fights with Frankie too, when he brings Emily over after Wick goes to work. It's almost like before they got divorced, except that now Frankie talks back. He has the law on his side, so he can say what he wants.

I don't like for my granddaughter to hear all the fighting, so when Emily comes over, I carry her into the bedroom to watch TV with me. We have three TVs now. The big one in the living room. The old black-and-white in the bedroom, and Sammy's new color portable that keeps him company while he's working on the apartment. Sometimes everything is going on at once. All the arguing, Sammy drilling and sawing, and the TVs going full-blast. I get such a big headache I have to put cotton in my ears. Only Lurline doesn't mind the noise. She hums and sings songs that don't make any sense.

Lurline knows when people are sad, because they forget about her. Sammy says to lock her in the room so she doesn't bother Wick, but I can't do that. I can't. I let her wear my clothes, my shoes, anything she wants. She likes to put on my crinoline and dance in front of the TV. She trashes up my room, pretending she is me.

I'm glad Wick doesn't come home until Frankie leaves and the noise dies down. I don't like to think about what Frankie tells his mother. Not too much, I hope. I might have to show my face at the clubhouse one of these days.

I lie in my bed listening to the dark, enjoying the quiet. The TVs all off, no rain on the window, no water rushing down the canal, no dogs barking. I'm so full of nothing that I don't even hear Sammy walk into the room.

He says, How come Beatrice sleeping on the couch?

I say the first thing that pops into my head. She has cramps. Don't wake her up.

He grunts. Woman talk embarrasses him.

How come you up so late?

Cannot sleep.

Too many night owls in this house.

He takes off his shorts and climbs in bed. How long has it been. I've lost track. I have toilet paper wrapped around my hair, so my perm will last. Toilet paper plus a hairnet and six bobby pins. And I'm wearing my pink shortie nightgown that's ripped under the arm. Even in the dark I can tell his BVDs are new. They feel different. Silk, he tells me. Hand wash. He bought them two for one on sale, and later on I can see what color but not now. He's wearing a new shaving lotion too—Jade East—I know because Wick uses it too.

He says Alice before he starts, and I'm so shocked I can hardly breathe. He never says my name anymore, at least not like that. Then he's touching me all over and saying Alice the way I like, and pretty soon I'm calling him Slop Boy and not worrying that he might go too fast.

It must be the hormones I am taking. Tomorrow my hair will be a wreck.

I don't care if the shower wakes them up. Surprise, surprise. The water feels so good running down my front.

Hard as I try, I cannot remember the bombing. The closest bomb to me was the one that fell across the street from the governor's house that morning. I didn't see it, but I heard it, and now the sound of it is gone. When I think in my head, December 7—any December 7, not just that one back in 1941, when the Japanese attacked Pearl Harbor—what I remember is Annabel Lee with hairpins falling and the two red carnations she threw on my bed in the dorm. The stems were broken, the flowers all crushed, but she didn't even care.

She said, Did you hear it? The bomb.

I nodded, but I couldn't say the word back. My lips were numb, my mouth dry.

She said, I didn't even go over to look at it. I should have, but all I could think about was, I better come back because you might be worried. The Sisters saw me with these damn carnations. They know I stole them, but what do I care? I should have looked at the bomb. We're going to die!

Don't say that.

Don't be stupid! I heard people talking about the planes. It's the Japanese. They're trying to kill us. Now we have to fight back.

She grabbed the carnations and twisted off the broken stems. She put one flower in her hair and the other one in mine. The way she dug the bobby pins in. Right into my skull.

We can't wear these to church, I told her.

Who said anything about church? Sister Mary Clementine says we have to stay here. We're stuck in this room. We're trapped.

The pepper scent of the carnations in our hair, which she squashed when she hugged me. The sticky wet on my cheek. Her pins dropping on the floor, one by one.

Stupid, stupid, stupid.

Sammy rode all the way from Palama to make sure we were all right. He begged Mizu the cook to send somebody up to get us. We had to sneak downstairs to talk to him. He'd borrowed his neighbor's bike, but the bike was too short, so he looked like he had grown a foot overnight. We talked through the wrought-iron fence.

This is for real, he said. I seen the rising sun. Planes flew right over our house. Look, you can see the smoke down by the harbor. No look good.

Maybe it's just practice, I said. We should wait until we get more proof.

I nearly got hit, said Annabel. How much proof do you want?

She told Sammy about the bomb that fell across from the governor's house. How we could have been killed because we usually walked that way after church. She was smiling when she told him how scared she was. I started smiling too, and pretty soon I was trying not to laugh.

This isn't funny, said Annabel. We could be dead.

I know, I said, but we both started giggling.

Sammy said, Listen, I heard there was parachutes too. They looking for the guys now. So stay inside. I gotta go Wahiawa. Help my uncle with the chickens.

Annabel said, On this bike? You'll never make it.

Have to, he said. Hens going be laying left and right. Nervous from all the bombs. No joke.

But you have to go by Pearl Harbor, she said. And Schofield. You might get hit.

She wasn't smiling anymore. Sammy moved away from the fence. Hit, she said. Killed. I couldn't believe this was really happening.

Annabel said, Alice, go ask Mizu for some food. Please. For Sammy.

I ran to the kitchen. I practiced the words on the way. Mizu, Mizu, you have to help.

I stood there shaking as our Japanese cook squeezed the rice into perfect triangles. I wanted to shout, Hurry up, Mizu, but I wanted everything to be just right too. He wrapped each triangle of rice with a strip of black nori and then placed two giant musubi in a brown paper bag, along with one chicken drumstick, one wing, and a shiny orange. I thanked him, bowing as I spoke. Arigato, Mizu. Arigato. Then I ran back out to the gate.

But when I got there, they were gone. I thought, Parachutes, oh no, but then I heard Annabel calling me from the other side of the mock-orange bushes.

Over here, she whispered. Sister was coming, so we had to hide.

They were holding hands. Annabel's eyes were big and shiny, her cheeks flushed pink. They dropped hands when I walked up. No wonder she looked so happy, and there I was scared out of my mind. Why did they run away from me? What if Sister had caught me and I couldn't say goodbye? Were they kissing while I was in the kitchen, getting this damn food? I shoved the bag into his hand.

Guess I better save it for later, he said. He didn't even look inside.

Annabel hugged me. Good girl, she said. Thanks.

Yeah, thanks, said Sammy, but he wouldn't look me in the eye.

I nodded, but I couldn't speak. Everything was spoiled. I knew I would cry if I opened my mouth. I wanted to hug him, but I couldn't, not now. He turned to get back on his bike. He tied the bag of food to his front handlebars with string. I worried about the rice balls getting squashed.

We watched until we couldn't see him anymore. Annabel squeezed my hand so tight that my fingers grew numb. Her palm was sticky from him, and she made me that way too. We smelled like him, like dirt and sweat and fear.

That night in the dorm, we couldn't turn on the lights. No candles either. Had to wash in the dark. Luckily, we'd laid our clothes out on the beds. Our whitest and prettiest brassieres and panties, clean flannel nightgowns. We brushed our hair out, no braids or pincurls. We painted our lips dark red. Nightshade.

Annabel said we might as well forget about hiding under the bed or in our trunks, like the other girls were talking about doing. She said, Dream something good, so if we die in our sleep, they'll find us smiling.

Before we climbed into our bunks, we said the prayer that always scared me. The one about lying down to rest and dying before I wake and praying to the Lord for my soul to take. But I didn't want to die, and I didn't want anybody taking my soul someplace it might not want to go.

Don't cry, said Annabel after the amen, or your eyes will get swollen and you'll look ugly when they come.

They, they. Like most people, I knew about the Japanese and worried they might attack, but I didn't really believe it would happen. All the ships, all the men in uniforms walking around town and in Waikiki, had made me feel safe. Now some of those men really were the pak gui my mother called them. White ghosts, not saviors. Dead.

When Sister Martha Verity came around to check on us, I hoped she would say a prayer, but instead, her light shone on Annabel's face and then on mine.

Painted hussies, she said.

She made us wash our faces in the dark. The soap made me sick. I threw up in the toilet, and then afterward my lips felt chapped, as if they might crack wide open. But back in bed, Annabel brought out the lipstick again. She held it out to me, across the floor from her bed to mine.

Let them kick us out, she said. If we're going to die, we might as well look good.

The Sisters sent all the boarders home. Still numb, not believing, but we had to move fast. Glad to be leaving the dorm, but not like this. Clothes, books, papers thrown all together. My father dragging my trunk down the steps, thump, thump, and nobody caring about the noise or the man in the hall, not even the nuns. Trying to say goodbye to Annabel and the other girls, and my mother yelling at me, Hurry up, hurry up. She was too scared to wait outside in the car by herself. She didn't want to keep my brothers waiting too long. They might be standing on the sidewalk, out in the open, wondering if we were ever going to come.

The ride home was not slow and lazy like before. People weren't strolling or sitting around. They were rushing, like they had to be somewhere fast. Some of them were huddled on street corners talking, trying to find out what was going on. There were jeeps, soldiers everywhere, holding rifles with bayonets, their faces like stone.

I didn't have to see Pearl Harbor to know we were at war.

All the way home, my mother worried about food. She had sent my brothers to wait in line at three stores: the Piggly Wiggly, Kaimuki Supermarket, and Kapahulu Grocery. Lucky for us, my mother had never gotten over the habit of stocking up, so we had plenty of salty and dry foods to eat when we ran out of fresh. The main thing was rice. The other problem was the icebox. How do you stock up on ice? I was hot and thirsty all the way home just from thinking about drinking everything warm. No more ice water, no cold soda, no shave ice.

.   .   .

Because of the rumors of enemy paratroopers, my father made latches for the windows and doors. Up until then we had never locked the house, not even a hook on the back door.

We ate supper before the sun went down. I wasn't hungry, but my mother said, Eat, you better eat, so I ate, forced the food to go down even when it didn't want to. Then we sat in the kitchen after washing the dishes, our ears pressed to the radio, trying to pick up something besides static. Answers to what was going on, to what was about to happen.

The islands were placed under martial law. That meant curfew, blackout, listen to the soldiers or you could be shot. My mind kept skipping back to school, to my friends. Annabel and Sammy, all of them. I prayed that Sammy made it all the way to Wahiawa. I wished that I had paid more attention in chapel, so that I had better prayers to say. Ones that would work overall, so I wouldn't sound too selfish in what I asked for.

My mother didn't want us to open the windows, even though it was so hot. I took a shower, but felt sweaty again as soon as I stepped out. The windows were wet. The whole house damp.

We slept together that first week, all of us, on the floor of my parents' bedroom. My father dragged the dresser across the window, and my brothers pushed the bed up against the door. We lay on the floor, my mother and me in the middle, with my father and brothers on both sides.

I was glad to be the baby, the girl, but I was so hot, lying in the middle, barricaded by my family. My mother cried, softly at first, then louder, as if it was such a relief. My father was quiet, like my brothers, only the sound of them breathing.

Finally, my father stood up and pulled the dresser away from the window. He went through the house, opening up the windows, banging the glass so it rattled each time, and every time my mother jumped a little and cried. Fresh night air poured in. It felt so good. I waited for my father to come back and scold her, but instead he

pulled my mother close to him and rocked her back and forth. He hummed in a singsong voice until she quieted down.

My father, the bone doctor, all those bodies and feet he had massaged and healed, and I had never seen him embrace my mother, never seen them hug, not even touch, until that night.

It came to me then. Pearl Harbor was us. Not just the Navy or the U.S. government, but my father, my mother, my brothers, me. If we were attacked again, the bombs might hit our house. Even if we got away, where would we go? The island had never felt so small. It was stupid to hide, to think a shingle roof and thin, wooden walls could keep us safe.

I leaned against my mother, and my brothers leaned on me, and we fell asleep like that.

All of Honolulu was black. All of Oahu, all of the islands. No lights shining, everything shut down, everything quiet. I pressed my face against the screen and strained to see in the dark. The night sky punched with stars. The moon hiding too. A few cars creeping by with blue paint on their headlights or black paper, like big eyelids, with only a little bit of the white eyeballs showing.

Days like mountains and you can't see behind them, just one mountain after another. All the questions in our heads, all the things we had to do without knowing why. Nights like water, like in a dream where you move too slowly to get anywhere and you try to wake up so it will be over. Something awful about to happen, somebody watching all the time, but you don't know what or who or when. Like playing hide-and-seek, but who was It and why was everybody hiding near goal?

If I should die before I wake. If I should live, what will I see?

At school the soldiers came to take away Mizu, our Japanese cook. The Sisters told us at chapel, and then we prayed. He was so small and kind. Giving us extra servings, sneaking food to us. We sat around the coral cross, held hands, and cried. Nobody knew where they took him, not even his wife.

No more of my favorite chop suey, no more perfect rice balls for snacks. We ate more macaroni and cheese than ever, and I hated—hated—macaroni and cheese.

My mother made window curtains out of heavy blue denim. She had enough fabric for only the kitchen windows, but it was too hot to cover all the windows, so we learned to live in the dark. To cook, eat, and wash up fast. To pay attention to where we put things, so we could find them later. To trust that what was there was there. To live without knowing or understanding what was going on. What we couldn't see, we had to imagine. We saved our candles for when we really needed them. We learned not to look directly at the light, so that our eyes would always be ready for what waited for us in the dark.

My mother crocheted with her eyes shut, so she didn't have to depend on the light. She made white doilies as if they were her last will and testament. Circles, ovals, squares, with plenty of ruffles. I watched her pile them into four equal stacks. Counting under her breath and then picking up the crochet hook for the next one. As if she would never have enough.

My father moved so quietly that my mother jumped when he showed up suddenly. Oh, you like one ghost, she said every time. He didn't surprise me, because I could tell it was him, by his clothes, his skin, and me, his daughter, knowing his smell, which my mother would know too if she were breathing right.

School was not the same. We were all day students now, so the place felt half empty, and there was a big hush behind the chatter. Words weren't enough, numbers were a joke. History a terrific lie. Always before, I felt the promise, that we could learn from the past, from our mistakes. But now my hope was a ball thrown high into the sky and falling, falling. My classmates were excited, almost happy,

talking about how they were going to help the war effort. But the ground was shaking under me. Where would I land?

Annabel's father insisted on painting the windows black. Every single window, on both floors of their house up in Maunalani Heights. This took place on the anniversary of Dora Kaiulani's death, Annabel's eighteenth birthday. Annabel had no candles, no cake, and my mother was afraid to let me go up the hill by myself.

If I had gone, I would have seen Sammy. Annabel told me he pedaled his bike all the way up there. He had his own bicycle now. Something he found at the junkyard and fixed up.

Don't get mad, she said. He brought me three stalks of sugarcane. But we couldn't visit. He spent the whole time helping my father and my brothers paint the windows black.

We studied the evacuation plan. A line divided Honolulu into two zones. In case of emergency, women and children on the makai side of the line had to evacuate to a location on the mauka side. If you didn't have friends or family to stay with, then you had to go to a refugee camp.

Annabel said my mother and I could stay with her. She said not to worry about preparing evacuation kits. She had lots of clothes and food and water. Everything we might need.

My mother was so grateful, she sent me to school with little gifts for Annabel. Something each week. Doilies, of course. Chewing gum. Ribbons for her hair. Rubber bands. Fresh slices of lemon. Gifts of appreciation. Insurance.

I felt amputated, but it wasn't a limb I had lost. I missed Annabel, living in the dorm, reading out loud in bed, falling asleep to Browning and Poe. Instead, there was my mother telling my father one more time to get up and check the windows and the doors. And the wooden floor creaking as he crept from room to room.

•　　•　　•

My brothers Russell and Michael went to work at Pearl Harbor. Their jobs were classified, top secret. All we knew was they were helping with the clean-up. They came home exhausted and wouldn't talk or look at us when we greeted them. They stripped down outside and then spent a long time scrubbing themselves. They shared a small sliver of soap and a bucket of water. The neighbors couldn't see them because it was dark when they got home. My father wouldn't let my brothers come inside until they had washed themselves twice.

They ate at the kitchen table in the dark, while my mother hovered around them, refilling their plates, urging them to eat plenty. If my mother lit the candle so she could check their plates, one of my brothers blew it out.

Russell stopped eating anything with bones. My mother had to strip off the skin and shred the meat so that it didn't look as if it came from a chicken or a duck or a cow. Michael didn't want to eat meat at all, but he knew my father would beat him if he didn't. So he shoveled the food in fast, scraping his plate so we could hear.

Late at night, when I heard Michael vomiting, I took him some rice and tea. I begged him to tell me about the harbor. What was it like? What did he do all day?

Michael said, You know I'm not supposed to tell.

But he told me anyway, after I promised I wouldn't tell a soul, not my parents, not Joe-Joe, not even Annabel Lee. He said Pearl Harbor was a mess, everything blasted apart or burned down. He and Russell had to pick up the scraps, what was lying on the docks or floating in the harbor. They paddled around in a boat, and what they couldn't pick up they had to haul to shore. That meant anything that blew up in the attack, not just parts of ships or buildings but bodies too. Arms and legs mostly, only a few heads so far.

I was so shocked I couldn't even cry. I kept thinking, If I hadn't asked, if he didn't tell me, then maybe it never really happened.

Every evening I saved a little bit of my rice and set aside a cup of tea.

.   .   .

They were out there. The eyes, black and straining like mine to see in the dark. Not the enemy, I hoped. But for sure the MPs with their rifles, the same men who stared at me in the daylight with their blue and green eyes, on the streetcar, in Chinatown. Not ghosts, but saints. Glad for them all.

We lined up for everything. Gasoline. Rice. Sugar. Gas masks. We waited all day to get our identification cards. How tall are you? Five feet. But still growing. How much do you weigh? One hundred, but losing, losing. My stomach felt full all the time, but not from food. Not hungry anymore. Let the boys eat my rice.

They pressed my fingers into ink and then rolled them on the paper. My fingerprints like the rings of a tree. My fingerprints were all I had to show the world. Not my face, or my low forehead or baby cheeks. Not my hair that wouldn't curl or my short legs or my black silk stockings with too many holes.

How do you carry a gas mask? Around your neck. Over your back so it doesn't flop against your stomach. Tied to your waist so it bangs against your hip. Diagonal, across your shoulder, like a bag. It sits beside you at chapel, in class, on your lap on the bus ride home. It even has a little pocket for lipstick, so you don't need to carry a purse.

When Annabel Lee and I graduated from the Priory, along with the rest of the Class of 1942, all of us dressed in white, we marched down the aisle of the cathedral with gas masks slung across our breasts.

My brothers and I dug a hole in the back yard for a bomb shelter. We dug until the dirt turned to mud and clung to the shovel and water began seeping into the hole. We stood there looking down at the brown, wet hole—a puka in the ground, a puka not even deep enough to be black.

Joe-Joe said, I not going in there. I no like drown.

It's only dirt, said Russell, but he didn't look as if he was in a hurry to try it out.

You could get stuck in that, said Joe-Joe. Just like quicksand. You could sink right in.

Throw more dirt inside.

Then going be too shallow.

So just sit down and cover your head. Good enough.

We threw a tarp over the hole, so we could start building the roof. But as soon as we tossed dirt on the canvas, the whole thing caved in. So then we had to start all over. First, we laid sticks across the hole, then put the tarp over that, but then the hole really was too shallow.

Finally, Michael said, Wait, I got an idea. The next night he and Russell came home from Pearl Harbor with a car roof tied to the top of the old Ford.

They placed the car roof over the hole, and we crawled inside the bomb shelter to check it out. My brothers were so excited. Joe-Joe kept hitting the roof with a stick. Ping. That's how the bombs would go. Ping ping.

We stocked the bomb shelter with canned goods, water, blankets. It was a tight squeeze with everything. We couldn't move around or stand up. I knew my mother would never go in there.

As we shoveled dirt on the roof, Joe-Joe said, Just like one grave.

Tough, said Russell. That's all the deep we can go.

I don't know about you guys, said Joe-Joe, but me for one I no like die in one lousy puka in the ground.

My mother gave us some sweet potatoes to plant on top of the shelter, for camouflage, but every time we watered the sweet potatoes, muddy water ran down the side of the mound and into the hole.

When the air-raid siren went off, none of us used the bomb shelter. Instead, we hid in the house, under the beds, inside the closet. The neighbor kids poured ketchup on their bodies so the Japanese would think they were dead already. After the siren stopped, they came outside to spray water on their red faces and legs and arms. They laughed and joked, as if it was just a game.

Joe-Joe said, Look at those hot dogs. Think they smart.

Annabel's brothers put their bomb shelter in the dirt floor of their garage. It was shallow too, but deep enough for a tarp and an old mattress. They didn't have to worry about rain inside the garage, so they covered the whole thing with the top of their Ping-Pong table. Annabel pasted scraps of fabric all over the tabletop. Finally, she had a pupule quilt. Her own brand of camouflage.

Every night I sat in the dark, by the window, watching for anything that moved. I was suspicious of all light, even the faintest, barely flickering light. I didn't trust the stars, the moon, if it really was the moon. The night wasn't quiet to me anymore. It was full of sounds I had never heard before because I had never really listened. It took a war for me to really hear the ocean, only a mile away, and the warm Kona wind blowing through the coconut and mango trees, and the crickets chirping in the heat.

The mesh of the window screen scratched my nose and cheeks. My tongue tasted like metal.

My mother said to make sure people knew we were Chinese, not Japanese. Show your card. Race: Chinese. Point at your name. Lum. Wash your hand, your face. Comb your hair. No make me shame. Make sure your panty no more hole.

Glad I was Lum, not Mizu. Not Harimoto not Fukunaga not Toma. Glad Annabel was Lee and Sammy, Woo. Not Hiraki Inoshita Inouye Kamei Matsunaga Matsuo Mizuno Suma Toda Todoki Watanabe Watasaki Yoshioka.

Annabel Lee wanted us to be first and second in line to buy fabric. Third and fourth was no good. If not for the curfew, she would have made us camp overnight in front of the store. Instead, she spent the night at my house, and then at dawn we caught the first bus to Chinatown.

Look at the line, I said, as we walked down River Street. The line was already winding around the block, all the ladies waiting with their shopping bags or furoshikis tied in bows over their arms. Annabel recognized a few of them, the ones who were dressmakers like her mother's seamstress, Winnie.

See how they're looking at us, said Annabel. They're trying to decide if they want to copy our clothes. That's why I never dress up when I go shopping.

I carried the basket while Annabel threw bolts of fabric into it. I let her choose for me too, because I could never decide.

Go for the color, said Annabel. Don't stand too close. Squint a little bit. If still looks good, grab it fast. Color counts the most.

The colors she liked were bold, loud. Red and orange and yellow. Blue and green if they were bright enough. Not the cool, dark blues and browns, the solid, plain colors that I preferred, that were better for hiding behind.

Her father complained: Why you need so much clothes? Why you waste money? Use up what you have in the drawer.

But Annabel wanted more than party dresses and suits. She needed work clothes, street clothes. Cotton, not only silk, and not the wool her mother had saved. Since we weren't allowed to leave the islands, she couldn't travel. She had to be practical for a change.

Whenever we had a free afternoon, we walked past the Royal Hawaiian Hotel, so Annabel could see what the haole women were wearing, the few still here in the islands. She drew quick sketches on the bus ride home and then gave the drawings to her mother's dressmaker, who translated them into patterns for Annabel to use.

Annabel hated the girls and women who got sent to the mainland after the attack. She pointed out that all the ones we knew were daughters or wives of plantation managers or rich businessmen. Haoles, all of them. She said they were traitors, cowards. She resented their passport to freedom: the color of their skin.

•   •   •

Annabel's older sister, Emma, eloped. She married a soldier, an enlisted man, but not an officer. Stupid girl, grumbled Mr. Lee. If she had to marry haole, then why not an officer? When Emma came home to visit, Mr. Lee wouldn't talk to her. Then the war broke out, and Emma's husband sent her to live with his family in Florida.

Annabel and I checked the globe in the library. Florida was much farther than San Francisco, not just across the ocean, but across the whole United States as well. To get there, we'd have to take the boat and then the train. Annabel said we could stay with Emma until we found an apartment. I was silent when Annabel talked about the apartment. I knew my mother would never approve of us living on our own.

The trip was Annabel's idea, not mine. There were alligators in Florida. Swamps too, with leeches and quicksand. I couldn't imagine traveling that far.

Annabel asked how far *would* I go? Was it the money? We could work two jobs after graduation. But it wasn't the money. It was how I thought of myself. Even when I lived in the dorm, it was never just Annabel and me. There was always my family, my home. But now everything was sliding away. Living in the dark made me realize how it might feel to live alone. Could I live without my family and my friends? Could I live without my home? If we lost the war, if I lost everyone I loved, could I go on?

The war woke Annabel up, pulled her out of mourning. She said, Alice, I'm going to San Francisco and Florida and then to New York. You can come with me if you want, but I'm still going, no matter what.

Mr. Lee spent most of his time at his restaurant in Chinatown. He slept on the floor behind a propped-up dinner table. He had a gun, although nobody knew about it, just Annabel and me. He didn't paint the restaurant windows black, because he wanted everybody to see inside, to know the owner was Chinese. He hung red, white, and blue paper in the window and painted CHINESE RESTAURANT CHI-NESE RESTAURANT WELCOME G.I. in big red letters on the glass.

Sometimes he came home to shower and change clothes, then went right back out before dark. He slicked his hair back with pomade and splashed cologne on his face and under his arms, so Annabel suspected a girlfriend. Some pake who was after his money.

After Dora Kaiulani died, Mr. Lee went back to being Chinese. Now everything could be only one way, the way of the old folks, his way. He prayed at the temple, at an altar in the living room, and burned so much incense that their house began to resemble my father's back parlor. He also filled the house with bowls of oranges, but nobody was allowed to eat them, so the oranges rotted. Later on, when oranges were hard to come by, he filled the bowls with carrots and pumpkins and candied squash from Chinatown, whatever was the color of orange, as if color alone performed the magic.

My father quit the shoeshine business one year after the war started. My mother did nothing but complain. How could he quit when there were more shoes now than ever before? How could he sell the shop without telling her? The boys could have taken over the business after the war. How could he be so stupid? When that didn't work, she tried a new attack. Rubbing his feet, sewing a cushion for his back, telling him what she saw when she went to the market. How the soldiers asked for him. How sad their shoes looked. All scuff. No shine.

But those were shoes going off to fight. Shoes touching blood, killing, being killed. The soldiers frightened my father, the way they stomped up and down the sidewalk, drunk, laughing. Now they looked at him as if he might be the enemy. As if he was *Mizu*, not Lum. Mizu, Mizu.

My father retreated to the back parlor again, back to his real profession, setting bones. At least people paid him money now. Money and little cans of rations that my mother loved. She added sardines and peanut butter and strawberry jam to the supply of dry and salty food that she hoarded in the cupboards. The Spam we ate right away. Fried Spam over rice, sometimes even on top of noodles or steamed with squash if we couldn't get ham. My mother believed eating Spam was patriotic. God bless America, she said every time she opened a new can.

I followed my father one day. He went down an alley in Chinatown and through the back door of an herb shop. Not the one he used to work in but a different one. Very small and dark. I went inside, but he wasn't there and the shopkeeper wouldn't tell me where he had gone. I couldn't figure out how my father could have left the shop without my seeing him. It was as if a hole in Chinatown had opened up and swallowed him, and I had to wait until it spit him back up again. I went outside and sat on a bench. When he finally came back out, through the same door, his eyes were half shut and his clothes smelled sweet. I stood in the middle of the sidewalk, right in his path, but he walked past me, didn't even recognize his own daughter.

How can I not be scared when scared is all I am. Waiting inside for what's out there is bad enough. But to be bumping into each other in the dark, thinking we've run into the enemy.

Here he comes, I whisper to my mother, when I see the shadow move behind her.

I talked to shadows too. It's just me, Alice. Hear me? Smiling. See me?

My brother Michael showed me a painting that he made. He said it was a self-portrait. One half of the face was black, the mouth open, screaming. The other half was blue turning to purple turning to red, then bursting into yellow flames against a gray, swirling sky.

Sammy Woo came by my house one night after curfew. I was sitting by the window looking out when I heard him calling at the door. Alice, Aay, Alice. I thought for a minute that Annabel was with him, but he stood there all alone. He had a black eye and a cut on his forehead. From banging into a door, he told me. In the dark.

He'd run the whole way, jumped behind the bushes every time he spotted soldiers, but the eggs were still whole. The eggs he brought us, brown with speckles all over, white ones too, a little bigger. Get plenty extra, he said. Chickens been busy, just like I told you.

My mother thanked him over and over for the eggs. She heated up a pot of jook and then searched the cupboards for something to feed him. Saloon Pilot crackers. Dried fish. Watermelon seeds. She also scolded him for coming over after dark.

Bum-bye shoot. How come your eye stay black and blue?

This time he said he'd run into a chicken coop.

She said, Your folks no worry?

He told my mother his parents were dead, that he lived with his grandparents in Kalihi and with his uncle in the country, on the chicken farm. Orphan, he said, and my mother nodded and nodded. I was afraid to ask what had happened to his parents, afraid he might shut up. The dim light of the candle must have made it easier for him to talk. He told us his mother had passed away giving birth, and that his father died later, in a warehouse accident. Before we knew it, my mother was frying up the cold rice she was saving for the next morning, and pretty soon we were all eating again. Eggs fried sunny side up, a can of Spam. Everything tasted so good, especially the eggs.

He slept overnight on the floor in the living room. Joe-Joe slept beside him, to keep him company.

My mother came into my room after she thought I was asleep. I felt her standing over me, like the Sisters at school. I tried to match her breath. In, when she breathed in; out, when she breathed out. I smelled the cornstarch on her hand, what she patted all over her body at night. She stroked my head with cold fingers before she left the room.

The next morning I got up early, while it was still dark. Sammy was already up, standing by the back door, getting ready to leave without saying goodbye.

I whispered, How's your eye?

He pulled me outside. He said, I wen lie to you.

That's okay.

I got into one fight. This guy he wen call me Jap. I asked my goong goong to teach me kung fu, but he no like. He teach all my cousin, my uncle them, too, but not me.

Ask my brothers to teach you. Ask my father.

No. Cannot.

He left, first walking, then running, as the roosters crowed and the sky grew light again.

My father taught my brothers to shadowbox. They practiced outside in the yard at the break of dawn. I watched from the bedroom, my face pressed against the screen. They danced in slow motion. First, they were holding an imaginary ball, then strumming something like a ukulele. They scooped and pushed and kicked the air as if it was heavy and alive. They moved like clouds, across the lawn.

What I loved best was when they stroked the horse's mane. Not a tame horse, one you could pet and ride, but a horse still loose, still free. You had to sweep your hands across his mane, stroke without fear. You had to believe he was tame and already yours.

11

THE LEIS THEY SEWED

Sammy takes Wick fishing way out beyond the reef, and the poor boy gets seasick and spends the whole day throwing up. He looks just like Sammy the first time Sammy went fishing on Maui almost thirty years ago. Red eyes, blue lips, white tongue. But of course Sammy has a different memory of that time.

Wick gets out of the Scout and heads straight for the outside bathroom. Doesn't even help unpack the boat, so I know Sammy is going to come in squawking.

But Sammy is all smiles. He cracks open a cold can of Bud, gulps it down fast, and then says, Where he went? I like show him how for clean aku.

Before I can stop her, Lurline runs to get Wick. She finds him sitting on the toilet with his pants still on, his head down between his legs. She drags me over to look at him. I close the bathroom door and tell her, Leave him alone, go get me a bottle of 7-Up.

Wick says he's not hungry. He'll eat later on, at the hotel, when he goes to work. He's all clean now, just one Band-Aid from shaving, and he's combed his hair back behind his ears in the movie-star way that Beatrice likes.

He tells me, I'm doing fine, Aunty Alice. Don't wait up for me now. Beet and I have a date tonight after work, and I know one thing: we're not going dancing.

Then he kisses me on the cheek.

I hope, I hope, I hope so much.

Beatrice used to be a hippie, but she's happier now. I kept my fingers crossed when she shacked up with the English professor. Sammy said that man was too old for her, robbing the cradle, but to me it was more like the cradle needed rocking. At least she wasn't in one of those hippie communes where she could get VD and drugs. Besides, the professor was good to her. He taught her how to drive, and she started eating again and didn't have to work. If she wanted to bake bread, she could bake bread, and if she wanted to weave, she could weave. Sometimes I wonder why she moved back home. Maybe she got bored with such an easy life. She came home on her twenty-ninth birthday and never went back. An old maid, but at least she wasn't pregnant.

Lucky for her Frankie Chew beat the draft. He was going to be a conscientious objector and run away to Canada, but he never got called, so he bought a motorcycle and drove all over the country. Then he went back to Santa Fe to work in a Chinese restaurant. He still has the leather jacket with decals from thirty-five different states. He wore it when he came back to see his family three years ago. He showed up at our house wearing Army boots and tight jeans and that leather jacket, even though it was so hot that night. Beatrice put on her black miniskirt and told him she was hungry for saimin. I thought Sammy wouldn't let her go, but he did. He even loaned Frankie our car, because he didn't like the looks of the moped Frankie had rented. They didn't come home until four o'clock that morning. I lay awake the whole time, wondering how Sammy could sleep. Frankie didn't look that safe to me anymore. Not in those boots.

When they were in high school, he used to send her poems. What he wrote. What other people wrote. I found the poems everywhere. In her pockets, on the floor, inside her books. She made fun of his poems, read them on the phone to Amy Toad, both of them laughing at the corny parts, but she went steady with him anyway, until her freshman year in college. They broke up because Frankie didn't want her to date anyone at Berkeley and she didn't want to be stuck in the dorm for three more years. I don't know all the boys she went with after that. Mostly haoles, I think, because she mentioned them only by their first names in the letters she wrote to me. But I know she still cared for Frankie, because she saved all his poems. I found a whole folder of them when I was cleaning under her desk. She never threw them out, even when she moved back home. If there was anybody she loved the whole time, I thought it was Frankie, not Wick.

I should have known. When Annabel Lee came to visit, Beatrice and Wick played together so well. She cried and cried when it was time for him to leave. Annabel and Wick returned to the islands only twice after the flash flood on Maui, when Beatrice was ten and fifteen years old. Wick was still small for his age, and the neighborhood kids picked on him and made fun of the way he talked. Beatrice always got into fights trying to protect him. As if she could. That girl, she still doesn't know her size.

Annabel Lee hated staying with her father because of the women Mr. Lee married and then divorced, one after the other. She couldn't stand to see her stepmothers wearing Dora Kaiulani's jewelry and showing off dresses made from her mother's fabric, from the drawers and drawers of beautiful cloth that Annabel left behind.

When Sammy invites Wick to go fishing again, to my surprise, the boy says yes. Even bigger shock when Sammy lets Wick drive the Scout. It's another one of Sammy's jakala cars. Heaven to him is a free piece of junk. The top came off an old Toyota that Sammy hauled from the junkyard and welded on backwards. The windshield wipers swing down from the top and go hiss every time. All the hubcaps are different because he found them in ditches, and the rear bumper fell off our old Dodge Ram. The driver seat is higher than the others, which makes Sammy feel like a king. He's proud when the locals crowd around to admire his creation. He says nobody has the nerve to steal it because it's one of a kind.

I'm nervous that Wick will get sick from the exhaust that leaks through the hole around the shift stick. Part of me's thinking Sammy expects Wick to give up after driving one block, but Wick is still at the wheel when they come home. He's smiling too. Not dizzy, not even seasick. Beatrice says not to tell Sammy about the Dramamine.

They sit out on the lanai afterward, talking about how they caught their fish and drinking the Heineken beer that Wick bought. Sammy makes me bring out the long-stemmed glasses the girls gave him for Christmas. Those two. Boys. Salty and sunburned and toasting each other because they caught themselves a big one. A marlin, almost three hundred pounds. Sammy says Wick is the one who caught the fish, and Wick says he couldn't have done it without Sammy's expertise. Sammy likes that, expertise. He goes to the box in the freezer and brings out two cigars. Wick says, No, thanks, but Sammy says, Just hold one for the picture and then give it back. They make Beatrice take a whole roll of film. First, both of them together with the fish, then one by one with the fish, then the two of them alone, then for all the rest of the pictures just the fish by itself. Sammy gives me a big chunk to take over to the Todamas. All the other neighbors get some too, and Sammy puts a large piece in the freezer to give to Frankie the next time he comes by the house.

Sammy teaches Wick how to talk pidgin. How to say Howzit, brah, instead of Good morning. Hannabuttah instead of snot. Blala and boddah and teetah and manong, and all those words I don't like for them to use. Annabel will scream when she hears Wick talking like that. Her sweet mainland boy with a broken mouth.

We're going to the airport tonight, because Beatrice's best friend, Amy Toad, is coming home from India. Beatrice bought two leis in Chinatown, even though I told her I had plenty of time to make some. She says we can't make the kind that Amy Toad likes. The double-strand kind, ginger and pikake. All that perfume makes my sinuses ache.

Amy Toad doesn't know anything yet. Not about Frankie and the divorce, not about Wick. That's what she gets for being gone for three months. Beatrice says Amy Toad will blow her mind when she takes one look at Wick. Amy Toad hardly goes out at all, because her standards for men are so high in the sky. But Wick is right up there. That's for sure.

I hardly recognize Amy Toad when she gets off the plane. She's wearing jeans and a halter top, not even a bra. I was hoping to see one of those Indian wraparounds. The fabric is so beautiful in those saris. Silk and real gold.

Amy Toad has an earring stuck up her nose. A little red ruby. At first I think it's a lump of blood, but she tells me it doesn't hurt at all, not even when she sneezes. I'm glad Sammy took Mits Todama to the Red Carpet Room to get him high before the plane landed. He and Mits are too busy talking story to see why I am patting Gracie's arm.

Could be worse, I tell her. A lot worse.

She pats me back and nods.

Amy Toad gives Wick a great big hug before she even hears the whole story. She has to tiptoe to reach him, because she's even shorter than Beatrice.

She says, Call me if Beet changes her mind.

Beatrice laughs and says, Don't listen to her, she's full of bullshit, but I see her pulling Wick away.

Beatrice and Amy Toad walk to the baggage claim area with their arms around each other, talking and laughing the whole time. Wick follows behind them with Amy Toad's backpack slung over his shoulder. The pack is embroidered all over with peace symbols and beads and little round mirrors. Lurline skips along behind Wick, looking at her face in the mirrors and shaking her scarab bracelet. Every time I see that bracelet I think of what I'm supposed to tell Sammy and can't.

She points at the little circles. I see what she sees. Pieces of herself, broken into bits. An eye, a mouth, a nose. I see my own face too. All of her, all of me, bouncing around, loose.

• • •

Sammy moves upstairs a little bit at a time. First, clean shorts and a T-shirt. Then his toothbrush and toothpaste. His electric razor. I can tell when the plumbing goes in, the wiring too, just by noticing what he takes.

I go over everything on the dresser and in the closet, to see what's still left behind. The biggest thing missing from the Take List is me.

I cannot sleep. I lie in bed and pray for him to come back down and ask me to go upstairs. Maybe then I'll tell him what his Aunty Ethel said about his being Japanese. I haven't told anybody, cross my heart and hope to—but I can't say the Die word, not for something I want this much.

Over and over I rehearse what Aunty Ethel wants me to tell him. *You're not an orphan. In fact, your folks might still be alive. And you have at least one brother, maybe sisters too.* My heart skips a beat just thinking of what this means. He's always saying that all he has is me and the girls, that we're the only ones who love him. What will he do when he finds out he has more than us? And how can I tell him the rest? That he isn't Chinese after all.

People always tease Sammy when they see the picture of him in his Army uniform. They say, Who's that Japanese boy? That's what I thought when I first saw the picture.

People joke about his bowlegs too. They say, Sure you not Japanese, Sammy? You get the legs.

Sammy laughs and shuffles around in his slippers, showing off his legs, but sometimes I catch him staring at the photograph, looking at it closely, as if he might see something he couldn't see before.

If the way you look makes so much difference, how come we didn't know? And when we guessed the truth, why didn't we believe? What made us blind? And will the truth make Sammy feel better? Or just more mad than he already is? And what about the girls? I have to tell them too. Lurline won't understand, but I'm afraid of what Beatrice will say. That her father is getting what he deserves.

So many secrets. So much to hide. And yet there it was all the time. What we would have seen if we'd been looking.

Sammy wears clothes I don't even recognize. New shirts, golfing shirts, even though he doesn't golf. Pressed blue slacks from the dry cleaner's just to go to the Red Carpet Room with my brother Joe-Joe. They go once a week now and pretend they're waiting for flights to arrive. The girls at the front desk know them by now and just wave them through. It's not like going to a bar, he tells me, because the drinks are free.

Sammy wants Wick to go with them, on the nights he doesn't have to work, but Beatrice says, No, he's busy with me. This makes Sammy mad, of course. He tells my brother that Wick is pussy-whipped. But Wick doesn't look whipped to me. His skin is getting darker and his hair, almost blond on top from all the sun. His muscles are bigger too. He surfs almost every day now, and Amy Toad goes with him sometimes. Beatrice too, on her days off. They wear their skimpiest bikinis, and I can just see them, strutting down the beach arm in arm, for everyone to see.

I wait up for Sammy. I can crochet in the dark, just like my mother. I make turtles for Emily and for any babies that might be coming along someday. Yellow and blue and red turtles. Striped. With different colors for the heads and feet. I make them the same way as caps, stuffed caps with bottoms. I start in the middle and cro-chet around and around until I reach the brim. Babies' heads are bigger than you think, so I use my own head for a pattern. This way I don't have to count the rows. All I have to do is try it on now and then. And when I hear the car in the driveway, I can run into the bedroom without worrying about where I left off.

When Sammy comes in to me, I pretend I am sleeping. He likes it better if I don't move too much. I smell only liquor and cigarettes on him, nothing strange. He's still good-looking, even with his extra weight, and you have to watch these airline girls. They go after older

men. It scares me the way he falls asleep afterward. Like he has no bones.

In the morning, when he's taking a shower, I check his shirt for lipstick, his pant pockets for receipts and credit card slips. Then I make him coffee, strong, the way he likes, and pour him a big glass of tomato juice with lots of Worcestershire and Tabasco sauce. I should tell him about what his Aunty Ethel said, before he starts reading the comics, but I don't.

Annabel Lee and me, Alice Lum, sitting in the kitchen at my house in Kapahulu, sewing leis for our football friends, Howie Harimoto and Milton Mau. The war was only six months old, high school graduation over, and the boys were going off to fight. We alternated yellow plumeria with purple vanda on the string, trying to stretch out our limited supply of flowers. We didn't want to play favorites by giving an orchid lei to one of the boys and a plumeria lei to the other. Flowers were getting so hard to find. We went from house to house with our paper bags, but the neighbors didn't have enough to share. They were too busy making their own leis for the boys they knew. Sometimes we had to make short leis. Short was better than no leis at all.

The leis we sewed:

Vanda orchid, for my brothers Russell and Michael, plus red carnation leis bought in Chinatown at discount.
Maile and vanda orchid, for Annabel's brothers, Gordon and Edward Lee.
Vanda mixed with plumeria, for Iolani quarterback, Howie Harimoto, and McKinley halfback, Milton Mau.

We were tired of saying goodbye. First, our brothers: Russell, then Gordon and Edward. They all left on the same Liberty ship. When

Michael came home with the enlistment papers in his hand, my father made him go outside and sit in the bomb shelter, mud and all.

Might as well cover you up, said my father.

My mother just stood by and watched. Do something, I told her, but all she did was walk away. I found her later in the bedroom, crying into one of her doilies.

I told myself it was just a matter of time. Michael would have gotten drafted if he hadn't signed up. What really made my father mad was that Michael could choose to leave.

My fingers turned yellow from the flower sap. I poked myself with the lei needle, but the point was too dull to draw blood.

Annabel was glad she hadn't gone steady with Howie Harimoto. Otherwise, she might have gotten knocked up like Barbara Chew.

I came that close, she said. She held up her thumb and her forefinger to show me how close. She looked up from the lei she was sewing and said to me, If the Sisters only knew.

I said, What do you mean, what did you guys do, but she wouldn't tell me any more.

I wanted to ask her about Sammy. Would she go with him if he asked? How much did she do with him? But I couldn't ask. I wasn't sure I wanted to hear her answer.

Annabel said, Let's make crackseed leis too. Crackseed will be good on the boat. The salt can settle their stomachs if they get seasick.

But we weren't allowed to give the boys those leis. Crackseed was food, and food had to stay in the islands for us to eat. We couldn't even give them chewing gum. As if that was all we needed to live on while the boys were gone—salty plums and spearmint gum.

I took Barbara Chew some lichee from our tree. Our lichee was big and sweet and crispy. I filled up a whole bag. I gave her a small book too, for writing in, not a baby book, just something for any occasion. Annabel brought a plastic ketchup bottle wrapped with a red bow. It wasn't really a ketchup bottle, just looked like one, red with a white screw-on top that you couldn't unscrew. A bank is what it really was, with a secret slot just above the label, so nobody could tell there was money inside. If you wanted to take out the money, you had to break the plastic. This seemed like a waste of a good bottle to me, but Annabel said, That way you save, you can't take the money out any old time.

Barbara Chew's eyes were red and swollen. She held a crumpled handkerchief under her nose. I tried not to stare at her stomach. She didn't look that pregnant to me. Just sad and very worried. I wondered how much baby food you could buy with one ketchup bottle full of money. How many diapers. How much evaporated milk. I thought about how Barbara Chew always let me have the cherry off her ice cream sundae, as if she wanted to be my friend, and me, I just took the cherry and ate it as if it was nothing but a cherry.

Barbara Chew didn't have a chance with Howie Harimoto until Sammy Woo came along, and then Howie went after Barbara to make Annabel Lee jealous. But Annabel says she wasn't jealous, so it wasn't her fault that Barbara got pregnant. Now Barbara's parents wouldn't let her marry Howie because he was Japanese. They were afraid he would get sent away.

Howie Harimoto was going away all right. To fight the Japanese. Him and the other Hawaii-Japanese boys, so many of our friends, I couldn't count.

Annabel told Barbara Chew, I want to make you a dress. With covered buttons down the front. I have plenty of extra fabric. Just tell me what color you want.

Barbara Chew started crying again. Not bawling, but whimpering. An animal sound.

Blue? asked Annabel. Robin's egg blue. Or maybe royal. What do you think, Alice?

Royal.

Alice is right, said Annabel. Royal will be just right.

.   .   .

We took some flowers to Dora Kaiulani's grave on the way home from Barbara Chew's house. Annabel's mother was buried in the Lee family plot in the Chinese graveyard near Punchbowl. When Mr. Lee died, he would be buried next to his wife, Dora Kaiulani. So would Annabel and her brothers too.

We got off the bus on the road that ran through the graveyard. The hills above and below the road were littered with tombstones, some new, some already falling over and turning black with mold.

As we walked down the steep slope, I started counting from the second plumeria tree. Five rows down, then fifteen graves across. On the day of her mother's funeral I memorized where the grave was, because I knew Annabel would have a hard time finding it again.

Everything was up and down the day of Dora Kaiulani's funeral.

Down from the cars to the grave for the burial. My shoes slipping on the hillside, the wet grass soaking through my stockings, my white shoes turning brown.

Back up to the car to get the lei of baby roses I made to throw on top of Dora Kaiulani's coffin at the last minute. I wanted to throw the lei myself. Yellow roses with the leaves still on.

Up to get water for Annabel Lee when she got dizzy.

Down again, and Annabel was weeping very loud by then, and I forgot all about the lei until they covered up the grave, so I had to throw the baby roses on top of the dirt.

Up to the cars, but then Annabel Lee wanted me to go down and make sure Sammy was coming to dinner in Chinatown at Fat Lee Wo.

Down to find Sammy, but Annabel was already racing past me to tell him herself.

All the way up to the car, and her father wanted to know where Annabel went, and I didn't want to go back down there.

I was hot and tired from the climbing and the crying and the confusion, but I did it, I went down the hill again.

.   .   .

Sammy was the only pallbearer who wasn't related to the Lees. He showed up at the house as soon as he heard the news. He cut school and insisted on helping out. He mowed the yard while the whole family went to the funeral parlor to pick out the coffin. He scrubbed down the lanai and watered all the plants too.

Annabel Lee sat with her aunties at the funeral. As a pallbearer, Sammy stood across the aisle, behind Mr. Lee and his sons. I sat in the second row, with the Hawaiian cousins.

But now, two years later, I couldn't find the grave. I couldn't figure out how I could have gotten the numbers wrong. I couldn't believe Annabel had waited this long to visit her mother's grave.

Annabel said, I should have counted myself. I shouldn't have relied on you.

The graves were so close, the tombstones practically touching one another. Many of the graves were lined with concrete. I hurried along the outside edge of the graves, reading the names on the stones, trying not to step on the grass. They were the wrong names, somebody else's mother, somebody else's father. I felt bad rushing by them so fast. All I wanted was to find one grave, Dora Kaiulani's, so we could leave our flowers and go home. The sun was dropping behind the trees, and I worried about the curfew. If we missed the bus, we would have to walk home and hope the soldiers didn't shoot us.

Annabel Lee finally found her mother's tombstone in the middle of a grassy area, the Lee family plot. She just stood there, didn't even call me to come. When I looked up and saw her crying, I ran up the hill as fast as I could. Every time I stepped on a grave, I said, Sorry, sorry, sorry.

More leis we sewed:

Stephanotis, for Benny Soares, who let me play his ukulele.
Tuberose, for Leonard Pang, who I had a crush on in fifth grade.

Plumeria, for Sonny Boy and Leonard Mahikoa,
Annabel's cousins on her mother's side.

Single white carnation, for Danny Wong, McKinley
fullback.

Maile and vanda, for my brother Joe-Joe, and for the
slop boy, Sammy Woo.

Sammy gave Annabel Lee his mother's jade bracelet to keep safe
for him. He was afraid his aunties would steal it if he left it at home,
and he didn't want to hide it under a rock, in case he didn't come
back. He brought it over to Annabel's house in a small pouch he'd
made from an old rice bag. Annabel showed it to me later that
evening, by candlelight, before she began sewing the maternity dress
for Barbara Chew.

Try it on, she said, handing the jade bracelet to me. It's too small
for me, but maybe it will fit you.

But it didn't fit me either.

Annabel said, We can use soap, but I said, No, might get stuck.

She said, I can't keep it for him.

Why not? I asked. I was so hurt that he had asked her and not me.
It was the final proof that I had no chance with him.

She said, Because I might not be here when he comes back. I told
you, I'm going to visit Emma.

I was sick and tired of hearing about Emma. Emma the wife.
Emma in Florida. Emma with her in-laws. I hoped the alligators
would eat her up.

Annabel said, I promised I would help her when she got hapai.

She's pregnant?

Not yet. But pretty soon she might be.

But what about Sammy?

What about him?

I bet he wants to marry you. Why else would he give you his
mother's jade?

Here, she said. She stuck the bracelet in my hand. You keep it for
him.

Me?

Yes, you.

I don't want it. He gave it to you, not me.

I threw it back at her. Lucky thing she caught it.

She said, Listen, Alice. If you don't keep it for him, who else is going to?

But what's he going to think?

He'll think you love him.

Me? He's not my boyfriend.

I hate when you act like that. I hate when you pretend. Like I'm supposed to feel sorry for you. Why can't you just fight for what you want?

I wanted to tell her I hated her too, but I started crying instead.

Sorry. Look, just take it. You don't have to tell him until he comes back. It'll be safer with you.

She held it out and looked right into my eyes. I couldn't believe she was doing this. It would make a difference, a big difference, and she was right, it was better off with me. But Sammy would be so hurt. I'd have to lie to him. I realized then that that was what she wanted. She wanted me to lie for her.

I ran my finger around the inside of the band. The jade was colder and harder and heavier than I had expected. But I knew it would break very easily if I dropped it. I had to guard it now, with my life. I knew exactly where I would keep it. In the parlor, where my mother never went, in the upholstery of my father's throne, where it would always be safe.

Annabel and I went down to the wharf when Sammy left. It wasn't like Boat Day, when we watched the *Lurline* and the other Matson liners leave from Aloha Tower. We weren't allowed to go up to the ship, so we arranged to meet him at the tower. He was so handsome, even with his hair cut short. When he saw us, he ran over and hugged us both. First Annabel Lee, then me. I looked around, because I hoped to meet his family, but he was alone.

I gave him a pair of socks that I had knitted with my mother's help.

Annabel gave him a wool scarf. She wanted to knit him a scarf, but knitting was too slow, so she didn't even try. Instead, she cut a wide strip of woolen fabric she found in her mother's dresser. She didn't even hem the edges, just sewed the two long selvages together and turned the whole thing inside out so it was twice as thick. Sammy hugged her and wrapped the scarf around his neck to try it out.

You look like you're all neck, said Annabel.

No, I said. *No* neck.

We laughed so hard we started crying. Annabel blew her nose and said, Don't throw your leis in the water. Wear them, and then let them dry out on your cot.

She was thinking about what people often did when they left the islands by ship. They tossed their leis into the harbor, and if the leis floated back to shore, that meant they would return soon. But if the lei went the wrong way, makai, then what?

Afterward, we caught the bus back to my house. With Emma and her brothers gone, it was only Annabel Lee and her father at home, and he was sleeping at the restaurant most of the time. My mother fed us chicken soup, and then we took turns reading *Anna Karenina*. Which the Sisters hadn't let us read in school.

Annabel and I stayed up late at night sewing. She cut the candlewick short, so the flame didn't burn too bright. I loved the sound of her Singer sewing machine. The hum was comforting, like a lullaby. But Annabel didn't like to use the treadle. She turned the wheel with her right hand while she pushed the fabric through with her left. She sewed one stitch at a time this way, up one seam and then down the other. She had a funny kind of patience, for seams but not for hems. But she was used to sewing that way. She and her mother used to do this, sew until late at night without waking anybody up. I hated to remind Annabel that it was just us now in her house.

I was in charge of the candle. When she didn't need to see, she told me to blow it out. She pinned a whole seam in the dark without poking herself with the needles. She pinned only the straight seams this way. The bust darts and armholes were harder because of the curves, and Annabel liked for everything to be just right. If the seam came out crooked, she ripped it out and started all over again.

She would have sewn in the dark too, but I lit the candle when I heard her cranking the wheel. I didn't want her fingers to get caught in the needle.

12

KEEPING THE BEAT

When my former son-in-law comes over to our house to pick up his daughter, the water is boiling on the stove, but the crabs are running around loose on the kitchen floor. My best friend's son and my younger girl are crawling on the floor, trying to catch the crabs so I can cook them. My older daughter and her best friend are sitting at the dining table drinking tequila with lime and salt and cheering for the crabs to win. My granddaughter is kicking and screaming from her high chair, because she wants to play too. My husband is killing flies, catching them with his bare hands and throwing them out the back door.

When Frankie walks up, Sammy says, Good, you just in time for eat. Guess what we're having? Your favorite.

Frankie looks at the family circus in my kitchen, at me by the stove. I nod at him. Stay. Stay. I know he doesn't like coming in the house when Beatrice's boyfriend is around, but my mother tells me Frankie is starting to go out again at night. Maybe he's ready to be friends. It doesn't hurt to ask.

I miss Frankie so much. Miss having coffee with him in the morning, miss the omelettes he used to cook for me. Spanish omelette, Denver omelette, even crab omelette if we had leftover crab. I know he misses me too. His mother, Aggie, won't eat eggs because of all the cholesterol. Frankie says she fixes him and his father frozen gourmet. Frankie won't cook Chinese for her, because she criticizes too much.

She says the carrots are tough, the choy too limp, the shrimp too old. So Frankie goes out to eat after work. When he comes by to pick up the baby, I see the box from McDonald's on the front seat of his Datsun. Only six months divorced, but he drives a sports car now that it's just him and Emily. It's a secondhand car, Model 1600, with two bucket seats only, and he's souped it up. Beatrice doesn't like the idea of her daughter riding in a car with a soft convertible top, but I know that's not the real reason. She's thinking, Why now, why not with me?

Cars, cars, my whole life full of cars and trucks, and I don't even care about them, just the men they come with, the men.

Maybe it's the Datsun with its new paint job. Maybe it's the sight of Wick on his hands and knees, chasing after crabs. Or Sammy, so eager to be friends. But Frankie looks at me, just me, and he says, Well, I might have to eat and run.

Sammy says, No problem, and before Frankie can change his mind: What can I get you for drink, the usual?

He shuffles over to the refrigerator in the garage, where we keep only beer and soda. He digs in the back for the ginger ale.

Frankie says, I could go for a little Cutty Sark too.

Sammy pulls his head out of the fridge. He looks to see if Beatrice is watching from the kitchen window, then he says, One Cutty with ginger coming right up. He's all smiles, reaching for the bottle in the liquor cabinet over the washing machine.

The girls spread newspaper on the living-room floor. This is the only time Sammy doesn't complain about not having rice. No rice, no vegetables, just the crab and all of us together like this for the first time without somebody yelling and somebody crying. I'm glad they're all trying for Emily's sake. Beatrice is already high, giggling and being silly with Amy Toad. Frankie's got a cool head, working on his third highball. It's only Wick who's looking nervous. He hasn't lived here long enough to know how to let bygones be gone, especially when it's time to eat.

Sammy takes his favorite nutcracker out from behind the glass case on the wall. He likes to show off this nutcracker that one of his service buddies gave him, a naked lady with long silver legs that open up wide to make way for the nuts. Frankie used to be the victim, but now it's Wick's turn. Sammy squeezes a crab leg between the legs of the nutcracker and says to Wick, Here, you try now.

Wick laughs and turns a little red. He looks at Beatrice.

No, thanks, he says. That bugger looks dangerous.

Everybody laughs. Poor boy, he tries so hard, but he still can't say buggah.

Sammy doesn't like no. He continues to wag the nutcracker in front of Wick.

Beatrice says, Daddy, don't, but Sammy ignores her.

To my surprise, Frankie says, Here, gimme that thing. He takes the nutcracker from Sammy and starts dancing it around in the air. He opens the legs, then slaps them shut, again and again. Beatrice and Amy Toad give each other the eye. They're wondering what is Frankie up to now? Sammy grabs a crab leg with a good-size pincher and waves it at Frankie.

Try this one, he says.

Frankie squeezes the nutcracker, and the pincher falls into Amy Toad's lap. She throws the pincher back at Frankie. He ducks, and the crab goes sliding across the floor.

Frankie says to Wick, Well, it's a little dangerous, but I survived. He holds out the nutcracker. Care to try it now?

Care to, he said. Care to, in his finest mainland accent.

Wick nods slowly and smiles at Frankie. He reaches out for the nutcracker.

Y'all are nuts, says Wick. But what the hell.

I'm so happy I have to go into the kitchen and wash my face. When I come back out, Amy Toad is saying, Come here, you sexist pig.

She's trying to crack one of Frankie's toes, and Frankie is saying, Quit it, eat your crab, but he's enjoying the attention, I can tell. How different he is now. Not waiting to see what Beatrice wants. Why couldn't he be like this before?

It might work out, this full house, this deck of wild cards. Frankie could marry Amy Toad, Beatrice could marry Wick, and we could all be together. We can live upstairs, downstairs, be neighbors, take up the whole block. Then Sammy could see that it doesn't matter what family he's from. Everything gets mixed up anyway, in the end.

After Frankie and Amy Toad leave, the rest of us lie down on the floor to watch TV. I'm crocheting a dish towel with variegated yarn—brown and yellow and white cotton—to add to my supply of Christmas gifts, when Sammy says to Wick, You and Beatrice can have the master bedroom when your mother comes to visit.

I drop a stitch.

Wick says, I already reserved her a hotel room.

Sammy scolds, Why waste money when we got so much room over here?

Can't see what I'm doing. So frustrated. When I ask him if Annabel Lee can stay with us, he won't even answer. Now he talks like I don't care. Like I'm selfish and mean.

Beatrice says, But what about Mom?

Sammy says, She'll be upstairs with me. Annabel can have your room. That way nobody has to sleep on the couch.

Upstairs. That's what he calls the apartment. That's how he tells me where I am going. Upstairs.

Annabel Lee is coming. She'll be here in two weeks. Maybe she can help me figure out what to tell Sammy. I need a clear head, the right words.

Better clean the house from top to bottom too, plus get a perm and buy a new muumuu with a low bodice.

Annabel sends me a check for three hundred dollars and tells me to get tickets ahead of time for whatever I want her to do. So much money, and she wants me to choose. I lie awake all night, trying to decide. Maybe she wants to go to the Polynesian Cultural Center to see the hula dancers. Maybe she wants to visit Foster Gardens and the Waiole Tea Room. Don't know what she likes anymore, and I have no idea how much tickets cost for anything. Don't even want to go with her, but she'll get mad if I stay home.

Wick says his mother always has to plan ahead. She doesn't know how to relax and just let things happen.

I don't like when he talks about her like that, even if it's true. I wish she had made the check out to him instead of me, but she knows her boy. The money would be gone before she arrives. Wick has too big a heart.

Wait till she sees her son, a real kanaka now, walking around barefoot, eating poi and lomi salmon, going surfing. One thing for sure: He knows how to take one day at a time. I wish Beatrice could be more like that. Wish I could be too.

Annabel Lee calls at midnight East Coast time, while we are eating curry stew. She says, As soon I get there, we have to go shopping for bathing suits. I don't like the ones we have up here. Besides, I don't know what's in style.

I don't want her to see what I wear to go swimming. Sammy's old white T-shirt and a pair of old shorts, because I hate all my swimsuits. They don't fit like I want them to. My breasts are big enough—that's not the problem. It's being short. The good parts don't look as good when squashed. Stretch is what I need to do. Stretch, and let Beatrice take her shopping. Beatrice can pick out something nice for me too.

I clip out pictures of swimsuits from the Liberty House catalogue to send to Annabel Lee. Also the calendar of events from the *Sunday Advertiser*. I tear up her check and put it in the box with her letters. If I let her pay for anything, Sammy will be so mad.

Wick says, Let's take her to see Don Ho. Beatrice groans. Wick says, She wants to play tourist, so why not? We can take her disco dancing too.

Oh boy.

Wick says, She's in pretty good shape, you know. She takes aerobics and karate.

Beatrice says, Why don't you take her to the clubhouse, Mom? She'll get a kick out of that.

Bet she will. I won't even tell Aggie Chew ahead of time. We'll just show up. Annabel Lee will laugh when she sees those old futs trying to do the tango. She can probably still do the lindy hop. The Charleston. Even air flips. Bet she can.

Beatrice sees me going through my chest of drawers. Opening, closing, slamming. So much to do. She says, Mom, can I help you pack something? Wick can help you carry things upstairs anytime.

Can't even speak, just shake my head.

Oh, Ma. She sits down on my bed and says, You don't have to move if you don't want to. Wick and I can get a condo now instead of waiting. We should have done this when we first came home.

No, don't go. We have plenty room.

Okay, okay. Don't get excited. But it's true. We need our own place. I don't know why I've waited so long. You know what Frankie told me last night? He said he's going to buy a house. Just for him and Emily. His parents are giving him the down payment. I can't believe it. He said the store made him department manager. I'm so pissed off. Sorry, but I am. He was the one who didn't want to move. Not me.

You don't have to pay us for the mortgage. You can stay here for free.

I don't care about the money, but if we leave, then Daddy can move back downstairs with you.

Daddy loves upstairs.

Oh, Mom, I should have known. You've been waiting for him to ask you to go up there. It's true, isn't it?

She gives me a hug, but my arms can't come up and hug her back.

She says, Listen, Mom, you're a free spirit. You can go up there any old time. Anytime. You don't have to wait for him to ask. It's your house too. Don't be so old-fashioned.

•   •   •

Free Spirit, she calls me. Some people call me Worry Wart and Not Feeling So Good and Quiet Type, but they never call me that.

Free Spirit leaving behind everything on my dresser. Everything in my closet and chest of drawers. Just a brush and lipstick and a small mirror in my purse. Free Spirit rolling my blue negligee with the peekaboo lace into a little ball and stuffing it into my purse so I don't have to come back to my room. I can go straight up there. Free Spirit squeezing into my red dancing dress and the matching gold sandals I've worn only once.

Beatrice plucks my eyebrows and helps me put on the eyeliner and eyeshadow. She says, You can drink Shirley Temples all night. And you don't have to dance if you don't want to. You can just sit and watch and keep Lurline company, unless of course somebody asks her to dance. They just might, who knows.

She says they might ask me too, but I can say no. I can wait until the time comes and then decide. But one thing for sure: she and Amy Toad are not bringing me back until after Sammy comes home from the Red Carpet Room.

Beatrice says, Let him wonder where you are. Let him worry.

Can't look at her. She knows how I wait for him to come home.

I have to go to the bathroom again before we leave. Check the mirror one more time. My eyebrows hurt a little, but my eyes look bigger, and I like the color of the lipstick that Beatrice has brushed on my lips. Vixen, she calls it. Red and orange mixed together.

You look so foxy, she says to me.

Foxy. Foxy Free Spirit looking back at me from the bathroom mirror. Go, she says. Have fun. You're still a spring chicken, no matter what.

When Annabel Lee was a baby, her father wanted her to go to Punahou School, where all the rich haoles sent their children, but Dora

Kaiulani said, No, we have enough haoles in this family, and what good did it do?

I often wondered what Dora Kaiulani would have said if she saw her daughter and me sitting in the Punahou library, with the high ceilings and the dark wood and the pillars and the books all around? After we graduated from the Priory, we went to work for the U.S. Engineers, who occupied Punahou School after the attack on Pearl Harbor.

One of the young engineers, a mainland boy, told us they were heading for the University of Hawaii but stumbled across Punahou along the way. He laughed when Annabel told him it was a school for haoles, not girls like us. He said to her, They can't be as pretty as you. He looked at me. Or you.

No, I said, not me.

Yes, you, he said.

He had red hair and freckles all over, but he was still kind of cute. I couldn't stop smiling all the way home.

We worked in accounting, tallying up the figures, checking the totals. The cost of trucks, guns, ammunition. We didn't pay attention to the words, just added and subtracted until the numbers came out right.

Numbers running through my head like water, in through my eyes, out through my fingers. The echo of typewriters and adding machines bouncing off the walls. Fingers resting on home row, reaching for the upstairs and downstairs keys without ever leaving home completely.

You had to listen to the beat. Same as when dancing. You had to think not just with your head but with your fingers, your feet, your whole body. Slow slow quick quick. Not stiff. For fox trot, you were supposed to be relaxed. Slow slow quick quick.

We practiced dance steps under the desks, tapping the beat with our toes. Slow slow quick quick. Slow quick quick slow. Fox trot, jitterbug, tango, cha-cha, all the dances we knew.

The beat, the beat and the numbers running through us. Carrots, rifles, jeeps, sardines. Slow quick quick slow.

Annabel Lee and me, keeping the beat while walking down the street, waiting for the bus to come, eating lunch, punching keys. Slow quick quick, slow quick quick. Slow quick quick slow.

After work we went dancing at the YWCA, at the USO. To the Richards Street Y, the Army and Navy Club on Hotel Street, Maluhia at Fort DeRussy, The Breakers in Waikiki. We went to every dance we could reach by bus, sometimes even as far away as Waimanalo or Haleiwa, wherever dance hostesses were needed. Most of the dances took place in the afternoon, because we had to be home before curfew. At least we didn't have to be inside by dark now. The curfew hours had changed, so we could stay out later, until seven or eight o'clock, and then catch the last bus home.

Lei makers took over my father's old shoe-repair shop. Aunty Vicki and her girls made camouflage nets now instead of leis, dyeing them green and brown. The walls of Annabel's father's restaurant were covered with camouflage colors too. If you looked closely, you could see a few coconut trees and chickens and dogs, not just blobs of color. The barbershop across the street had an Uncle Sam poster pasted on the door that made me stop to look every time. It said, Women Can Help Win the War.

That was us. Annabel Lee and me, Alice Lum. Working for the engineers, helping at the Red Cross, but what we cared about most was dancing. To us, that was as important as folding bandages and knitting, maybe even more. Like Annabel said, If you asked them which they'd rather have before they died, do you think they would choose socks?

I had to lie to my mother when we went dancing. Had to make up some excuse, and more often than not, that excuse involved going to the Red Cross or up to Annabel's house to sew. My mother worked now too, at Dole pineapple cannery and at Piggly Wiggly, so she was too tired to worry about me. At least she seemed happier now that

she was bringing home some money and not just hounding my father.

I cashed my paycheck and gave all the money to my mother, except what I needed for bus fare. The bills felt good in my hands. Each one- and five- and ten-dollar bill with the HAWAII stamp. Money I worked so hard to earn. The whole U.S. of A. counting on us, counting on me.

In the ladies' room at work, Annabel and I changed into party dresses that we'd stuffed into our big handbags. We wore shorts under our skirts, black and tight and not too long. We rubbed our legs with thick liquid foundation and drew lines down the back of our calves to look like stockings. We shared lipstick, digging down into the tube with a lip brush, to make every bit of it last. Our favorite was Russian Sable by Revlon. So dark it was purple on our lips instead of red.

The buses were crowded, but we never had to stand. Sometimes the men fought to give up their seats. They said, Dance with me, sugar. Save me a dance.

Annabel ignored them. She sat straight in her seat with her knees together and stared out the bus window.

She said to me, Don't look at them, Alice. Don't answer.

But I couldn't keep from turning to see who they were talking to. Was it Annabel Lee they were calling sugar or was it me, Alice Lum? Were they blond or dark? Tall or short? Would they follow us off the bus? We fought for the window seat. I hated sitting in the aisle seat, with the men pressing against me as they moved down the aisle.

When we got off the bus, Annabel said, Don't look back, walk fast.

All those eyes on the bus and more on the street. The front of me grew bigger, the back of me too. My ankles felt weak and my knees shook, but I followed Annabel down the sidewalk. Quick quick quick quick. Gas mask spanking my hips, but I kept on walking and didn't look back.

•   •   •

We made up names for ourselves, borrowing from the movie stars. Irene Dung, Claudette Choy, Ginger Rodriguez, Marlene DeLima, but never Annabel Lee, never Alice Lum.

We danced with blond, brown, redheaded servicemen with big feet and rough hands and hair on their arms, most of them smooth talkers, some clumsy and shy. I worried about my slip showing, my heels breaking, slipping on the slick floor, my underarm odor. I thought of what Sister Martha Verity used to say about how a lady perspires, a lady never sweats.

Most of the boys couldn't dance fancy, just step together, step. Boring, and my side ached from moving the same way all the time. We retreated to the restroom from time to time to wipe the smudges off our dancing shoes.

I told Annabel Lee, My toes are so sore. If one more guy steps on me, I'm going home.

Tap the beat on their shoulders, Annabel said. When the music starts. Not too hard, just tap. One two three four, so they can feel the rhythm.

Dance with me, soldier boy.

Never mind who's watching. Just close my eyes and dance dance dance.

Before the band played the last song, we excused ourselves and went to the powder room, where we changed back into our work clothes and climbed out the window or sneaked out the back door. Sometimes we ran barefoot on the hot sidewalk because our feet were too tired for shoes. We ran quick up the steps of the bus, quick down the aisle, dropped into our seats, our hearts beating. Quick quick quick quick.

We met Mary-Jo Starr in the bathroom at Fort DeRussy. We were waiting for her to finish powdering her nose so we could climb out the bathroom window. We couldn't escape through the back door, because there were soldiers waiting for us out in the hall.

That lady. She took her sweet time. First, she had to add another layer of black mascara to her eyelashes, then put on fresh lipstick and rouge, both of them more violet than red. She pressed a tissue between her lips, then smiled at us through her reflection in the mirror. She dabbed perfume behind her ears, on her wrists, between her breasts. Perfume, not cologne. I recognized the scent. Taboo. Her hair was short and fluffy and orange, and swept back from her head and up to one side like a wave getting ready to crash. She wore a peacock-blue dress that clung to her curves. I couldn't stop staring at her.

You girls having a good time? she asked.

I said, Yes. Annabel dug her elbow into my side. I looked at her. What? Annabel shook her head.

Then the woman said, I'm Mary-Jo Starr, but you can call me Mary-Jo. She snapped her cosmetic case shut, then turned around to face us.

She said, Roy spotted you first. He said, Mary-Jo, look at those two young ladies over there. They really know how to dance. You go on over and tell them I said so. And I was just about to, but here you are.

Annabel and I looked at each other and laughed.

Have you been dancing for a while? Mary-Jo asked.

I looked at Annabel Lee. She didn't answer, and I kept my mouth shut this time.

Mary-Jo Starr said, Roy can always spot the good ones. Even if the boys you're dancing with aren't that great. She rolled her eyes as she said this. Some of them sure need help, don't they?

I glanced at Annabel Lee again. She was nodding now.

Roy says you're just what we're looking for, and I must say I have to agree with him. If he hadn't seen you first, I'm certain I would have.

Annabel looked at me. She raised her eyebrows, our signal for it's time to go, soldier boys or no.

Roy Ladare is my business partner, said Mary-Jo. We're instructors for Arthur Murray. If you come down to our studio, we'll give you some free lessons.

Free? I asked. Annabel tugged my arm.

You bet. We'll teach you steps you're not going to learn out there. Mary-Jo Starr tilted her head in the direction of the dance hall.

How come they're free?

Well, I'll be honest with you. You're nice girls, I can tell. You see, we just won this big government contract, so we need to hire more dance instructors. Otherwise we can't possibly teach them all.

Them? Who's them?

Those sweet boys out there, said Mary-Jo Starr. She waved her arm in the direction of the dance floor. She moved her left hand slowly, so we could see her long red fingernails. She wore rings on three fingers, but not the wedding finger.

You look like smart girls to me. You're both attractive and poised, and I bet you're hard workers too. I can always tell. I told Roy, Girls like that are the reason we are going to win this war, and we're going to win, you know. I know this with all my heart.

I nodded. Didn't even look at Annabel.

Mary-Jo Starr said to Annabel, By the way, I love the skirt you're wearing. May I ask where you purchased it?

She sewed it, I said. And I helped her with the hem.

You did? My, my. What pattern did you use?

She made the pattern too.

Well, now I'm really impressed.

Annabel Lee finally spoke. She said, You want to hire us to teach dancing?

That's right. All you need to learn is a few more routines, as well as our teaching method, but I'm sure you'll catch on right away. And it won't cost you a thing. Then when you start teaching, we'll pay you.

You'll pay us? asked Annabel.

Of course. We wouldn't ask you to do it for nothing. I bet you can use some extra money too.

Mary-Jo Starr didn't wait for our answer.

Listen, she said. You don't have to give me an answer right now. In fact, you really ought to think it over for a while. We still have a few openings, so there's no big rush. I'll tell Roy you need some extra time. I'll be here at the dance next Tuesday. Or you can come by our studio and take a free lesson, if that will help you make up your mind. Here's my card.

How much are you going to pay? asked Annabel. She refused to look at me. If she had, she would have seen me shaking my head. Don't ask, don't ask.

Why don't we talk about that when you come in? said Mary-Jo Starr. She brushed past us on her way out the bathroom door, leaving in her wake the faint odor of Taboo and cigarettes.

We hurried past Fat Lee Wo, past the herb shop and Aunty Vicki's lei stand, past the market and the prostitutes in the doorways. The Arthur Murray Studio was on River Street, one block from where we bought fabric, between a pool hall and a barbershop. Big fans spun from the ceiling of the studio, but the place was still very warm.

I felt sorry for our dance instructor, Roy Ladare, all dressed up in a suit and dress shirt and necktie. Beads of sweat clung to his temples, but he never took off his jacket. He wiped his face and neck with a pressed white linen handkerchief, which he folded and refolded carefully after each use.

What Annabel Lee loved best was the big mirror on the wall. She liked to dance close to the mirror. She didn't care if people caught her looking at herself. She moved like a cat back and forth across the room. Slowly, so light on her feet.

Me, I hated that mirror. I tried not to look into it or even think about it. I focused on my feet, on Mary-Jo Starr or Roy Ladare, on the footsteps on the floor, the ones we were supposed to follow if we wanted to learn the dance routine.

Mary-Jo said, Dancing is an art, even walking is an art. She showed us how to stand and walk like models. She taught us to put tiny taps on the heels and toes of our shoes so we could sound like professional dancers. She said people loved to hear the clicking sound, that it was tantalizing. She crooked her hands as if she were a ballerina. She had perfect calves, firm and shapely, and slender ankles. Tantalizing.

I loved to dance with Roy Ladare. He made me feel like a feather. Light and floating, free. Slow slow quick quick slow. Pivot turn, brush off, rock back. Slow quick quick. Slow quick quick. Parallel walk, chase, cross step, kick. He smiled and looked right into my eyes the whole time. He had the most beautiful green eyes I had ever seen — that was before I met Coy. I couldn't help but stare right back. He smelled like pumpkin pie, although Annabel said it was cloves I smelled, not pumpkin. She said he sucked cloves to cover up his cigarette breath. I almost didn't want to dance with him after that.

Roy Ladare looked best when he danced with Annabel Lee. They made a handsome couple, even more than when he danced with Mary-Jo Starr, especially when Annabel wore her emerald-green dress that matched his eyes. He always saved Annabel for last. By then she'd memorized the new routines, and when she danced with Roy Ladare, it was as if they'd been dancing together for years.

Pick me, pick me, haole boy whose face changes every time. Sailor on the bus, soldier at the dance, Roy Ladare. Spin me around, dip me way back. Watch my hips swing. Quick quick quick quick. Look but don't touch until I say touch. Look but don't talk until I say talk. Slow quick quick slow. Dance with me last. My eyes wide open, looking at you looking at me. Hold me close so I can't think. Take my breath away. You can't win the war without me, boy. Not too fast. Go slow. Slow quick quick slow.

13

DANCING THE BOY'S PART

It takes four of them to carry the bed upstairs. My brother Joe-Joe and our neighbor Mits Todama pulling from above, and Sammy and Wick pushing from below. Sammy likes to joke about the bed, that it's older than most people's marriages these days. We bought it twenty-five years ago when we moved back to Oahu after the flash flood on Maui. What he forgets is that we have to buy a new mattress every ten years, because the old one sags, and I'm not about to remind him.

They take our dresser upstairs too, with the clothes still in the drawers. They carry Sammy's aloha shirts and pants, my dresses and muumuus, still on the hangers. Only things left in the closet are my shoes, which I need to go through so I can throw some away, plus my sewing machine, record albums, and cigar treasure box.

The back of the closet is covered with mildew, so Sammy tells me I better scrub it good, with vinegar, not Ajax.

I can do that. I can scrub with vinegar. They can move the bed and the dresser and all my clothes, but I'm not going up there. I'm not. He knows I can't, especially not now, with Beatrice and Wick moving out. I can't leave Lurline down here all by herself. Plus, what happens when Emily stays overnight?

But still I want him to ask. As if it's just him and me. Boy-girl. A simple combination with love in the middle.

*   *   *

Beatrice says, Daddy's so hard head. How can you can stand it?

The vinegar hurts way up past my eyebrows. I hate when she talks about her father like that.

She says, You have to talk to him, Mom. I can't do it. It has to come from you.

No worry. I can sleep on the floor. I like to sleep on the floor.

She says, Why don't you take my bed? We have to buy a bigger one anyway, so Wick can have more room for his feet.

But I'm wondering where is Annabel going to sleep? She's coming to visit, but I don't know exactly when. She keeps changing her plans. Soon is all I know. Maybe too soon, because I'm not ready. All the confusion, everybody going separate ways, and me stuck between the elevators.

Beatrice says, Aunty Annabel can sleep in Lurline's bed, and Lurline can sleep on the floor.

No, Lurline needs her bed. The rest of us can move, but not her.

Beatrice says, I give up. Do what you want. Just don't make me feel more guilty than I already do. You know I've been wanting to have a place of my own for a long time now.

No worry. Just go. We'll be okay.

She says, Wick only drinks to make Daddy feel good, you know. He just wants Daddy to like him.

She wants us to come and visit their condo and help them celebrate. We're not supposed to bring anything, no potluck or booze, just ourselves. They're going to fix everything, haole style. All we have to do is come and eat. She can finally use the tablecloth and napkins that Annabel gave her years ago, now that she has someone who will appreciate them. Beatrice says not to look so worried. They'll cook something Sammy likes. Maybe Wick can grill some porterhouse steaks, and Sammy can put on as much salt as he wants.

She looks so excited, like a new bride, although I know I can't say that yet. Ever since they started looking for a condo, they've been so lovey-dovey. Lying outside in the dark, naming the constellations, or going to bed early instead of watching the late movie. Too bad they have to rent a condo instead of buying. Wish I had the money to give them for a down payment. Beatrice says never mind. When Wick gets a better job, they'll be able to afford a mortgage. For now, she is just happy to be doing something instead of waiting around, and for what?

Beatrice isn't as scared of the water anymore. She still doesn't surf, but at least she goes in the water now. She hangs on to Wick so tight it squeezes my heart to watch. The way he carries her, like a baby. The way he never splashes water on her face and never forces her to go in deep.

Before she leaves the house, Beatrice says, Do you want me to go upstairs and bring some clothes back down for you?

Clothes. He has all my clothes, and I don't even know what I want. Can't decide that far ahead. If I can't have them all, might as well have nothing.

She says, Tell me what you want, and I'm thinking, What I want is more than what she can bring me.

No answer, she says. Okay, I'll just pick out something, then it's up to you to go up there and get the rest.

She brings down my favorite red muumuu. My blue negligee. The yellow silk dress she gave me that I have no place to wear. My sleeveless blue housedress with the zipper up the front that makes my arms look fat. Two panties, two bras. My brown Bermuda shorts and white cotton eyelet blouse. My jewelry box. The nerve he has. Taking my jewelry box upstairs.

I have room for my records now. Plus my sewing machine and my yarn and all my crafts. But I like how empty the bedroom feels. Now that I've vacuumed and mopped, the floor looks brand-new where the bed stood. I'm an explorer. Where I am, nobody else has been before. All the clutter, all the weight is gone.

Wick says Beatrice knocked on his heart, and once he opened the door, he couldn't shut it back up. Beatrice says it was serendipity that brought him into her life. Serendipity is all over, everywhere. You just have to recognize it. She says most people's lives are loaded with serendipity, but their eyes are shut. They're too busy worrying about their jobs and their kids and their house payments, so when something good happens, they don't even see it.

This from my customs inspector daughter, whose job is to search for what people are hiding. She takes away what is forbidden. Undeclared jewelry, agricultural products, drugs. What people want. What they're not supposed to have. What they think they can get away with for free.

While Beatrice was in Georgia, she had obligation on her mind when she phoned Annabel Lee. She only called her aunty because I begged her to do it. But Annabel wasn't even home; she hadn't even read my letter. Wick answered the phone, and he called Beatrice right back when she ran out of quarters. They talked for two hours long distance, and before they hung up, he said he was coming to see her. He drove day and night, and all the obligation inside her went right down the drain, as if somebody was pulling the plug, and then all of a sudden she was filling back up again.

She says they didn't even know what was happening until it was too late to stop. He rented a motel room, and he went back home only once, to pack his bag and arrange for the neighbors to water the plants. The amazing thing is that Beatrice didn't flunk her course. When it was time for her to leave, Wick bought a plane ticket for the same flight, but only as far as Los Angeles. He planned to get off and hunt for his father while Beatrice was trying to work things out at home. He had an old address for Coy that he found in the kitchen drawer. One minute they were talking about what to do about Coy and Frankie and Emily and the rest of us; the next minute they were both crying, trying to say goodbye, and then the door to the plane was closing and Wick was still on board.

He wouldn't let go of my hand, she says. He said what if he couldn't find his father, then what? We just sat there crying. Sad and happy and so relieved to have the decision made for us. Next thing I knew, the stewardess was bringing us a bottle of champagne that the

passenger in the seat in front of us had ordered. It was a haole man, about Daddy's age.

He paid for Wick's ticket too?

No, of course not. We charged it. The pilot said he'd had the urge to do the same thing sometimes. So did the man sitting in front of us. Everybody was so nice. They treated us like we were Romeo and Juliet.

She smiles. I never know what Wick is going to do next.

He's like somebody I know.

No, she says, Wick is not like Daddy. Don't tell me that. That's scary.

Those words come out so fast they scare me too, because it's not Sammy I'm thinking about.

The roof opening up. The sky falling into my room. Moonlight, stars. So many memories.

I'm glad for Beatrice and Wick. Glad they're not letting family obligations get in the way. Better to have a place of their own, where they can be alone. Of course, I want that for them, but all the coming and going is getting me down. Them moving out, Sammy upstairs, Annabel on the way, Emily with me three times a week, but even that's changing, because Frankie is letting Emily stay with Beatrice overnight now.

Beatrice wonders who Frankie is dating. She says, I bet it's that clerk at Long's. She's had her eye on him. He has so many girl friends, it's hard to tell. Just friends, my eye.

Poor Emily. I'm not the best popo these days. When I babysit, I have only half a mind. Don't have patience like I used to. Can't keep track of everybody's schedule.

Thank goodness for my room. Sometimes I even have the whole place to myself, if I can keep Lurline occupied. I can watch TV with the sound turned off. The actors say what I want them to say, and if I don't want them to have troubles, they don't. Even on *All My Children* and *As the World Turns*.

Sleeping on the floor feels good. The wood is smooth and shiny and not that hard, with my built-in padding and the cushions from the couch. I'm a little sore, but not that much. Not enough to make me move upstairs.

Beatrice buys me a futon. She says I can roll it up when I'm not using it. She almost bought a single futon because she was mad at her father, but Wick said why make trouble, so she bought one big enough for two. Sammy won't like the futon anyway, because it's Japanese, but I don't want to bring that up. Beatrice hates when Sammy doesn't like something or somebody because of race. That time he got sent to court because he called one of his Negro workers Boy, I didn't dare tell Beatrice about it. Lucky thing she was at school in California, so I didn't have to lie. Just as well, because he watches his mouth a little more now. Good thing Wick is only part haole. Sammy can just shut his mind to that half.

Beatrice is sweet to her sister too. She says Lurline can have whatever's left in her room, including her *American Bandstand* poster. The one in the closet, all covered with dust. She grabs Lurline's hand and they start dancing. The two of them doing the Mashed Potato. Beatrice squeaking barefoot, and Lurline sliding on the floor on her stocking feet—she likes to wear my hose with garters.

I make Beatrice take some papaya and a loaf of sweet bread and some Portuguese sausage to fix for breakfast. Wick loves Portuguese sausage. He likes all the local food. He tries everything, even the pig's-feet soup I make for Beatrice at her time of the month. The soup is a little tart because of the vinegar, and the color makes him nervous—black.

But he says, You're real ono, Aunty Alice. I wish my mom could cook like you.

I'm so stunned, I don't know what to say.

Beatrice says, Hey, haole boy, you just called my mother delicious. It's the pig's feet that's ono, not her.

Poor Wick. There's always something.

Sammy follows me into the kitchen and pats my okole as I am putting the dishes in the sink.

Ono, ono, he whispers to me. He licks my ear.

Don't, I say. Not now. But I don't say it too loud, only so he can hear.

What this boy has started. He has no idea.

Gracie Todama loves when Wick calls her Ma'am. He gets that from his father, so polite. Gracie laughs and hides her face so he can't see her buck teeth. She sends Amy Toad over with mochi and sushi and everything she wants Wick to taste.

She makes me ask him to go pick seaweed at Ewa Beach. She even lets him drive their new Corolla. We pick too much seaweed, because Wick doesn't know when to stop. Then there's sand on the carpet and the trunk gets all fishy, and Gracie's afraid that Mits will get mad. Wick helps her vacuum, but the car still smells, so he says, Why don't I take it in for auto detail, get it cleaned up good.

I'm watching from the bedroom when Mits Todama comes home and sees the rental car sitting in his garage. When Mits calms down, Gracie tells him the story, and Mits says, Son of a gun, I always wanted to drive a Lincoln Continental.

Mits takes Sammy out for a ride. When Sammy comes inside the house, I'm waiting for the music, but he says, That kid not cheap. He even bought collision insurance.

Wick has to work double shift to pay for everything, and then he gets in the doghouse with Beatrice for that.

Wick tries so hard to pass for local, but of course people can tell right away that he's not. He doesn't tuck his shirt in except for work, and he can wear slippers now without limping, but that's not enough. He won't sit down at the table until after I sit, even when Sammy says, No wait, eat before the food gets cold. He opens the car door for me and the girls, and he holds my arm when we cross the street. He gives shaka to the beachboys at Waikiki and says, Howzit? How are y'all doing today? And they know, of course they know. He could go naked with tape on his mouth and they would still know.

I wonder if he can be who he wants to be.

When he and Beatrice leave for their condo, Wick gives me a special hug. A long one, all mine, and then he says, See y'all bum-bye.

What can I do but love?

I'm making a mural. Part crochet, part appliqué, maybe even part weaving, if I ever learn how. Beatrice says this is the way to go if you hate to follow patterns. You can make all the pieces separately so they're easy to carry around, and then in the end you can stitch them together like a quilt, except that when you put it on the wall, it's not a quilt. It's a wall hanging.

But my wall hanging is going to cover so much wall, I have to call it a mural. It hangs on the wall where the dresser used to be and then stretches all the way over to the window. I don't know the whole design yet. All I have is one piece here, one piece there. I hammer them on with nails. The rest I can fill in later on.

Beatrice says my mural is an excellent idea, and I'm so creative, why didn't she think of that?

It just fell out of my head and into my fingers. Like that.

Besides my futon, Beatrice's loom is my only furniture. It's been sitting outside in the garage under a tarp ever since she brought it home from the mainland. She doesn't use it anymore, because it brings back memories of her professor boyfriend. I polish the loom up good with Johnson's wax. Beatrice says she'll get me started and then I'm on my own. I feel like a pioneer with my loom. I lie awake thinking of what I'm going to weave. A skirt for Lurline. A bathroom rug for Beatrice and Wick. Pieces to fill in the big holes in my mural. Some islands, maybe an ocean.

Amy Toad taught me how to make yarn pockets for my shells. So you can see them, just like you can see the little mirrors on Amy

Toad's backpack. She says it is a Pakistani technique that will help me incorporate found objects into my mural.

Incorporate. I like that. Now I have something to do with the treasures in my cigar box.

Dance bid. One-dollar bill with the HAWAII stamp. My old ID card with fingerprints. My Mickey Mouse watch. My brother Michael's drawing of Chinaman's Hat. Pupule quilt swatch. Dried-up corsage with pink ribbon in an envelope. Can't tell it's carnation anymore. Shells, pieces of coral. Sardine-can key. My silver whistle, all rusty.

Serendipity brought them to me, and now it's up to me to find them a home.

I wonder if Frankie still has his old shoes. He dresses so different now. I don't know what it is at first. Not the colors. Still dull. Beige and black and taupe. Finally, I figure it's the size. Everything fits him just right now. He has a chest and muscles from lifting weights, and he's wearing a new pair of shoes every time I see him, as if he's trying them out for the store. I want to ask him if this means he's finally thrown the old ones out, but I'm afraid to find out the answer.

When I look at my own shoes—my high heels that I have kept since the war, the taps all gone, the soles worn down, the leather scuffed—I wonder why I am still hanging on to them. Thought I knew why, but can't remember now. I even have my saddle oxfords from the Priory that I hated so much at the time. I have only one pair of shoes that still look good. My navy-blue pumps. I was saving them for going away. I never told Annabel, and now they don't fit, because my feet have spread so much.

That night we went dancing, me and the girls, my Free Spirit night, my feet were so sore. I danced too much, with the girls at first, especially Lurline. I was relieved when the boys started asking her, so I could sit down. But when they turned to me, I couldn't say no every time. Funny how it all started coming back. Most of the men were lousy dancers, but I remembered how to help them look good. Then one of them got a little too personal, so I refused to be his partner again. I looked around and noticed all the women who were sitting down, and realized I was taking up space that one of them could use. So I said no after that and wouldn't get up again, no matter who asked. It was better that way, just sitting and watching. I loved the disco ball that flashed light all over everything and everyone. It was like the celestial light Beatrice gave me at Christmas to put under the tree, except bigger. I wanted to lie down on the floor, like we did at home, and watch the stars whirl across the ceiling and the walls.

When we got back to the house, I put on my blue negligee in the garage before going upstairs to Sammy. I didn't even go to my room first, because I was scared I would change my mind. I put my bag on the hood of the car, and the hood felt warm, so I knew Sammy hadn't been home for long. I called out as I climbed the stairs. It's me, Alice. Not too loud, just so he wouldn't think I was a burglar. No answer, but the door was unlocked, not even closed all the way. The light in the bathroom still on. Like he was waiting for me to come.

To my surprise, the place was clean. Everything tidy. A broom and dustpan in one corner, the floor swept. No sawdust, no nails or tools lying around. The ceiling and walls were fresh with white paint. No cigarette butts, ashtrays, or bottles.

He was sleeping on a mattress in the middle of the living-room floor. On Beatrice's old twin mattress, which we stored out in the garage. Blue cotton sheets. Blue, like the ones he bought for Beatrice and Wick that first day. And he was wearing silk BVDs. Not black this time, but burgundy. Burgundy.

I poked around, looking to see what was what. The TV on an orange crate. A lamp on the floor. Matches from the Red Carpet Room in a jar, a carton of Camel cigarettes. A small refrigerator full of beer, a single hot plate on the counter. One small pot with a shiny copper bottom. A blue coffee mug with white ducks on it. In the bathroom, I found a new white towel folded into thirds. A see-through plastic shower curtain with red and yellow fish swimming all over it. A bar of Dial soap, the kind I can't use because I am allergic.

A part of me was mad that he could sleep like that, that the apartment was clean, without my help, but the rest of me felt so relieved I just wanted to cry. I tiptoed out the door as fast as I could and hurried back downstairs before he woke up.

He's up there now, on a bigger mattress, ours, and I'm still down here, lying on a hard futon, contemplating my mural. Part of it on the wall, the rest still growing inside my head. The sections I have finished look like islands waiting to be connected, but maybe I won't join them after all. Maybe it isn't one big continent I'm making but many little places you can visit and leave whenever you want.

There's a big blue football and white pom-poms that I crocheted when we took Wick to the stadium to see Kam play Punahou.

A koa bowl and all the fruit that goes inside—mangoes and papayas and bananas. Apples and oranges too.

A white-and-pink conch shell. I plan to stuff it and then hang puka shells from the bottom, so it makes a noise like chimes.

This big black one with the tiny hole, that's my first record. I'm going to make some LPs, some 45s. And I'll sew the names of my favorite songs on them.

"Night and Day."

"I'll Be Seeing You."

"They Can't Take That Away from Me."

Thank you is what I whisper. Thank you for my girls, my futon, my mural, my treasures. For all the serendipity still waltzing into my room.

We forgot the war by dancing, Annabel Lee and me. Forgot the blackout, the martial law. Forgot who was gone and who wasn't coming back.

It was just the two of us at Annabel's house. The radio blaring in the upstairs parlor. "The Way You Look Tonight."

Annabel saying, Hurry, let's go upstairs or we'll miss this song.

She moved so quickly, I barely heard her feet on the steps. The stairway was dark, but she knew the way. I crept behind her, one hand on the railing, my other hand on the wall. Her house gave me chicken skin, especially in the dark. I kept expecting Dora Kaiulani to brush past me, to call out my name. Annabel said she could feel her mother sometimes.

It's like she's pressing against my chest, said Annabel. Like she's holding me. I can hear her too, singing on the lanai. One time I thought I heard something out there, so I went outside to look. My father was standing by the bedroom door, his face all white, like he had heard something too.

The Lees didn't use the upstairs parlor much, not even when Dora Kaiulani was alive. Annabel Lee covered the lamp with a blue silk scarf that she found in a trunk. It was her tutu's scarf, which Dora Kaiulani never wore. Blue silk with white peonies. The bulb was only twenty-five watts, and the scarf made the lamplight even dimmer.

The room was crammed with Chinese furniture and figurines, a black upright piano too. I loved the little ebony tables that slid under one another, from small to big, like a close-knit family. Photographs of Mr. Lee's relatives covered the walls and squatted on top of the piano.

All those eyes staring at us. Mr. Lee's father with his cane, sitting on a high-back chair. Mr. Lee's mother standing by his side, carrying a baby, and her stomach already big again beneath her long cheongsam. And Mr. Lee's brothers and sisters, most of them still living in China. Aunties and uncles and cousins. All of them watching us dance. What would they think of Dora Kaiulani's girl doing the jitterbug? What would they think of me?

We pushed the furniture aside and carried the porcelain Buddha and Kwan Yin into the bedroom. Annabel Lee carried the Buddha, because I was afraid to touch it. My mother believed that if you rubbed the Buddha's stomach, you'd get pregnant. She said it worked for her every time. But Annabel didn't believe in superstitions like

that. She stuck her finger in her mouth and rubbed it on the Buddha's belly before she picked it up.

How many babies does that make? she said. Forty-three, forty-four? I've lost count.

Rubbing the Buddha was part of her ritual before dancing. Just like I had to turn over the photographs on the piano and dance so I didn't face the pictures on the wall.

Annabel wore a new red skirt. It was gored, not gathered. Gored was fancier, trickier to sew, but it showed off her hips better than gathered. I wore an old pair of slacks, navy blue and faded from too many washes, because I thought we were going to sit on the floor and sew.

She danced the lead first. She knew I hated to be the boy.

Close your eyes, she said. Pretend you're in San Francisco in a big ballroom and the ceiling is so high you can't see the top. Go ahead, lean back. I won't let you fall.

I don't feel like it.

Just pretend. Come on.

Sometimes she whispered in my ear, tickling me, as we danced. Her voice got real low, and she sounded just like her mother.

Dora Kaiulani, dancing with her mother and father in San Francisco, in a big ballroom with white pillars and tall glass windows and gold satin curtains tied with silk rope. She liked to tell us the story again and again.

She said, Mama liked to lean way back and look up at the ceiling. Louis had to hold on tight so she didn't fall down. He waltzed with me before they went out dancing. He carried me in his arms so I could pretend. He turned one way and then the other way, so I wouldn't get dizzy when he stopped. He was so handsome in his tuxedo and bow tie. Mama wore a gown with a low neckline. Her dress had a bustle in back. A bustle is a fake okole that haole people used to wear to look big back there. Louis loved that dress.

•   •   •

As we danced, I thought about Sammy Woo and Howie Harimoto and Milton Mau and all the boys we didn't dance with anymore because they were off somewhere, fighting in the war.

I wrote to my brothers, but only Joe-Joe answered. His letters said nothing about the war or where he was stationed or if it was rainy or cold. His envelopes were taped shut and the paper inside all cut up. Big holes, pukas, where there should have been words. What passed the censors dangled from my fingers like paper dolls with their arms and legs chopped off and their hearts cut out.

My brother Michael's birthday was coming up in two weeks. I wondered, Would he spend it in a dark, cold trench? I couldn't even bake him a cake.

Heaven. I was not in heaven. I was not dancing cheek to cheek.

Annabel fussed with the radio dial, trying to find the music, the big bands, not all the talking. We were tired of the talking. She wanted a fast song, something wild.

Lucky for me all she could find was another fox trot, because it was my turn to dance the boy's part.

Come on, she said. Try. I don't want to be the boy all night.

I can't see what I'm doing.

Just feel the steps with your body. I'll help you. Start with your left foot.

But I was already stepping back with my right. We jerked away from each other.

Never mind. Start again.

I hate this.

What? Do you want me to change the station?

No. I just don't want to be the boy.

Okay, okay. She sighed. She pulled me toward her, spun me around and around.

The next song was Annabel's favorite. Tommy Dorsey and his orchestra playing and Frank Sinatra's voice filling the living room and Annabel and me crying like we would never smile again. She turned off the light so we could dance in the dark.

· · ·

Sammy, come back. Slop boy, slop boy.

I thought of the two of us dancing at Annabel's birthday party. His strong hand on my back, his hand that carried the slop can, his arm all muscle and bone. No talking, just his breath on my neck.

The fog made Mama cold, said Dora Kaiulani. She couldn't take me swimming in San Francisco Bay. She missed the warm salt water and her poi and laulau, so we came home. Louis sent us back by boat. Mama said it was my fault, because I cried all the time. But I never cried. She was the one who cried.

Dizzy, dizzy and aching, one more night.

When the song ended, we opened the windows. Nothing but wind blowing into the room. Warm air, thick with the scent of ripe mangoes. We crept downstairs in the dark.

The Lees' bathroom downstairs had two doors, neither one with a lock. I could never relax in there. Had to hold on to the knob of one door while I sat on the toilet and prayed nobody would come through the other door, the one I couldn't reach, the one that opened into Mr. Lee's bedroom.

I thought I heard him snoring. He might have come home while we were upstairs dancing. But maybe it was just my breathing, so loud in the dark. I tried to go quietly, holding back the stream as much as I could, so that I made only a little tinkle at a time. Afraid to flush, afraid not to. The sound like a gun going off. If he was there, he was awake by now.

I opened his bottle of shaving lotion, put a little on my throat, then wiped it off with his towel. Didn't want to run the shower, so I gave myself a sponge bath in the sink. Held my washcloth under the hot water first and then under the cold. Hot and then cold, hot and then cold, ending with cold, so that the cloth was lukewarm against my skin. I rubbed the bar of soap between my fingers. The soap felt good, slippery and warm. Washed my face and neck, then rinsed with the towel. Then under my arms. Then down between my legs. His soap. Tiptoed to rinse myself. Cold, then hot, then a little more cold. Wiped myself dry. I still felt sticky, but smelled like soap now instead of sweat and everything else.

Annabel was already lying in bed.

Are you still awake? I asked.

She didn't answer, but I knew she wasn't sleeping. We lay there for a long time, neither one of us breathing very loud, until finally she whispered.

Alice?

What?

Do you remember what Mary-Jo Starr said about how being the girl wasn't all following?

You mean, when she said you can't just go limp?

Right. She said you have to give the boy something to push against, something to pull. Otherwise it doesn't work.

Yeah, I know. She said following isn't waiting. You have be ready to go where he wants you to go.

I recalled how we'd laughed about this on the bus ride home. Annabel had said, I'd be afraid to go where some of those boys want me to go, and I'd agreed.

But she was serious now. She said, Well, I'm ready, Alice.

Ready for what?

For the next step. I'm ready to start living my life. And you know what?

What?

I'm not going to sit around and wait for some boy to take me wherever he wants me to go.

Oh.

Do you still want to be a nurse? she asked. Do you still want to go away to school?

That was before the war. We can't go now.

Why not?

You know why not.

If we could go, when we can go, would you still go?

What about Sammy? I asked.

What about him?

Aren't you supposed to write to him?

I can't. I told you that already. Answer my question.

It's late. We better go to sleep. We have to work tomorrow.

Don't you hate doing what people expect you to do? Don't you ever want to just run away?

Where would I go?

Away. Off this rock. Doesn't matter where. As far as you can go. I'm going to have enough money pretty soon. I have all what I make from sewing clothes for the girls at work. I only give my father half my paycheck. Plus there's the money we're going to make from dancing.

We haven't made any money yet from dancing. I'm starting to think we're never going to make any money that way. Besides, we should be buying savings bonds.

Why? she asked.

What do you mean why?

Why should we buy savings bonds? To keep on fighting?

You shouldn't say that. You shouldn't think like that.

You know what?

What?

You know what we are? We're ladies-in-waiting.

No, we're not. We're working. We're career girls. You said that yourself. We're helping to win the war.

No, she said. We're ladies-in-waiting. That's all we're doing. Waiting.

Night, still night, and I was never going to fall asleep. Not now.

Finally, Annabel said, You hungry? Let's go find something to eat.

With all the banging she made in the kitchen, I was pretty sure her father wasn't home after all. It was just us. She brought out the small box of chocolates that she'd been saving for a special occasion, plus some candied orange slices that she found in a tin above the icebox. She even dug out a bottle of rum from the back of the cupboard, where the pots and pans were stored.

Rum? Your father has rum?

He doesn't know. My mother hid this from him.

Your mother drank rum?

Sometimes. Why not?

All I'd seen Mr. Lee drink lately was Five Islands gin. My father drank it too. Because of the liquor ration, they couldn't get any of their favorite whiskeys.

Now is when we need it, said Annabel Lee. No sense saving it for later on because later on might never come.

I wish you'd stop talking like that.

Just try a little. So we can make a toast.

Okay.

To the boys, she said. May they all come home. See, I'm not that mean.

I know you're not.

She drank half a jigger. I took a little sip.

And now, to us, she said. To all the ladies-in-waiting.

Are you drunk? I asked.

Not yet. But I'm going to be pretty soon. Now let's eat the candy. I'm starving.

Annabel fell asleep right away, but the rum and candy kept me awake. She lay on her side, with her back touching my left arm. I could see the curve of her hips under the sheet and feel her hair falling on my shoulder. She had taken out her braids while we were drinking in the kitchen, so her hair would really be tangled and wild in the morning, the way I loved best. I brought my right hand up to my breasts, slowly, quietly, so she wouldn't hear me, wouldn't turn and see me feeling my nipples, hard under my nightgown. My eyes closed now, trying not to think, her bare back pressing heavy on my arm. My hand moving down, between my legs, then back up every time she stirred. Still wide-awake now, pretending we were dancing, Annabel and me, Annabel and Sammy, Sammy and me. Worrying about Sammy: would he come back alive, who would he want? Trying to remember his face, trying to feel his arms around me. Wishing

I had his mother's jade bracelet with me, so I could hold it. Hoping it was safe where I hid it last.

I had moved that bracelet so many times since its first hiding place, tacked to the bottom of my father's chair in the parlor. I hid it inside an old sock in the back of my drawer, in a box I stashed in our bomb shelter, inside a shoe in the back of my closet. No place felt safe enough, so I kept moving it around.

Sammy's mother must have been a very small woman, or she had worn the bracelet when she was a child. There was nobody to ask, so I could only imagine. Her wrist must have been weak and fragile. She was like a flower just beginning to bloom, when the stem snapped.

Snap. That's what might happen if I tried to put on the bracelet. I wanted to wear it so badly, even if for just one time. I didn't want to wear it in public or show it off. It wasn't mine to keep, just to protect.

Is that what it means to love? To hide and worry and want?

I tried using soap and a little water on my left hand, because it was smaller than my right. If I pressed my thumb against my little finger, I could make my wrist even smaller, and the bracelet might slip over my knuckles.

I squeezed and pushed and almost got it on, but I had to stop. Afraid I might succeed, and then I wouldn't be able to get it off again.

My hands traveled up and down my body. The trip felt new every time.

Which is harder? Jade or bone? Jade or bone.

BIRDCAGE

Frankie brings me parakeets. I'm lying on the couch in the living room, listening to the refrigerator and the clock, when I hear him calling from the back door.

Alice Mom. You home?

Alice Mom. That's my new name, because I'm his friend, not just his ex-mom. Ex. X. Like I'm supposed to cross him off my heart.

Seven o'clock in the morning, and I haven't even made coffee. Have to sit up slowly. Wait for my head to stop spinning around. Try and think why he's come. Am I supposed to babysit today?

Frankie walks in carrying Emily and a big birdcage with two parakeets inside. He puts the cage on the coffee table. It's huge, taller than me when I'm sitting up.

Frankie says one parakeet is a boy, the other one is a girl. You can't have just one or it gets lonesome. The parakeets are green with yellow masks. He says you can tell the boy from the girl by the blue band across his face.

Plus the girl is more bossy, Frankie tells me. Look how she nips my finger when I stick it in the cage. She thinks I'm a stick for her nest.

I ask him how come he brought me this cage, what is it for?

He smiles. Gotta have reason?

No.

Well, then. I just want you to have it.

Frankie holds Emily in his arms. He sways back and forth, and I sway too. That's how we talk, like we're standing in a boat. Me and Frankie and Emily, and the living room bobbing up and down.

Emily holds out her arms. She wants to come to Popo. She feels soft and warm against my cheek. She smells like sour milk. She likes when I tickle, when I pretend to bite her leg. I cover my teeth with my lips before I put her little calf inside.

This little piggy's going to eat you up. Oink. Oink.

Frankie says his hippie friend Polo made this cage. That's what Polo does for a living, makes birdcages and welded contraptions that move. You drop the metal ball in and it falls from one place to another and goes like a roller coaster all the way to the bottom. As I listen to Frankie, I'm wondering where he gets the money to buy a house and a car and now this birdcage. No wonder Beatrice complains about the child support she's paying.

Frankie says he dreamed that I wanted a birdcage, so when he woke up he had to go get this one for me. He says it didn't cost that much, because he's helping Polo set up shop. Writing brochures and letters, plus a little bookkeeping, and in exchange, Frankie gets to use all the tools and welding equipment. He wants to make jewelry—like the dangling earrings Amy Toad wears. He can sell the earrings in Polo's shop. When they have the grand opening, Frankie's going to read poetry and they'll have a big party. He wants me to come and help them celebrate—the whole thing is free—and I can bring anybody I want. He says he has been writing poems like crazy since Beatrice and he split up.

It's beautiful, I tell him. Best birdcage I ever did see. I always wanted one.

He says I must have been visualizing this cage, that's why he dreamed about it, that's why it's standing here in front of me. He says if you really want something, all you have to do is picture it inside your head. You see what you want and then it comes true.

Like this birdcage. Mine.

The metal is silver, not shiny like the toaster, but raw and dull and bent into circles and curves that go all over the place. The boy parakeet sits on a carved wooden tree branch, and the girl rides a little swing that tinkles because of the bells.

Frankie whispers in Emily's ear. Bird, bird, bird. Say bird for Popo. Emily hides her face in his neck.

Then he says to the parakeets, Say, Hi, Alice. Say, Hi, Alice Mom. But they don't answer.

Frankie says, They're nervous, that's why. New house. They can't talk like parrots, but the man in the pet shop said they can learn something. Just keep it simple when you teach them.

Me?

Sure, why not? Everybody talks to you.

What should I make them say?

That's up to you.

I'm Emily's popo, I tell him.

That's what you're going to teach them?

I'm Emily's popo. I'm going to babysit no matter what.

He stares at me for a moment, puzzled, then he says, Oh, I get it. You think this is a thank-you for watching Emily.

Nod.

Want to touch the wire, see how it feels, but scared to get too close. Always wanted parakeets, but Sammy says they're waste time. If they fly away, they won't come back, not like homing pigeons. Don't dare remind him of all the pigeons we lost on Maui because Sammy named them after fish. They didn't come back because they forgot who they were.

Frankie says, This is not for taking care of Emily. If it has to be for something, then think of it as a birthday gift.

But my birthday isn't until Saturday. After Annabel comes.

Close enough, he says. I want you to have them because you're so good to me. Sometimes I think you know me better than my own mother.

Don't want him to start talking about her. Ask him, You coming to my party?

He shakes his head. I don't think so.

Why not? You and Beatrice still fighting?

No, not that. I just feel funny, with Wick and all.

But I thought you and Wick were pals.

Only for Emily's sake. Besides, if I get along with him, he just catches hell from you-know-who.

Don't know where she gets her temper. Not from me.

He laughs. That's for sure.

Sammy can't help it when he drinks.

Frankie shakes his head. He won't say anything bad about Sammy. He says, Well, I better be going. You okay in the house by yourself?

Not by myself. Lurline is with me. She went to the market with Gracie. My head too sore.

You not feeling so good?

Shrug.

Frankie kisses the top of Emily's head. He squeezes her, then he says to me, Beet told me the flash flood happened just before your birthday. When was it? Is today the day? The anniversary?

Flood in my head. No, pretty soon. Go over to the chair and sit down.

Emily squirms in Frankie's arms. She wants down. She points at the cage.

Frankie says, Bird, bird. Say bird for Popo.

Emily wobbles over to the cage. She grabs the bars with her little fists and rattles the cage back and forth. The parakeets squawk and fly around. The cage might fall. The cage might break. Why doesn't Frankie make her stop? The birds might bite and fly away, and I haven't even named them yet.

Frankie says, How come nobody talks about the flash flood? Beet doesn't even remember what happened. She says she was only five years old. So that means Lurline must have been about Emily's age. That's twenty-seven years ago. Long time.

Feels like yesterday. Lurline only a baby then. Still a baby. Pray for Emily to grow. Get up, Alice. Make coffee. Kitchen bobbing up and down.

Alice Mom. You okay? I'm sorry I brought it up.

Frankie follows me to the kitchen. His voice is louder. Worried.

Bend over to get the percolator. Dizzy. Better sit back down. Frankie means well. Don't make him scared. Pretty birdcage. Parakeets mine. Have to name them. Let the cold water run. Fill the pot. Five scoops of coffee. Put the lid on. Plug it in.

Seven-thirty a.m. Twenty-six flash floods, and one more coming up. Half an hour and two days from now. On the day my best friend, Annabel Lee, arrives.

Annabel Lee, Annabel Lee, what a good dancer she was. She taught me all the steps I knew until we started taking lessons at the Arthur Murray Studio. We went there two, sometimes three, times a week during the war. It was our haven, our secret place. We never told our parents or our girl friends from the Priory. How lucky we were, making money for doing what we loved best. So what if the pay came only when we gave lessons. So what if we taught steps we just learned ourselves that day. We gave group lessons at the USO dances, then handed out coupons, and the men came down to the studio to cash them in for private lessons with us. The first time was free, but not the times after that.

Don't forget to smile, girls, said our dance instructor, Mary-Jo Starr. Talk with them. Flirt a little. All they want is a little company. And remember, it doesn't hurt to look good.

Looking good was easy for Annabel, but not the rest. She ignored the men who stared at her, didn't smile or try to carry on a conversation. But the way she lifted her chin, the way she raised her arms and spun on her toes, caused the men to line up for her anyway.

They wanted to dance with me too. Not the Alice who wanted to run home and hide under the couch, but the other one, finally blossoming, my breasts full size now and my hips just right. I even had a waist, from all the running around. No time to eat, just work and

dance, work and dance. My hair finally held a curl, with Annabel's
help and a beauty shop perm.

One Alice dancing, men with arms full of muscle holding me
tight, rocking me from side to side. The other Alice rushing past my
mother in the kitchen, the steaming pots on the stove, to the bathroom, to my bedroom, away from my mother's sensitive nose. She
sniffed my hair, my skin, my clothes. Her nose, her eyebrows all
scrunched up. She scolded in Chinese first, then in English. What
kind smell this? I let her words float right by. Like my father, a clam.
Shut.

Alice the Pig, no longer loyal. Hiding some of my work money
instead of giving it all to my mother. I counted the cash on my bed.
Made two piles. Theirs. Mine. One Alice, indulging in small luxu-
ries—lipstick, cologne, costume jewelry. The other Alice, saving for
something bigger, but exactly what, I didn't know.

Alone in my bed, the wild scent still with me. Feeling my breasts,
my stomach, all the way down. Smelling my fingers. Falling dizzy
into sleep.

Annabel didn't work in the restaurant anymore, but her father
never complained. She didn't dance the hula either, at least not in
front of me. Her ti leaf skirt, brown like paper, lay forgotten in one
corner of her room. Her uliuli silent, the red and yellow feathers covered with dust. Her hinahina lei, dry and crumbling on the dresser,
next to the faded photograph of her mother.

We met Coy Whitlow at the May Day dance at the Central
YMCA. He was standing in the refreshment line in front us, and the
scent of our pikake leis made him turn around.

It was the biggest dance of the year so far, and it was just for
defense workers. No servicemen. Instead of wearing leis, we were
supposed to buy war bonds. But Annabel said what was wrong with
flowers? The flowers were going to fall off the bush if we didn't pick
them. She made two leis, one for me and one for herself. She picked

some pikake to put in our hair too, so we didn't need to wear perfume.

I didn't want to go to the dance. Most of the defense workers were from the States. Haoles, not local boys. Many of them were draft dodgers, military rejects, who came to the islands to make a killing. We'd seen them hanging around town and in Waikiki. They didn't shave. They were losers, bums without uniforms. The lowest of low.

But Annabel said, Don't forget we're defense workers too. All you have to do is dance. You don't have to take them home.

I made her promise we could leave anytime, that she wouldn't make me stay.

She said, Our brothers were defense workers. Wouldn't you want somebody to dance with them?

Maybe you can be open-minded when you're dating an Army lieutenant like she was, someone she met at Punahou. She only went to officers' dances with him, and not every time he asked, because she didn't want him to get too serious. If you dated an officer, you weren't supposed to go out with anybody else. Not a private, not even a sergeant, and especially not a war worker from the States.

I don't know why she discouraged the lieutenant. He could have been transferred Stateside, and if they fell in love and got married, she could leave with him. Then she wouldn't have to wait for the war to end. But Annabel said he wasn't that great a dancer, and he could only think of one thing—getting his hands inside her panties. When the other girls at work talked about getting married after the war was over, Annabel got up and walked away.

We thought Coy was joking when he said he came from a town called Sweet Home. Sweet Home, Georgia. But later on, when we couldn't find it on the map, we figured it must be true. How could he make up a town like that? We decided his name must be real too. Cornelius Wycliff Whitlow the Second, not Junior, because his family expected a Third.

But, he said, don't call me that. Coy is enough.

That first night, we gave him our movie-star names, Vivien Lee and Myrna Lum. We didn't bother to change our last names because there were so many Lees and Lums in town.

He smiled like his name. Coy. A little bit rascal, but shy and embarrassed when we smiled back, his lips thin and quivering when he spoke.

It was hard to believe he drove a truck. He delivered food and supplies to Schofield and Fort Shafter, all the items we totaled up every day on our adding machines. He didn't look like a loser to me. His face was shaved smooth, his hair wavy but not too long, his slacks a little baggy but tapered at the ankles, his white shirt fitting just right. His shoes, black-and-white wing tips.

He wanted to know what kind of perfume we were wearing and couldn't believe it when we said it was the pikake. He asked where he could find pikake. He wondered why, when he tried to make a plumeria lei from flowers on the Punahou campus, the flowers kept falling apart in his hands. This sounded very strange to us, a man who picked flowers and tried to sew a lei.

He said, Are you hula-hula girls? Did y'all see *Waikiki Wedding*? Do you know "Sweet Leilani," what Bing Crosby sings when the pig comes barging into the shack?

He sang it then, right there in front of the refreshment table, his voice bright and clear, while holding Annabel's pikake lei between his shaking fingers.

The music was fast, a jitterbug. Annabel's lei flew across her neck, and her dress rose high on her hips as Coy spun her around. Her eyes lit up when she realized after only a few seconds on the dance floor that he knew what he was doing. They didn't talk, not even during the slow songs. I couldn't keep my eyes off them, even while I was dancing with other men.

The way he stared at her, not nervous now that they were dancing. And her, not looking bored, not making eyes at me as she usually did when her partner was a dud. They danced six songs in a row before they finally came over to the punchbowl and Annabel dragged me outside with them to cool off.

Out in the courtyard Coy told us he wanted to learn how to dance the hula. He said, Boys can do it too, can't they?

We laughed, but he said, I'm serious, I'd like to try. I seen the hula girls down in Waikiki. Y'all are much better than in the movies. Can you teach me how to do that? He looked at Annabel and then at me, then down at the ground, his voice trailing off into a whisper.

Annabel said, Well, maybe. I don't know.

Her face was flushed, as if she was embarrassed.

He shook his head and grinned. Well, never mind. It was just a thought. Now it's my turn to dance with Miss Myrna. Will you do me the honor?

I looked around, and then I realized he was talking to me. Using my Myrna Loy name. I turned to look at Annabel. She smiled, nodding.

I said, I would be pleased to dance with you, Mr. Coy Whitlow.

Hey, none of that. It's Coy, you hear?

I held out my hand. Coy.

He led me back inside, to the dance floor. I didn't even try to hold my dress down. Just let it fly.

Annabel's father didn't ask where she was going anymore. He didn't even look up when we walked into the house. I said hello to him anyway, my voice loud so he could hear. When I stayed overnight at Annabel's, I always brought Mr. Lee something. Herbs or rubbing liniment from my father. Sweet potatoes and vegetables from my mother, from her victory garden. She taught me how to cook the potatoes for him. She told me to wash the dishes and clean house when I was over there and not to eat too much. It embarrassed her to give food to a restaurant owner. That's why she sent raw vegetables—or crocheted doilies—so she wouldn't insult him.

Sometimes Mr. Lee nodded or grunted when I put the gifts on the table, but he never said a word. He sat on a plump upholstered chair in the parlor, resting his elbows on the white doilies from my mother. He stared at the wall and puffed his pipe. Even when the tobacco was all gone, he kept on sucking. Air rattled through his pipe like the plumbing first thing in the morning.

The Lees' house felt musty from being closed up during the day. When Annabel came home, she went through the house, opening up the windows and doors, turning on the few lamps that still had lightbulbs in them. Sometimes she kissed his cheek. I wished I could kiss my father like she kissed hers. Wished I could walk away like she did, not minding when he ignored her.

My father was silent too. He stayed in the back parlor long after his customers were gone. Not like my mother, who gossiped on the phone with her sisters, her friends, with whoever came on the party line.

They were lost to the night, my father and Mr. Lee. Shadow men.

Put on my new Tommy Dorsey record, said Annabel.

She brought out two bowls, two plates, two pairs of chopsticks, and put them on the kitchen table. Mr. Lee ate at his restaurant, but he brought leftovers home for us. Annabel and I opened all the boxes. Picked only what we liked. Warmed the food up on the gas stove, except for the rice, which we ate cold. The squid was like rope, the chicken like rubber, the rice so dry the grains fell off my chopsticks. She turned the Victrola up so loud that I could see our mouths moving, but I couldn't hear the chewing even inside my own head. Annabel pushed the food around her plate. She hardly ate anymore. Peck, peck. One small bite, then another, and the rest she scraped into the garbage can.

While I washed the dishes, Annabel practiced ballet. She took lessons now, from the mother of one of our Priory friends. Mrs. Kaleikini was haole, the daughter of a wealthy Honolulu merchant married to a Hawaiian musician, but she refused to leave when the other rich haole women and children were evacuated from the islands. Annabel sewed dresses for Mrs. Kaleikini in exchange for ballet lessons twice a month.

Annabel showed me how to stand, how to hold my hands out in front of me and then bend my knees so my back was still straight but my toes pointed out. All that at once and her correcting me the entire time and me thinking, Why bother? How could I lift my whole body with just my toes?

She danced ballet to all kinds of music. Tchaikovsky, Sinatra, didn't matter. Annabel was good at capturing the mood of the music, whatever it was. If the step wasn't right for the song, she changed the way she moved to make it fit right. She flung blue and red scarves over the lamps for atmosphere. She draped flowers and leis everywhere, on top of the piano, on the stove, even on the toilet. She lit candles and squirted perfume in the air and danced with her shirt tied at the waist. Her skirt was made of gauzy cotton so thin you could see right through to her long brown legs.

Sometimes when the record stopped, she kept on dancing, and all you could hear was the needle scratching and the floor creaking and the windows rattling and the echoes of her feet bouncing through the house.

All those rooms, full of furniture and clothes and photographs, but no people, no sounds but our own. Annabel and I knew each other so well, we didn't need to talk. I could let my thoughts drift. Even with all the music and the dancing, it was always nighttime in that house.

When Coy showed up at the Arthur Murray Studio, our dance instructors, Roy Ladare and Mary-Jo Starr, were demonstrating the tango. He stood by the front door watching, hands in his pockets. Annabel and I waved at him from across the room, and he thought we meant for him to come in. He didn't realize we were taking lessons.

As he walked over to us with long, quick strides, Mary-Jo and Roy began to exaggerate their moves, so we could see what the tango should look like when done with the true feeling in mind. Coy grabbed Annabel and started to imitate our dance instructors. Mary-Jo saw them, and when she and Roy stopped dancing, she turned to Coy and said, Well, look at you. Want to give it a try?

Coy looked around. Pardon? Are you talking to me, ma'am?

I surely am, said Mary-Jo. I see you already know a thing or two. What's your name?

Coy Whitlow, ma'am. I only know a little.

Show me.

He wiped his hands on his pants before he took Mary-Jo in his arms and stood very straight until the music started. He began with simple steps, like he did with Annabel and me at the May Day dance, and then moved quickly into more tricky patterns. They used the whole room, every bit of floor. They looked into each other's eyes the whole time. When the music ended, my heart was pounding and I felt Annabel's hand squeezing mine and me squeezing back.

Mary-Jo turned to Roy Ladare and said, Well, it looks like we have a ringer here. I guess I better teach him myself.

Roy Ladare said, Don't be silly. The other girls want to dance with him. We don't want to play favorites anyway.

Mary-Jo Starr just laughed. She was still holding Coy's arm. Coy looked at us and then back at Mary-Jo.

She said, What do you think, Mr. Whitlow? What would you like to do?

Coy said, Well, ma'am, I just want to dance is all. I came to dance with my friends. Miss Vivien over there and Miss Myrna.

He pointed at us. Mary-Jo and Roy looked puzzled. They knew us by different names: Veronica Lee and Rita Lum.

Roy said, No problem, Whitlow. You can dance with anyone you want.

Roy put his arm around Coy and pulled him away from Mary-Jo. Roy said, Where the heck did you learn to dance like that? Why don't we step outside and have a little chat.

Mary-Jo didn't like that. Her heels pounded across the studio floor. She scratched the record while yanking off the needle, slapped a new record on, and then pulled one of the soldiers onto the dance floor.

We told Coy our real names afterward, when we saw him waiting for us at the bus stop. He was smoking a cigarette, but when we walked up, he crushed it against the wall behind him. He looked a little upset, but all he said was, Thanks for inviting me, sorry if I caused a fuss, and then we were saying, No, no, that was fun, hope you come again, and then him saying, Maybe, I'd like to, I guess, if it's all right with you.

Annabel said, We have something to tell you, Coy. Can you keep a secret?

What? he said. A secret? Sure.

She whispered into his ear and then motioned to me. I whispered into his other ear. We told him our real names.

He looked at us, one at a time, then said, And here I went and told y'all my whole goddamn name.

We were still laughing when the bus came. As we waved and shouted at him from the bus window, several of the soldiers on the bus waved too.

Goodbye, Coy, they chimed in high voices. See you later, Honey Pie.

We had a code name for him. Louise. Like Louis, but a woman's name, so our parents didn't get suspicious. We're going to fold bandages with Louise. Louise invited us over for dinner.

This was his pattern. He came early for the lessons. Then later, when we danced with the men, he spent half an hour with Annabel and half an hour with me. Sometimes me first, sometimes her, depending on who was free. Then he went outside to wait, so he could escort us to the bus stop.

Coy and Annabel danced the complicated version of the jitterbug, the lindy hop. Nobody else could do it besides Roy Ladare and Mary-Jo Starr. I knew a few of the basic steps, how to kick away and do heels. I did a little Charleston too, but they knew even more. All the tough moves. Aerials. Back flips. Mary-Jo's black panties showed as her skirts flew up. Annabel's too. She didn't like to wear shorts underneath her skirts anymore.

All eyes stared at Coy and Annabel. Nobody watching Mary-Jo Starr and Roy Ladare.

Annabel was not her usual royal self, quiet in public, serene on the dance floor. She was laughing out loud, practically screaming. She and Coy matched what Mary-Jo and Roy were doing, plus added their own twists and shakes.

Afterward, Annabel ran over to me. I hugged her.

Feel my hands, she said. I think I'm going to faint.

She held out her hands. They were damp and hot, her fingers limp. She breathed heavily and leaned on me, her strength used up.

She talked about him all the way home on the bus, her voice high and shaky.

I felt sick to my stomach. It was happening again. I decided right then and there that she could have him. She could have all of them. Sammy Woo, Howie Harimoto, all the officers and engineers in the whole United States Army, all the men who came to the dance studio. Coy Whitlow too.

I would be nice to him. Be friends. Listen, smile. But that's all. Milton Mau used to say to me, Annabel may be good-looking, but you're the one with the nice personality.

That was me. Personality. Alice, so nice. Alice, so sweet.

It was a race to see who would reach Coy first when he walked into the studio, Mary-Jo Starr or Roy Ladare.

Mary-Jo said, Let's dance.

Roy said, Let's talk.

They hovered around him, contradicting one another. We made bets to see who would win.

I told Coy, Do something fancy with me. I want to try.

Baby, he said, swinging me out, you're asking for trouble.

He did what I asked. Inside and outside turns, back to back. Shuffles and twists, all over the place. He lifted me up, practically carried me across the room. My body felt so light, my feet barely touched the wood. And me hanging on, going wherever he led me. We danced slow too, so close the silver whistle he wore around his neck pressed against my forehead, but I didn't mind. Not that, not even the sweat of him that rubbed off on me.

Annabel's eyes on fire, but me not looking at her, not sorry.

He called me Baby. Not sorry at all.

I scrutinized my body in the mirror when I got home. I practiced looking sultry and mysterious. I put my hands on my hips and made my lips look full and pouty like Annabel. Like Scarlett. Jezebel.

He said, I like dancing with you, Alice. It's so relaxing.

One Alice blushing, acting all embarrassed; the other one, churning, burning inside. You want to relax? Go home and take a bath.

One day in the studio, Annabel rushed up to me and said, Hurry up. Louise is going to give us a ride home.

A ride? I couldn't figure out why she was using his code name.

Don't ask, she said. Come on.

We had a rule never to accept rides from or date any of the men we danced with. It was a rule we'd made from the beginning, even before Mary-Jo Starr recommended it. It was a rule that was supposed to keep us safe.

Act like you don't see them, said Annabel. She yanked me past Coy and Roy Ladare, who were standing outside the door, smoking. Roy had his arm on Coy's shoulder. Coy slumped, with his arms folded.

I heard Roy say, Why not? Just one drink.

Annabel practically dragged me down the block.

Just keep walking, she said. Don't look back.

We turned the corner, and then Annabel pulled me into one of the shops.

Let's wait here, she said.

A few minutes later, Coy appeared. Annabel called to him as he walked past the store.

He grinned when he saw us.

Come on, he said. He led us to his car, farther down the block. It was a green Studebaker, not new, but clean and polished. He opened the front passenger door. I hesitated, so Annabel climbed in first. After I got in, Coy closed the door and ran around to the driver's side. He pulled away from the curb, then looked at us, and we all burst out laughing.

Holy shit, he said. That queer don't know when to give up.

I gasped, but Annabel just laughed some more.

Coy lit a cigarette, passed it to Annabel. She inhaled deeply, then blew smoke right at the windshield. He had held that cigarette between his lips, but she acted as if it was nothing. She handed it back to him, didn't even offer it to me.

Coy took another long drag, then held the cigarette out over Annabel's lap. My turn.

Annabel said, She doesn't smoke.

I said, Sure I do. She raised her eyebrows at me.

I took the cigarette, sucked hard, and erupted into a cough. Many coughs.

Both of them laughing, and Coy saying, Never mind, you got the right idea.

Glad for the air blowing across my face. Glad for Coy lighting up two more cigarettes in his mouth at the same time and passing one to Annabel and sharing the other one with me, so I didn't have to smoke it all myself.

We were two chatterboxes, Annabel and I, talking about whatever popped into our heads. The movies we'd seen recently, the songs we liked. We made him drive by the Priory so we could show him the school and the cathedral and point out our dorm. We sat low in the car so the Sisters wouldn't see us. We took turns telling him about the times we almost got expelled.

Coy smiled and listened, didn't say much at first. But when he did, it was mainly questions, like what was it like to be around girls all the time, did we feel closer to each other as a result? They were deep, personal questions, what we weren't used to being asked.

When we reached Wilder Avenue, Annabel said, Turn right here. Alice lives down on Kapahulu. You might as well drop her off first, so her folks don't worry. It's a long way up to my house.

Coy said, Is that okay with you, Alice?

Yes, I said, but of course it wasn't. Her alone with him. Nobody spoke again until we were right in front of my house.

Don't stop here, said Annabel.

She made him drive around the block so the neighbors didn't see us. As Coy got out to open the door for me, she squeezed my hand.

Talk to you later, she said, her eyes half closed, a faint smile on her lips.

When the car pulled away from the curb, I noticed that she still sat in the middle of the car seat, next to him, that she hadn't moved closer to the door, as I would have. As I think I would have.

My mother said I was wasted motion. She said it took me so long to do anything because I spent so much time walking back and forth, opening cupboards and drawers, forgetting what I was looking for.

Yoo-hoo, she said, waving her hand in front of my face. Where Alice stay? Anybody home?

We looked for him at dances. When he didn't show up, we left early. Any little thing sent us fleeing to the powder room or out the back door. A hand in the wrong place. A whiskered face trying to nuzzle our cheeks. Too many scuff marks on our shoes. A soldier pulling rank. We stopped using our movie-star names and started calling ourselves Chastity Lee and Prudence Lum, and then watching as the smiles froze on their faces.

Coy didn't join the Navy because of a heart murmur.

Annabel said, A heart murmur is when your heart beats funny. It makes you weak.

But Coy didn't seem weak to me. A little shy and nervous at times, but never while dancing.

Annabel said, I guess you can go for a long time like that and it doesn't show.

But even before he told us about the heart murmur, I knew he was different. Like something inside him was waiting to break.

Break apart or break loose. I wasn't sure which.

We started meeting him in Waikiki, at the Natatorium or Kuhio Beach. We wore kerchiefs and hoped we wouldn't run into anybody we knew. If we did, we would tell them that Coy was a friend of Mr. Lee's. Annabel's father had a lot of servicemen as regular customers now.

One day Annabel finally gave Coy that hula lesson he wanted. He took off his shirt and rolled up his pants. Without his shirt, he looked less boyish. The skin on his chest was smooth and tan, no hair. His muscles bigger than I thought. I tried not to stare, not like Annabel.

She showed him how to bend. Low, with his knees pointed out.

She said, You have to be bold. Stick out your chest. Open your legs more.

Men stopped to watch us. At first I thought they were admiring Annabel, but then I realized it wasn't just her they were looking at.

Coy didn't hold back. He thrust his hips and slapped his chest and shouted, like Annabel showed him. She wasn't shy either, demonstrating how to dance like a man. But as he got better, she started dancing like a woman again, shaking her hips real close to his. When he started to follow her, she shook her head.

No, keep on going, she said. You're the man.

Dora Kaiulani's spirit came to visit me at night. Through the open door of my room. The house dark. Only the sound of my parents snoring. The sheet falling off my bed, the breeze cooling my skin. I heard her whisper, I felt her fingers graze across my face, my chest. The jade bracelet pressed against my belly button. Warm, and getting warmer.

• • •

One afternoon we met Coy at Waikiki. He was sitting on the sand in front of the Royal Hawaiian Hotel, watching the surfers and waiting to take a lesson.

How long have you been here? asked Annabel.

Too long. All morning. They said I should have made an appointment.

Appointment? We turned to look at the surfboard rental stand. The beachboys were talking to two haole women in swimsuits, one blonde and one brunette, Army nurses, we decided. Soon the women were following the beachboys down to the water.

Annabel said, You could be waiting all day.

Shit, said Coy. He stood up and walked over to the Hawaiian guy who was watching the surfboards. He said, What about me? I been waitin' since nine.

The beachboy ran his eyes down Coy's body. He smiled, You like surf, haole boy? Okay. I make one exception for you.

Ho, listen to him, said Annabel. Exception. Not as dumb as he looks.

Quiet, I said. He might hear you.

She laughed. We watched as the beachboy selected a long board and ran into the water as if the board were a wing carrying him, rather than the other way around. Coy threw his shirt on the sand and ran to catch up. The beachboy made Coy lie on the board first, then hopped on behind him, and they paddled out like that.

I wondered out loud, Why didn't they take two boards?

Good question, said Annabel. I was just thinking the same thing myself.

As we watched, I asked how come she didn't go out with Hawaiian boys. Didn't she like them?

She said, You think that guy wants to go out with me? You saw him. He likes haoles.

As if we don't.

Yes, but this guy acts like he owns the beach. I just hope he doesn't take Coy out too far.

The surf was down, so they kept paddling farther and farther out. But the water was too flat. They wouldn't stay out long.

An hour later they were still out there. Waiting. Standing on the board. Taking small waves. Falling, jumping, diving off the board. Swimming around.

When the other beachboys came back, they weren't too happy to find their surfboards unattended. They stood in a circle, grumbling, saying things I didn't want to hear. I was afraid they'd go after Coy, beat him up.

Annabel said, No worry. He has a bodyguard now. Let's go. I'm tired of waiting.

She stood up, brushed the sand off the back of her legs, and walked toward Kalakaua Avenue. I picked up Coy's shirt, shook it out, and draped it over the trunk of a royal palm, where I hoped he would see it.

One dream, two men.

This Hawaiian guy. Tall, full of muscle. Thick, dark skin. Handsome. Asking me to dance, but my legs can't move, so he carries me through the jitterbug and the tango. He wears nothing but a bow tie.

This haole guy. Growing taller the closer he gets, taking off his shirt. Grinding his hips. Wearing nothing but a grass skirt.

I woke up sweating, my legs tangled in the sheet.

Coy didn't show up at the dance studio for two weeks after that. When he finally turned up, he waved at me, but asked one of the other girls to dance. He didn't even look at Annabel. She pretended she didn't see him, as if she didn't care. At the end of the session, he came up to me. We danced for a while, without talking.

Finally I said, Where were you? We missed you.

He said, Oh, I was a little under the weather.

What?

Sick. Not feeling so good, you know?

Oh, sorry. I could have brought you some chicken soup.

He laughed and squeezed my shoulder. We didn't talk, just danced, and that felt good. He left right after that, didn't even stay to dance with Annabel. She came up to me after he walked out the door.

What was that all about? she asked.

He said he had another engagement.

What engagement?

I don't know, he never said. He's been sick.

Sick? Did he apologize about the beach? Sick, my foot.

She was hurt because he talked to me, danced with me. Me but not her.

Annabel looked up every time a man walked into the dance studio. I told myself not to expect anything. Nothing made sense except that he was tired of us.

When he showed up again, he didn't come into the studio but waited outside the door. Annabel saw him when she went out to get some fresh air. They sat in his car and talked. As we walked down the street to the bus stop, she told me about the conversation.

He said he's been working lots of overtime. He has to think things over. Sounded to me like he was confused, but he wouldn't tell me why.

Confused about what?

I don't know. He wants to know if we'll still go out with him.

Oh.

She grabbed my hand. Her eyes were watery. She said, He wants to see both of us. Not just me.

Don't worry, I said, pulling my hand away. I don't have to go. Tell him I don't want to. You can go out with him all by yourself.

No, she said. He wants you to come. He insisted.

You can have him. I'm not that hard up.

She shook her head. Come on, Alice. Don't be like that.

It wasn't like her. Begging.

He wanted to drive over to the windward side, to Kailua Beach. Annabel wouldn't talk, so it was just Coy and me, chatting as if

nothing was wrong. Annabel sat by the window and let the wind blow in her face.

We had to crawl through an opening in the barbed wire to get to the water. Sentries with rifles and bayonets strolled up and down the beach. They didn't smile, just waved us past.

Coy said, Shit, they make me feel like I'm the goddamn enemy.

Annabel was a good swimmer. Her strokes were long and smooth. She hardly splashed any water, even with her feet. Coy and I sat on the beach, watching her.

He said, She's pretty good, ain't she, and I said, She's good at everything, and then he said I shouldn't let her get in my way. Shouldn't act like I was her shadow, because I wasn't. I was my own self.

It felt very strange and wonderful talking like that. For once in my life somebody understood me. But I felt guilty too, talking behind her back.

He said, Don't worry, I like her. I like both of you a whole lot. Y'all don't whine. Not like them Southern belles. Calling a fella sugar and all that.

We laughed. The wind felt good, blowing through my hair. He leaned against my shoulder as we talked. I wanted Annabel to keep on swimming forever.

She stood in front of us, dripping. I held out a towel, but she shook her head. She pulled her long, wet hair to one side and twisted out the water.

Coy smiled as he watched her. He said, You're so goddamn beautiful. I wish I could draw. I'd draw nothing but you all day.

She glared at him. I couldn't understand why she was mad, not after what he just said to her. By the tone of his voice, I knew he wasn't joking.

He said, Too bad you had to quit, 'cause I was just about to ask if you wanted to race. Now that you've blown off some steam.

You, she said. You. She kicked sand at him, then turned around and ran back toward the water.

He got up and ran after her. Both of them splashing water all over each other, then diving in. She swam faster than he did, so she had to slow down to let him catch up. But when he got close, she pulled ahead again. Then he gained on her, and they swam side by side straight out to open sea. Finally he stopped and waited for her to turn around. When they came out of the water, they fell on the sand, both of them gasping for air.

Me by the window on the way home, her next to him. None of us talking, only smoking. Ashes flying in my face and I wanted them to sting, wanted them to hurt.

Barbed wire behind me, above me, all around. Them in the cage, swinging from the treetops, shouting, Aay Alice come here come here. And me treading water, so I couldn't wave back. Could barely keep my head above the surface.

His daddy was a Navy man. Almost an admiral, but not quite.
Coy said, He beat the shit out of me when I told him the Navy didn't want me. I just stood there and let him hit me. I knew if I fought back, one of us was going to die. That's when I knew I had to get the hell out. I was planning on going to New York, but when the Japs hit Pearl, I changed my mind.
He reminded me of my brother Michael shining shoes, sitting in the bomb shelter. Of Sammy carrying slop, watching his cousins practice kung fu.

My mother told me that Annabel's parents had helped pay for my Priory tuition. None of my mother's society friends knew. Even Annabel didn't know.
I carried this secret to work the next day. A dull knife stabbing me in the belly, where my hurt lived.
When Annabel asked me to lie again—one more afternoon with Coy, one more night of dancing—I didn't even call my mother until

after dark. And when she came on the phone yelling, I handed Annabel the phone so she could make up the story.

Annabel told my mother only the true parts. That her father was working late again. That I was going to cook dinner and then help her sew.

She said, I can't sleep with the house so empty. She lit a cigarette and handed it to me. I sucked deep and passed it back over the phone. Red stains on the cigarette paper. My lip marks on top of hers.

Coy liked to watch people. He liked to watch locals better than haoles. People who were old or fat or poor, not tourists, not servicemen, not even good-looking women. People who didn't think they were anything to look at.

Like that lady over there, he said. She's a beaut.

It was a fat Hawaiian woman, but he wasn't making fun of her. He liked watching her hips sway and her stomach jiggle. He said natural was beautiful, and our bodies were the most beautiful things we would ever own.

He liked to feel everything. It was his way of looking. He rubbed his fingers on the backs of chairs, along railings. When we walked on the beach, he was always picking up something, giving us a piece of coral to hold, a rock, a shell. Even sand was worth feeling. Sand between toes, falling on skin. He never wiped himself dry after swimming, not even his face, because he liked to feel the water evaporate.

He stood close when he talked, so near the air still smelled like him after he walked away. Sometimes he touched us, not grabbing or pressing up against us like the sailors on the bus or men at the dances, but blowing in my ear when he walked up from behind because he knew I was ticklish there, or winding Annabel's hair around his finger and then watching it spring back when he let go.

The war still going on. Like a drum that never stopped beating. Always in the back of our minds. And the three of us, sitting on the shore, letting the waves and the sand wash over our legs. Holding hands, so the ocean couldn't suck us in and carry us away.

I hated when they talked about New York. About how they wanted to study modern dancing, not just ballroom, plus take acting and singing classes. When Coy told Annabel she was good enough for Broadway, that's all she could talk about for weeks. How she and I could go to college in New York and rent an apartment next to Coy's, so we wouldn't be alone. It would still be the three of us.

I told her I wasn't going to New York. I said it right in front of him.

Annabel said, But you want to go. You told me you wanted to.

No, I didn't.

Yes, you did.

No.

Okay, I'll go by myself. It'll be just me and Coy. See how you like that.

Coy said, Come on now, don't fight. I don't want to hear. I'm leaving, see? I'm getting the hell outta here.

The private rooms in the dance studio. Like closets. The hands on me. Like handcuffs. The music slow, my body sluggish. The men handed over their coupons and the meter started ticking, but never fast enough. Taxi dancers, that what we were. Giving rides to nowhere, that's all.

My mother wanted to know where I was going all the time. She stuck her nose in everything. My purse, the underarms of my dresses, my shoes.

She said, You just like your father. So many secret. You watch out. Bum-bye get baby. No come crying.

Baby, my God.

I shouted back: You the one drove him away. All your talk talk talk.

Baby. Had to laugh.

•   •   •

Coy and Annabel began dancing together. Not ballroom dancing, but the other kind of dancing that Annabel was doing at home. Not ballet but modern. It wasn't easy finding places where we could be alone but with a lot of space. Sometimes at the YWCA, on the basketball court, or in an empty room. Or at the dance studio, when Coy managed to get the key from Roy Ladare. Coy wanted me to come too, even if I didn't dance.

You can be our audience, he said. We'll dance better if somebody's watching.

He always brought a little something for me. An orange, a pen, a magazine — most of it stolen from the crates he hauled. He danced in his undershirt, let me hold his whistle, so it wouldn't bang into Annabel's face.

I felt funny at first. Clumsy, awkward, just sitting there while they danced. No music, just grunts and thumps, heavy breathing. But after a while I forgot myself and became a part of the music in their heads. A palm tree swaying, a wave crashing on the rocks, a tomcat on the prowl.

Coy came over to talk to me, saying, What do you think, how do we look? Did you like that last part? Am I lifting her high enough?

They didn't talk about New York or Broadway, at least not in front of me.

Afterward, they gave each other lomi-lomis. His shoulders and back. Her legs. Massaging each other as if it was nothing.

My body, not hers. My hands, not his. The only music the scratching of my nails on the pillow I clutched at night.

He showed up at the studio one afternoon. Annabel was dancing in the back, so she didn't see him. He pulled me out onto the sidewalk. His eyes were shining and he slurred when he talked.

He said, Listen, Alice. I been thinking. We should go out on a real date. I mean a double date, none of this trio shit. You and me, and I'll find somebody for Annabel. We can go out to dinner, to a picture show.

I didn't know what to say.

He said, I know you think I'm drunk, but I'm not. Come on, say yes. Don't you want to, don't you like me?

No, I should have said, but I nodded yes. Glad we weren't dancing when he asked me, because my legs felt weak.

What about Annabel? I asked.

I told you. I got somebody for her. This guy I work with. Wren. He's smart, gonna be rich and famous someday. Smooth talker and not bad-looking either, nice body 'cause he works out. She'll like him, I know she will.

But why me? Why don't you go with her? She's cuter.

That's why I love you, he said. You don't know the meaning of cute.

He laughed and kissed me on the forehead, right there on the street.

Don't worry, he said. I love her too.

He put his finger to my lips. But don't tell, or we'll both catch hell.

HIGH TIDE, LOW TIDE

Annabel Lee is coming. Tonight, nine o'clock, United Airlines Flight 37, Gate 11. Just in time for the anniversary of my flash flood, which is today. Just in time for my birthday, but not my thirtieth. I can't get used to the number. Fifty-too-much. As old as the nuns, and sometimes I feel like one too.

I wonder how she looks. Still good, I bet, if she's going out with a plastic surgeon. I changed clothes four times, until Sammy said he wasn't going to wait, so Beatrice told me what to wear. This long red calico muumuu with a white lace yoke and cap sleeves. The neckline is high, like a dog collar.

My eyebrows, my eyelashes stiff from hair spray. Trying not to rub my itchy eyes, so my eyeliner doesn't smear. Took two pills before we left the house. Hope they don't wear off too fast.

Her plane is already one hour late. Sammy stands over by the escalator, smoking a cigarette and checking his watch. He was hoping to take her to the Red Carpet Room after her plane arrived, but it's getting to be too late. Now he's thinking he could have been sucking them up for one more hour, if he knew he was going to have to wait.

But here's the plane, pulling up to the gate. Beatrice covers her baby's ears, to protect Emily from the noise. Wick hugs both of them from behind. They fit so snug, right under his chin. Lurline clings to

Wick's arm, making him sag a little bit to one side. She waves at the plane like I taught her a long time ago.

Beatrice scolds, Let go his arm, don't hang on to him like that.

But Lurline won't stop unless I go over and pull her hand down, and I'm not going to. Don't want her to start screaming. Hope Beatrice won't slap her. Wick hugs Beatrice closer and kisses her head. He whispers something in her ear. Never mind, I hope he's saying. Never mind because of love. Beatrice lifts Emily up in the air. Emily's fist goes open shut open shut.

I hope Annabel can see them. Our babies, all of them, alive and well and happy, waving at her through the glass.

This morning Wick and I drove up to Tantalus to pick white ginger for Annabel's lei. My head was so sore I didn't want to go, but he said fresh air would do the trick, besides he didn't know the way for sure. Beatrice took him up there once, but it was dark.

He liked the winding road, wanted to take it all the way up and then back down Round Top Drive, but when he saw my face, he said, We can turn around after we get the flowers. He couldn't believe how beautiful it was up there. Like what he expected Hawaii to be. Lush and tropical. Not so many houses and cars and hotels. Exotic. Exotic. He said it twice.

I prayed for his Volkswagen not to overheat. Beet Two's engine made a squealing sound when he shifted to low gear. My bucket seat slid back and forth every time we went around one of the hairpin turns, and there were so many. I put my hand on the dashboard so it would stop rattling and hoped I wouldn't throw up.

He said, I guess this buggy still needs work, but doesn't her paint job look good?

He got a special deal from one of the moonlighting bartenders who works in a body shop. Now Beet Two is blue with white waves on the doors and yellow and orange fish on the trunk. A real surf-mobile.

Wick pointed out the window at the red torch ginger growing in the ditch.

He said, What about that pretty red flower? I bet Mom would like some of that.

No good for lei, I told him. Graveyard flower.

Oh. I guess not, then.

You can take some to your popo's grave, though. Dora Kaiulani loved torch ginger.

That's a good idea. I'll do that.

You can go with us to the graveyard. I'm sure your mom wants to go.

He said, You're the best, Aunty Alice. I don't think I ever told you how grateful I am. The way you and Uncle Sammy took me in and all. You know, in spite of everything.

No trouble. I'm glad you came.

You see what I mean? Anybody else would have kicked me out. I wasn't really thinking when I got on that plane. It was like something was pulling me over here, and I'm only finding out now that it wasn't just Beet. It was something I've been feeling all my life, you know? Oh, don't worry. I love her. I really do. And I can't wait till I can call you Mom. You going to let me call you Mom?

You and Beatrice getting married?

If I can talk her into it. She wants us to live together for a while.

Good idea. No rush. You know what happens when rush.

I guess. Maybe I'm being selfish. I don't want to start a family when I'm too old.

You want babies?

Sure, why not.

Does Beatrice know?

Well, I'm working on it.

Is that why you fight?

That's part of it. But we're getting along better now that we're in our own place. No offense. Nothing personal.

I know. Lurline doesn't understand. You have to pull her hand away. Not too hard.

I don't mean that. I've figured her out. Lurline is like a puppy dog. She doesn't hide what she's feeling, not like the rest of us.

Lurline's a good girl. Both my girls are good.

I love Beet so much. I really do. I just wish it was enough. I don't know what she wants.

Me too. You have to give her time.

We picked enough ginger for two leis. I sewed one. He sewed one.

He said, This is my first lei! My very first! Wait till Beet sees this. Do you think she'll like it?

His lei was very sad, the flowers all brown where he squeezed too hard. His father, Coy, would be so proud.

So many people coming off the plane. Honeymooning couples holding hands, fathers carrying babies and diaper bags, women my age wearing scoop-neck T-shirts and wraparound skirts. Signs waving in the air. All About Paradise. Waikiki Escapes. Every now and then, when somebody local walks through the door, their friends and relatives push their way around me. Excuse, excuse, sorry, yeah? Leis. Kissing. Hugging. So many people, so much noise. My head throbbing. Scared of what will happen, who will walk off the plane, thinking about Beatrice coming home with Wick. Have enough surprises to last me for a while.

Wick, he says, Mom likes to sit in back, near the bar, where she can talk to the stewards. She's always the last one off. She likes to make a grand entrance.

I shouldn't be nodding. He doesn't have to tell me.

There she is, he says. Behind that guy in the leisure suit. Wearing the straw hat. Mom! Mom!

Mom, Aunty, Mrs. Coy Whitlow, Sissy Miss Prissy, Vivien, Veronica, Chastity, Annabelle with the curlicue *e* under her name. Annabel Lee. My very best friend. She's here. At last.

Her hair is so red, more red than I remember, and it's short. It sticks out from under her hat, not like an Afro, but wavy and scary in a beautiful way. Her suit is wool. Cream-colored wool, not white. The jacket is three-quarter length, the skirt stops way above her knees. Her legs are still long. Perfect. She's wearing a turquoise blouse that clashes with the pink carnation lei that Beatrice bought for her. I told Beatrice not pink, make sure not pink, but she wouldn't listen to me. The carnation lei squashes Wick's ginger, but maybe it's just as well.

Annabel says, Oh, Alice, it's so good to see you. You haven't changed one bit.

But she looks surprised. Her eyes wide open as if she's just heard something she can't believe. Not a single wrinkle on her face. Her skin so smooth, the color of coffee with milk. And when she talks, it's like when I open up my jewelry box. Open the lid and the song comes out. Every word a bell. Every sentence a chime.

She says, Ginger, my favorite! You're so sweet. You didn't forget. I can't get over how grown-up the girls are. I hardly recognize them. Your hair looks good. You must have just had a perm. But you shouldn't let them tease your hair or put so much spray.

You look so young, I tell her. Even younger than before.

She laughs and says, All you need is a face-lift. Can't you tell? It's my fiftieth birthday gift to myself. That's how I met Judd. Not before the operation but after. He's my doctor's best friend. Used to be anyway. I'll tell you about him later. Oh, we have so much to catch up on.

Her red lips sear my cheek.

Look what I did.

She rubs my face. Her fingernails are long and tickle my skin. Her perfume is the same as mine. White Shoulders. Wick gave me some for Mother's Day.

She looks at Wick and Beatrice and Emily. She says, You, look at you. Oh my. Then she's hugging them all and saying, I'm almost a grandmother now, don't make me cry. I give her my handkerchief so she can blow her nose.

Lurline, she says, come here and let Aunty look at you. Oh, how pretty you are. How did you get so tall? Speaking of tall, where's Sammy? Oh, I see him. Sammy! Hi, Sammy! What's he doing way over there?

She walks so fast, even with high heels on and in that skirt. I have to hurry to keep up with her. Sammy just stands there when she kisses him, doesn't even kiss her back. She grabs him by the arm and pulls me with her other hand.

Come, walk with me, both of you. Tell me about your new house, Sammy. Well, okay, your new apartment. I hear it looks real nice. Wick says you've been working so hard.

Sammy doesn't answer, but I can tell he's pleased. He offers her a cigarette.

She says, No, thanks, I'm trying to cut back.

We go over to the baggage pickup like this, Sammy and me with Annabel in the middle, everybody else spread out beside us, taking up the whole walk, like the wings of a giant bird.

Annabel says to me, I have to wear high heels because of my clients. You can't sell a house wearing flats, or nobody will buy from you. I always wear a suit and heels and nylons. I never wear polyester, even if it doesn't wrinkle. Polyester looks cheap, and it gets too hot. Plus, you know me, I always go for color. Ivory is my newest color. Not white. White shows dirt too fast. Even this Panama hat is ivory, not white. I better take it off. Squashes my hair. The trick is to accentuate, so you don't look faded. I think I own a million scarves. But I don't need a scarf today. These leis are better than scarves. I bet you made this ginger lei. You didn't buy it. I can tell.

This is our house. This is the kitchen. This is the living room, Lurline's room, Beatrice's room, where you can sleep. Nothing fancy. Beatrice left you the bed. You have to keep the blinds closed or the sun comes in, but you can turn on this fan if you get too hot. Are you hungry? What did you eat on the plane? We have chicken left over, or I can heat up some jook in the microwave. Sorry, I forgot you hate jook. Salad, you want salad? Wick says you like vegetables.

Talking too much. Need another pill.

She walks through the house, checking everything out. Hope her nylons don't pick up too much dust. Vacuumed twice, but I can still feel crumbs. She's not as tall as I remember, not in her stocking feet. She looks at everything two times. She pats the couch cushion. Bounces on it. Fingers the drapes. Peeks behind them, through the picture window I forgot to clean. She says, Not much view, too bad you can't see Diamond Head from here. She flips the switches, one by one, and watches the lights go off and on.

Wick says, Mom, this house is not for sale.

Annabel laughs. She says, Sorry, I can't stop working. How much does a house like this cost anyway? I don't mean this one in particular. But in this neighborhood. I'm not trying to be rude. It's my job to know. Just a ballpark figure.

Mom!

Never mind. I bet I can guess. But I better look at the apartment first. I have to see what it looks like inside.

She rattles the birdcage. Well, look at you two. Polly want a cracker?

They're parakeets.

I know that. What do you call them? Do they talk?

When I tell her I don't know their names and they don't talk yet, she says, Well, we'll have to do something about that.

Later on they stay up drinking. My husband, Sammy; my best friend, Annabel Lee. They drink Jack Daniel's straight, not the Southern Comfort or the sloe gin that Sammy bought in case Annabel wanted something sweet. Sammy likes a woman who can drink like a man. She bums cigarettes off him, saying, God, I needed this, I just can't quit.

It's okay, I tell myself. She has jet lag, she won't last long.

Her voice like a bell, ringing again after so many years. A flood in my head, but this time it's real. Even when I put my pillow over my head, the ringing doesn't stop. The waves are coming at me from both directions and dragging me down, down, down.

The next morning she is slow. I am slow. I make coffee and toast, but she doesn't want butter, so I have to start all over. She needs more hangers, where is the ironing board, the iron, her clothes are all wrinkled, she has to press what she's going to wear. Where is her eyeliner, where is her bra, she can't remember where she packed anything.

By the time we leave the house, it's already hot, almost lunchtime. Lurline goes next door to watch TV with Gracie Todama. We'll have to sneak out the back so Lurline doesn't see us, but once we're gone, she'll forget.

Dear Gracie, she is so shy. She doesn't even talk when I introduce her to Annabel, just nods and smiles. Annabel raises her eyebrows at me. She's thinking which one of us does the talking when we're together, but I just ignore her and hand Gracie the plate of sushi that I made. There's only one Japanese woman I could make sushi for, and Gracie is that one.

Annabel can't believe when I get in the driver's side of the Ford.

She says, I thought you were too scared to drive.

I tell her I go all over the island with her son. Even now he still takes me to the beach with him, except when he's going someplace too windy. That shuts her up, the fact that me and Wick are friends. Last night she invited him to come shopping with us and then go swimming, but he said no, he already had plans to go surfing with some of his friends from work. That made her mad, that he made plans when he knew she was coming.

I take her to Ala Moana Shopping Center, where she buys three bathing suits at Liberty House. One bright yellow with criss-cross straps, a turquoise bikini that she holds by the natural light in the window so she can make sure it's really turquoise and not plain blue or green, plus a white strapless one-piece for when she gets more tan. White not ivory. For bathing suits white is better, because ivory looks too much like sand.

She says, The older I get, the less I go for understatement. When my hair is all white, I'll buy a purple swimsuit. You'd be surprised how good purple looks on mature women. But now I still have enough color of my own to show off.

She wants me to come into the dressing room with her, so I can help her decide what to buy, but I won't go in.

I'll stand outside the door, I tell her. Not enough room in there.

She says, Pick out something for you too. Just try it on, you don't have to buy.

She wants us to wear our swimsuits under our clothes and then go right across the street to swim after we're through shopping. But I refuse to try anything, not while she's looking, so she goes to get the clerk.

Put it on my card, she tells the clerk. Whatever she wants. I'll be right back. I'm going to take a peek at the dresses.

I hate to look in the mirror, hate to take off my clothes to try on swimsuits that won't fit anyway. If I had known Beatrice was going to fall in love with Wick, if I had known Annabel was going to come home so soon, I would have lost weight, I would have gone dancing, done my stomach and leg exercises. But Sammy likes me this way, with something to squeeze, not skinny like her. Besides, I'm not even going in the water.

I suck in my stomach and tell the clerk, Blue, one piece, size ten if the top has plenty room. Otherwise twelve. Plus could you please bring me a T-shirt? A man's one is good. Plain white. And make sure it's big enough.

She nods, but she's only nineteen or twenty, probably a size three. She has no idea how big is big.

When Annabel comes back, I'm at the cash register and the clerk is trying to figure out how Annabel can sign the charge slip when she's not there.

Here I am, says Annabel. Oh, you bought something. Good. Where is it? Show me.

I have it on, underneath. You said.

Oh, that's right. I better go put mine back on. Come and look at this dress I'm thinking about buying.

It's a jungle print and it's strapless, a tight fit. The print isn't too Hawaiian, could be Caribbean or African, so she can wear it when they go on cruises. Judd likes for her to dress Hawaiian, but she hates to, because it makes her feel out of place, so this is a good compromise. She pays for the dress, then we have to find something for Lurline in Lingerie. By the time we're done, it's way past my lunchtime, and I tell her if I don't eat pretty soon, I'm going to fall down.

Yogurt is all she wants. Yogurt and an apple and maybe some carrots. But they don't have that kind of food at Chang's Chinese

Kitchen, so she goes over to Foodland while I sit on the bench and eat my plate of crispy gau gee mein. I'm so hungry I don't care if she eats rabbit food. The gau gee is crunchy and ono, and the noodles don't fight me going down.

She asks about everything and everybody. She remembers everything I tell her, everything I have ever told her. As we walk back to the car, she says, Doesn't Beatrice's ex work here? What's his name? Franklin? Didn't you say he works at Reyn's? I need to buy some shirts for Wick. Maybe we can go there and see if they have something good on sale. Maybe he can give me a discount.

We shouldn't bother Frankie.

We won't bother. Come on. I think I remember where the store is.

Frankie's busy with a customer when we walk into Reyn's. Annabel walks straight to the sales rack in the back of the store. I peek through the shirts. Frankie's customer is wearing a business suit. A Chinese guy, good-looking, Frankie's age, flashy dresser. His old shoes still look new. There must be two dozen shoe boxes on the floor around him. Loafers, dress shoes, black ones, brown ones, conservative shoes, not the kind that goes out of style. Frankie kneels and ties the man's shoes on. He presses the toe and says, How does that feel?

The man stands up and walks around the rug.

Frankie kneels on one knee, pencil behind his ear. He says, That looks good. That one and this one.

He lifts a pair of black dress shoes. He says, This is what I would buy if I were you, Quent.

Okay. Say no more. I'm sold.

Whispers. I can hear them laughing.

The man follows Frankie over to the cash register. He says, How's about a drink later on, Frank? What time you pau work?

Annabel pokes me with her elbow. She says, How come you didn't tell me?

She's standing behind me. She's been listening and watching the whole time.

Tell you what?

Frankie looks up. He says, Alice Mom. What are you doing here? Oh, this must be Aunty Annabel. When did you get in?

Annabel says, Franklin! So good to meet you. Alice didn't tell me you worked here. I've heard so much about you. I guess you've heard about me too.

He looks at me.

A little, he says. Not much.

His left eye is twitching. Just a small tick. Annabel offers her hand to him, and when he shakes it, she pulls him toward her so she can give him a hug and a kiss.

She says, I'm so sorry you had to get hurt. I'm sorry if my boy hurt you. That's what he is sometimes, just a big boy.

Frankie pulls away. He says, Well, I guess it's just one of those things. He looks at me. Arms crossed now.

Annabel says, I'm glad you feel that way. I hear you've been taking it real well.

You have? He looks at me again.

The man buying the shoes says, Well, Frank, catch you later. Call me, yeah? Later. He nods at Annabel and me.

Frankie waves. Sure, Quentin, thanks. Hope those work out for you.

Frankie turns back to us. Smiling, but not so much.

I look at Annabel and say, We better go. Before there's too much traffic.

Wait, she says. I saw a shirt I might want to buy. Frankie, come tell me what you think.

She grabs him by the arm and drags him to the back of the store.

It's too late to go swimming. We'll catch the traffic, and I don't want to leave the packages in the car. Plus Sammy is fixing teriyaki tonight. He won't like it if we come home late.

Annabel says, Okay. I give up. We can go swimming tomorrow.

Cannot. Tomorrow's my birthday party. At my parents' house.

Well, we can go swimming before! You people. All you can think about is food! I didn't come here to eat. You know, Alice, you should go away sometime. For a long time. Then when you come back, you'll know what I mean.

Before we go to the car, we stop at Sears, Roebuck, where we pretend to be shopping for dresses so we can take off our bathing suits. I feel like a shoplifter turning myself in, but at least I can breathe again.

My head is sore, so she has to drive. As she pulls out onto Ala Moana Boulevard, she says, So how come you didn't tell me Frankie was gay?

What?

Gay. Mahu.

I know what gay is. Frankie's not gay. He's not mahu.

How much you want to bet?

But he was married. To my daughter. They have Emily.

So? I was married to Coy, don't forget. And I have Wick.

That's not the same. I wish you wouldn't talk like this. You shouldn't make things up.

I'm not making things up. Believe me, I know how shocked you are. Now you know how I feel.

Frankie's a good boy. He's just nice, that's all. He doesn't like to fight.

Oh, so that's why he doesn't care about his wife dumping him. I'm telling you, Alice, it's not normal.

She swerves the car into the right lane. She says, What's wrong with these people? Why do they hog the left lane?

She guns the engine and passes the car that cut in front of her.

I say, You don't know Frankie. He's sensitive. He's a writer.

I know what I can see with my own two eyes. Frankie likes men.

If you're so smart, then how come you were so blind before?

What do you mean?

How come you didn't know about Coy?

Oh, Alice. I *did* know.

But I thought—

What did you think?

When you came to Maui that time, I thought you just found out.

She says, I can't talk like this while I'm driving. Let's find a place where we can get a drink.

But Sammy's waiting for us.

Forget about Sammy. Let him wait.

She turns off Nimitz and heads back into town. She wants to go someplace where we can have cocktails and talk about all this once and for all. At least she hasn't mentioned Waikiki or going to see Wick at the Moana Hotel bar. I look at my watch. Four o'clock already. Wick doesn't start work until five o'clock, so he's safe.

Not Chinatown, I tell her. I won't go Chinatown.

Okay, okay.

We park the car downtown on Fort Street and walk to the bar of the Alexander Young Hotel. It's cool and dark in there, and the air conditioning goes right up my nose. When the bartender comes, I let Annabel order for me.

Margarita for my good friend, she says. And a double vodka martini for me. You got the real Russian vodka? No olive.

The salt on the margarita glass makes my lips sore, but it tastes good, so I lick off the rim before I drink.

Annabel says, I was young, I didn't think it would matter—the way he was.

It takes a while before I figure out she's talking about Coy. I'm afraid to say anything. Afraid she might stop.

She says, All I thought about was New York, New York. I hated staying with Emma in Florida. She was too domestic for me. She wouldn't go anywhere or do anything. That scared me like hell. Being a housewife. Coy was so good, coming to visit me, even though he had to drive so far. He didn't care that I was pregnant by Wren. He treated me like the baby was his. And then when I lost her, he helped me get back my strength. You know what a good dancer he was. I still haven't met anybody who can dance like him.

You were both good, I tell her. I could have watched you two all night.

The margarita is getting to me and I'm only halfway through.

I guess that's why we lasted so long. Maybe things would have been different if we didn't have Wick.

I want to know how they did it, how she got pregnant, but the words are stuck inside. Maybe it was different with her. When the words finally come out, they hang in the air, like feathers falling. It must have been so hard. Stuttering now. Telling Wick and all.

She says, I need another drink. You too. Waiter, one more round.

After the drinks come, she says, Coy showed up one night, drunk, and he wanted Wick to go out with him. Wick was only twelve. I said, No, he can't go with you, and Wick started crying, and Coy called him a sissy, a mama's boy. I couldn't believe it. I was so mad, I said, Look who's talking. I didn't want to tell Wick about Coy, but I had to after that.

Oh no.

Oh yes. And he was still wetting the bed. I should have waited.

Terrible. Shaking my head.

No, just as well, because I stopped feeling sorry for myself then. And it was out in the open, so I didn't have to lie anymore. I told myself I wasn't going to let him make us suffer. Hurting me was one thing, but not my boy.

She tells me she went out with plenty of men after she and Coy split up. Promiscuous—that's her word, not mine. They were all pretty good in the sex department, but none of them as talented as Coy. Some of them stopped asking her out when they found out what a good dancer she was. Like she intimidated them. Coy never made her feel like that. Not about dancing anyway. Her eyes get wet when she talks about the dancing.

She says, Don't look at me like that. I'm over him. I made a mistake, okay? I thought I could live without sex, but I couldn't. So what of it?

Everybody looks when she raises her voice, but I lift my glass in the air. So what of it? I repeat.

She laughs. You drunk already? You never could hold your liquor. We better go. I haven't told you everything yet, but we have two more weeks to talk. We can go out tonight after supper if you want. Just you and me.

•   •   •

Go out, go out, that's all she can think of. I haven't told her everything either. What happened with Coy in her parents' garage. What I
know about her and Sammy, what they did on Maui while I was laid
up in bed, after the flash flood. And I haven't told her the real truth
about Sammy, the truth of his birth, the truth of his race. I'm afraid
she'll say I can't keep this a secret. She might even tell him herself,
and when she goes back to the mainland, I'll be stuck picking up the
pieces.

If Wick knows about his father, then Beatrice must know too. I
wonder if it's true about Frankie, or is Annabel just trying to get back
at me because she was wrong about Coy? If Frankie's gay, does Beatrice know? If so, she must have told Wick and even Amy Toad
by now.

So many secrets, and yet, to my mind, not enough.

What is the good? Most things, if you wait long enough, they take
care of themselves. The tide goes in, the tide goes out. If I could
write everything I worry about on sand, if there was room enough on
the beach, then maybe the waves could erase everything. The
heartache, the secrets, the lies.

I'm sick after dinner. The lime from the margarita was too sour for
my stomach. So Annabel goes with Sammy and Beatrice and Amy
Toad to visit Wick at the Moana Hotel bar, and Lurline stays home
with me. When Annabel walks out onto the lanai wearing her new
sundress with the strapless bodice and the tight-fitting skirt, Sammy's
whistle is so loud, I can tell I'm in for another long night. At least Beatrice and Amy Toad will be there to chaperone. I can see them now,
my husband and my former best friend. Her still after him and him
acting like nothing is happening. I wonder if she'll make him dance.

Former best friend. Am I really thinking that? Now, when we have
a chance to be close again? Why can't I say what I want to say? I've
shut myself up for too long.

I'm the parakeet who doesn't talk.

Annabel left for the States on a Pan American DC-4. Her father bought her a one-way ticket to San Francisco for $195. The flight was twelve and a half hours long, and after that she was going to take the train to Florida, to her sister Emma's house. She took only what she could carry, one suitcase and a cosmetic bag. Four trunks followed by boat. Lucky for her the war was over. We toasted the victory with tea instead of champagne, since Annabel was already feeling nauseated. People shouting on the streets and buses, laughing and crying for happiness, and the two of us relieved because now Annabel could leave the islands before her baby was born.

I helped her pack. All the outfits she had made over the years for this long-awaited trip, plus three of my dresses for when she started showing. After she got to Florida, she could borrow Emma's maternity clothes, and there would be plenty of time to sew for the baby. Mr. Lee had the car packed and ready to go to the airport, but Annabel was still in the bathroom throwing up. I worried about her, how she was going to fly in her condition. I gave her a salty li hing mui to stick in her mouth.

Suck on this, I said. The salt will settle your stomach.

I gave her a whole bag of dry, salty plums to suck, plus some herbs to brew for tea.

She said, I'm going to call my baby Maile. What do you think of that?

I thought you were going to give her a movie-star name.

We had gone through them all the night before. Bette, Ginger, Irene, Veronica, Olivia, all of our favorites.

But Annabel said, She'll be happier with her own name, don't you think?

But what if it's a boy?

I know it's a girl. She already answers when I call her Maile. I can feel her moving inside me even when I just think her name. Like she's already reading my mind.

Maile Lee. That sounds funny.

No. Not Lee. Maile Stevenson.

Stevenson?

This is a hapa-haole baby, remember? I'll tell people her father was an admiral and he died at Pearl Harbor.

No.

You're so honest. Gullible too. That's why I love you. Too bad I made all my dresses so tight. Thanks for lending me yours. Emma can help me put the hems down. Good thing I like things short. I'll send them back to you as soon as I can fit my own.

No worry. Take your time.

What if I save them for when you come to visit? Come after Maile is born, so you can see her.

We'll see. We better go now. Your father is honking and honking.

Maybe I should name her after you.

Don't you dare. Maile is better.

Maile Alice Stevenson. That way I can remember you.

I hugged her.

Don't. I might start throwing up again.

Her face was pale, and her hands shook as she handed me the tube of lipstick. Put this on for me, okay? I don't want to get it all over my teeth.

Louis was what Annabel called Coy Whitlow after he went back to Georgia. Louis or RLS. She wrote his name everywhere. On her notebook, on her leather purse, on the tables in restaurants. Louis, for her grandfather who didn't come back from California. RLS, because he left without telling her he was going. Because he was her dream, her big adventure.

She would never forgive me for knowing first.

It was on another Sunday morning that Coy came to tell me good-bye. It was seven o'clock. Half an hour later and I would have been on my way to church. My mother walked into my room looking worried. My first thought was my brothers, but she said, Your boss sent one driver. His name Clark Gable, just like the actor. Funny, yeah? He say you have to go work. Must be emergency.

I was confused. I ran out to the living room. When I saw Coy, my heart skipped a beat.

Don't worry, Ma, I said. There's nothing wrong. We just have a big job to finish up from Friday. I forgot to tell you.

My calm voice surprised me. Trying not to look at him, wishing he wouldn't stare. I grabbed my shoes and purse and followed him out the front door. We didn't speak until we were inside his car. As soon as we turned the corner, he pulled me closer to him.

Hey you, he said. Don't be mad.

Clark Gable?

Sorry, he was the only one I could think of. Right accent, you know.

When he turned up toward Kaimuki, I thought we were going to Annabel's house, but he headed for the university instead and then up into Manoa Valley. The air grew cooler and light rain began to hit the windshield. Neither one of us said a word until he finally pulled over to the side of the road and parked.

My father had a heart attack, he said. He's dead. I got a telegram last night.

I started to speak sorry words, but he said, No, don't say it, I didn't come to hear you tell me that. I'm glad the bastard is gone.

Bastard, he said. I didn't like hearing him talk like that.

He said, Listen, I don't have a whole lot of time. I'm flying out at 1100. Today. I just found out about the flight. Wasn't easy getting on it. I'll have to find my way from Frisco. I'll miss the funeral, but I don't care. I'm not going back for that asshole anyway. If it wasn't for my ma, I wouldn't be going back at all.

His eyes looked tired. I put my hand on his arm. Pushed my fingers up his sleeve. He pulled away.

He said, Where you been anyway? I ain't seen you in weeks. You got me worried when you didn't show up at the studio. Annabel said you weren't feeling good. She didn't look so great herself. Kept disappearing on me.

I didn't tell her about us.

I know. I'm not saying you did. I wouldn't care if you did.

I started to cry.

What's the matter? What did I say? Christ, the way you just sit there. Did I hurt you the other night? I was only trying to make you feel good.

I moved away, put my hand on the door handle. His voice got soft.

Shit. You're scared, ain't you? You think I don't care. And now you think I'm taking off. Shit.

He patted the seat next to him. Come here. He grabbed my hand and pulled me over. Put his arm around me.

Listen, he said. I'll always be your friend. You're beautiful, you know? Don't shake your head, it's true. Your kind of beauty don't fade. No matter what happens, remember that, okay? I have to go home. Been away too long, but I'll be back. I promise.

He kissed my forehead, my cheek.

Do me a favor, he said. His voice hoarse now. You got to tell Annabel for me. I don't have time or I'd tell her myself, but I had to come see you first. Tell her I really wanted to see her, okay? At least we got to dance together night before last. Tell her I want to remember her that way. Look, here's my address. Put it someplace safe. I want you to write to me, okay? Annabel too. Both of you. And if you go to Florida before I come back, I want you to look me up, Georgia ain't that far. Don't cry, come on now, smile like I like you to. We should be happy, the war is over, damnit.

Coy dropped me off at the cathedral. He parked right in front, but I didn't care. He said, Pray for me, Alice. I need all the help I can get. I love you. Tell Annabel I love her too. And y'all be good to one another.

He took off the chain he was wearing around his neck, removed his whistle, and pressed it into my palm. Here, he said. You're too damn quiet.

The services had already begun. I sat in the back instead of walking up the aisle to join Annabel. Didn't want to take Holy Communion, but I had to or she would be suspicious. The wine tasted bittersweet in a way that reminded me of blood. Coy didn't know about Annabel, that her menses hadn't come. Dear Lord, forgive me. I forced myself to swallow the wine.

I told her in the courtyard. She looked so beautiful, even as nauseated as she was. I kept the story short, told her I ran into him at the bus stop and left out the part about the drive up to Manoa.

She said, How could you let him go without my saying goodbye? I thought you were my friend.

Her words slapped hard. I am telling you, I said. I couldn't do it in church.

Yes, you could have.

She ran inside to use the church phone. There was no phone in Coy's dormitory, so she called the motor pool, where Wren worked.

She said, Tell Coy I need to see him before he goes. Ask him to come down to the school. He knows which one. No, I can't go out with you. Just tell him.

She didn't care that the church secretary was listening. She said to me, I told myself I was never going to call. Look what you made me do.

I pulled her outside. I said, Coy wants you to write. He wants you to look him up when you go to visit Emma.

No more lies. Tell me the truth. Is that really what he said? He wants me to write? He wants to see me? What about you?

He said both. You and me.

How come he told you but not me?

I finally confessed that he'd taken me for a drive, that he said he loved both of us as friends. But I didn't tell her what had happened that last night we went out together—her and Wren, me and Coy. I didn't show her the whistle. I couldn't, not with her like that.

Bleeding and bleeding. My monthly bleeding wouldn't stop. Stained my panties, my nightgown. Stained right through the sheets to the mattress pad and the mattress underneath. I slept with my knees up to my chest. My mother made pig's-feet soup and brought me a hot-water bottle. She was especially good to me at that time of the month, because she was so relieved that I wasn't pregnant.

The baby was Wren's. The girl kicking inside Annabel was Maile Wren, not Maile Stevenson. But she didn't want Wren to know. She refused to go out with him again, even after Coy was gone. She made me promise not to tell anyone who the father was, but she said, You could have told Coy, you should have told him.

But you didn't know for sure.

You could have told him anyway. If you had, then he might have stayed.

But he had to go back because of his mother!

Bleeding and bleeding. Why her but not me? Why me but not her?

My brother Russell came home first, on a medical discharge because of his leg. When my father saw Russell sitting in the wheelchair, he went into the back parlor and wouldn't come out.

My mother said, Alice, take him the medal. Make him look at it.

Russell said, Leave him alone. Leave us both alone.

My father mourned Russell's leg for three weeks. He didn't come out of the back parlor until after everyone had gone to sleep. Only then did he sit down to eat the food my mother left for him on the stove. One night Russell went into the kitchen to sit with my father while he ate. I heard Russell thumping along with his crutches, the scrape of my father's spoon in his bowl, but no voices. Another silent night, but not as long.

Annabel's brothers Edward and Gordon arrived on the next ship, both with German brides. Mr. Lee wouldn't talk to them for one whole week, but when he finally spoke, he was full of plans for a joint wedding reception at Fat Lee Wo. He liked the way the German wives doted on him, cooked sauerbraten and cleaned house, called him Papa Lee, Papa Lee. He liked their big chests too, liked watching his sons hug their wives. He made a big deal out of going out at night, and hinted that there was more than one lady interested in him. He told the German girls, Call me Sing, I not you Papa. Sing Sing Sing.

Finally, my brothers Michael and Joe-Joe returned. Joe-Joe wore a nifty gold watch and gold chains that he'd acquired on the black market. He'd gained some weight, from muscle not fat. No longer a shrimp, he strutted around the house looking so proud. He gave my father a chess set, my mother a set of teacups that he'd bought in England. For me, what I'd always wanted, a necklace with a locket that opened up.

You can put your boyfriend's picture inside, he said. If you can decide which one.

I wondered if he knew something, but when I looked up at him, he was grinning. I punched his arm.

You terrible, I said. He picked me up and spun me around before he put me back down.

I hugged Michael the longest. We went outside to pick mangoes while Joe-Joe taught our father how to play chess. We picked mangoes that were still green for us, red and yellow ones for everybody else.

Michael said, I don't have anything for you. Only this. He handed me a notebook full of drawings. He said, I tried to write you, but I couldn't, not after your letters came to me all cut up. I couldn't stand the thought of somebody reading over my shoulder.

I stayed up late that night looking at his drawings, again and again. The pictures were small and tidy. He used black ink, not pencil, as if he was sure about what he saw. They were all the places he'd been to. Munich. Heidelberg. London. I could see what people wore. The cars they drove. The churches. The shops. Even the food. Like all that time away from home was one big art excursion.

I said, How come you didn't draw pictures of the war? Where are all the soldiers and the guns?

You don't want to know about that.

Yes, I do.

You just think you do, but you don't.

I tried to read his face. His jaw and cheeks and forehead were all angles and lines, not round like my other brothers'. But his sadness made his edges sag. Like a house that might collapse at any moment and there would be nothing inside. As close as we were, I still didn't know what he was thinking. He had our father's heavy eyelids. Like shields.

He said, You know what I want to do? I want to drive around the island. Just you and me. I want to see everything again. The beaches, the mountains, everything. I used to lie awake in my bunk and try to remember all the little details, but I couldn't. My home, and it was just one big blur.

I got up extra early to pack lunch. Cone sushi, leftover chicken, slices of mango, canned apricot juice. For breakfast, I fried steamed sweet-potato pudding dipped in egg and filled a jar with hot tea. We could eat in the car. I wanted to get away before anybody else decided to come along. I wanted my brother Michael for myself. Sadness and all. Maybe he would talk to me. Really talk.

We stopped at Diamond Head, Hanauma Bay. At Sandy Beach, Makapuu, Waimanalo.

Finally, Michael said, We better not stop for a while or we'll never get all the way around.

When we passed Chinaman's Hat, the tide was out. I could see the rocks, the shallow water all the way out to the island. I turned to look at Michael, to see if he was remembering the day he almost drowned.

I said, You know, all of us could have drowned that day. Not just you.

He said, That's right. How long did it take you to figure that out?

Why does Dad pick on you?

He's not happy.

But why you? Why not Russell or Joe-Joe? Why not me?

I don't know.

The night before, I had heard my father scolding Michael, berating him again. There was Russell, sitting like a vegetable in the back parlor. Joe-Joe, coming and going whenever he felt like it, always with some new deal cooking. Only Michael helping my father sell herbs the day after he got back, and yet my father still had nothing good to say to him.

Michael said, That's okay, I'm going away pretty soon. I'm going to school in Michigan. Uncle Sam is going to pay. Dad can't complain. He always wanted me to become a doctor. Maybe I'll become a psychiatrist. Serves him right. I can take art classes on the side.

That night I dreamed about Chinaman's Hat at high tide. All of them swimming away from me. My brother Michael, Annabel Lee, Coy Whitlow, Sammy Woo, and Annabel's baby, my namesake, Maile Alice, all of them leaving me on the rock. I tried to yell at them, but every time I opened my mouth, it filled up with water.

When I awoke, all perspiring, the house was quiet except for Joe-Joe's loud snoring, which came through the wall. I heard footsteps in the kitchen, not heavy like my mother's or shuffling like my father's, so I got up to see who it was. I found Michael, standing by the stove, waiting for the teakettle to boil. On the kitchen table, I saw his notebook and pen.

Are you drawing?

Drawing and writing.

You write too?

Sometimes, if the picture isn't enough.

Can I see? May I?

He showed me the page. I recognized Chinaman's Hat right away.

I told him about my dream, how everybody left me alone on the island. He leaned back in his chair and listened as I talked.

I said, I'll tell you more—real stuff, not dreams—if you promise not to tell. But you can't write it down. You can't even draw it. Okay?

He smiled. Okay. He tossed his pen over the table, into the garbage can.

I told him about how we went dancing, me and Annabel Lee. How we caught the bus downtown. I told him about Sammy Woo and the jade bracelet I was hiding. About the Arthur Murray Studio. About Coy Whitlow, but not everything. Just what a good dancer he was and how Annabel and I loved to dance with him. I told him about how Annabel wanted me to come visit her in Florida. He

frowned when I told him about her baby. How she wanted to name it Maile Alice Stevenson.

I said, You know, after Robert Louis Stevenson, because he went away.

Michael coughed. What? he said.

I stopped talking then. I felt like a wind-up doll that finally ran out of wind.

Michael grinned. He said, All that happened while I was gone? And you the one who's jealous because you don't have adventures?

You think I should go to Florida?

Do you want to?

Yes and no.

What do you mean yes and no?

I want to, but I can't.

Why not?

I don't know. I have that bracelet. I have to wait for Sammy Woo to come back.

Come and visit me, then. When I go to Michigan.

How can you go there? You don't know anybody in Michigan.

That's why I'm going. Come and visit. We can ride the train all over the country. Just you and me. Explorers.

I received a Western Union telegram.

MARRIED YESTERDAY STOP MOVING TO NYC
AFTER MAILE COMES STOP BE HAPPY STOP VISIT US STOP
LOVE COY & ANNABEL STOP

I sent a telegram back.

CONGRATULATIONS VERY HAPPY STOP
LOVE YALL ALICE STOP

I embroidered towels for a wedding present and crocheted a blanket for the baby and sent them by air mail, not ship.

•   •   •

My brother Joe-Joe ran into Sammy Woo at the PX. Joe-Joe told us at suppertime, while we were eating fish. My father was scolding Michael, telling him not to eat so fast, be careful of the bones, why was Michael always in a rush. The rest of us were quiet, trying to swallow our food.

Finally, Joe-Joe said, Guess who I saw today? Sammy Woo. He was looking pretty snazzy too. He get one watch just like mine.

Joe-Joe snapped his watchband.

What did you tell him? I said.

I told him come by the house. Told him somebody I knew would be happy to see him. I wonder who's that.

Oh, you didn't.

Why not?

Did he ask about Annabel?

He already knows about Annabel.

What? What does he know?

He said he went by the house and Annabel's father told him she went away. Annabel no stay, Annabel no stay. That's all Mr. Lee could say.

Did you tell him the rest?

Joe-Joe squirmed. You never tell me it was secret. Besides, he already knew about the baby. From her brothers.

My mother said, Enough. Eat your food. She didn't like talking about Annabel that way. And not in front of my father.

Joe-Joe said, What's the big deal? The baby's father married her anyway, right? Well, he did, right? It's not my fault the baby died. No look at me like that.

I didn't want to see Sammy, but I had a promise to keep. I wrote a letter explaining to him that I had his jade bracelet, that Annabel had given it to me for safekeeping before she left. I didn't say how long before. Just could he please write back and tell me what to do.

One whole week I waited for an answer. I couldn't eat. I couldn't sleep. My cramps were bad. My bleeding heavy again. I thought of Annabel, how sad her own bleeding must be, now that she'd lost poor Maile. That was the saddest part. The baby really was a girl, just like she'd hoped.

Sammy brought me goldfish. Two of them in a jar. I cried when I saw the fish. He put the jar down on the table.

He said, Sorry, only goldfish. I didn't know what else for bring.

I shook my head, couldn't speak. I handed him the little rice bag with his mother's jade bracelet inside. He looked at me, then took the bag. He pulled out the bracelet, held it up to his cheek, then pressed it between his hands.

Thanks for taking care of it, he said.

My mother came into the kitchen.

She said, Sammy Woo, it's about time! How you?

She saw the bracelet in his hand. She looked at him, at me.

She said, Jade. Goldfish. Aiiyaa. She put her hand over her heart and sat down.

Sammy got a job at Hickam Field, working in the maintenance shop. Joe-Joe told me what Sammy really did was clean the luas and mop. Shit work. But Sammy never talked about Hickam or toilets and floors. He didn't talk about the war either, just about his escapades in Europe, in England, Germany, and Italy. He told me funny stories, about gambling and traveling by train and looking for places to eat rice.

We went out with the gang—his war buddies and their girlfriends. All of them locals. Chinese, Japanese, Filipino, Portuguese, Hawaiian. No haoles. While everyone danced, Sammy and I sat and held hands. He said the war gave him two left feet and I could dance with the other boys if I wanted to because he liked watching me.

No, I said. I'm staying right here by you.

He gave me his Mickey Mouse watch. I knew he'd bought it in San Francisco and that he'd really intended to give it to Annabel Lee, but I thanked him for it anyway. There were a lot of girls he could have given it to, a lot of girls with their eyes on him. He was taller, better looking than ever, and wise in a way that I could never be, because of where he had been and what he had seen and done. Even when he appeared to be lost in his thoughts, his face as dark as my father's, I was glad to be there when he returned and found me. Still waiting.

One day he came by my house after supper. His face was grim, and he shook his head when my mother invited him to eat, so I went outside to see what was wrong. We sat on the wall, and I listened while he talked.

He said, When I came home from work, they were taking pictures. My whole family. Them all dressed up and me so dirty and the photographer getting ready for shoot. He wen look at me like, who this guy? They never even let me take a bath or change my clothes. I had to stand far away so they couldn't smell how stink I was.

He started to choke up. I tried not to cry, but the tears kept coming and coming.

Some people live outside their families. They never belong, no matter how hard they try. They spend their whole life fighting for love, for happiness, for something, but they can never get enough.

One week later we were engaged.

My brother Michael left for Michigan before my wedding. Everybody went to the airport to see him off. They piled leis on Michael, up over his ears. My father was stiff, so Michael didn't touch him. Michael hugged my mother, Russell, Joe-Joe, and then, last of all, me. He yelled so I could hear him over the airplane engines.

Remember, he said, you can come anytime. No need ask.

I yelled back, I wish you could stay for my wedding.

Don't forget, he said. Married or not. Anytime.

Sammy hated church, so I told my mother, No church wedding. She didn't argue. She was so relieved to have a local boy for a son-in-law, a good Chinese boy, a soldier, even though Sammy was only a private first class and a public school graduate. A man who brought his future wife goldfish and showed her his mother's jade was plenty good enough.

Joe-Joe was our best man. I asked Barbara Chew Harimoto to be my matron-of-honor. My mother threw her apron over her head. So many nice girls to choose from, why pick one who had a baby out of wedlock?

But she's married now, I told my mother.

Sure, Howie Harimoto come back war hero. Big shot.

She was jealous because Howie Harimoto came back with arms and legs too, plus a brand-new Chevrolet that he brought over for my brothers to admire. When Howie saw my brother Russell in the wheelchair, he said, Come on, Russ, I give you one ride. He scooped my brother up, leaving the chair behind, and marched out to the Chevy. My mother screamed at them from the kitchen, He might fall down, he might fall down. When they came back from their drive, four hours later, Russell was holding a basketball, dribbling it, as Howie carried him back into the house. After that Russell wouldn't stop talking about Howie and sports and going back to school so he could coach.

My mother didn't like this kind of silly talk. Dream cloud, she called it. Bum-bye you dream cloud bust, she said. Water all come out.

Let him dream, I told her. Why not?

But it scared her, watching Russell do pull-ups and sit-ups, watching the top half of his body grow bigger and tougher. Like he really was going to pop one day, and be horribly disappointed.

I confided my mother's worries to Barbara. That's how Barbara Chew and I became close again, after all those years when I was too busy working and dancing to go and visit her and her baby.

Russell can take care of himself, said Barbara. He's one tough guy. Worry about your own dream cloud.

I knew what she meant. My fears came tumbling out. That Sammy didn't really love me. That he only wanted me now that he couldn't have Annabel Lee.

But Annabel could never love him, said Barbara. Not like you do. And he knows it too.

You think so?

In all those years Howie was away, don't you think I worried that he might never come back? And if he did, that he might choose someone younger and prettier? He could have married me, you know, before he left. We didn't have to listen to my parents. But he didn't push me to go against them, and I didn't want to beg.

Do you worry that he only married you now because of the baby? Because it was a boy?

All the time.

But you still married him.

What else could I do? I had to think of the baby.

But what about love?

I've always loved Howie, but I'm not dumb. I know he will never love me as much as I love him.

Don't say that. It's not true.

It is, but I don't care. I love him anyway. Look at what he's done for Russell. Did I choose wrong? Maybe I was stupid, getting pregnant so fast, but if I had to do it over again, I would.

Talking to Barbara made me more sure than ever. I thought of my brother Michael. How he cut the rope and swam away, even knowing he might drown. Even Russell needed to take the chance.

I threw myself into the wedding, small as it was. Selected a white store-bought suit, practical, so I could wear it again. To work. On a trip. Wherever life took me. My lipstick red. Yours Truly. My corsage, a white cattleya orchid with white net and ribbon. We took plenty of pictures to send to Annabel and Coy.

Sammy bought me a fake diamond ring, because we wanted to save our money for a house. We didn't want to live with my parents forever. But we splurged on the hotel that night, the Royal Hawaiian, where I had always longed to stay. All those days and nights of strolling on the sand, past the pink hotel, envying the honeymooning couples sipping their drinks on the lanai, eavesdropping on the orchestra music, and now I was the one being serenaded and kissed.

As soon as we got to the hotel room, Sammy reached into his duffel bag and pulled out his mother's jade bracelet. I couldn't believe he had brought it to the hotel.

He said, I almost sold this so you could have one real diamond, not fake.

No, I said, you can't sell it. That's all you have.

He pulled me down to the bed and tucked the bracelet into the top of my blouse.

Keep it for our daughter, he said.

The daughter we made that night or the next morning or the next day at home, in my room, our room. Me, Alice, and Sammy, the slop boy. One of those times, but I don't know which.

ALL THE MONKEYS IN THE ZOO

As old as I am, my mother still throws me a birthday party. At first it was because she was glad we moved back from Maui after the flash flood, because my girls and I were still alive, but now it's because she refuses to believe I hate the attention. People looking at me, talking about me, how I look too young to be anybody's popo, all those candles and gifts, the whole production.

Just going to my parents' house is bad enough. We have to take the barbecue grill and extra chairs and whatever else my mother tells us to bring. The phone rings all morning with instructions. Stop by the store. Bring ice. Buy charcoal. And we can't go to the house in Kapahulu without taking Lurline to the zoo, so it's a very long day every time.

Add Annabel Lee on top of all this, and it's no wonder my head won't stop throbbing. When Gracie Todama sees me watering my orchids, she knows I need a rub. She stands on the stone wall and gives me shiatsu on my head. I close my eyes and let her press all my troubles away. Could be my only peace and quiet. All I want is for the day to end.

First thing Annabel says when I walk in the house is, Let's drive by my old house up in Maunalani Heights. Then go swimming at Waikiki.

No time, I tell her. If we go to the beach, we have to take towels and extra clothes. And then we have to take a bath at my parents' house, or we'll be stink for the party. Plus, Sammy reminds me, what about the barbecue meat? How are we going to keep it cold for so long? We can drop it off at my parents' house first, but that makes too many trips. We'll never have time to get out of the car. And one thing for sure, if we don't go to the zoo, Lurline will be cranky all day.

Annabel says, Stop, stop, I don't want to hear any more. Let's just go swimming tomorrow. Tomorrow for sure.

What Lurline loves best are the seals. The rocks they climb, their big swimming pool. She likes the way they slide on the wet concrete and flop on the stones. The way they slip into the pool without splashing, swim underwater, and then leap for fish. She puckers her lips and flaps her arms as if she's trying to swim like them. My daughter, who swallows the world and spits it back out in the only way she knows.

Sammy loves the orangutans. He likes to watch the male orangutan scratch his balls. All he does is scratch and eat, eat and scratch, like some people I know.

The giraffe is Beatrice's favorite. She, who ended up with my short legs, who hates not being able to see over people's heads. My granddaughter, Emily, likes the camels. I help her feed them grass. She's not scared, that girl, to put her face up close. Those lips could cover her with one big smack. Wick goes for the parrots, I can tell. He admires their red and orange feathers, the way they talk, but when he sees the panther walking back and forth in his cage, he says, Oh my God, he's a beauty, how can they lock him up? The way they pace, the two of them, looking at each other through the fence.

Me, I like the tortoises. The ones hiding in the tall grass, looking like boulders. The big, old ones. Some of them are over two hundred years old and still moving, even though you can hardly tell. I like the way they tuck their heads inside their shells. Wherever they go, they always have a home and a place to hide.

Annabel says, Why do you have to be so predictable, why don't you love flamingoes? You never see pink as pink as them, and besides, they're elegant and they fly. She says if I want to see real flamingoes, not just the zoo kind, I have to go to Florida. She says we can all come visit—me, Sammy and Lurline, Beatrice, Wick and Emily too. We can stay in a condo on the beach, one of the places she rents out for clients. If a condo is empty, then we can stay for free, but we have to promise not to tell.

Sammy likes free. He puts his arm around me and says, What you think, Ma? You like go Florida?

I don't like when he calls me Ma. When he asks me right in front of her.

Annabel says, If Alice won't come, you come by yourself.

Sammy says, Maybe, I'll think about it. I always like go travel.

My foot, I'm thinking. My foot he like go travel. I pull away from him and walk over to look at the ostrich. That's an animal with the right idea.

Annabel says, Who wants shave ice? I'm buying.

Everybody orders the biggest size, three flavors each. The whole time we're eating, Annabel complains about the ice, how it's too coarse, not smooth and fine like the shave ice we used to eat when we were young. Sammy says she has to go School Street or Waimanalo to get that kind. He says we can all go and get real shave ice before Annabel has to go back.

Before, before. I'm already flooded with the list of things to do and places to go before Annabel leaves. I'm hot and sticky and tired. My tongue the color of a bleeding rainbow.

Lurline clings to the fence with her fingers and toes. She's strong, that girl. She has dents all over her face, where she pressed too close to the cage. The zoo animals want to come out, but she wants to go in, and so do I.

My parents' house. This is the same house they have always lived in, although it has a new concrete foundation because of termites. The neighborhood has changed. Apartment buildings dwarf the house, bus engines drown out the TV, and there's always kimchee and garlic in your nose because of the Korean restaurant next door.

The traffic is so heavy, we can't let the kids walk to the beach any-more. The parking is bad too.

Inside the house, my father, Dr. Lum, greets everybody from his throne. His hair is completely white and he has a skinny goatee that he's very proud of. My mother rubs gel on it to shape his little bit of hair into a point. He's shrunk from the height he used to be, so he wears his pants pulled up to his armpits. My mother makes him sit in the front living room, and he's too weak to argue. He thinks we are all his customers—these relatives of mine and our closest friends, all of us moving past him like water flowing around an island. He reaches out, as if he's trying to find our sprains and broken bones. He sways when we kiss him, but his cane keeps him from toppling over.

He reminds me of the plastic Bozo the Clown punching bag that my brother Joe-Joe gave the girls for Christmas one year. There was sand in the bottom, so that when you punched Bozo on his nose, instead of falling over, he bounced right back. Sometimes I think Sammy liked Bozo more than the girls did. I'd come into the living room late at night, and there he would be, hitting the clown, again and again.

It's hard to tell how much my father understands anymore. He refuses to wear his hearing aid, so when we walk into the house, we have to stand in front of him while my mother shouts. THIS ONE BEATRICE! ALICE DAUGHTER! THIS ONE ANNABEL SON, WICK-LIFF! LOOK HOW BIG! THIS ONE ANNABEL! SHE STAY FLORIDA! ORANGE JUICE, YEAH? COME ALL A WAY FOR ALICE BIRF-DAY! YOUR DAUGHTER! ALICE! WE GOING HAVE CAKE! BIRFDAY CAKE! YOU LIKE!

My father nods at everything she says. He nods at everyone and everything. At Annabel, her son, at Perry Mason in a wheelchair on TV, at the Bugs Bunny carrot bib my mother ties around his neck to protect his shirt.

Lurline leans on his lap. Her skirt rides up, showing her red panties. She puts her face next to his, and he nods and she nods too. It's as if she knows what he is thinking.

My mother scolds. Her skirt so short! Her hair so long!

I kiss my father, his wrinkled face covered with freckles and tiny black moles, what Sammy calls fly shit.

I kiss my brothers too. My brothers number one and three, Russell and Joe-Joe. They're both grandparents too. Russell teaches at McKinley—mathematics and PE. He coaches the track team, even without a leg. He says the boys run for him because they have no excuse. Joe-Joe sells real estate, insurance, mortgages, whatever you need. When he sees Annabel, I'm afraid he's going to try to sell her life insurance. But what he wants to know is are there any good investments in Florida, can she give him some inside tips? Not for him, of course, but for some people he knows who have a little extra cash.

Even Frankie's parents are here. My mother will deny that she invited them to my birthday party for the purpose of causing trouble. She doesn't think in that way. Aggie Chew sits by my mother in church every Sunday, both of them without their husbands. They tell everybody they are related. I can just hear them talking to the other church ladies, each one trying to outbrag the other about their mutual granddaughter, Emily.

Aggie Chew is wearing her Big Hair tonight, what Beatrice calls the Elizabeth Taylor wig. It's very black, and Aggie's face is very white, like pie crust, and her lips pink pearl. She walks right up to Annabel first thing and says, Alice tells me you dance real good. Make her bring you by the clubhouse, and you can show us a thing or two.

Annabel takes one look at that crumbling face and says, I'm booked up every day so far, but I'll check with my appointment secretary.

They both look at me, but I'm walking away. I have enough to worry about.

Annabel's own son, for one thing. Poor Wick. He doesn't know what to say to all these people. And he can't sit down, not with all these old ladies bobbing up and down, so he drinks his Primo standing up. He's wearing the aloha shirt Annabel bought for him at

Reyn's yesterday. It's a reverse print, with the bright side of the fabric on the inside, not the out. Frankie says all the local boys like this kind. Dull. Color that is no color, because local boys don't like loud. I wish Wick brought his banjo, so he could play "Fireball Male" and show them all the true meaning of loud.

Wick gives me a plumeria lei that he made all by himself. The flowers are bruised, but I love my birthday lei. Beatrice says he went to the neighbors with his paper bag and begged for flowers, just like I taught him. Beatrice wears plumeria too, in her hair, which is growing long again and turning brown from going to the beach so much. Her T-shirt is a low scoop-neck, black. Aggie Chew's husband, Cyrus, leans over to read the words printed on my daughter's T-shirt, over her left breast.

High Voltage, he reads. Ha ha, he says. What a scream.

The way Cyrus stares at Beatrice's chest and then at her legs, I know what he's thinking: How could Frankie give up that? Cyrus Chew looks at Wick, all six feet two; then at Beatrice, petite and sassy; then at his wife, who is glaring at him. He rolls his cigar around in his mouth. Every time I see him, he has a cigar. Sammy says it's probably the same cigar, because Cyrus never lights it.

My mother waddles from room to room. My mother, the chicken, the duck, the Pig. Plump, full of energy, her hair still black and not from dye, she wants everyone to know. She looks puzzled, as if she's trying to remember what she's looking for. A serving spoon, but where is the dish? A can of tea, but where is the pot? A photograph that she promised to show someone, but who?

Annabel and I go to the kitchen, where pungent odors rise from the old gas stove. My mother has been cooking for weeks. She tells everybody no potluck, and then she panics, so now we have everything she made—pork with oong choy, sweet and sour spareribs, shrimp with black beans, squid with sin choy—plus what she orders from Kapahulu Chop Suey, chef special noodles, ginger chicken, char siu pork, San Francisco *and* Peking roast duck, black mushrooms with bamboo shoots and water chestnuts—plus roast turkey, baked ham, and sweet potatoes, because she's afraid Annabel won't eat Chinese food that doesn't come from Fat Lee Wo. And people still bring food. Sushi, teriyaki, lavosh, taco salad, namasu. Feeding time is six o'clock. In the meantime, everybody's eating pupu. Lumpia, ahi poke, cuttlefish, sour-cream-and-chive potato chips.

My mother's afraid I'll drop her good dishes, so Annabel helps her wash the platters and serving bowls. This is my mother's precious Hong Kong china which I'm supposed to inherit one day. The dishes are painted red and blue, with pink chrysanthemums and gold around the edges. I'll get only the dishes. My brothers will inherit the vases.

My mother tells Annabel that my butterfingers are why she has only five teacups left out of a place setting of eighteen. These are the English-style teacups, so thin you can see the light right through them, not thick like the Chinese cups. My mother forgets all those parties when she used those English teacups to impress her mah-jongg friends, who were high on rice wine, 80 proof.

My mother says to Annabel, You like my china? I like you hair. Teach Alice how for make you hair.

Annabel says, Alice has sensible hair, easy to take care of, not impossible like mine. She flips her hair with the back of her hand when she says that word. Impossible.

They talk about me as if I'm not here, and I don't care, because I'm not.

I'm back out in the living room, where Wick is playing the piano that my mother bought for her sixtieth birthday. She told us all she didn't want a party because all her friends would find out how old she really was. Then she went and bought this piano for herself. I felt bad, because I didn't know she loved music so much. She's been taking lessons for almost twenty years now, but she still won't play in front of anyone.

When Wick starts to play a song like sprinkling rain, what he calls water music, my mother and Annabel Lee come rushing out of the kitchen. I wave at them to stand behind him, so he doesn't get up. Beatrice sits by him on the bench, and my mother and Annabel and

I sway behind them like trees in the forest, rain falling out of his fingers, falling only on us.

Outside on the lanai, my brother Russell tends the barbecue, with Sammy supervising. The other men drink beer and play cards. Frankie's out there too, with Emily. She plays on the concrete with her little cars. She has ten cars, four airplanes, a carpenter set, and only one doll, a Raggedy Ann. No Barbie dolls. Beatrice wants Emily to grow up thinking like a boy and save herself from a lot of grief, and Frankie doesn't complain.

Frankie stands up when he sees me. He's here because of me. Because of his mother and my mother. So many mothers. He kisses me and whispers, Happy birthday, Alice Mom. I have something for you. Here.

He puts a little box in my hand. It's all wrapped up. Gold paper, yellow ribbon.

But you already gave me parakeets. You already gave my birdcage.

Never mind. Go ahead, open it. I have to leave pretty soon.

They're earrings, and I know right away what they are. Little lifesavers hanging from tiny ropes. My very first pair of dangling earrings.

Did you make these? I ask him.

Sort of. I had a little help from Polo.

I give him a big hug.

Wear them when you come to our grand opening, he says. I'm putting you at the top of the guest list.

Then a car honking out front, and Frankie says, That's for me. I better get going.

I'll walk you out.

No need.

No, I want to. Here, let me have Emily.

She'll cry if you come out front.

Who's picking you up? I ask him.

My friend Robin, he says. Bye now, gotta go.

He kisses me on the cheek, and then he's gone. Robin, I'm thinking, a bird's name. It tells me nothing I want to know, but it's what I deserve for asking.

At dinner, Annabel talks to the women about her father's house up in the heights. What a zoo it is, she says. Kids and dogs chasing each other. Statues and garage-sale junk littering the yard. The rock wall falling down. The house is a disaster area too, painted yellow with red trim. Red and yellow together—imagine that! Rooms added on every which way, the roofs all different levels. She blames the whole shebang on her father's wives.

Mr. Lee married and divorced three times after Dora Kaiulani died, and each new wife was even more Chinese than the one before. The last wife, number five, came with a whole village. So many children and grandchildren that Annabel's brothers tried to get their father to sign a prenuptial agreement, but he refused to sign and kicked them out of the house. He died last year, while Annabel was visiting Greece, so she missed the funeral, but Sammy and I went with my mother. My mother spent the whole time trying to figure out which children and grandchildren belonged to which wife. The three ex-wives showed up at the funeral to make sure their kids would inherit something.

This makes Annabel mad. She says they will never be family to her. She warns Wick to stay away from the house, or they'll ask him for money, as if they didn't get enough from the old man.

She says, I don't care about the property, but what makes me mad is they gave away all my mother's clothes. Even my tutu's wedding gown hanging on the wall. And they used up the fabric—all of it—without even asking me if I wanted anything.

Aggie Chew and my mother are all ears, of course, but Annabel doesn't care. In less than two weeks, she'll be gone, and she won't have to listen to the gossip when it comes back around.

She pushes the noodles into circles on her plate, making one puka here, another puka there. The only thing she eats is a piece of chicken that falls into a hole. She chews so slowly, and when she swallows, I can feel the lump going down. I worry about her not eating, only drinking. She blames her poor appetite on the big shave ice she had this afternoon, but I saw her throw half of it away. She finds no joy in food, not like the rest of us. What fills her up, I wonder. What keeps her going? Wick was like her when he first came to the islands—only snacking, not that hungry come dinnertime—but now he's keeping up with Sammy, and Beatrice is complaining about Wick getting fat. I look around the house at my family, at everybody chowing down. We are one giant mouth, one big puka into which everything goes.

A knock at the front door makes everyone stop talking, because nobody knocks, nobody comes in that way. Lurline runs to the door. It's a delivery boy carrying a green vase with roses. Long-stemmed roses. Red. A small white envelope is pinned to the ribbon, also red. My name written on the outside of the envelope. I grab it before Lurline can rip it open. Inside, I find a card.

It reads, For my favorite Pig. Love from Your Brother the Ram.

I run to the door, down the walk, but all I see is the blue florist van pulling away. When my mother sees the flowers, I have already stuffed the card into my pocket.

They're from Sammy, I tell her. The message is private.

She laughs and claps her hands. Good boy, good boy.

Annabel sniffs my roses. She says, These aren't hothouse roses. I'm impressed.

Real smart, Alice, I'm thinking to myself. Look what you did now.

Sammy nods, but he looks confused. He never buys gifts for my birthday. It's always, Look what I did, fixed the washing machine, built you that table you wanted for cutting fabric. He won't say no to what comes his way by mistake or accident or even somebody else's bad luck. The quarter on the ground, the fallen hubcap, the check he wrote at the store that he finds later on in his bag, along with the receipt and a new pair of socks. They're all part of his missing fortune. What he has coming to him from someone, somewhere. What they owe him. Anyone. Everybody.

.   .   .

I'm mad at my brother Michael for sending the roses here, where my mother can see them. Doesn't he know how sad it makes her? All the gifts he sends me but not her. It's a mean thing to do, punishing her, when it's our father he should hate. I used to blame her too, until I married a Hard Head myself.

I guess Michael is a Ram in more ways than one. He's true to his horoscope—wise and gentle, kind to the underdog, good at art—but he still has his boxing gloves on.

Michael lives in Minneapolis now, where he teaches doctors at a big university. Psychiatrist doctors. He paints pictures for children's books too, but there's no money in books, so he has to keep on being a doctor. My father should be proud—Michael is making more money than any of us—but my father still criticizes.

The last time Michael came home, eight years ago, my father beat him with his cane. When we came to the house for dinner that night, there was my brother, tall and handsome, the hair on his temples turning gray. And there was my father, poking Michael with his cane, poking him like a dog, a rabid dog, and Michael not saying anything, standing with his arms raised in the air, tears streaming down his face. Before he left the house, he said, Sorry, Sister. I'm too old for this crap.

I didn't know where he went. To stay with friends, to a hotel. I didn't even know what flight he was taking back to the mainland, so I couldn't go down to the airport to say goodbye. I would have followed him, but Sammy wouldn't give me the car keys. He said I might crack up the Dodge. That piece of junk. I'm glad it's gone. I begged Sammy to help me, but he was drunk. The whole time my father picked on Michael, Sammy sat outside in the lanai and drank.

My mother pretends Michael is coming home any day now. The same way she pretends that all the lickings, all the lectures never happened. She thinks he'll just show up and say, What's for eat, Ma, and she can feed him until his hunger is satisfied. Hungry, that's him all right. Stalking us at every party. Watching us through the bars.

Michael usually sends me money for my birthday and at Christmas too. Twenty-, fifty-dollar bills. He says use the money for only you. I write him every time. Don't send me cash in the mail. Might get lost. But still he sends me crisp new money. Naked in the envelope. No paper hiding it. I spend some of the money on my crafts, the rest on my girls, so Sammy can't squawk. Once Michael sent me a plane ticket. Round trip to Minneapolis, so I could go visit him. Sammy said I should cash it in, but I couldn't do that, so I mailed it back.

Sometimes Michael sends me books. Travel books. Adventure books. He knows what I like. Books about climbing mountains and paddling canoes on the Amazon. Books by Robert Louis Stevenson. *Treasure Island, Kidnapped, The New Arabian Nights.* He remembers, he remembers. He writes my name in the front so I can't give the books away to somebody else. As if I would. He writes something special inside each one.

For my sister Alice, who loves adventure.

For my sister Alice, who saves us all.

That last one bothers me. I haven't saved anybody for a long, long time. Just my babies, but nobody else. Saving yourself. How does that count?

Annabel asks, right in front of my mother, as if she's reading my mind, Whatever happened to your brother Michael? Did he get married?

I almost drop the plate I am carrying to the kitchen.

My mother's face lights up. I know what she's thinking. Michael could marry Annabel, and they could both move back home and buy a house, and we would all be happy and related. She thinks it's that easy.

Michael has a girlfriend, I tell her. A haole girl. From Connecticut.

Oh yeah? They shacking up?

He's been with her for ten years now. They might as well be married.

My mother is upset. She doesn't like this talk of shacking up, and she's mad at me for discouraging Annabel. She's dreaming double wedding—Michael and Annabel, and Wick and Beatrice—one big nine-course dinner with twice the gifts. But she acts as if Frankie and his parents are still part of the family. She can't subtract and divide, only add and multiply.

Annabel helps my mother light the candles on my cake. Too many, because my mother believes you need one candle for every year, no matter how old you are. Everybody forgets to sing, because they are too busy watching me blow out the fire. Then Wick starts playing the piano. His voice is loud and in tune, so my birthday song sounds better than ever. When they come to the second part, though, he doesn't know the words.

> All the monkeys in the zoo
> Send their best regards to you.
> Happy birthday to you.

Wick says, Y'all sing that different than we do back home.

Annabel says, Well, this is your home now, so you better learn.

Wick lifts his mother up and gives her a big kiss on both cheeks, and then sets her back down.

Everybody laughs, because Annabel is so embarrassed. Her face is all flushed.

Goodness gracious, she says, just like a haole, and everybody laughs again.

These are my favorite presents:

The roses from my brother Michael that make Sammy quiet. He's wondering who they're really from, and I'm not going to tell him. I've already torn up the card into little bits and buried them in the garbage can.

The lifesaver earrings from my son-at-heart, Frankie.

Two little chairs that Lurline made with Wick's help from the metal tops off champagne bottles.

A big wooden comb from Beatrice for weaving tapestries without a loom. This time she's really going to show me how.

A tambourine from Wick, so I can play music too. He tied rags between all the little cymbals so the box wouldn't make any noise when I shook it. My leg is already black and blue from where I hit it with my tambourine, but I don't care. I love the sound of my sound.

And from my oldest and dearest friend, Annabel Lee, a beautiful slip, royal-blue silk, and it's not from Liberty House. She bought it in New York, not at Macy's but at Bergdorf Goodman, which I never heard of, which she says is even more high class. She makes me put the slip back in the box, so people don't touch it with their greasy fingers.

She says, You can try it on later, when we get back to the house. I have one just like it, in green.

But we don't go straight home, because Annabel wants to go disco dancing while the night is still young. Beatrice and Wick say they'll take her, but Sammy says, We all go, you too, Ma. So we head for Rumors in Waikiki, me wishing I had worn something short. How can I dance in my long muumuu?

But not to worry. Sammy plants himself at the table. He says, I'll just sit and watch you folks, so Wick has to dance with us ladies all by himself. Beatrice makes him ask Annabel first, then me—I have to hold up my hem. Then he dances with Lurline, and finally Beatrice, for three dances in a row, before he starts over again. But Annabel doesn't sit around waiting for her turn. Men approach her left and right, young and old, good-looking and not-so-good. She sends some of them over to ask me. They already know my name when they walk up. I tell them all no, thank you. I say no to Wick too, on his third time around.

I wouldn't mind keeping Sammy company if he would put his arm around me like Wick does when he and Beatrice are sitting down. He doesn't even have to talk, just act like we're a couple, not only married, but still in love, in love. But he won't even look at me.

He smokes and drinks highballs, one after the other, and watches the dance floor. Watches Annabel Lee.

The disco light chops everybody into pieces, so they aren't people, just their parts. Like what you get from the butcher. Rump, breast, neck, thigh. Every piece a different price.

Sammy hated the job he got at Hickam after the war. He didn't like to tell people he was a janitor. Machinist was better, or mechanic or welder, but Sammy had trouble getting along at work. His boss said he was too cocky and had a problem with authority.

Authority, Sammy said, what is that? People always telling you where to go, what to do. Cannot think for yourself. Always stuck at the bottom.

Same thing happened when Sammy was in the service. All his good ideas ignored. Unfair treatment because he wasn't haole, so he had to find other ways to get ahead, and not all legal. That's why he came out the same way he went in. Still buck private in the end.

Every night I listened to him complain, my stomach in knots. We lived with my parents and had no place to talk, just in the bedroom, and there was always Beatrice crying in my lap. Sometimes he got so mad, he grabbed her and put her outside the bedroom door, where my mother found her. Then it was my mother pounding on the door and scolding, in addition to Beatrice screaming at the top of her lungs.

He hated birthdays, hated Christmas. All the gifts that my family gave to us, but we got nothing from his relatives. He grumbled at me when he saw all the presents Beatrice received.

I'm an orphan, he said. I got nothing, nothing.

On Christmas Eve he got drunk and repeated over and over, Fuck Santa Claus, fuck Santa Claus.

So when his war buddy Sylvester Kaleheo said, Come Maui fish, I said never mind my family or buying a house or Beatrice's school. Let's pack up and go.

·   ·   ·

The cottage in Hana was filthy. Sylvester said we could do anything to it, nothing could make it worse, so I threw out the rotten
lauhala mats, scrubbed the linoleum, the walls, the windows,
washed everything until my hands were raw. Luckily I didn't get
pregnant with Lurline right away, so I could clean without throwing up.

That was my second-honeymoon time. Those first three months
on Maui. Sammy came home tired every night, but that didn't stop
him from wanting me. He took a shower outside, under the spigot he
rigged up by the side of the cottage, where the neighbors couldn't
see because of the ti leaves. That first time I watched him from the
window, the sight of his body getting stronger made me ache so
much that I forgot the rice on the stove. The smoke filled the house,
and we had to sleep with the windows and the back door wide open
to get rid of the smell of burnt rice. In the morning we were covered
with mosquito bites, but we made love again, scratching and all.

Sammy loved catching fish. Fish still alive and jumping, fighting
up until the moment they died. He brought home fish every night
for us to eat. He recited the numbers. How many, how heavy, how
much money we saved by eating what he caught himself. Sylvester
paid him in fish, and we traded what we couldn't eat for vegetables
and rice and a chicken now and then. Sammy liked our life away
from Honolulu, away from the big town. No cash register, no price
tag, no chain of command. Everything direct, from the ocean, from
the land, from his hardworking hands, right into our mouths.

After I got pregnant with Lurline, all I could hold down was rice
and a little bit of tofu, so Sammy ate my fish. He didn't like for anything to go to waste. He plucked the eyeballs out of the fish and
swallowed them whole. He said as long as he ate the fish eyeballs, he
would never have bad eyesight, not like me. He wouldn't let me
wear my glasses to read. He said I had to train myself to see without
them or I would need them for the rest of my life.

The rest of my life. The days and nights so long. I had my records and Annabel's phonograph which she gave to me before she left, but listening to our dance music made me cry deep down inside. The Hawaiian music that Sylvester Kaleheo and his cousins played at night made me sad too. There was no music inside me, no dancing. Just babies and rain and my husband, who was still full of hurt that even an ocean couldn't take away.

He kept me up late in the kitchen talking about his mother, his family, how they were all so mean to him except for his grandmother. He talked about the war too, the same stories but with more details. Bragging that he never once got caught stealing cigarettes or liquor and selling them on the black market. Other Hawaii guys he knew weren't so lucky. They got court-martialed, but that was because they were stupid, not clever like him. He held Beatrice on his lap while he talked. She didn't understand him, but she laughed when he laughed, and he liked that, being her one and only hero. Me, I just sat and listened. His stories didn't seem that funny to me anymore.

One night he told me he wrote to Annabel during the war, but all his letters came back marked REFUSED. He thought maybe she had died or gone to the mainland. I cried, I was so hurt. Annabel had never told me about those letters.

I blurted out, Why didn't you write to me, I would have written back.

He said, How could I ask you about her?

Her! I cried some more.

Never mind, he said, What's gone is gone. I have you now. I don't care about her. Coming home to you was the best thing ever happen to me, he said. Fuck Annabel Lee. Fuck her.

He didn't always talk to me. Sometimes he sat outside and talked to his pigeons. Before he let them go, he whispered in their ears. I didn't want to know what he told them. Every bird he let go that didn't come back was like punishment to me.

My life was dictated by feeding times. The girls, Sammy, the pigeons, the rabbits, the garden.

I made up stories for Beatrice, stories with happy endings that made me hate him even more for taking me to Hana, taking me away from my family and my home, so I would be alone, like him.

And the rain, always the rain.

When Annabel called to ask if she could come visit, I didn't have the heart to tell her no. She was crying on the phone, and I could hardly understand what she was saying. Something about Coy leaving, and this time it was for good, she couldn't take any more. I told Sammy we had to let her come. She had no place to go in Hawaii that was home anymore. She wouldn't stay with her father, because of his new wife. Her sister, Emma, still lived in Florida, and her brothers, Gordon and Edward, had fled the coop too—one in the Philippines, the other somewhere in Alaska. The war carried them away, scattered them, like broken coral on the beach.

She has no family, I told him. Just like you.

He didn't say anything, and after dinner he went outside to sit in the yard and talk to his pigeons. He took a bottle with him. When I came out to get him, he was already drunk. I slept with Beatrice that night. The two of us on her cot.

The next morning, he was already gone when I woke up. Our bed was still made. He didn't make love to me for a whole month, and when he finally did, he forced himself inside me and then yelled so loud I thought for sure the neighbors would think one of us had died.

BIG WATER

This is my house, quiet, except for my husband and my best friend, still talking and drinking in the kitchen as if a quarter of a century has not gone by. Annabel's voice hasn't changed much, just a little husky from all the cigarettes. Sammy's, the same as always, low and rumbling, which scares the babies the first time they meet him. I can hear them all the way from my room. Laughing and joking. You'd think Annabel would be tired from disco dancing until 2 a.m., but no. Sammy says, How's about a nightcap, and pretty soon they're drinking again. Cognac and B&B this time.

Lurline sleeps on the living-room floor in her new baby-doll pajamas, white nylon with fur around the hem, that I bought for her the other day. I bought white, not red, so she looks like an angel. My angel, my baby who will always be with me. So little it takes for her to be happy. Nobody appreciates her like I do. They think she's too much trouble. They think she's dumb. They don't hear what I hear, the song in the way she moves her body. They don't see what I see, the wings from never being scared.

My parakeets sleep in their cage, under the blue silk scarf that Annabel gave me a long time ago, one of Dora Kaiulani's scarves that we used to drape over the lamp when we danced in the Lees' living room during the blackout. I have names for my birds now. Petey and Tweety. Real bird names for real birds. Not movie-star names, not fish names, not the names of famous writers.

This is my room. The moon is hiding behind the clouds, so everything is black. Black is the floor. The wall. My crocheted mural. The pukas are even blacker. So many holes I still have to fill. Only my bed is white. My futon, a white boat floating on the black, black sea.

Me and my girls—Beatrice, almost five; Lurline, still in diapers. Three of us floating makai, riding out to sea in the pickup, Cock-a-Roach. The sun came out this morning, but up in the hills the sky is still crying. Tears falling, running under the ground, filling up the pools, the streams. Big Water rushing down the valley and out to sea, and Annabel Lee is coming, coming to our cottage on Maui. Sammy's playing baseball with the boys, and I'm floating with my babies out to sea.

Her voice like a bell.
Don't bother Aunty Alice BONG let her sleep, she almost drowned. Stay in the yard BONG don't fight, don't go out on the street.

Drifting in and out of sleep.
Sammy ties a message to my leg before he lets me fly out of the pigeon coop. When I look down, he's waving at me and his mouth is moving and I'm afraid he's going to yell my name. My real name for everybody to hear. Not Aku or Ahi. Not Myrna or Veronica, but Alice. Alice.

They're coming for me. Birdie, birdie fish girl. Shark, dolphin, stingray, eel. Coming for Alice, birdie fish girl. See them flying in the sky. Coming for me bye and bye.

Can Alice come out?
Alice no stay.
Where Alice went?
Alice went away.

•   •   •

How come you waiting in the yard, Sammy Woo? How come you
looking up at the sky?

My pigeon lost. My pigeon no come home.

Which way home?

Where I am lost.

Which way lost?

Where I am gone.

Her voice like a bell when she calls long distance. Static. Her
words all choppy, broken up by waves, by clouds, by everything lying
in the way.

Alice, I have to come see you. I'm bringing my boy. Wycliff. Louis
not coming. You know, RLS. I can't say his name. I'll tell you about it
when I see you. Can't talk on the phone. Too many ears.

She calls him Louis, RLS. Not Coy.

Something wrong. He's gone, he's gone.

My nin-nins sore.

Pump your milk BONG you can feed her later.

Lurline's eyes still shut. Rattle my nipple on her lips. Suck, baby.
Drink milk. Pinch her leg a little bit. Drink more. Her eyes, her
mouth shut tight.

Wrong. Something wrong.

Is he coming back to me?

Who?

Louis, RLS, Coy.

Don't think like that. Look what happens when you do.

Seaweed floating in and out.

Hold your breath, blow the bubbles out. Don't cry, don't think,
don't let go.

Shark come get you by the toe.

• • •

Wycliff BONG you and Beatrice go BONG play nicely, don't fight.
You have to let her go outside, Alice. You can't keep an eye on her
all the time. You just making her more scared than she already is.
BONG BONG BONG

Nipple keeps popping out. Stick it back in.
Annabel standing by the bed with a mayonnaise jar.
Pump your milk in here, Alice. Squirt in the jar. Let me help you.
Her fingers so cold. Squeezing. Sore.

Sammy's pokey face on mine.
The girls, the girls.
Shh. Annabel's with them. Just like hold you.
NO NO NO.

Big Water still falling inside, my whole body crying, but it won't
come out.

I'm going to wash your hair, Alice. I'll do it right here on the bed.
You don't have to get up. Don't worry. I'm just going to lift your head.
I'm only going to make it a little bit wet. Don't cry. Close your eyes. I
promise I won't get water on your face. There. Good. Now I'm going
to put on a little shampoo. Baby shampoo, so it won't hurt your eyes.
Let me rub your head. Feels good, I know. Keep your eyes closed. I'm
going to rinse you off. There. All pau. Now you smell so sweet.

Cock-a-Roach, Cock-a-Roach.
How did Alice swim back?
Cock-a-Roach, Cock-a-Roach.
How did Alice save her girls?

Pretty panties, who gave you that?
You.

Who?

Aunty Annabel.

Me? I gave you those panties? Are those the ones I sent you? Only now you fit them. I see. Pretty. You look so pretty.

I'm already five.

Big girl. Come over here. Let your mama sleep.

BONG BONG BONG

Don't cry, don't fight. Close your eyes and kick. Birdie fish nose. Birdie fish toes. Show the little fishies how you kick.

You know, Alice, you really should take Lurline to a real doctor. Not just some hick. That's how come I have scars. When I gave birth, that horse doctor tore me all up. Feel my scar how bumpy. Keloids. That's how I am. Takes me so long to heal.

The rope I lay me down to rest.

The inner tube I pray the Lord to take.

Lurline sleeps with me. Beatrice sleeps with me.

Annabel's boy wants to sleep with us too.

Okay, you can climb in bed with Aunty. Don't kick her now. Beatrice, here's your quilt.

His little feet so white. Hapa-haole feet. His toes on mine. His feet on mine. His eyes so big. Like his daddy's. Big and green and staring at me. Fish eyes.

This is what I remember about that night. We all went out on a double date. It was the third time. Me and Coy Whitlow, Annabel and Wren, but we didn't know Wren's first name. Coy said Wren, and Wren said Wren, and that was good enough for us. Annabel had just turned twenty-one, and I was still twenty, and the war was still on.

Annabel starting it all, telling Coy and Wren she wanted to go home, she didn't care to dance to lousy music and a band that couldn't keep time. She didn't say it, but I knew she was tired of Hotel Street, Fort Street. The low-class places we were stuck with going to because the boys weren't in the military. Empty beer bottles rattled on the floor of the Studebaker as Coy steered his car around the curves up to Annabel's house in Maunalani Heights. Me, sitting in the front seat with Coy, hugging the door, so I didn't slide into him. I didn't want to move close to him until he asked. But Coy was quiet. Neither one of us talking, because of them going at it in the back seat.

It was like that the first time too, on our first double date. Annabel and Wren in the back seat, and me and Coy in the front trying not to look. She didn't like when Coy gave me a pink carnation corsage and Wren handed her baby roses. They were yellow roses. Coy must have told him what she liked best. But they came from the wrong man. She didn't like me being with Coy and her stuck with Wren. Not that first time or the two times after that. She got into the back with Wren without saying a word and was quiet all the way to the dance. I didn't dare look around. Coy and Wren did all the talking. When we got out of the car, Wren was already holding her hand. That's how fast it went. Wren wasn't as good a dancer as Coy, but Annabel didn't complain, just let him hold her tight and rock her back and forth, slow dancing like the men at the dance studio always wanted. And Coy and me, dancing as if we didn't know how, with our arms stiff, holding each other far apart, and the words inside me evaporating as soon they reached my lips. We sat out the fast dances to keep them company, but they didn't pay any attention to us. Just laughed and whispered as if we weren't even there.

After that first night, I told her I was sorry, it was Coy's idea, not mine.

She said, I'm not sorry. Wren is twice the man.

But I could see how hurt she was. She stayed up all night sewing and wouldn't let me help her. She continued to dance with Coy, the modern kind of dancing that they did, but she wouldn't let him joke around. If he talked too much, she left. She said it was up to me if I wanted to watch. I did, but only for one last time. Seeing them so quiet and serious, and yet dancing together better than ever, was more than I could stand.

And now, on our third double date, she was saying to Coy, Park the car up past the house, near the trail, so the neighbors can't see. Don't worry about my father, he's sleeping at the restaurant tonight. It's just Alice and me. We're supposed to be sewing.

When Coy parked the car, I didn't even wait for him to let me out. I headed for the bushes, to the path that led to her back yard. I could hear Coy following me, not even asking me to slow down, as if he wanted to get away from them too. I was glad for the dark, for that thin slice of moon. I didn't want Coy to see how scared I was. A spiderweb fell across my face, and I stopped in my tracks. He stumbled into me. His voice husky, saying, I'm right here, keep on going. His warm breath on my neck.

I poked my fingers through a hole in the back-door screen to lift the hook. Mr. Lee didn't bother to lock the house anymore. It was dark in the kitchen. An empty lightbulb socket in the kitchen ceiling. I found some matches in the drawer next to the stove and lit the candle on the table.

Coy said, I'm hungry, what they got to eat in here?

He opened the icebox. Stale, warm air spilled out.

Where's the Chinese food? I thought her father owned a restaurant.

I opened the cupboard and brought out a few cans.

Which you rather have? Spaghetti or corned-beef hash?

He walked over to where I was standing. The air in front of me grew thick, almost suffocating. The heat of him. His chest in my face as he felt in the cupboard behind me. His underarms. Him saying, What about liquor, they got any liquor?

Me saying, We can't drink Mr. Lee's liquor. He'll find out. You have to ask Annabel when she comes, if she comes.

And Coy saying, They sure hit it off, didn't they?

Him laughing nervously. Standing close again, too close. My back pressed up against the counter. The light from the candle formed a halo around him. This was her house, her kitchen, but him, my own guardian angel.

I said, Annabel has some rum, but it's a secret. I'm not supposed to tell.

He said, Y'all are full of little secrets, ain't you?

It's not a real secret. We just don't tell anybody.

But that's what a secret is, what you don't tell nobody. A secret should be something you care about, something which if you told could hurt somebody. Like if your parents found out y'all was going dancing instead of sewing, if they found out you were here with me, which you are, and I'm glad.

I ran all my words together too, the way he did. Saying, I can make you some corned beef if you're hungry, I can fry it up, I can cook some rice.

He said, I'm not saying it's bad, keeping a secret, I'm glad to know you have a mind of your own, I know it wasn't your idea, coming here. God, I'm hungry, corned beef and rice sounds mighty fine.

We heard steps on the porch then, and Annabel and Wren came crashing into the kitchen, their arms wrapped around each other. Her words cut through the dark.

Well, I hope we're not interrupting anything.

I remember breathing then, like I'd just learned how. One big gulp followed by the next.

She walked over to the cupboard next to the stove, knelt on the floor, and starting pulling out pots and pans, banging the lids. Then she pulled out a paper bag and lifted out the bottle of rum. It was a new bottle, not even open. She placed four glasses on the counter and filled each of them halfway.

She said to Wren, Come on.

More banging as Wren followed her into the living room, stumbling into the table and chairs along the way.

Coy grabbed two glasses for us and said, Leave the candle, but I brought it with me anyway and followed him into the living room.

The lanai door was flung open, and the breeze felt good, cool on my hot skin. Annabel and Wren collapsed on the sofa, him whispering, her laughing. Coy took Mr. Lee's chair, a big soft one. I sat in the rocking chair and watched the candle wax drip. No sounds except for the chair squeaking on the wood floor and them at it again on the couch. Kissing and moaning and kissing again.

Finally Coy said, Getting stuffy in here.

He pulled me out of the rocker. The candle went out as soon as we walked outside. He lit a cigarette, put it between my lips for us to share. Whispered, Do you want me to take you home, they won't even know we're gone, I can come back for Wren.

One Alice wanting to say, Yes, let's go, but the other Alice saying, Do you play Ping-Pong, do you want to see the Ping-Pong table, it's in the garage.

I remember thinking I could smell him all night. Rum, tobacco, skin.

Me leading the way again, this time over the gravel path to the garage. Most people's garages were open on the sides, but Mr. Lee had added walls to his, on all four sides, after Annabel's brothers dug the bomb shelter inside. He couldn't park in there anyway, not with the hole. We found the kerosene lantern just inside the door. Coy showed me how to turn the wick down, so the lamp didn't burn too bright.

I said, There are candles under there. I pointed at the Ping-Pong table lying in the middle of the dirt floor.

Coy said, What's it doing down there, what happened to the legs, what's that on top?

He knelt down to touch the fabric that Annabel had glued to the tabletop.

What the hell is this?

A pupule quilt.

What's that?

Something you make when you're crazy.

When he lifted the cover and he saw what was inside, he whistled and said, This is crazy all right.

The bomb shelter still looked pretty good. A box of food. Jugs of water. Candles, candlesticks, and matches. Folded blankets. Extra clothes. Wooden planks and a canvas tarp on the floor of the shelter. And an old mattress on top. No water in the hole, like in my family's bomb shelter, down in the valley. No rats because of the neighbor's cat.

Coy stepped into the hole. He said, Kinda short, wouldn't you say? Have to lie down if you want to hide in this foxhole.

He looked in a box and brought out a bottle. Clear liquid. He sniffed.

Gin. I'll be damned, I like this even better than rum. What else is there—crackers, what do you know, I don't suppose they have sardines.

We lit two candles, turned off the lantern, and placed the candles on opposite ends of the bomb shelter. Then we laid out the feast. The gin, a box of Saloon Pilot crackers, a can of sardines, then peanut butter and grape jelly, scooped from the tins with our fingers. We took turns feeding each other. I stood on the ledge above him and fed him down in the hole. Him laughing and reaching for sardines with his mouth, sucking my fingers, one by one. When he reached my last finger, I closed my eyes. It was like the movies, better than the movies.

He said, That was fun, now I need a butt.

The camera inside me died. I wanted to crawl away. The candles too bright all of a sudden.

One Alice saying, I'm going back inside the house.

Him saying, You don't want to go back there right now, trust me.

The other Alice saying, Are you wishing I was Annabel? Are you sorry you're not Wren?

What, hell no, what are you talking about?

Me babbling now. How come you didn't keep her for yourself, I know you like her, how come you set her up with Wren?

Him saying, No, hush, don't talk like that, don't.

My knees shaking as he pulled me down into the hole.

Don't go, stay here with me, I want you to. You're like a sister to me.

My body like glass waiting to break. His words like rocks, a whole skyful.

I don't want to be your sister. I have enough brothers.

You too? Shit, I thought you had a boyfriend. Annabel told me about him—Sammy Woo—that's not a bad name, you know. I wonder if he'd like to trade?

She told you about him?

She said you're gonna marry him when he gets out.

That liar. She's a liar!

I told him the truth about Sammy then. How I never really had him, how he wanted Annabel, but she didn't care about him. Not him or any of the other guys she could have had. Just you, is what I told him. She only wants you.

No, he said. Not me.

You're wrong. You don't know the half of it.

I know there's something else she wants.

A dance partner.

That too, guess again.

He was so calm when he said this. His voice almost cold, making me feel disloyal, cheap. Betraying my best friend by telling on her and somehow betraying him just by being there. I turned to get up.

He started to touch me then. His hands in my hair, on my neck, over the front of my dress, and me crying, angry, confused, but not wanting him to stop. He kissed me everywhere, but not on my lips, and when I tried to kiss him, to touch him back, he pulled away.

No, he said, let me, just me.

He talked to me the whole time, telling me not to be scared, he wasn't going to hurt me or get me pregnant, all he wanted was to make me feel good, I just had to lie back and relax.

All I could think of was, I'm no good at dancing, not as good as I want to be. I can't sew because I can't follow patterns. I lose at Ping-Pong. All I can do is let.

I closed my eyes and let his fingers go where they wanted to go, where I wanted them to go. My buttons, too many of them. His hands inside my dress, under my bra, my slip. He lifted me so I was lying on him, on my back, with him underneath. Took off his belt so the buckle wouldn't hurt me. I thought about Annabel and Wren on the couch in her living room, and it was me on the couch, me inside her body, but Coy's hands moving down the front of me. All I could see was her face, her lying in bed next to me, her hair falling across my arm. They might come looking for us, her and Wren. One Alice wanting him to hurry, turn me over, put it in. The other Alice afraid he might, he might.

His voice like a prayer: Come on, baby, that's it, I can feel it.

It wasn't just me humming, singing all in one breath. It was her too.

Prayer, while I was sinking back into myself. He rolled me over to his side. Let me watch while he did what he did to himself. It was so beautiful, the way he kept his eyes on me the whole time, and me, staring, not wanting to miss a thing. His eyes so dark, as if there was no bottom. When I tried to help, he said, Don't, please don't.

I think of him when I'm alone, when Sammy's on top of me, when I'm trying to push her away, out of my head. Annabel Lee, and sometimes her mother, Dora Kaiulani. One of them dancing, the other half naked.

His eyes green in the flickering candlelight. Prayer, then confession. His voice loud and clear. Telling me what I didn't want to hear, what I didn't understand until years later, when it was too late. What he said at the end, shaking his head, finally shutting his eyes.

You don't know me, baby. You don't.

Two more pigeons lost. Sammy let them go four days ago, before the flash flood, and they still haven't come back. He and Annabel sit in the back yard and wait.

First, he mixes martinis. Clink, the ice in our silver mixer. Green olives. Our wedding gift martini glasses with the stems.

He sits in his chair. She sits in mine. Her boy stands between them, leaning on her leg. She whispers to Wycliff. He runs back inside the house. Screen door goes slam.

Mommy says too many mosquitoes out there. She says come inside and play with Beatrice.

He tugs her arm and I slap him. Hard.

NO NO NO

What are they saying, what are they doing?

Rash on my breasts, on my stomach, all over.

The rope still tight around me.

Listen to my babies breathe. Slow quick quick slow.

Sammy climbing into bed, babies and all. Gin on his breath. Reaching for me.

NO NO NO

BANG. The cupboard. BANG. The drawer.

I don't know how you can stand living out here. I can't believe there's no bakery in this town. Do you know how hard it is to cook in somebody else's kitchen? Where do you keep the vanilla? I can't find the measuring cups. I want to bake a cake for you. We should do something for your birthday, even if we can't go out. Do you want to go to church? It might make you feel better. Where's Sammy? When I woke up this morning, he was gone. I guess he went fishing. He has to go back to work sometime. Can't stay home with you forever. Should I take Beatrice to church with me too? How do the women dress in this town? I hope they dress up, because I don't have anything plain. You know me, I can't stand plain.

BANG BANG BANG

Her voice like a bell.

Let's light a candle. You must have candles in this house.

Babies all around me. Annabel's. Mine. Sleeping so sweetly on my bed.

Them sitting in the kitchen. Drinking, smoking.

BONG it's so good to be here, Sammy, I'm so glad we can finally talk.

Rumble, rumble, like a train.

Smoke filling the living room, coming into the bedroom, through the open door.

BONG how come we never talked like this before.

Sammy shaking the ice. Shaking and pouring.

BONG, I want to tell her, but how can I BONG it's my fault they almost drowned BONG don't tell me not, my husband doesn't want me BONG everybody I love goes away BONG I miss my mother, she loved you, Sammy, she always loved you.

BONG BONG BONG

So quiet now, except for the rain. Rain falling on the roof. Waves breaking on the rocks.

I can put on my robe. I can get up and make breakfast for them. Whole-wheat toast and scrambled eggs. Surprise, everybody. Surprise, I'm awake.

The door closing. Somebody closing it.

Everybody I love. Rain falling on my island. Waves crashing on my reef.

And I'm floating, floating out to sea.

My robe is periwinkle blue, chenille, from the Sears catalogue. I cried when it came. Dull and drab, not blue like the sky. But now it's just right. Heavy on me, hiding the real blue, the Big Water running deep inside.

The moonlight shining through the louvers, and all the little mirrors on my mural glowing like baby moons. I know what I'm going to crochet when Annabel leaves. Sardines swimming in a bowl of fire. A small camouflage net. Brown and green, and shaped like a glove.

They're not in the kitchen anymore. Lights clicking off. Footsteps in the hallway. Her voice like hell. Hoarse from too much smoking, too much talking.

Sweet dreams, she says. Tell Alice not to wake me up, tell her not to fix me breakfast, I don't eat breakfast anymore. After you reach a certain age, you have to give up something. You know what I mean?

Laughter, muffled.

Yeah, says Sammy. Sleep tight.

Then quiet. Them kissing, I'm sure. Hugging too. All I can see is the outline of Sammy. He's not wearing a shirt. He hardly ever wears a shirt at home, but she doesn't know that. She goes into the bathroom. The toilet flushing, but where is he?

Sorry, she says, when she comes out of the bathroom and stumbles into him. Why are you sitting on the floor? Good night.

No kissing this time.

Sammy goes into the bathroom. The shower running and running.

When he walks into my room, he's naked, not even wearing BVDs. He climbs onto the futon, the side that's empty, the side I don't sleep on out of habit.

This is my husband. This is my bed.

Who am I to him tonight? Me or Annabel? Me or his mother?

And the other question: Who is he to me?

The father of my children. A good provider. A little boy. Hurt, angry. A drunk. All these years and we're still together. He gave up fishing, gave up Maui, after the Big Water almost took me and the girls away. Was it for love? Or because Annabel went back to Florida?

And what about me? What did I give up?

Don't want to think about the answer. Don't know him, and he doesn't know me. He doesn't even know himself.

But here we are. Him, pulling up the sheet, putting his head down on the pillow, his back facing me, like I'm a lump in the bed, just ignore it. He doesn't even notice I'm wearing my new royal-blue silk slip that Annabel gave me for my birthday. Trying it out, trying to make myself feel better. He's here because she's in the house. He comes to save face. He comes for love, but what is that—sleep, sex, company, what?

One Alice, aching inside, wanting him to climb on top of me, wanting him to be rough and loud, so she knows this is my room, this is my house, my husband. But is it really him I want? The bedroom door is wide open, so she can hear us. He left it open, and I'm not closing it.

The other Alice, doing nothing, waiting. My camouflage is fading after all these years, but they're not looking, so they don't see me.

When he finally rolls over and touches my nipples hard under my blue silk slip, I'm not there. I'm watching the moon fill the pukas, the holes in my mural. The pukas are white, white so dark in this dim light that you have to believe in the white for it to be real. You have to carry the light in your heart.

ON THE BEACH

When I wake up, Sammy's gone. The Scout and the boat are missing too. I thought he was going swimming with us this morning, but I guess he's not. Annabel will be disappointed when she finds out he went fishing without asking her to go along.

Sammy never takes women fishing, only men. Beatrice says that it's a chauvinist-pig thing to do, but she doesn't care about fishing and neither do I. The last place we want to be is on a boat. Plus I like when he's gone. I don't have to listen to him grumble, I can hang the laundry in the garage and play my music on the stereo real loud.

I put on my Paul Anka album, the one that Beatrice gave me to keep when she and Wick moved out. Paul Anka has a sweet, high voice, not like an opera singer but like a boy next door singing over the fence. "Put Your Head on My Shoulders." "You Are My Destiny." If Mits Todama sang to me like that, Gracie would have to lock the gate. I sing along as I scrub the toilet, the sink, the bathtub, and then I run the vacuum down the hall and into the living room, where Lurline is talking to the TV with the sound turned off.

Annabel Lee opens her bedroom door and staggers out into the hall. Her hair lies flat in back, where she has slept. Her eyes look wide awake as always, but the rest of her is still groggy.

She groans. How can anybody sleep with so much racket? Don't tell me you're cleaning house on a Sunday morning? It's only seven o'clock!

I switch the vacuum off and turn down the stereo.

Forget it, she says. I'm up. I'll sleep on the beach. I can't go back to bed now that I'm awake.

When she hears Sammy has gone fishing, she looks relieved. She says, That's good. I don't have to put my face on right away.

I plug in the percolator and say I hope she doesn't mind having fish for dinner. Fish and leftovers from my birthday party. But Annabel doesn't want to think about food. All she wants is black coffee and orange juice. She says, after all she ate last night, she doesn't need to eat for the rest of the time she's here. I want to remind her that she hardly ate anything last night, just picked at her food. I want to remind her about the calories in the alcohol she consumes, the alcohol that drags her down this morning, but of course I don't. I notice that underneath her eyes, her skin is dark, almost like it's bruised. She sees me staring, so I say, That face-lift must have hurt.

No, she says, I'm paying the price for spending so much time in the sun when I was younger. The Florida sun is different, more yellow, more acidic. She says the plastic surgeon could take away her wrinkles, but not the color of her skin, and that's why she has to wear heavy makeup all the time or dark glasses, even when she goes swimming.

She's been here for only two days now and already I'm counting.

It's different talking to her than to Wick or Frankie or even Beatrice. I'm afraid to say too much, because once I get going, she'll pump me until I'm reading Empty. With Annabel, it's better not to even start. But there's so much I want to know myself, so much I have to ask. The trick is to get her talking about herself. That way she leaves me alone.

So after I pour her a second cup of coffee, I begin with her boyfriend Judd. Is it serious with him? Is she going to get married again?

She says, Marry Judd? And spoil everything?

She tells me Judd is a playboy, and the only reason they've stayed together this long is because she's still married to Coy.

All these years and they've never gotten divorced.

She says even Wick doesn't know that they're not divorced, and now it's too late to tell him. He won't understand. She says, It just happened. I didn't plan it this way. And then I realized that if I don't get divorced, then I can't do anything foolish—like get married again.

But didn't he want—I mean, I thought Coy fell in love with somebody else.

Yeah, but he wasn't going to *marry* the guy. Besides, he had more than one lover. I just told you about the one.

You didn't tell me. You told Sammy.

Well, how could I? You were a nut case after that flash flood. But that's why I went to Maui. To tell you. You know that.

She's starting on me. I get up from the table. Walk over to the refrigerator.

What do you want to eat for lunch? I ask her. I have to pack food for the beach.

There you go again, she says. You're using that *f* word.

All the food in this house and more of it coming. What Wick and Beatrice are bringing from my parents' house, the leftovers we couldn't take home last night because we were too busy dancing.

Too much trouble, she says. She wants to buy plate lunch when we get to the park, so we don't have to take a cooler or pick up ice.

The only thing I won't let her talk me out of bringing is bread for the pigeons I feed every time we go to Waikiki or Ala Moana. The birds eat right out of my hand and try to sit on my lap, as if they know me and remember how I used to wait for them to come back home. I have a plastic bag of Love's bread in the freezer ready to go. The ends of the bread that nobody wants.

I put the bread into my plastic purple and yellow-daisy beach bag, along with a bottle of suntan lotion and two towels for Lurline and me. Annabel packs her own bag, a big straw one. She doesn't want a towel, because she has a terry-cloth robe that can double dip. We take only what we need from our purses. Driver's license and insurance cards. Keys. Kleenex. Gum. Lipstick. Comb. Money—four quarters and one ten-dollar bill apiece. I slip in an extra ten since

we're buying lunch. No wallets. We put everything in Baggies to keep them dry.

Look at us, says Annabel. We're bag ladies.

Bag ladies changing into our swimsuits. Me in my new swimsuit and T-shirt. The blue of the swimsuit fades from dark to light the farther up you go. Plus there are fish on the top. The whole thing is like a big fish tank.

Annabel decides to wear her turquoise bikini first. She shows me her hysterectomy scar again. It's horizontal, like a tiger smiling, a tiger with a beard. She says her whole life changed when she became like a man at the age of thirty-eight. No periods. No sanitary napkins. She could do whatever she wanted at any time without the worry and the fuss.

Water-ski, jog, dance, she says. And you know what else.

I'm glad Sammy's not home to see her prancing around the house in her new bikini. She doesn't want to put the rest of her clothes on until the very last minute, because it's already too hot. She wants to know how come we don't have air conditioning in our house. She couldn't live without it in Florida, that's for sure. She says I can try on the see-through yellow blouse she's going to wear over her bikini, but I don't feel like taking off my T-shirt after looking at her. She has matching yellow shorts and a turquoise chiffon scarf for tying down her straw hat. When I see her bring out a pair of high-heeled sandals, I add a pair of rubber slippers to my bag, for when her feet get sore later on.

Lurline sits outside on the back porch, waiting. I don't even have to tell her where we're going. That girl can smell the beach. She's wearing the orange polka-dot bikini that she loves. What Beatrice found marked down four times at Ritz. She wears my chiffon duster over her bathing suit, even though I told her it was for sleeping, not for going out. She wants a see-through top, like her aunty's.

When I walk to the garage to get the beach mats, I spot a manila envelope lying on the ground. It's addressed to Sammy and it's ripped down the side, the way Sammy opens envelopes. Inside are some papers that I recognize. The birth certificate of a Japanese boy,

Hirao Murata, whose parents were Hideo and Michiko Murata, and papers for the adoption of Hirao Murata by Sammy's Chinese parents, Woo Wah Tuck and Florence Nyet Yuen Lee. There's a copy of Sammy's birth certificate too, the one he already has, with the same birthday as Hirao Murata and with his Chinese parents' names. It's like a jigsaw puzzle. The pieces look almost the same, but they're not. These are the same papers Sammy's Aunty Ethel showed to me that day she came to our house. But there is one thing I haven't seen: this letter from her lawyer.

Dear Samuel Woo [it reads],

Your maternal aunt, Mrs. Delbert Pang, née Ethel N.M. Lee, requested that my office deliver the enclosed documents to you in the regrettable event that circumstances beyond her control prevented her from presenting them to you herself. The papers herein convey familial information that Mrs. Pang has held for safekeeping at the request of her brothers and sisters. Her untimely death in our motherland providing sufficient cause herewith, I am therefore releasing said items to you pursuant to her instructions. As you can see, these documents confirm that you and Mr. Hirao Murata are believed to be one and the same.

Please accept my humble condolences on the passing of your aunt. If you have any questions or if I may be of further assistance, please do not hesitate to call.

I remain
Yours very truly,
Herbert Y.C. Ching, Esq.

When Wick and Beatrice arrive, I am lying down on the couch, in front of the fan. Annabel is mopping up the hallway, where I threw up. My head feels like a gun went off inside and my skull was

too hard for the bullets to come out. There were two shots. One aimed to the left, the other to the right.

I'm deep in a box canyon. Voices all around me. Ambush, and there's no way out.

My God, Wick, do you know what this means? I'm only half Chinese. The other half of me is Japanese. I can't believe it. Wait till Toad finds out.

What a way to find out! Why do they wait until now? I don't blame your mother one bit for being upset.

But how did he get this second birth certificate? It looks like the real thing.

What do they do, just fake these things? My God!

Poor Uncle Sammy. He must be upset. I wonder if it was a good idea for him to go fishing.

Better that than stay home and drink. This is what he gets for being prejudiced anyway. He hates the Japanese.

How can you say that, Beet? He has Japanese friends. Like Mits Todama.

Mits Todama is our neighbor, Wick. He has to be nice to him.

I can't believe you're talking like this about your father, Beatrice.

Yeah, Beet. Think of how he's feeling right now.

Think of how I'm feeling too. This just blows my mind.

No, Lurline. No, we can't go to the beach right now. Beet, you better explain to her what's going on.

Leave Wick alone. Let go his arm. Let go!

Slap. Lurline crying, climbing on the couch.

Maybe we should go look for him. Alice, what you do think?

He's probably already out on the water. He could be out there all day.

Oh, I hope he doesn't do anything stupid.

He wouldn't, would he? Mommy?

Well, I might as well get out of this swimsuit. We can go swimming some other time. It's too hot by now. We'll just get sunburned.

Are you sure, Mom? I can take you down to Ala Moana, if you want.

No, I can't leave Alice by herself.

Go.

You sure?

Go.

Why don't you come with us too. The fresh air will be good for you.

No. You go.

Listen, Wick, take your mother. I'll stay home with Mom.

What about Lurline?

Fuck Lurline. Take her too! See if I care.

Oh great.

Beatrice. Go.

Mommy.

Everybody. Go.

Aunty Alice, are you having one of them migraines?

Mmm.

Here, Alice, take these. They're just some mild tranquillizers. They'll help you relax.

Oh, Mom, don't give her that shit.

You watch your mouth, young man.

She has pills of her own, Aunty Annabel. Where are they, Mom? In your room?

Maybe she can lie on the beach.

No. Go.

She's right. We're making too much noise. Mommy, do you want to stay out here or in your room?

Aunty Alice, shall I carry the birdcage in there for you?

Put the scarf on top so they don't make noise.

Here are your pills, Mom. Just take two.

We'll just go for a quick swim, Alice, and then we'll bring back some lunch. What do you want to eat?

She can't eat when she's like that. Mommy, we're going, okay? Take a nap, okay?

•   •   •

So quiet. The house sighing now that everybody's gone. It's just me and my parakeets, Petey and Tweety. When I pull the scarf off the cage, they're so happy to see me. They chatter and squawk and fly from branch to branch.

All I have to do is say the same words over and over. Nothing too fancy. Frankie says you have to keep it simple. They're not parrots after all. But first I have to separate them, just like in school, so the boy doesn't try to learn what I want to teach the girl.

I open up the cage door and stick my finger in. Tweety is too scared to come close, but Petey hops right on. Thinks he's so smart. I close the cage door and take him into my bathroom. Put the toilet cover down. Fill a little water in the basin, for him to drink. He's scared, but when he sees the water, he's happy again.

Hi y'all, I say to him. Hi y'all. Hi y'all. Hi y'all.

I'm crocheting an ocean and all the little fishies I can think of. All I have to do is make a big blue blob with white ruffles for the waves. Doesn't need to be a perfect oval. Better tight in some places and loose in others, so it doesn't lie flat, just like the water. Then fish in all different colors. Tack them to the blob. Don't even need to buy new yarn. I can use the scraps I've been collecting all these years. It's not for the wall, it's for the floor. So you have to cross the ocean to get from the door to my futon.

While I crochet, I talk to Tweety. Nice and soft, so she listens. Just two words, but not what I taught Petey. I repeat the words again and again. Put down my yarn and my crochet hook. Lie down. Listen, Tweety, to what I have been saying for forty years. I need you to help me. Only two words.

Slop Boy, Slop Boy, coming for us.
Hi y'all, hi y'all, birdie fish girls.

My silence, a knife in his back, in her back.

Slop Boy, Slop Boy, flying in the sky.
Birdie fish nose, birdie fish toes.
Slop Boy, coming for his birdie fish girls.

. . .

Who am I protecting? Why am I hiding?

What kind of friend am I? What kind of wife? What kind of woman?

The tide comes in, the tide goes out.

And me, Alice, still stuck on the beach.

The back door slams. Lurline flings herself on my futon and me. Wet swimsuit and all. Taste her. Like salt and strawberry soda water.

The house like a plate-lunch wagon. Curry stew. Teriyaki beef. Chicken katsu. Macaroni salad. Kimchee. Daikon. An extra plate of curry stew in case Sammy's come home.

But no Sammy. Sammy gone, Sammy no stay. Cover the plate up good with foil. Put it in the icebox. Take out the leftovers. Heat it all up. The chicken. The duck. The chef-special noodles. Serve the ice cream and cake. Big piece of cake that Annabel saved for me. Too excited to eat it last night. Devil's-food cake with cream-cheese frosting and scarlet letters on top, spelling my name.

Hard Head. Tight Lip.

When Annabel comes into the bedroom to keep me company, I'm ready to confess. It all rushes out. What Aunty Ethel told me. What I was supposed to tell Sammy but didn't. And now he's alone, he's drowning, he's lost.

She says, Pass me that crochet hook. I'll help you make one of those fish.

I blow my nose, then give her a number five hook plus two balls of yarn, one orange, one pink.

She says, It's amazing what you end up doing when you have too much time on your hands. The first time Coy stayed out all night, I began to crochet a doily, a round one, like the kind your mother used to make. The stitches were all lopsided, and it wouldn't lie flat, but I didn't care. When it reached doily size, I kept on going. I figured it could be a tablecloth. He still went out, and then I ran out of cotton crochet yarn, so I had to use string. String was cheaper anyway and already wound into a ball. It looked stupid, but I didn't care. Before I knew it, I was thinking even bigger. A bedspread. A canopy. A tent.

As she's talking, I'm thinking that fish is going to end up bigger than my ocean in the end.

But she picks up the scissors, clips off the yarn, and hands the fish over to me on the end of the crochet hook.

Here, she says. One fish kabob. I know when to stop now.

Then she stands up. She says, It's not your fault, Alice. That family is sick. Where does Sammy keep his cigarettes? That's what you need. A really good vice.

My best times have been my guiltiest. My worst times too. What I don't understand is why it doesn't always have to do with what's good or what's bad. Take love, for example. I have felt bad but not guilty, and I have felt guilty but not bad. What really makes me sick right now is that I'm not just feeling guilty and bad. What I'm also feeling for Sammy is pity. Pity.

Maybe that's why Annabel gets along so well with him. Because she doesn't have to live with him. Because she can walk away anytime, and he knows it.

Nobody has an appetite when suppertime comes. We heat up all the leftovers in the microwave, but most of it goes right back into the refrigerator or into the garbage can. When Frankie comes by with Emily, every single light in the house is turned on, but we're all sitting outside in the garage, watching TV. Mits Todama is out with the boys, even though it's Sunday, so Gracie and Amy Toad come over to sit with us too. We jump when we hear the car drive up, and then sit back down when we see Frankie's Datsun.

After we tell Frankie what happened, he says, Don't you think you better call the cops? He never comes home from fishing after dark.

No cops, I tell him. Sammy hates cops.

Annabel says, Oh, Alice. He's right. Listen to him.

Tell you what, says Frankie. Wick and I can drive out to Kaneohe and look for him. If somebody can watch Emily for me.

Beatrice says, But I want to go too.

Amy Toad says, I'll watch her. You go with them.

We can't all fit in my Datsun.

Then why did you buy that stupid car?

Beet, don't. We can go in my VW.

As if that's bigger! You guys!

That's enough, says Annabel. Just take the Fairmont and go. Toad, you go too, so they don't fight. If you don't find him, we'll call the police. Here, Emily, come to Aunty. That's a good girl. Look at her, isn't she sweet? Ouch, don't grab my hair like that.

Frankie calls from the dock. There's no sign of Sammy or the Scout or the boat. They're coming back home.

Annabel calls the cops.

Well, let's see. He's about five-nine, five-ten. How much does he weigh? How do I know? Alice? Just put down 150. That's close enough. Doesn't it say all this on his driver's license? The car? Well, all depends. It's supposed to be a Scout, but the roof is Toyota. Welded on backwards. Or is it Dodge? Wait. No, that's the bumper. What? Green. Sort of lime, but closer to apple. It's a very odd shade. No, I don't know the license number. Can't you get that from your computer? He's not my husband. I'm just calling for my friend. My name is Whitlow, with an *h*. Can't you just look for the boat? There can't be that many of them out there right now. What kind of boat? Alice? Here, you talk to them. Go ahead. Just tell them what you know. Don't be shy. Talk.

Talk, that's all we do, Annabel and me. Talk and drink and talk some more. We sit in the kitchen, not in my room, because we're getting too old to sit for long with our legs crossed. I'm tired of being in my room anyway. Yarn all over the place. So many pieces started and not completed. All I want to do is vegetate. Vegetate. That's a good

word that Beatrice taught me. Annabel is a carrot drinking Southern
Comfort, and I'm a tomato imbibing—another good word—sloe gin
and 7-Up. Sloe gin isn't slow, not like I thought, and I like the sweet
taste and the color. Fuschia.

We haven't had a chance to visit like this in a long, long time. Not
since the war. We haven't had time. We haven't been alone. Even
now the house is full. Wick, Beatrice, Amy Toad, and Lurline are
camped out on the living-room floor. Gracie went home to wait for
Mits. Frankie left too, with the baby. He swore he wouldn't say anything to his mother, and I promised to call him as soon as we heard
something. The TV is still going full blast. Annabel tells me to leave
it on so they can't hear us talk.

She's full of good stories. About the people she meets while selling
houses, about the men she went out with before Judd. Even her stories
that aren't funny make us laugh. We have to keep our voices down so
we don't wake up the kids, but we're pretty good at laughing without
making too much noise. Raise the eyebrows, drop the jaw, throw back
your head. It's our Priory training. From the hours we spent sitting in
chapel, lying awake in the dorm, hiding from the Sisters.

We start to get a little sentimental when we talk about school and
the war that followed. We sound like the Priory grads I hate to run
into, the ones who only talk sweet about our alma mater. We're bad
Priory girls, Annabel and me. We don't even go to church anymore.
But as we remember our pranks and lies and the sneaking around,
I'm thinking we're no different than Beatrice and Amy Toad when
they talk about their hippie days. Or Sammy with his war escapades.
We have our own battlefields. We survive in our own way.

Annabel tells me about the boardinghouse she lived in after Coy
left her. She didn't want to work full-time because of Wick, so the
boardinghouse seemed like a good idea. That way they would have a
place to live, and she could cook and do chores during the day and
let one of the boarders babysit at night, in case she got a dancing job.
But she soon discovered how naive that was when she noticed how
the men stared at Wick. He was a beautiful child, but he was too

trusting. Even at school he was like that. Making friends quickly. Always following the other children home.

That's when she decided to move back to Florida. It meant giving up her dream, taking a job as a secretary, and leaving Wick with her sister, Emma. Three strikes and she was out. Coy would never return to Florida, and she didn't want him to. She lied to her family. She told them Coy ran away with a waitress from a truck stop, just like what I made up. We shared the same mind, even so far apart. Then she called me. On Maui.

But I was all a wreck on Maui.

You're telling me. But I must say you had a pretty good reason. Not everybody gets washed away in a flash flood.

That's not funny. Don't make me laugh.

But she laughs anyway, and so do I.

I was so jealous of you, she says, wiping her eyes.

Me? I was jealous of you.

Why?

I heard you. You and Sammy. I heard you in the kitchen, late at night, on Maui.

We were just talking. Why?

You sure that was all?

What else? Oh, Alice, you didn't think we—

I nodded.

Oh boy, she said. You mean to tell me, all this time. I don't believe it. You know, I've gone out with married men, but that was the one time I couldn't do it. Not that I didn't want to. I was so horny. But you would have found out. He's way too honest. Takes after you. Oh, Alice. Don't you know me by now?

Sometimes I think I don't know you at all.

But you do. You just don't approve is all.

I didn't tell you about Coy.

You mean what happened that night at my house? Out in the bomb shelter?

You knew?

Sure. He told me.

What did he tell you?

Enough. It's okay. I'm glad. I was thrilled in fact. Not at first, but later on. I think it helps you understand me better. Why we lasted so long.

I knew right away what she meant. It was the real reason why she didn't sleep with Sammy, not then, and not last night, because he wanted her too much. That's why she married Coy, why she's still married to him. Because, in his own peculiar way, Coy knew how to love her. They were perfect for one another. Both of them able to be only so close.

Maybe that's how it is with Sammy too. He's afraid I might go away, so he keeps himself far. Maybe that's why I didn't want to tell him he was adopted. Because then I'd have to listen, and I'm not sure I can anymore.

All we had to do was talk. Annabel and me. But did we do it?

Even now, I'm listening with only one ear.

Sometimes far is where you have to go.

The light in the kitchen flickers for a moment. Then the house goes silent and dark. Then the power comes back on again and the TV starts blasting. Then off and on again. Three times. Everybody who was sleeping wakes up. The rain starts pounding on the roof.

Wow, says Annabel. What was that?

God must have heard us.

What? she roared. Oh, we're in trouble now!

I said, Tell me, whatever happened to Wren? That guy who got you pregnant.

Wren? Annabel shrieks. Wren?

Wick comes into the kitchen. He says, What's going on? Did they find him?

Find who? We both answer at once.

Uncle Sammy, who else?

Annabel and I burst out laughing.

He stares at us. Beatrice wanders into the kitchen, rubbing her eyes. She says, Is he home yet?

It's a parade, firecrackers. Sammy lost, and Annabel and me, we're both laughing. Hysterical.

Finally, Beatrice says, How can you two be so wide awake? I'm hungry. Don't you have anything to eat in this house besides left-overs? All I want is something simple. I'm sick of all the rich food.

Three o'clock in the morning and Annabel and I are punchy from all the talking and drinking and laughing. We stumble all over the kitchen trying to figure out what to eat. Tupperware containers open, tops all over the counter, on the floor. The drawers, the cup-boards, the refrigerator door banging.

Finally Beatrice says, Why don't you two go and lie down, and Wick and I will fix breakfast. We'll call you when it's ready.

Annabel and I go into my room and collapse on the futon. I intro-duce her to my parakeets again. This time I tell her their names, and then I try to get them to talk.

Slop Boy. Come on, you can say it. Hi y'all. Hi y'all.

When she hears what I'm teaching them, she screams so loud, the light goes on in the Todamas' house, and before we know it, Gracie and Mits are knocking on the door.

We're in the kitchen, eating scrambled eggs, Vienna sausage, and toast when the call from the police finally comes. They've found Sammy's Scout and the boat parked in an alley in Palama, but they don't know where he is. The cooler on the boat is full of dead fish and empty beer cans, and there's a whiskey bottle on the floor of the Scout.

I call up Frankie, like I promised. He comes by to get Wick, and they go to Palama to wait for Sammy, so the neighborhood kids don't climb all over the Scout or steal fishing gear or parts off the boat. So they can be there when Sammy comes back.

Awake and still eating, awake and still talking. Gracie went home to get more food for us. Cold fried chicken, hot broth with udon noo-dles and slivers of pink fishcake, fresh slices of orange.

I am so hungry. Annabel too. Both of us so, so hungry.

What did you do with that tent? I ask her. The canopy.

Annabel says, You mean the tablecloth. I gave up before it got that big.

Everybody's listening, but they don't know what we're talking about.

I stuffed it in a trunk, she says. That trunk I hated, that belonged to Louis. I sent the whole thing to my father and his third wife. For a wedding gift.

Oh no!

I'm laughing, holding my stomach, which is sore from eating and drinking, from being awake all night.

Terrible, yeah? But felt so good. She even sent me a thank-you note.

Then she's laughing too, and everyone else is staring at us, wondering what the hell is going on, when the phone rings again. Like it's our laughing that makes it ring.

It's Sammy this time. The police have arrested him for peeking into somebody's living-room window. He's slurring his words. They made him take a breath test, but he says it doesn't count, because he wasn't driving. He's more worried about the Scout and the boat than anything else.

He says, I guess you better call a lawyer. Tell him I never steal nothing. I was just looking for my mother and father. I got a right under the Constitution. Tell Wick go look up for me which one.

When I hang up the phone, Beatrice says, We can call my lawyer, the one who handled my divorce, but Annabel says, You think your father wants a woman for a lawyer? Beatrice shakes her head.

Call her anyway, says Annabel. Ask her if she knows somebody who wants to defend a Peeping Tom.

Nobody says anything when Sammy saunters up the driveway and gives us that why-are-you-looking look. Mits Todama follows close behind. Both of them looking as if they stopped somewhere on the way home. I knew I should have gone down to the police station to get him, shouldn't have let Mits go by himself, but Mits insisted that Sammy would be embarrassed if everybody showed up.

Sammy goes straight to the garage to check the boat. Wick and Frankie have already hosed it down. The cooler is sitting in the middle of the driveway, because it stinks so bad. Sammy tells the boys to take the whole thing to the dump. Cooler and fish. Throw it all away. Then he takes a shower and goes upstairs to the apartment, without eating the bowl of udon noodles that I fixed for him. All he wants to do is sleep.

Beatrice calls Sammy's boss at Hickam. She puts on her customs inspector voice and tells the boss that Sammy has caught the Asian flu and has to stay home for at least a week. Then she and Wick leave, and everybody goes home who has another home, and I take the phone off the hook.

Sammy sleeps all day, and so do the rest of us, until it gets too hot in Lurline's room and she comes into my room to wake me up. Annabel wakes up too when she hears the record playing.

The Beatles? I hate the Beatles, she says. We might as well go to the graveyard. This day is shot.

She calls Wick and tells him to meet us there.

I'm hoping we can find the graves. There are a lot more people buried in that cemetery now. Two hills full. As I remember, we have to count from the second plumeria tree, then five graves down and fifteen across, in order to get to her mother's grave. We can visit Annabel's father's grave at the same time. Sing Lee is buried right next to his wife, Dora Kaiulani.

But Annabel says, No, that's where we went wrong the last time. It's the third plumeria tree. You always get the numbers mixed up.

I can't concentrate, because Lurline is stepping right in the middle of all the graves. All that bad luck and she doesn't need it. Fortunately, Wick finds Dora Kaiulani's grave without even counting. He says he remembers where it was from the one time Annabel took him there, when he was only ten years old. Plus he looked for a more recent tombstone, the one marking his grandfather's grave.

He says, I figured this had to be the one, because of all the incense and candles and bowls of food. He had all those wives and children, and you said they were real Chinese.

Annabel shakes her head. She says, From now on, Son, this is your job. You can remember for us.

On both graves they put torch ginger, which Wick picked up at Tantalus, plus some orchids from my back yard. Then Annabel set out our bowls of food, most of them in front of her mother's grave. Dora Kaiulani must be really hungry, looking at all that food on her husband's grave for so many years, but none on hers. Our food is not leftovers from my birthday, and not takeout from Fat Lee Wo, since the restaurant is long gone, but oranges for Sing Lee and fresh, hot manapua for Dora Kaiulani which we bought in Chinatown from a restaurant whose name we do not utter out of respect for the dead.

On the way back to the car, I ask Annabel, Why did you guys name Wick after Coy's father? Coy hated his father.

It was my idea, she says. I wanted Coy to feel like he wasn't alone. Plus I thought it would keep him with me always. If the boy had his name, Coy wouldn't go very far.

But it didn't work.

Didn't it?

She looks behind us at Wick, who is carrying Beatrice in his arms and Lurline on his back and staggering up the hill.

Look at that load, she says. How can he carry both of them all by himself?

Next day, Sammy hires a private eye. He wants to find his parents, if they're still alive, in case they have something for him to inherit. He doesn't want to know about brothers or sisters, and he doesn't want them to know about him, so they won't come after his estate, his money, his jewelry. His jewelry, of course, meaning mine.

He won't talk about being Japanese. All he says is that it explains a lot. The way he was treated. Like a second-class citizen.

But that's all. When Annabel asks him how he feels, he says, I feel like a Scotch on the rocks, how about you?

Beatrice says, This is so weird. Now he's into denial.

Wick says, But think of what it's like, finding out everybody's been lying to you for so many years.

Beatrice says, I can't imagine.

Annabel says, We need a trip. Let's go to Maui.

But Wick can't take the time off. He's already in trouble for not showing up for work the night Sammy was missing.

Beatrice says, Well, count me in anyway. Me and Toad. And Emily.

Annabel asks Sammy, because I won't ask him myself, and he says, No, cannot. Private eye could call any day now.

Annabel says, Well, Alice, I guess it's you, me, and the girls.

Wick says, Maybe I'll come anyway. Let them fire me. I can always get another job.

Oh no, says Beatrice. You and I can go to Maui some other time, by ourselves. Don't get mad, but I think this trip needs to be just us women.

Annabel looks at me. Well, she says, you coming?

Sammy looks at me too. He expects me to stay home and keep him company while he's waiting for the private eye to report. All of them waiting for my answer, but I'm not talking. Just going into my room, taking my birdcage along.

We catch an early plane that morning. Leave the house at 5 a.m., before Sammy wakes up. I write him a note. Tape it to the boat. Hamburger casserole in freezer. Heat one hour at 350°. Frankie coming for dinner. Back tomorrow night.

Annabel reserves a suite for us at a fancy hotel in Kaanapali, but the beach in front of the hotel is filled with too many beautiful women.

This is like *Love Boat*, says Annabel. And look at these men, all panting like dogs. Let's get out of here.

She wants to go exploring. Not around Hana, because I won't go, but out to this beach that Amy Toad tells us about—Little Makena. So we drive out past Lahaina, past Kihei, until the road turns rocky and shakes up the rental car. It's starting to give me the creeps—this road and the direction we're taking. I don't want to go out to where the Big Water hit.

But then Amy Toad yells, Stop. Back up, we just passed the trail.

We have to hike through bushes and weeds to get to the beach. I can't believe I'm doing this, and for what? Little Makena Beach lies right next to Big Makena Beach. So? And then we see why the girls are smiling. Everybody on Little Makena Beach is naked. It's a nude beach, where all the hippies go.

Annabel is thrilled. She says, This is great! How come I didn't know about this?

She takes off everything but her dark glasses. So does Amy Toad, and so does Beatrice, and of course, Lurline follows what the rest of them do. Beatrice undresses Emily too.

Beatrice says, Just close your eyes, Mom. It's not that bad if you can't see them looking at you. That's what I did in the dorm at school.

What?

Oh come on, says Annabel. Just let it all hang out.

I am. My mouth is wide open, my tongue is dangling. I'm gawking, that's what I'm doing. I don't want to look at these naked men, but I can't help it. Annabel's happy because there aren't as many women on this beach. There are more of *them* than us.

The girls take turns rubbing sun block on each other, on Annabel and the baby too. Rubbing and laughing and making jokes. I take off my T-shirt so Beatrice can rub lotion on my back.

Amy Toad says, Cool swimsuit. I haven't seen that one before, have I? Look at all the fish! I love it!

Beatrice says, Yeah, it's the real thing. The original tank suit.

Shut up, I tell them. Stop talking about my suit.

Annabel says, Well, take it off, then. Nobody's looking. Besides, I'm almost a black belt. Did I tell you? I'll just kick them in the balls if they give us trouble, like this.

The way she kicks the air, her legs still pretty strong for her age. The way she lies down, not on her front but on her back, so everything shows. Her tiger scar roars at anyone who dares to come close.

But the men aren't even looking at us. We're the only ones who are paying any attention.

Annabel and the girls calm down at last. Beatrice wants us all to be quiet so Emily can take a nap. Under the umbrella so the sun doesn't roast her.

The sun, like a broiler oven. I'm the only one who is blue like the sky because of my fish-tank suit. The ocean green, then blue, then black, the farther out you go. The waves are way too big for me, but I'm not going in, so I don't care. All I have to do is keep Lurline on the beach.

But Lurline isn't running into the water. She's lying on her back like Annabel Lee. Her eyes closed. Her long hair fanned out around her. Her arms and legs wide open. Why do I worry about her? At least with her nothing changes.

My eyes are tired from all the brightness. I have to close them, just for a minute. Just for a minute, I don't have to worry. All I have to do is take off one strap. Push it down over my shoulder. The other one is easier. It just follows.

MAKAI

Annabel Lee flies from Honolulu to the island of Martinique in the French West Indies. Her doctor friend, Judd, has rented the imperial suite, where Prince Napoleon once stayed. She promises to send me a postcard and a photograph of Judd, maybe even one of him sunbathing, if she can sneak a picture. He's a little self-conscious, she says, because of his bald head. After that, she's flying to Miami to coach some seniors for a ballroom-dancing exhibition. And then she'd better start selling real estate again before her money runs out.

Why don't you move back home? I ask her. You can sell houses here and go dancing at the Ala Wai. I know a few senior citizens who could use a lot of help.

She says, Why don't you go back to school and get your nursing degree? Might as well have a title to go with what you've been putting up with for all these years.

Touché, I tell her. That's my latest favorite word. That keeps us both laughing, in spite of our tears.

Sammy's been sleeping downstairs since Annabel left, since the private eye told him there's no family alive. His Murata parents passed away over thirty years ago, and the neighbors say the children are gone too—a son, who would have been Sammy's older brother, dead from leukemia in his early twenties, and a daughter, killed in a car accident while on her honeymoon. No grandchildren, no heirs, no estate.

Sammy's really worried now. Bad genes in the family. Bad luck too.

Beatrice comes home crying. Frankie wants them to have joint custody, and she can't say no. If they take turns keeping Emily for two weeks at a time, then it will be easier when the girl starts school. Now Beatrice has all this responsibility, plus Wick wants a baby of his own. But he doesn't like staying home with Emily, and he gets mad when they can't go out. All he can think of is surfing and playing music. They had a big fight when he came home with a guitar. Here she's trying to save money and he wants to learn slack key. She kicked him out and told him not to come back until he gets his shit together. That means get a real job, not all this fooling around, pretending he is some kind of royal act. She doesn't want a beach bum for a husband, and she won't give up her career for changing one more set of diapers.

Beatrice is jealous too, because Frankie has a live-in babysitter, Robin, who turns out to be a girl after all. Too young to be a hippie, but she likes to think she's one. Hair too long, halter tops, no bra, peasant skirts. She's spoiling Emily, Beatrice says. Now Emily always wants to be carried, and she won't go to sleep until late. Frankie has another roommate too, a former classmate, now a stockbroker, Quentin Liu. Beatrice is suspicious, wonders if this is some kind of ménage à trois.

My ears are burning from this eruption, this explosion of hurt and accusation. I don't want to hear. I have enough, enough. She says all that to tell me this: she wants to move back home. Into the apartment over the garage, since nobody's using it anyway. She can't afford to pay for the condo all by herself. Plus—and my eyes are closing now—she needs somebody to babysit.

Sammy's not talking. It worries me, the way he sits outside in the dark, not even grumbling to himself. He doesn't go to the Red Carpet

Room with my brother Joe-Joe, just stays home and drinks. He takes the boat out every weekend, but doesn't bring home much fish. Sometimes Wick goes with him. They meet down at the dock, so Beatrice doesn't know. Wick tells me all this when he comes by for coffee while Beatrice is at work. He says Sammy's still catching fish, just letting most of them go. They don't talk, but Wick says, Don't worry, he'll say something when he's ready.

Me, I just nod and nod and nod.

Wick invites me to have lunch at his bachelor pad in Waikiki. It's a studio in an old apartment building that's about to come down, so the rent is low. The landlord is the uncle of a guy Wick met while surfing. Wick says Lurline can come too, but Lurline can't keep a secret, so I send her over to Gracie Todama and go to visit him by myself.

I take the bus. It winds past watercress farms and sugarcane fields on its way into town. Past the pineapple canneries, the pool halls at Aala Park, then slows down in traffic in Chinatown. The fabric store is still there on River Street, but the dance studio is now a butcher shop. Tourists, servicemen, and shoppers stroll along the busy sidewalks. The markets are crowded with baskets of vegetables and fruit, fish stare from beds of ice, chickens and ducks dangle from hooks. A woman bends over to feed her young daughter a piece of red barbecued pork. An old man squats in front of a shoeshine stand, picking his teeth.

Wick is living like a monk. Simplifying his lifestyle is what he tells me. Sleeping on a lauhala mat on the floor, rolled-up sweatshirt for a pillow. The rest of his clothes neatly folded in two piles—T-shirts in one, shorts in another. Underwear in a shoe box. Slippers and a pair of brown loafers by the door. A short red hapi coat hanging over the only chair. What's spooky is the mirror that covers one whole wall. Wick says a dancer used to live there, but he's dead now. Drug overdose.

I ask Wick, Have you heard from your father? Beatrice told me you wrote to him.

No, he says. Not yet.

Now is a good time to give him the presents. A new silver whistle on a strong chain, plus a crocheted dishcloth.

He fixes me ramen for lunch. Plus there's sushi and nishime that he bought from the market at Ala Moana. We sit on the floor to eat, on cushions, Japanese style. He made the low table out of an old surfboard—a long one. He cut off the ends, sanded it flat, screwed on coffee cans for legs, and painted the whole thing black with wavy white, red, and yellow lines. Abstract, but still you can see it's supposed to remind you of the ocean.

He says, I got the idea one day while I was lying on the beach. It's what you see when you close your eyes in the sun. The colors inside your head.

I'm thinking, This boy is mine, his mother is me.

He says, Don't tell Beet, but I'm taking hula lessons. I'm going to start my own company when I save enough money from tips. I'm going to design custom-made tours, so people can do whatever they want. Surf, hike, dance, play music—even catch fish, if I can get Uncle Sammy to help. I'll call it Treasure Island Adventures. Do you think Beatrice will like that?

I can visit him only now and then, when I'm not watching Emily, when Gracie takes Lurline off my hands, when everybody else is at work. Sometimes he helps me practice my ballroom dancing, so I won't feel stupid when I go to the clubhouse, *if* I ever go there. He's very good, of course, since Annabel taught him, but he hasn't danced this way for a while, at least not fancy like this.

It doesn't feel like lying, going there. It's more like hope—my true Golden Age Club; two members so far. He wants to know everything, so what I remember has a place to go, and he's tracing his Hawaiian roots back to the royal days and has something new to share with me every time. A messenger is what I am. A translator too. And the mirror on the wall reminds me that it's only temporary, until my boy leaves the nest.

•   •   •

Annabel sends me photographs. One of Judd, who is bald on top, like she said, but hairy everywhere else, and muscular too. A handsome man, although not very tall, shorter than Sammy and younger too, and he's got two young women in bikinis holding on to his arms. Must be French-Indian girls, very pretty. There's a picture of Annabel too, dancing with the diving instructor. On the back she writes, He had flippers on his feet, I swear.

Then three more pictures. Older. One taken when Wick was a baby. It's Coy, throwing Wick in the air, both of them with their arms open wide and big smiles on their faces, as if they are hugging the sky. Another of Annabel next to the dress that hung on her bedroom wall up in Maunalani Heights. Her tutu's wedding dress. All you can see is Annabel's head, because she's sitting on the floor, and the empty dress is still without a body. And last of all, a picture of Annabel with her mother, Dora Kaiulani, just their heads, with their cheeks pressed together so they look like Siamese twins.

I can't believe she sent me the originals. I can tell because of the wrinkles and bent-up edges, from when she looked at them again and again. She trusted them to the post office, and now she trusts me to keep them for her. Or is it for Wick, when he's ready?

She sends me a dress too, a velvet dress, just like one she owns that the men all love. Hers is green, but mine is maroon, as royal as blue, but in its own way, maybe even more, because it's like blood, the way blood would look if it didn't hurt coming out. The dress has a low V-neck in front and a drapy collar, plus a tight-fitting skirt and a bare back. She sends me a brassiere too—backless, strapless, and push-up.

She writes, Don't tell me you have no place to wear this. You can always wear it at home.

She puts it in all capitals. HOME.

Home, where is that? Maybe the real question is who.

Beatrice gives Sammy and me her water bed to sleep on, because Sammy doesn't want it to fall through the garage ceiling and smash his boat. Sammy likes to keep the bed sloshy, not full, so you can hear the water moving inside and feel it too. Takes me a while to get used to this. At first, I roll into Sammy every time he turns, and then I hang on to the side, but that hurts my back.

But now that I know how to lie, it isn't that bad, and Beatrice is right about the one thing it's good for. When Sammy's on top of me, I'm floating, not sinking, and when I'm alone, I can lie right in the middle and bounce. Lurline likes to jump on the bed with me. We pretend we are riding in a boat and the mural on the wall is life passing us by. Sometimes I hum to her, like the wind, so we're on top of a mountain, up in the clouds.

I dream too. Real, vivid dreams, very wicked. In one of them I'm at Little Makena Beach, lying with my back to the sun, no swimsuit on, so there's nothing but a nice, even tan when I model my velvet dress for someone whose face I cannot see. Sometimes the heating coils in the water bed get too hot in one spot, and I dream that my skin is burning right through, and I'm like a calf getting branded. Then I'm back on the beach, this time lying where the waves land, and the mark on my skin is washing away. Fading.

One inch, one layer, one life at a time. Mine.

When the Big Water hit Cock-a-Roach, we were halfway to heaven, my babies and me. I yanked the rope off the truck door, climbed onto the seat and out the back window, through the shower curtain. I lifted Beatrice out first, then Lurline, still in her basket. I wrapped the rope around the inner tube lying in the back of the truck. Then I tied the rope around my waist and sat down on the floor of the truck, holding my girls. I crossed Lurline's heart, then Beatrice's, then my own, and we waited for the rest of heaven to come.

The driver-side door of Cock-a-Roach washed up in Hana Bay. The rest of the truck, like my red sling-back pumps, is still out there, providing a home for the crabs.

I don't remember swimming back to shore. All I remember is the inner tube, but Sammy says when they found me, the rope wasn't tied to anything but me.

They say it was luck, plus I have a pretty strong kick and a very loud whistle.

But Sammy is more practical than that. He says what happened is we caught the current just right. He says the current makes you go where it wants you to go. You can't fight the current. You have to let it take you out and then carry you back in again. He holds his fist out in front of him. He sweeps his other hand through the air. What takes you out to open sea. Makai. Then he grabs the fist that is waiting and pulls it toward him. What brings you back home. Mauka. He opens his hands and his fingers fly. Free again. Like doves.

ACKNOWLEDGMENTS

The writing of this novel felt like an ocean voyage at times. Years on a homemade raft, rough seas, fog, no map or compass, a few shipwrecks, rare glimpses of land, and an awful lot of wind. Fortunately, I was never really solo in this venture, thanks to those who fueled me with stories and facts or buoyed me along the way, including:

Members of my extended ohana—the Ah Cook, Ching, Chun, Drews, Knopp, Mau, Tyau, and Wong families—who continue to bless me with memories, generous hospitality, and perhaps more inspiration than they truly desire.

Priscilla Ho, Gladys Leong, Alice Lum-Lung, Eileen Mow, Verna Seiss, Florence Stanley, Marion Stanton, Carol Walker, and Carolyn Wedemeyer, for remembering the war years. James Cartwright, Mary Judd, Kawilani and Ladon Niles, Travis Pancayo, Jimmy Perry, Eddie Pu, Dick Tsuda, Gerri Watanabe, and Lisa Yee, for professional and timely kōkua.

Sally-Jo Bowman for blood quantum and the dress on the wall. Carol Fukunaga, my resource artery. Jim Hancock for his royal genes. Wyckliffe Malloy (Wyck) for letting me borrow (and misspell) his name. Gene and Kathleen Hashiguchi for dance lessons. Michael Mau, novelist and long-lost cousin, for coming home. Christy Vail for the flash flood. Gregg Kleiner, David Poulshock, Floyd Skloot, Tom Spanbauer, Tim Thompson, and especially Barbara Scot, for many dousings of faith and good counsel. Barb, thanks for treading all that water with me—we made it, my dear!

I am also grateful to Literary Arts, Inc., the National Endowment for the Arts, and the Oregon Arts Commission for financial and artistic support. Jennifer Hengen and Pat Kavanagh, my guardians in publishing, for finding me good homes. Rebecca Kurson for believing and helping me see my way.

And Paul Drews, mate in song and spirit, for luring me into the deep, for wings.

Mahalo nui loa. Me ke aloha.